Margaret Skea was born in Ulster, growing up there through the 'Troubles' but now lives with her husband in the Scottish Borders. An Hawthornden fellow and award-winning short story writer - credits include Neil Gunn, Winchester, Mslexia and Fish - her first novel, *Turn of the Tide*, set in 16th century Scotland, won both the Beryl Bainbridge Award for Best First Time Novelist 2014 and the historical fiction section in the Harper Collins / Alan Titchmarsh People's Novelist Competition. The sequel, *A House Divided*, was long-listed for the Historical Novel Society New Novel Award 2016.

For more information about Margaret Skea, or to contact her, please visit her website
www.margaretskea.com

sanderling

Also by Margaret Skea

Munro Series (Scottish Historical Fiction)
Turn of the Tide
A House Divided

Short Story collection
Dust Blowing and Other Stories

Katharina: Deliverance

Margaret Skea

Published by Sanderling Books in 2017

Printed by Anthony Rowe, Chippenham
Cover design by www.hayesdesign.co.uk

Cover image: Katharina von Bora by Lucas Cranach the Elder. Nationalmuseum (Stockholm) Photographer: Erik Cornelius (Public Domain) Wittenberg: 1546 engraving, photo: petervick 167/ 123RF

A CIP record of this book is available from the British Library

ISBN: 978-0-9933331-4-9
Sanderling Books
28 Riverside Drive
Kelso
TD5 7RH

The author acknowledges the support of Creative Scotland Open Project Funding Programme while researching this book.

Main Characters

The von Bora Family
Hans von Bora (father), died before 1523
Anna von Haugwitz (mother), presumed dead by 1504
Hans, Klement and one other – name unknown – whom I
    have called Franz (brothers of Katharina)
Katharina von Bora, born 1499
Frau Seidewitz, Hans von Bora's second wife
Johannes and Emil Seidewitz: it is known that Frau
    Seidewitz brought children of her own to the marriage,
    but not their details – I have named them here.
Magdalene von Bora, (later known as Muhme Lena) sister
    to Hans senior, a nun in the Marienthron convent at
    Nimbschen
Margarete von Haugwitz, Abbess of the Marienthron, a
    relative of Katharina's mother

The Luther Household at Mansfeld
Hans Luder (father)
Margarete Lindemann (mother)
Martin Luder, born 1483/4 (later changed his name to
    Luther)
Barbara, Dorothy and Margaret, (Martin's sisters)
Jacob, (Martin's brother)

Colleagues and Friends
Johann von Staupitz, vicar-general, Martin's superior and

chief mentor

Nicholas Amsdorf, professor at Wittenberg

Johannes Bugenhagen, pastor of Town Church, Wittenberg

Lucas Cranach, painter, printer and apothecary, Wittenberg

Barbara Cranach, his wife

Justus Jonas, dean at Castle Church, Wittenberg

Katherine Jonas, his wife

Andreas Karlstadt, professor, dissenter

Anna Karlstadt, his wife

Philipp Melanchthon, Luther's chief co-reformer.

Katharina Melanchthon, his wife

George Spalatin, secretary and chaplain to Elector Frederick

Philipp Reichenbach, town clerk, Wittenberg

Elsa Reichenbach, his wife

Jerome Baumgartner, former student of the University of Wittenberg

Herr Köppe, merchant and councillor, Torgau

Leonhard Köppe, his nephew

Gabriel Zwilling, pastor, Torgau

Other Notable Characters

Caspar Glatz, supporter of Luther

Thomas Müntzer, former supporter of Luther

Chancellor Brück

Albert, Archbishop of Mainz (elevated to Cardinal in 1518) – early opposer of Luther

Balthazar, Abbot overseer of the Marienthron convent at Nimbschen

Peter, Abbot overseer of the Marienthron covent at Nimbschen, after Balthazar

Nuns Who Escaped with Katharina

Magdalena von Staupitz, novice teacher at the Marienthron convent

Else von Kanitz

Lanita von Golis

Ave Grossin

Fronika and Margarete von Zeschau

Eva and Margarete (called by the diminutive, Marta) von Schonfeld

(Three others, unnamed)

Nobility

House of Wettin – Ernestine Line

Frederick 'the Wise', Elector of Saxony, 1486–1525 (Catholic)

John 'the Steadfast', Elector of Saxony, 1525–1532 (Lutheran)

House of Wettin – Albertine Line

George, Duke of Saxony, 1500–1539 (Catholic)

N

Mansfeld •

Eisleben •

Frankenhausen • • Allstedt

• Mühlhausen

Eisenach

• Erfurt

The Wartburg

R. Weere

Jena •

• Schmalkald

Worms 125 mL.

Thuringian

Forest

• Caburg

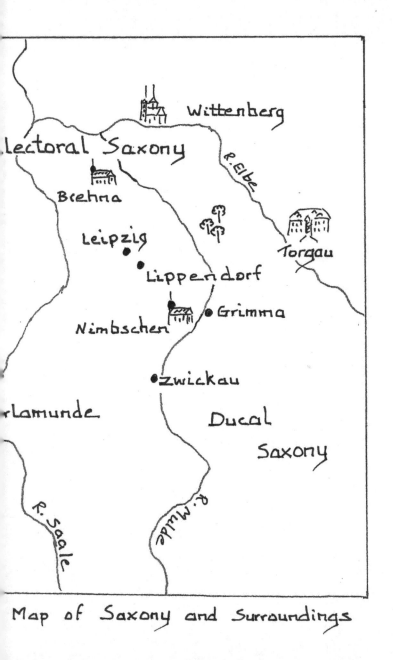

Map of Saxony and Surroundings

Torgau: September, 1552

It seems that I am dry, under me something soft. I search for the word to describe it, dredging it from the recesses of my brain: sheepskin. I am lying on a sheepskin. I want to stretch, but my right leg refuses to move, and when I try to shift onto my side there is a sharp pain in my hip, as if someone is thrusting a hot poker through me. I raise my arm; it at least works, as do my fingers when I wiggle them. But even that effort seems too much, and I let my hand drop onto the coverlet, my eyelids flickering.

When I next wake, it is to the half-light that creeps around the edge of ill-fitting shutters, augmented by a stump of candle flickering on the window ledge. Beside it, slumped in a roughly fashioned chair, a woman sleeps, and momentarily I feel a pity for her, for the sound of laboured breathing fills the room and I think she must be unwell.

She stirs, approaches my bed. 'Frau Luther?'

Her voice sounds normal and I try to pull myself up to better examine my surroundings, to see who else is here, but discover that without the aid of my legs I have not the strength to move. I content myself with swivelling my head, first one way, then the other, the small sideways movements enough to show me all there is to see, for the chamber is narrow, with barely enough space to walk between the bed and the hearth. We are alone, yet the rasping sound continues, and though my neck moves freely enough, I feel a clicking and a grinding as if there is gravel trapped between the bones. I lie, quiescent, trying to remember what brought me to this place, to find some order in the jumble

11

of places and faces that crowd in upon me. There is a rattle of rain against the shutters and it reminds me of another chamber, another time, and we three trapped indoors, bickering as children do. 'We none of us liked her,' I say.

The woman bends her head towards me, as if she is hard of hearing, but when her brow wrinkles and she queries, 'Frau Luther?', I see that she is confused.

I try to speak clearly, as if to a child. 'Seidewitz. Her name was Frau Seidewitz.'

CHAPTER ONE
LIPPENDORF, FEBRUARY 1505

'It is very shameful that children, especially
defenceless young girls, are pushed into the
nunneries. Shame on the unmerciful parents who
treat their own so cruelly.'

Martin Luther

Curled into the window seat, I press my face against the
rippled glass, watching the trees bending and straightening
before the wind, as the townsfolk do when Duke George
passes through the market square. Above the trees, clouds
pile, black on black, and I shiver. 'The rain is coming.'

Klement, standing behind me, whispers in my ear,
'The giant is coming. His footsteps shake the track
leading from the woods. Soon he will reach us and...' He
grips my shoulders, shaking me.

Hans leaps up from his chair, shoves Klement
backwards. 'Stop it!' And to me, 'It's only thunder, Kat,
and cannot touch us here.'

Another rumble, louder than the last, and with it a

distant rattle, like a cart on the cobbles in Lippendorf. The sky darkens, sucking out the light, Klement hissing, 'And darkness was over the earth from the sixth until the ninth hour…'

Hans glares at Klement again as a jagged line of light splits open the sky, the accompanying crack frightening. I cross myself and shut my eyes until the noise fades, then peep between my fingers and see the rain spiking onto the ground below the window, churning the semicircle of path that curves to our door into a river of mud. The tree outside the window is blackened and a curl of smoke struggles upwards against the falling rain.

Klement is triumphant. 'See? Next time it will be…'

'Shut up!' Hans spins round, claps his hand over Klement's mouth. 'Listen. There's a carriage coming. Can it be Father?' His voice has a catch in it that sends another shiver through me. 'Anna said…'

Klement is at my other side, mischief forgotten. 'Anna is a gossip. We shouldn't pay too much attention to what she says.'

I tug at Hans' arm. 'What did Anna say?'

He pats my hand, shakes his head. 'Nothing. Klement is right. It is but gossip and likely nonsense.'

We all crane to see as the carriage rolls to a stop, sending a wave of water arcing towards Anna, drenching her skirts as she waits in the open doorway. There is another flash of lightning as our father emerges and, holding the carriage door, reaches up to hand down a woman dressed in a burgundy cloak, her face shadowed by the broad brim of her hat. The padded velvet top is studded with pearls in the shape of a swan, its wings raised as if poised for flight.

'Rich, I suppose,' Hans says.

She hesitates on the carriage step, as if reluctant to soil her shoes in the mud, then, with a flash of ankle, she lifts her skirt and, holding onto our father, leaps the puddle between the carriage and the threshold of the door, slipping as she lands. He keeps his arm around her waist even when she's steady again.

I catch a glimpse of a silver buckle and shining leather, just like our mother's shoes she wore on Sundays going to Mass, and my stomach aches. 'Who's she?' I ask. 'And why's she with Father?'

'The wicked stepmother, I presume,' Klement says.

'Hans?' I jiggle his arm, but he stares at the floor, shrugs.

Anna appears, her voice husky as she sends the boys downstairs. She shakes her head at me when I go to follow. 'Not you, miss. I'm going to tidy you up first.' She fusses at my dress, running her hands down the skirt, straightening the girdle, tugging at the sleeves. Her grip on my hair is firm, the comb strokes rapid, the teeth biting into my scalp, but when I put up my hand to stop her she slaps it away.

'Ouch,' I say, hurt as much by her uncharacteristic brusqueness as by the action itself.

She sets the comb down and turns me to face her. 'Be good, Kat. Try to behave like a little girl, not a hoyden.'

'For whom?'

'For Frau Seidewitz. She's…' She takes a deep breath, the huskiness back. 'She's to be your new mother.'

I stamp my foot. 'We don't need a new mother. We have you.'

'Liebchen, your father thinks that you do. In his eyes I am only a servant.'

15

I stamp my foot again. 'I shall tell him different, then.'

She shakes her head. 'You mustn't.' A drip is forming at the end of her nose and she brushes at it with the back of her hand, something she has never allowed to pass without reprimand when I've done it. 'It will only convince him that you are becoming unmanageable.' Her eyes are shiny and she brushes at them too. 'If he is persuaded of that … there are worse things than a new mother.'

I want to ask what she means, but Hans appears in the doorway.

'You're wanted below.' He looks over my head at Anna and I see the glance that passes between them, and I know he's hiding something.

Anna gives one final tug to my dress, pushes me towards the door. 'Remember your manners, Katchen. Remember to curtsey.'

'So this is the child?' Frau Seidewitz looks me up and down.

I know that look. It's the one the priest has when he looks at my brothers' schoolwork, hoping to find something wrong. So, minding Anna, I dip in a curtsey and look down; it's easier than smiling.

'She's a good girl, clever too, and musical.' Father sounds just like Hans when he's caught in a fault, and it scares me.

'Clever? Then she will benefit from education.'

I glance at Father through a fall of hair and see that his fist is clenched tight, the knuckles white.

'She's still very young.'

Frau Seidewitz waves away his comment. 'Musical, you say? Then surely a choir school will suit admirably. And the younger she goes, the better prepared she will be.'

I want to ask, 'Prepared for what?', but from behind Frau Seidewitz, Hans signals me into silence.

She moves to stand beside our father, tucks her arm into his. 'No doubt they're good children, but they don't need to be privy to this discussion. I'm sure we can make the right decision for us all.' She removes her hat, shaking off the droplets of rain that glisten on the pearls and sweeps him towards the door. 'My clothes are somewhat damp and I'd like to change before supper.'

When they are gone, Hans releases his breath in a whoosh. 'The right decision for her maybe.'

Klement pokes with his toe at a loose end in the rag rug on the floor. His voice is unusually quiet, as if he too is scared. 'Will she have us all sent away?'

Hans shakes his head. 'Why would she? We are the cheapest labour to hand. Unkind she may be, but I doubt if she's stupid.'

'I don't like her,' I say.

'Well you'd better try, else…'

'Klement!' Hans sounds cross.

'Better she knows.' Klement's mimicry is perfect. 'The younger she goes, the better prepared she will be.'

This time I can ask. 'Prepared for what?'

'Consecration, silly. She means for you to become a nun.'

CHAPTER TWO
LIPPENDORF, MARCH 1505

Frau Seidewitz has been with us three weeks, in which I have crept about the house trying to make myself as small as possible, scurrying around corners when I hear her footsteps, as if I am a mouse and she a cat, ever on the prowl. It is 'Katharina this' and 'Katharina that' and 'Why can't you' and 'Don't', and it seems I never do anything right, however hard I try.

Anna, helping me dress, is unexpectedly gentle. 'There's no pleasing some folk.'

Hans and Klement fare better, for the most part managing to avoid her, spending their mornings shut up in the schoolroom with the priest, who stuffs their heads with Latin and geometry, and their afternoons helping on the estate. Klement, who showed little desire for either learning or labour in the past, declaring an inclination for both that surprises us all.

Father finds me in the nursery, hanging over the edge of the crib in which Franz lies, his startling blue eyes staring up at me, his mouth easing into what I chose to think is a smile, as I set the crib swinging.

'Look, Vati, he likes me.'

He pats my head automatically, but he doesn't look at Franz and his voice is gruff. 'No doubt, no doubt. But you cannot spend all your day here. I wish for you and Frau Seidewitz to get to know each other.'

'I don't like her.'

'Katharina! You must not speak so.'

There is anger in his voice and for a moment I wish I hadn't said it, but then I remember the hardness in her eyes every time she looks at me, and feel her nails biting into my palms as she marches me into the church for Mass, and I can't stop myself. 'She doesn't like me either.'

'Katharina' – he hunkers down – 'it is hard for her, to come as a stranger into our family, but I am sure she wishes to love you and you must try to love her in return.' He grasps my hands. 'Can you do that, for me?'

The crib slows to a stop and Franz opens his mouth wide as if about to wail.

'I have tried,' I mutter, pulling back my hands, about to start the crib swinging again, 'but…'

'Then you must try harder.' He speaks sternly, and Franz begins to whimper.

I bend over the crib again but Father grasps my shoulder, pulling me upright. 'Leave the babe to the maid.' At the top of the stairs he pauses, a softness returning, 'Frau Seidewitz and I will be away for a week or two, and when we come back she will be your new mother, and I wish you to treat her as such.' He sucks in his lip and I look up at him, searching his face, willing him not to say anything more, but he's not looking at me, he's looking at the painted plaque of the Virgin and Child and his lips are moving as if he seeks her blessing. 'When we come back

19

... you will have two more children to play with.'

CRXXD

I find my brothers leaning over the gate of the pasture, watching the mare nudge her new foal to his feet. He wobbles for a moment, then with a flick of his tail he burrows his head under the mare's stomach and, finding the teat, begins to suck so noisily that it nearly drowns me out when I repeat Father's words.

Klement swings round. 'He said what?'

'Frau Seidewitz has two children.'

'She must be very rich, then.'

I don't understand what money has to do with it, but it seems Hans does.

'I'm not sure.' He's shaking his head. 'The word in the kitchen is that...' He breaks off, letting his breath out in a sigh, his shoulders settling. 'We may hope the gossip is wrong, for the estate barely keeps us, let alone three more mouths to feed. If she brings no money, who knows what economies must be found.'

'We know one that she thinks of.' Klement glances at me and I remember what he said when first she came.

Hans glares at him and puts his arm around my shoulder, twirling a strand of my hair in his fingers. 'Don't worry, Katchen. If we all try to make them welcome, perhaps nothing will change. Maybe she has money no one here is aware of.' He pulls me against him. 'How long did Father say they're to be away?'

'A few weeks,' I whisper.

'Well then, let's enjoy them while we can.' He tugs on my hair, summons a smile. 'Who knows ... we may even

20

like her children.'

Klement snorts. 'Oh, yes. Especially if they favour her.' The mare leads her foal to the fence and noses Hans' chest, as if presenting him.

I slide my hand through a gap but the foal retreats, nestling into his mother's flank.

Hans reaches over and strokes the foal's neck. 'Well, we like this young one anyway.'

⬭⬭⬭

I'm in the kitchen, perched on a stool by the fireside, watching cook remove miniature spice cakes from the oven. There are two types of pastries already cooling on the racks on the table, but when I stretch out for one as I usually do, she slaps my hand away.

'Don't even think of it! Your father returns today with his new wife and I will not have her finding our storeroom lacking.' Then, relenting, 'But if there should be a misshape, or one that tumbles from the tray, it will be yours.' I cross the fingers of both hands behind my back, and wonder if a Hail Mary would help, or if it is a mortal sin to pray for cakes to be spoiled.

She is turning towards the table when the bell jangles right above her head, the tray tilting, the cakes sliding towards the edge. I see her eyes flicker to the statue of Saint Martha in the niche above my head, hear her muttered petition, and I hold my breath, pressing my fingers more tightly together, but though the cakes tip on top of each other she manages to rescue them. Dusting her hands on her apron, she nods at Saint Martha, as if in recognition of her help, and begins to lay the pastries out, then, as if sorry for her previous sharpness, picks up the smallest one.

'Here. But don't expect any more mind. And you'd best eat it quickly. You'll be wanted.'

◁◇◇◇▷

Anna ushers me from the kitchen, dipping her head to the crucifix hanging in the hallway as we pass. I dip my head too, as I have been taught, but I don't look up, for though I know the blood isn't real, the trails of red from the hands and feet and the ragged gash in the Christ's side make my stomach churn. Anna pauses before she opens the door of the Stube, to brush with her sleeve at the crumbs clinging to the lacing of my bodice. The boys are lined up in front of the hearth. Hans looks straight ahead, expressionless, his arms stiff at his side, but Klement's head has a defiant tilt, that I see, by the tightening of Frau Seidewitz' mouth, is noted. Her gaze slides over the boys, rests on me. She reaches out her hand and picks out a crumb from my dress that Anna missed, looking over my head at Father.

'You have been too lax with your servants. I see I shall have some work to do if your children are not to disgrace us.'

He flushes and I feel the heat rushing into my cheeks too, resentment boiling. Behind her, from the doorway, Anna opens her eyes wide at me and shakes her head. I'm biting so hard on my lip that I draw blood, while behind my back Hans' fingers close around mine and he presses, but whether it is a warning or comfort I'm not sure. There are two boys to the right of Frau Seidewitz, one as defiant as Klement, one staring at the floor. She thrusts them

22

forward.

'This is Emil, and this, Johannes.' She looks at my brothers, her tone like treacle. 'I trust you can all be good companions. My boys are well versed in city ways, while yours' – she turns her snake-smile on Father – 'can no doubt share their knowledge of the countryside.' It's obvious, even to me, which she thinks the more important. Beside me, Klement stiffens, his fist clenched.

Father is quick to intervene. 'Perhaps we should leave the children to get to know each other, while you, my dear, might wish to rest. The journey was, I know, somewhat tedious.'

For a moment I think she is going to contradict him, then she smiles again and moves to his side. 'I cannot deny you are somewhat remote here, but I daresay I shall become accustomed to the travel in time.'

Johannes moves to the window and leans on the ledge to look out. Beyond the glass the rain drips onto the outer sill, the sound magnified in the silence. He turns his head, says, 'Does the sun ever shine here?'

Hans and Klement both answer at once.

Hans is conciliatory. 'The rain won't last long. Look, the sky is lightening.'

Klement is combative. 'We *are* in the same country, our weather much as yours, I imagine, though perhaps in the city there is not the space to experience it.'

They are like a pair of dogs facing up to each other, hackles rising.

Emil steps forward, holds out his hand. 'We have none of us chosen this, but perhaps we can make the best of it.'

Klement ignores his outstretched hand, but Hans takes it, nodding once.

23

'We have nothing to lose by trying to be civil and nothing to gain by enmity.'

Klement snorts, turns on his heel, and is out of the door before Hans can stop him.

Johannes seems amused. 'Temper, temper. I see we shall have to watch that one.'

Emil sighs, darts a look of apology at Hans. 'Perhaps if you can mind your tongue, Johannes, there will be no need for watching.'

'As you see, my little brother is always the diplomat.' Johannes' lips curl. 'Or mealy-mouthed, whatever you prefer.'

The pressure in my chest is too strong to be contained. I throw myself at him, hammering my fists against his thighs. 'I hate you and I hate her and I hate Father that he brought you here.'

Hans grabs hold of me and hugs me close to stop me from struggling. 'Shush, Katchen, Shush.' He is rocking me back and forward as I sob into his chest, and when I raise my head he rubs with his hand at my cheeks.

'A wildcat, I see.' Johannes runs his hands down his clothes as if to remove all traces of me.

'Shut up, Johannes.' Emil is by Hans' shoulder and his eyes seem kind. 'She is only a child. You cannot expect her to welcome us with open arms. Especially not when you are so rude.' He lifts his hand as if to touch my hair, but I shrink away, burying my face again in Hans' chest, nursing my distrust.

Hans disentangles me and gives me a gentle push towards the door. 'There is only half an hour to supper. You'd best go to Anna and get tidied up, or there may be more criticism.'

24

I stamp my foot, think of Frau Seidewitz' critical gaze. 'I don't care what *she* thinks…'

He puts one finger against my mouth. 'But you care for Anna. If you are unkempt, she will suffer for it.'

Father says the prayer of thanksgiving before we eat, his hands placed like a steeple on the table in front of him, and I ache to have him take my hand, as he did for a time after our mother died, when, with my eyes tight shut, his unseen touch brought her back to me. These last weeks she has been slipping further and further away, and though I didn't understand why, now, as I open my eyes a slit and see that Frau Seidewitz' eyes are also open, and fixed on Father, I know it is her doing. That Mother will never come back. I'm not hungry and pick at my food, *her* voice droning on and on: about the city, the shops, the houses of those with means.

'Not that I intend any criticism, for I know a man does not notice these things, but really' – she waves her hand towards the rug on the floor – 'it is well worn and, indeed, threadbare in places. I know exactly the shop where we may find a replacement. And as for the tableware, we can do better than wooden platters, I think.'

'In time, my dear.' Father pats her hand. 'In time, perhaps.'

'We could do better without you,' Klement mutters into his plate.

Hans jerks, and I know he's aimed a foot at Klement under the table, but when Klement doesn't react and Emil's eyes widen instead, I realise that the kick has gone

25

astray. I hold my breath, waiting for the protest, but Emil says nothing. I smile at Klement and chuckle into my soup, glad that he says what I feel. Hans' foot flashes out again, accompanied by a fractional shake of his head, this time catching me on the shin, and I see the glance that passes between him and Emil. Resentment builds inside me again and I glare back, as if to remind him that he is *my* brother, Klement too, and Emil the enemy.

As soon as we are dismissed from the table I fly to the nursery, still angry with Hans. My shin is hurting, and my pride, and I hang over the crib, rocking it so vigorously that Franz stirs.

Hans follows me, refusing to be ignored. He places his hand over mine, stilling the motion of the crib. 'I didn't mean to hurt you, Katchen, only to stop you laughing. Don't you see…?'

I stamp my foot. 'I *do* see. I see that you care about making friends with Emil more than you do about me. And you *did* hurt me.' I pull up my skirt, show him the pink mark still visible on my leg.

'I'm sorry.' He bends down to rub at the mark, but I drop my skirt and jerk away. And though I ignore his sigh, I want his arms around me, want him to say that it's us that matters, not them.

I try, 'If we aren't nice to them maybe they'll go away and it'll be like it was, just us and Father and Anna.'

He sighs again, and hunkering beside me strokes my shoulders. 'Frau Seidewitz is a von Bora now, Katchen. We must make the best of it that we can.'

'I won't. Ever.'

'She is Father's choice. We must respect that.'

I pick at a thread on my bodice, worrying it loose.

'And Johannes and Emil, do they have our name too?'

'No, but they are her sons, and where she lives, they must live. It must be hard for them, to be uprooted from their own place and brought here. Emil, I think, wishes to be friends … at any rate he did not betray me when I kicked him under the table by accident, and Johannes…'

'Johannes is a bully and a braggart.' Klement is framed in the doorway. 'I shan't be going out of my way to befriend him, whatever Father says.' He glares at Hans. 'Neither should you.' He looks at me, his voice softening. 'Anna wants you, Kat. It's time for bed.'

Preparing to protest, I search his face for any trace of the usual pleasure that accompanies his reminder that I am younger than him, but his eyes are as soft as his voice, his unaccustomed gentleness frightening me more than his cross nature ever does.

CHAPTER THREE
LIPPENDORF, MAY 1505

They have been with us two months. The boys are at their lessons, the priest instructing all four of them together. I am working at my sampler, with every stab stitch thinking of Frau Seidewitz, who will never be my mother whatever Father may say. I thrust the needle through the cloth and catch my thumb, blood beading on it, spotting the linen.

Anna, who has been irritable since their arrival, shakes her head at me. 'Away you go. There's no use staying here to make a mess. I've more to do than spend time washing off your carelessness.'

Her sharpness stings me, but I'm glad to be released, and I go to the pasture, to climb on the fence and watch the foal. He's doing bravely now, his legs strong, and with each day that passes he runs around the field in ever-widening circles, kicking up his heels. The mare too, is drifting away from him, less patient when he nuzzles at her teats, allowing him to feed for only so long before she shakes him loose. As our mother did to us, the night Franz was born. I pull up clumps of grass and lean over, holding them out, hoping to entice him close enough to stroke the beginnings of his mane that stands up like the bristles of a brush all down the back of his neck. My hand is flat, the fingers tilted slightly downwards, so that if he does come he will be able to take the grass without nipping. The mare approaches, but I close my fist and pull my hand back. She is no longer my favourite. She shakes her head at me, as if to show she doesn't care, and begins to munch on the long grass that springs against the fence, the foal, gaining courage, coming alongside her. I hold my hand out again, rewarded by the nudge of his nose against my palm, the warm slobbery feel as he lips the grass.

'You've succeeded then.'

At the voice, the foal retreats and I turn round crossly, wiping my hand on my skirt. 'See what you've done.'

'I didn't mean to startle him, just…'

'Well you have, and now he mightn't come back and…'

'I'm sure he will.' Emil leans on the gate beside me and I sidle sideways to put distance between us, turning my head away.

'What do you know?'

'Nothing, really,' he says. 'Only I've been watching you, and he's come closer every time you try. Look, he's coming back.' I risk a glance. The foal is coming back, and I want to pet him, but I don't want Emil to be right. I don't want him here, with me, and especially I don't want to see the kindness in his eyes.

He lifts his hands. 'I won't move and I won't speak.'

The foal is dunting me so I bend down and pull another clump of fresh grass, and this time while he's chewing I touch his neck, and when he doesn't startle I slide my hand down the side of his face. He tolerates it for a minute and then, for no reason that I can tell, reverses and begins another circuit of the field.

'There's always tomorrow,' Emil says. 'You have a way with you.' He is staring past the foal to the line of trees that bound the river marking the edge of our fields. His voice is quiet as if he speaks without meaning to. 'You look just like her.'

'Who?' I say.

'Our sister.'

I don't understand, but I *am* curious. 'Where is she then?'

'She died.' He scrubs at his cheek and I almost reach out to touch his arm, but I remember in time that I don't want him here. His voice hardens and I hear Frau Seidewitz in it. 'A stupid accident.' Then, in his own voice again, but quieter still, and I think he has forgotten I'm here, 'She was always adventurous, wandering off, getting into mischief. Mother indulged her, *too much* Father said, *one day you may regret it*, he said. He scrubs at his cheeks again and I see the smear of damp on his curled fingers. 'He was right. She did regret it. We all did. Still do.'

In the silence I can hear the whisper of water as it flows over the rocks, the dangers in it hidden from any but the most experienced of watermen. His voice flows with it, and I feel a lump in my throat.

'If Mother hadn't given in to Maria's pleadings for a picnic, if she hadn't strayed too close to the river, if Johannes hadn't jumped out at her and startled her… When she fell in, Johannes screamed, and we all came running and Father jumped in after her. But the current was too strong and … they were gone.'

The foal has returned and is poking his nose through

30

the fence, nudging at my chest. As I bend to pull fresh grass he whinnies his thanks, and Emil turns and looks at me as if he has only just woken up.

'You look just like her,' he says again, and he stumbles away towards the house.

The catechism begins as we wait for Father to appear for supper. There are grass stains on my skirt and green under my fingernails, which my hurried run of my hands under the pump didn't shift.

She grabs hold of my skirt, spreading the folds. 'Where have you been? You didn't get these stains sewing.'

'Getting fresh air,' I say. 'Like you say we should.'

'Don't be insolent, child.' There are spots of colour on her cheeks, like the ones I've seen the maid make when she pinches herself before slipping across the yard to the stable. But the maid's eyes always sparkle. Frau Seidewitz' are hard, like pebbles. 'Have you no thought for the work you make for the servants?'

I look down and make the mistake of smoothing my skirt with my hand. She grabs it and raises it up, her eyes narrowing. 'And this' – she pokes at a nail – 'do you not know how to wash your hands?'

Emil comes to stand beside me. 'She was teaching me how to feed a horse without getting bitten, Mutti.'

Frau Seidewitz pulls her mouth into a tight line. 'When she should have been at her lessons, and you at yours?'

'We had finished for the day.'

'Indeed. And are the horses not capable of feeding themselves that you need to supplement their diet with clumps of grass?'

'It is but a childish pleasure and does no harm.'

She pounces on the word childish. 'I did not bring you here to revert to childishness. I expect more of my sons.'

I shiver, thinking of *her* watching us, and, perversely, though I had not wanted Emil's presence at the field, I don't want her to forbid it.

Father appears and looks at each of us in turn, his shoulders settling, but his voice is hearty. 'Well, well, apologies my dear for keeping you waiting, but' – he nods his head towards the window – 'it looks like a storm may be coming, so I went to bring the mare and her foal in from the pasture.'

'Of great importance, no doubt,' she says, sweeping past him.

The meal is eaten in near silence, Father's few attempts at conversation frozen by Frau Seidewitz almost before they have begun. We five say nothing, but instead we keep our heads bowed over the food, concentrating on eating. It's a relief when he dismisses us. 'You may all go. Your mother and I have somewhat to discuss.'

Klement hovers in the hall, but Hans pulls him away.

'We all want to know what is going to be discussed, but to stay here would be folly.'

'Speak for yourself,' Johannes says. 'I have no interest. Why should I?' He runs up the stairs, taking them two at a time. Emil, watching him, seems about to say something, then stops.

Klement heads for the small room that separates the kitchen from the dining room

'Don't blame me if you're caught.' Hans pushes me towards the stairs. 'You go up. It's not cold. We'll hide under the window outside.'

There can only be one 'we', and annoyed that he will take Emil, I say, 'Let me come.'

He shakes his head. 'Best not, Katchen. We'll tell you what's said.'

I start, 'Don't call me…', when we hear footsteps on the landing. Hans jerks his head at Emil, and before I can finish, they've gone. I tuck myself behind the curtain at the turn of the stair. The voices from the dining room get louder, but I can't make out the words until the door flies open. I peer round the edge of the curtain and see Frau Seidewitz in the opening, Father behind her.

Her voice is hard. 'I warned you, Hans, she's becoming unmanageable.'

My heart is thumping, and I clutch the curtain against my chest, afraid they'll hear it.

He touches her shoulder, softens his voice. 'She's only a child. Surely Anna…?'

'Anna allows her to run wild. Only today she appeared for supper, her dress ruined, her fingernails filthy.'

His brow puckers. 'I didn't notice…'

'Of course not, you're too concerned for your precious animals to see what a hoyden your own daughter is becoming.'

A new expression settles on his face, like the one he has when he argues with Klement, the same firmness creeping into his voice.

'She does no harm. A little schooling…'

'And where may schooling be found for girls in this backwater?'

'There is the priest. One extra child will hardly tax him.'

Ugly blotches of colour appear on her neck and her cheeks. 'I won't have my sons share a schoolroom with that child. Already Emil shows an interest in her that I have no wish to encourage. And she no doubt basks in the attention.'

I want to scream *I don't*, and so stuff the edge of the curtain in my mouth.

'Perhaps you could…'

'Perhaps I could not.' Her tongue flicks across her lips, and she presses her hand against her stomach. 'For I think Franz won't be the baby for long.'

Father looks startled, then stupidly pleased, like a dog who has just been thrown a bone, and his voice softens again. 'Oh, my dear.'

'So you see why she must go to school? And learn to be a young lady.'

He pats her arm, nods. 'Brehna, you say? I will make enquiries there.'

Chapter Four
Lippendorf, August 1505

Anna comes to my chamber and dresses me in my best dress, combing the tangles from my hair, setting me back on the edge of the bed while she empties the chest under the window. My thumb strays to my mouth as she places the remainder of my clothes in a saddlebag, along with a wooden carving of Our Lady, and though she sees me, there is no reprimand, so that I feel a sudden need and have to run behind the screen in the corner. When I emerge she is pulling the straps of the bag so tight that one splits. I catch half a stable-hand word, before she chokes it off, and ordering me not to move, she disappears for some cord to replace the broken strap.

When the bag is firmly shut, she kneels in front of me, pulling me against her chest, crumpling my dress more than I could have done myself, and making it hard for me to breathe; but when I begin to struggle she releases me, her voice cracking. 'Perhaps this is for the best, Liebchen.'

To begin with I'm interested in everything we pass, for I've never been further than Lippendorf: going to church or to gape with other villagers as Duke George passes through the square. But after a while the rocking of the cart makes me sleepy and my head drops, only to be jolted upright again when the track roughens. Squeezed between the side rail and my father, I feel the jab of his elbow in my side with every twist and turn. A river flows beside us, the water a muddy brown. At the crossing point, the horses plunge in, the cart lurching from side to side, water spraying up onto my hand. I jerk back, and Father, darting a glance at me, says, 'You needn't fear. The recent rains have made the river fast, but the water won't reach to us.'

I believe him, but my belly doesn't settle until we rattle up the shingle on the far side, water streaming from the wheels. The meadowland beyond the river is a patchwork of fields: some the soft green of new grass, others ploughed and ready for the sowing of barley. My eyes sting as I imagine Anna at harvest-time, carrying bread and beer out to my father and brothers in the field and think of the mice running between the lines of stubble, Klement chasing along behind, whooping when he manages to catch one. Who will plead for its release? For a moment I see Emil hanging over the gate of the pasture, remember the gentleness in his eyes as he watched the foal, and a warmth creeps through me, but I push it away. Why must I go while they stay? We turn onto a forest track, the trees closing about us, all around scufflings and rustlings and the high-pitched squeal of a weasel disturbed in the undergrowth. I lean into Father, needing to feel the rise and fall of his breathing.

36

We stop in the courtyard of the inn crowded with wagons and horses, men shouting and maids scurrying back and forth, carrying steaming dishes and trays piled high with rye bread.

'This is Leipzig,' Father begins, pride in his voice, then breaks off as a horse that is being led across the cobbles stops and lifts its tail, causing a stable-boy to sidestep to avoid the arc of urine, jiggling the pail of water he carries so that it spills down my skirt and over my feet.

Father grabs his shoulder, thrusts him aside, his voice unusually harsh. 'Watch what you're doing, boy.' I attempt to shake the water from my skirt, but he hurries me inside, demanding, 'A bedroom if you please, and supper and something to dry off the child.'

The girl who flounces up the narrow stair before us hovers in the doorway until Father reaches into his pouch and presses a coin into her hand. It cannot have been enough, for when she returns she offers only a tattered rag, and the bowls she slops down before us contain a greyish liquid, with lumps of what looks like gristle floating in it, globules of fat smearing the surface. Father dabs ineffectually at my dress and indicates for me to sit. I take one spoonful of the soup she has brought and manage with difficulty to swallow it down, but I promptly bring it up again, the gristle flying across the table to land on Father's lap, the liquid spattering his chest. I wait for the reprimand, my stomach heaving, but all he does is to close his eyes for a moment, then wipe at his own front with the rag before setting both bowls aside.

'Can't we go home?' I ask, but he shakes his head.

'It's only one night, Katchen.' He tears a chunk of bread from the half-loaf and passes it to me. It's nothing like Anna's, but better than the soup, and chewing on it takes away the empty feeling in my belly.

'Tomorrow you'll be at Brehna, and there will be other girls to share your lessons ... and your play.' He reaches out, tugging at a plait. 'They say it's famous for its music. You'll like that, won't you?'

I want to say, *No, I only like home*, but then I remember Frau Seidewitz' expression when she looks at me, and Father's stupid grin when he places his hand on the bulge beneath her waistband, Johannes pinching me every time I pass him and Klement, increasingly cross, and I bite hard on my lip; I won't cry. My head starts to nod, and Father takes me to the bed and we kneel down together as he recites the bedtime benediction that Mother used to say for us. He stumbles over the words, his voice hoarse, and I wish it was Anna with me, for her recitation is a comfort. When he is done I clamber onto the bed and the next thing I know he's shaking me awake and leading me down the stairs and onto the cart again, all around us the hustle and bustle of tradesmen and travellers eager to start their day.

The second day is longer than the first. We pass a farmhouse with a crooked chimney, just like ours, and I dart a glance at Father, risk, 'How long will I stay at Brehna?'

He chews on his lip. 'You're a clever girl. You want to learn and there is no school at Lippendorf. Brehna is famous for its schooling.'

I'm not sure if I do want to learn anymore, and the further we travel the more my stomach aches and I'm afraid I might have to ask him to stop and let me down into the bushes to relieve myself. We pass a cluster of buildings that Father says are weaving mills, his explanations of how it is that cloth is made failing to distract me from what lies ahead. I try to think about Hans and little Franz in the crib, but all I can see is Klement's face as he hissed, 'She means for you to become a nun.' On a hill in the distance I can see roofs poking out above a high wall and I shiver, thinking of the procession of monks I once saw disappearing into the monastery at Lippendorf. The gate clanged shut behind them and I never saw them again.

'Is that…' I ask, nodding towards the hill, biting on my lip to stop the tremble.

Father looks down. 'No.' He slips one arm around me, as if in encouragement. 'We have a ways to go yet,' he says.

I want to ask, 'How far?' but am too scared of the answer.

The sun is burning through my bonnet and itching my scalp as we pull up at a pair of tall gates half-smothered in ivy, a curving avenue of trees stretching away inside. Father leaps down and thrusts his hand into a gap in the ivy, the jangle of the bell startling the crows that are roosting in the trees overhead. They fly up protesting and I cover my face with my arms, remembering the dead lamb I'd once stumbled over as I ran to hide while Hans counted by the yard gate, and my fear as the crows that were picking at its eyes rose around me, flapping and cawing. There is a cry of welcome and I peer between my fingers as the gates are hauled back, the man within clapping my father on the shoulder and smiling down at me.

'Is this Brehna?'

My father shakes his head. 'This is your uncle's estate.

39

We will sup here. But Brehna isn't far away.' His tongue slides around his lips. 'So you see, you'll have family close by.'

The last part of the journey is least comfortable of all, riding in front of Father on a borrowed horse, the buttons of his jacket pressing into my spine, my bottom and legs aching from bouncing up and down. The leather of the saddle chafes my thighs, and though I'm frightened to arrive, I wish for the journey to end.

One moment we are in dappled sunlight, the next we stop in the shadow of a tall wall in front of a bleached oak door, studded with metal. The opening is deep-set, lined with alternate long and short stones, pitted with chisel marks, where slivers of stone have been chipped away. 'How can stones be dressed?' I'd said, when Hans told me that was what it was called.

And he'd laughed and ruffled my hair. 'It's just a name, Katchen, to show it's been worked.'

'Well it's stupid,' I'd said, cross that he'd laughed. If Father would only turn around and take me home, I'd never be cross with Hans again.

Instead, he lifts me down, holding me round the waist for a minute, then unties my bag and hammers on the door. It opens to reveal an elderly nun, her face creased and marked with dark spots, like an apple lain too long in store, and he pats me on the head and tells me, 'Be good, mind, and do all that is asked of you.'

I reach for his hand, but he slides free of me and turns away, his voice gruff, as if he has something stuck in his throat. 'You cannot be taught at home, Katchen, and I think you will be happy here, if you do but give it a chance.'

As the heavy door bangs shut behind me, blocking him from my sight, my stomach heaves. I swallow hard and stumble along the flagged path behind the silent nun and through another, smaller door, where she sets me down at a rough deal table, another woman thrusting a posset of warm milk and cinnamon into my hands. The last thing I remember: the warmth of glowing embers on my left cheek and a tuneless humming from the woman, as round as she was tall, dressed in a shapeless gown the colour of dead leaves, who stirred a pot on the fire.

Torgau: September 1552

I drift up from the darkness towards a line of light slanting across the floor. It beckons me with the promise of warmth and I see Paul haloed in it, his hair a nimbus around his face, his slim frame shadow-like. I stretch out for him, croaking his name, and he is by my side, capturing my hand in his. He drops to his knees, and leaning over me he places a kiss on my forehead, tears shining in his eyes.

'Mutti, you gave us such a fright.'

I tilt my head, fragments of something nudging my memory. 'Did I? I didn't mean to.'

He is stroking my hand, such a display of affection unusual, and I say, 'Have I been ill?'

His response is halfway between a snort and a sob. 'We thought you gone from us. But now' – he releases my hand and leaps up – 'I must get Margarethe.'

There are voices in the passageway outside and I turn my head towards the door, summoning a smile to mask my fatigue.

Margarethe is on her knees at the opposite side of the bed from Paul, wrapping her arms about me, and I think perhaps I must have fallen and bruised myself, for her clasp hurts me. 'You're awake,' she says, and I hear the pleasure in her voice. 'We thought…'

'Yes I know,' I say. 'But you are not to be rid of me yet.' It's the right thing to say, setting both of them laughing, and I laugh with them, though it hurts my chest. I press my hand into the space between my breasts, draw in my breath, Paul's laughter cut off.

'Does that hurt?' he says, and I nod.

'What did I do?'

'You had a fall, from the cart, when the horses…'

'Who was driving?' I see the look that passes between them, then Margarethe says, 'You were. Don't you remember?'

'It's hazy,' I say. 'Where were we going?'

Paul looks away, but Margarethe answers readily enough. 'To Torgau, with the college.'

It's my turn to look down. 'Oh, yes … of course.' I am searching for understanding. 'Why was your father not driving?'

Paul opens his mouth as if to answer, but Margarethe cuts in. 'He didn't come with us. Not this time.' She stretches behind me and brings my head forward. 'You look tired. Drink this, it will help you sleep.'

I drop my head back against the pillow as she pulls the blanket up to my chin and smooths out the rumples. In the distance a bell is ringing.

Chapter Five
Brehna, August 1505

'I always loved music: whoso has skill in this art, is of a good temperament, fitted for all things. We must teach music in schools.'

Martin Luther

The bell wakens me. My eyes fly open, but I press them tight shut again: against the darkness, against the creeping cold that makes my cheeks ache, against the soft shuffling as if of slippered feet that I can hear from somewhere outside. If Klement is ringing the bell, if it's another of his jokes, I shan't respond. Someone is shaking my shoulder, whispering to me to get up, but I burrow back into the bed, ignoring the sound so as not to give him the satisfaction of thinking he startled me. I go to pull the blankets up to my chin but find there's only one, and the mattress under me is hard and lumpy, the sheet coarse, scratching my legs. I open my eyes again, frightened now. This isn't my bed, my room. This room is long and narrow, a plain wooden crucifix hanging on the end wall, and there are six beds, not one. A girl is standing at the foot of mine, her voice low but insistent.

'You need to get up, or you'll be in trouble.'

The noise from outside increases, a steady patter of footsteps passing the door and the girl glances towards it. It's solid with a metal grill near the top, like the door of the prison cell in the town gaol that Johannes threatened me with when I dropped his mother's dish in the dining room and it smashed. Behind the grill, figures pass in ones and twos, bobbing up and down in time to a whisper of skirts. What if they're Klement's ghosts, if the door opens, if they are coming for me? What if the girl is one of them also? I thrust my head back under the blanket again and hold my breath until I hear a sigh, then the door closing. Cautiously I poke my head up again, breathe out in a whoosh of relief when I see that I'm alone. I'm still half-asleep, still at a loss to know where I am, when the door opens again, the hinges creaking, the base scraping across the flagged floor, as at home, and yesterday comes flooding back.

'Up, up.' The nun leaning over me has a sharp face and thin lips, a gob of spittle trembling at the corner of her mouth. 'Did you not hear the bell?' It is the call to Prime. She pulls back the blanket, grabs my arm, hauls me from the bed. 'I have enough to do without having to come for a child who is too lazy to get herself ready in time.' She thrusts me into my clothes, tugging at my bodice, smoothing down my skirt, and standing back she regards me through eyes like slits. 'You'll do.'

I scramble into my boots, my fingers fumbling with the lacing, leaving the tails uneven, so that I almost trip as she grips my shoulder and marches me along the corridor.

Her stride is so long that I have to half run to keep up with her and avoid going my length on the flags.

We cross the courtyard and I skid to a stop at my first sight of the church, the steeple, topped by a weather vane in the shape of a cross, reaching to the sky. She casts a glance at me, nods towards it.

'It can be seen from everywhere in the cloister. A reminder that God is always watching.'

A happy thought, which she turns into a scary one.

The church isn't big, but it isn't homely either, not like our one at Lippendorf. I loved its whitewashed walls and the vaulted ceiling that I thought sent the chanting of the psalms right up to heaven. I loved the crown-shaped lid on the baptismal font, and the way it glittered when the sun shone on it. Week by week Anna had fussed me into my best dress and cloak, saying, 'God likes to see you, Liebchen, and he's happy when you visit him,' so that I thought going to church was like going to the house of a kindly grandfather, who smiled on me as I hummed along with the music, though I couldn't get my tongue around the words; and who Anna said wouldn't expect anything other than that I fall asleep during the homily. I'd said that once to Klement and he'd snorted with laughter.

'No wonder. For who could stay awake with a windbag of a priest mumbling away as he does. I do suppose it's Latin, though it's hard to tell, as everything he says is punctuated with belches and hiccups.'

Anna, coming into the room in time to hear him, had shaken her head. 'You should not speak so. It is not fit.' But her words had come out half-choked, as if she, too, struggled not to laugh.

This is different.

In the entrance, two sober-faced men in gilt frames frown down on me, as if reminding me not to misbehave. All along the nave the walls are alive with pictures of animals, so very like that I shiver. Some I recognise – dogs and horses and prancing lions – and I feel very small, like a mouse they might pounce on, and so I shrink into myself in case they notice me. Others are fantastical creatures I know only from the fables my mother used to tell to me before I slept. There is a unicorn, but next to it are dragons and sea monsters and half-naked figures that I force myself to stare down as if I'm not frightened at all, rubbing at my eyes with my sleeve, afraid of what the nun might say if she sees a tear. I look up higher and am rewarded by the sight of angels and cherubs flying across the soaring arches from pillar to pillar. High above them the ceiling is star-studded, as if I am looking right up to the sky. Directly above me the broad face of a man wreathed in leaves grows from the stone. I know him. He is the green man and has a friendly face, so perhaps there is nothing to fear after all.

The nun tugs at my arm and I dip my head and concentrate on keeping my feet straight, on not tripping, until she stops and gestures me to stand with a group of other girls, all older, but like me dressed in ordinary clothes. The one who tried to wake me darts me a smile and shuffles sideways to make a space and I sidle as close as I dare, the ache in my stomach less.

In the beginning they laugh at me. At how I say certain words, how little I know. That I am not from the villages round about. It hurts, but I learn not to let them see it, for fear that will make it worse. I attach myself to Klara, the girl who first made space for me, following her around like a shadow, grateful that she doesn't laugh with them, instead standing up to those who delight in teasing me.

'Leave her alone. She cannot help how she speaks. And who knows but that she might outstrip us all in learning, and then it will be she who will laugh at us.'

She's nearly right. It seems I am clever and so enjoy the lessons. But I don't laugh at anyone, for fear of drawing more attention on myself. I concentrate on transforming my once shaky letters into a script that flows, unbroken, across the slate, and my heart swells the first time I am allowed to scribe a message to be sent to Father: *I am well and happy*. It's true in a way, though sometimes at night I cry myself to sleep, stifling my sobs under the blanket for want of my family. Hans I miss with an aching void in the pit of my stomach, the baby, Franz, a less sharp, but still noticeable loss, as of a doll that has been taken away, and even Klement's attentions I would welcome, though it be as a frog in my basin, or the body of a dead spider beside my plate. Once or twice, without meaning to, I also remember Emil and the kindness in his eyes.

The *Our Father* and the liturgy I learn easily, the Latin rolling around my tongue, the feel of it pleasing, so that the teasing changes, some of the older girls showing their envy in minor cruelties: pinching my arm, or jolting my elbow to make me slop my soup and so earn the wrath of the fratress. But it is for the music that I tumble out of bed in the darkness, chafing my toes until the feeling returns and presenting myself in the church in good order so that the chantress smiles on me. And that too is an offence against some.

Today is *the* day. I skip into the choir, harmonies ringing in my head, eager to answer the chantress' summons.

'Katharina! Reverence please. This is the house of God.' The reproof is belied by a twinkle in her smile.

'But I am to be in the choir.'

'Of course. I cannot refuse the linnet in our midst. Nor would I want to.' She places one arm around my shoulder. 'Come, here is your place.'

The choir gathers and I find I have been put beside one of the sterner nuns. I cast a pleading look at the chantress, but she busies herself with her music, ignoring me, and settles everyone down with a wave of her hand.

'Katharina is joining us.' She looks at the nun next to me. 'You, Sister Ursula, will have charge of her.' And to me, 'Listen well, Katharina, listen and learn.'

I hit the top note, clear and true, soaring with the music, as if to heaven itself. Beside me, breaking the illusion, Sister Ursula's voice cracks, and the chantress, who listens with her eyes shut – the better she says to hear the blending of our voices – snaps her fingers to halt us.

She comes over, and I want to say, 'It wasn't me,' but there's no need, for it's Ursula's stomach she presses her fist against. 'Breathe from here,' she says, 'not here.' She jabs at her throat. 'You must get under the note, rise into it. As the linnet does.' Her smile is for me. 'Sing it for us again, child.'

Her name for me has stuck, the early jealousies of some of the choir long since melted into a pride that, although not voiced, is understood by all, a chorus of smiles encouraging me as I begin the phrase again.

The abbess appears in the doorway, and I falter, the notes dying.

'I must speak with Katharina.'

Irritation flickers on the chantress' face, but she nods and I slip from my place, uneasy. In her chamber the abbess gestures for me to sit and smiles a reassurance.

'You are not in trouble, child. It is something else I have to say to you.'

I keep my eyes fixed on her face, remain still, but my mind is churning. For the past week I have been expecting just such a summons, for I have been four years here and few of us pass our tenth birthday without a decision on our future being made. I don't know if what I want matters, but if this is to be my life, if I am allowed to choose, I will ask to train to be a chantress.

The abbess leans forward. 'A letter has come, concerning you.' She pauses, and a chill settles on my stomach.

'From Father?'

'Not directly, though it does concern him. It's from a relative of yours, on your mother's side.'

I haven't heard anything of my mother's family since entering the convent and had supposed that Frau Seidewitz ensured that Father had little contact with them. The chill deepens. 'Is there ill news?'

'No, child, she writes of your future. Your father wishes for you to leave us.'

I don't know whether I want to laugh or cry. 'To go home?'

She shakes her head. 'To go to Nimbschen, near Grimma, to the Marienthron convent there. Your aunt is the abbess. A cart will come for you within a day or two.' She hesitates, as if what she must say next displeases her. 'Your father cannot take you himself, for there are urgent matters requiring his attention.'

'Why can I not stay here?'

She pauses again, as if she isn't quite sure how to

answer, and that also frights me, for I have become used to thinking the abbess knows everything. If she does not, then who does?

'Your father thinks Nimbschen more suited to your needs: nearer to home, two of your aunts already there, and others among the postulants that are also of your acquaintance. Aside from the abbess, your father's sister, Magdalene von Bora, is there. And mention is made of two von Schonfeld sisters.'

Marta von Schonfeld I can't picture, but Eva I can: a pixie face, hair that, Anna once said, with a sigh, curled without the need to tie it up in rags, and dark eyes that twinkled when she laughed. I remember chasing chickens with her in the yard, until cook saw us and shooed us away, and how we burrowed into the straw in the stable and found the newly born kittens to cuddle. I look up, smiling, but see the abbess' face has clouded and she's swivelling the plain gold band on her finger. There is something else to come and it frightens me.

She breathes in, out again, says, 'It is a Cistercian house. You understand what that means?'

There is a gaping hole in my stomach. 'We can't talk?'

'But for the *Divine Offices*, and the readings at mealtimes, no.'

'But how do…?'

'They communicate by sign language, and I believe you may write a note if something is of especial importance.'

I want to ask how I can make friends if we cannot speak to each other, how I can learn if not by repetition?

It's as if she knows what I'm thinking. 'Already you have a good grounding in music, in morals, in the liturgy and in Latin. It is only in the discipline of the order that

52

you must be prepared, and that you can only learn by living it. You would have grown beyond the education we can provide soon in any case.'

I don't think that's true, the feeling that I might have caught the abbess in a lie uncomfortable. The window of the chamber overlooking the convent garden is open, children's voices floating up from below, and I blurt out, 'Is laughter allowed?'

She answers slowly, as if she chooses each word with care. 'There will, I'm sure, be the chance for recreation and exercise, though how it will be organised I cannot say. But the regulations will not be so stringent for postulants as they are for those who have taken their vows.' She reaches across the table to touch my arm. 'We will be sorry to lose you, child, but no doubt your father wants what is best.'

There is a knock on the door, the chantress standing on the threshold. The abbess nods at me. 'Run along, Katharina, there still waits a half-hour before Sext. The sun is shining and it's a shame to waste it.'

I should do as the abbess says but I can't help hovering in the corridor outside, sure it will be of me they speak.

The chantress begins. 'You have news for the child?'

'Her father wishes her transferred.'

'To where?'

'The Marienthron at Nimbschen.'

'Why there?'

The abbess' tone is harsh, not as it had been for me.

'No doubt he thinks to save money.' A pause. 'It is an ill I have long despaired of, but the system of patronage is too engrained to be changed, besides that it's needed to ensure our houses can survive. If the von Boras cannot meet our requirements, in monies or land to gift, then a cheaper alternative for Katharina is inevitable.'

There is an uncharacteristic bitterness in the chantress' voice. 'And the Cistercians the cheapest of them all, their poverty, their determination to avoid any hint of excess, to be admired.' I hear her rapid footsteps criss-crossing the chamber, her voice rising. 'She has great promise, in music and learning both. Could we not bend the rules?'

'For myself I would, but I don't think our overseers would look kindly on it, however much promise she has.'

'But a silent order. For all that she isn't talkative, it will be a difficult transition. And for a ten-year-old, it is surely too much of a challenge.'

The abbess' voice drops and I strain to hear. 'What can we do? It is for her father to determine her future, our duty but to carry it out.'

The pacing stops. 'I will miss her. She has the voice of an angel.'

'I know. You chose a good name for her.' The abbess' footsteps are coming towards the door, and I scuttle around the corner lest I be discovered and their good opinion of me, which I hug to myself as I run, be lost.

Torgau: September 1552

Margarethe is here, her head bent over her sewing, her eyes narrowed, her lip caught between her teeth. I have told her so many times that she will ruin her sight, but she has always resisted wearing the eyeglasses Martin obtained for her. I understand it when in company, for even in a house such as ours where learning is valued, a girl does not always want to look a scholar. And she is of an age now when it is a husband she thinks of. I raise my head off the pillow, ask, 'Where are your eyeglasses, Margarethe?' In my head the words are clear, my voice loud, but there must be something amiss with my ears, for I cannot hear myself, only a whistle in my throat, barely audible.

She looks up, but doesn't answer, instead comes over and bends her head close to mine. 'What is it, Mutti?'

I say again, 'Your eyeglasses. You know you should wear them always, but especially for fine work.' Her forehead puckers, as if she still doesn't understand, so I wave my hand towards the sewing she'd laid down, reach up and touch my fingers to her eyes.

Her face clears. 'My glasses, Mutti? They were damaged. In the accident.'

I cough to clear my throat, ask, 'What accident?' but she ignores the question, instead puts one arm around my shoulders raising me up.

'Drink this, Mutti. It'll soothe your throat.'

I push away the cup. 'What accident?'

She sighs, lifting the cup to my lips again. 'Try, Mutti, please try.'

I don't want a drink, not in this bed, in this rabbit hutch of a room. I thrust aside the coarse blankets, put every ounce of strength I have into my voice. 'We should go home now.'

Although it is barely more than a croak, this time she seems to understand, but setting aside the cup, she settles me back against the pillow and takes both my hands in hers, 'Soon, Mutti, when the carter is come.'

Chapter Seven
Nimbschen, 1509

'The fewer the words, the greater the prayer; the more words, the poorer the prayer.'

Martin Luther

At the entrance to the valley the carter pulls up the horses. 'There it is. May not look much, but you won't go hungry and the sisters are said to be kind.'

I look at the clutter of low buildings crouching in the valley, the rough stone scab-coloured, and bite my lip hard, blinking to halt the tears that threaten. A gash, like an open wound, scars the hillside behind them, and the wagon driver, glancing at it, and then at me, adds, as if he thinks it the outside I fear, 'One thing's for sure, you'll be safe within, though why they needed the ditch I don't know, as if the hill isn't enough protection.'

As we approach the surrounding wall I hear the bleating of sheep and the lowing of cattle and above them the screech of geese.

'Plenty of livestock and farmhands and shepherds to

look to them.' A hint of amusement creeps into the driver's voice. 'As many workers as sisters I believe, so they're well served...' He breaks off, as if he's said something he shouldn't. 'But I daresay you won't have any contact with them' – he grins again – 'or not yet awhile at any rate.'

I don't understand what's funny, but I give him a small smile in return, surprised by the flush that spreads across his cheeks. The entrance is half-hidden, as if they don't welcome visitors, and my stomach starts to churn. As he lifts me down, I see my father hammering on the door at Brehna, handing me over as if I was a package to be delivered. I hadn't properly understood then what it meant. This time I know that when the door shuts behind me, it might never open again.

He pulls on the bell rope beside the gate. Used to the quality of the Brehna bells, the resulting jangle makes me wince. There is a pause, then shuffling footsteps before the door swings back. The man who opens it has a gnarled face, like the bark of an old oak, with a bulbous growth on the side of his nose. I stare at it and he narrows his eyes at me, far from welcoming.

'Yes?'

The driver pushes me forward, his touch on my back surprisingly gentle. 'Katharina von Bora. She's expected.'

With the giving of my name the gatekeeper's eyes soften. 'She'd better come in then.' He picks up my bag, the driver nodding as he turns away, his muttered, 'Good luck, child,' the last thing I hear as the gate shuts behind me.

As the bolts scrape home I shiver.

'You cannot be cold, child. When did you last eat?'

I'd managed a couple of spoonfuls at breakfast, but

58

they scarcely counted. 'Not since last night.'

'Hungry then, I daresay.' He shuffles ahead of me across the courtyard to a low door, the smell of potage making my stomach rumble.

He ducks his head through the doorway, calls, 'I brought you a new one, needs a bit of feeding before she's seen.' He thrusts me past him into the kitchen. There's a fire flaring on the hearth, a pot hanging from a bar over the flames, the contents bubbling away. My stomach rumbles again and I press my fist against it willing it to be silent.

The kitcheness spins round, the wooden spoon in her hand leaving a trail across the flagged floor. She's bandy-legged, almost as round as she's tall, with cheeks as red as a russet apple, her scolding I think for show. 'A knock would be a fine thing, to give warning before you barge in. Unless you'd care to clean the floor for me.'

His smile shows more gaps than teeth. 'Is that all the thanks I get for an act of charity.' He winks at me. 'You'd best look after her, for skinny as she is, she's kin to the abbess.'

The kitcheness grasps my shoulders, holds me at arm's length, her head tilted to one side. 'Well you'd best leave her to me then, and don't be passing the word around too soon.' She waves me towards a seat at the table, ladling me a bowl of the potage, and as if she thinks me afraid of the gatekeeper says, 'Don't listen to that old goat. You're not skinny exactly, though a bit more flesh on your bones wouldn't go amiss.'

I blurt out, 'You spoke to him.'

Her laugh is hearty. 'If I did not, there's more than you would go hungry.' She slides onto the bench opposite me. 'Silence is a rule among the sisters, but not the lay helpers.' She leans towards me as if it is a secret she shares. 'Though sometimes that would be an advantage. Eat up now. Rumour spreads faster in this place than a spillage of soup. The abbess will be wanting you before you know.'

Rapid footsteps approach the door and I shovel the soup down, afraid I won't have time to finish.

The nun who enters comes straight to me, and raising me to my feet she wraps her arms around me, squeezing me tightly, the discomfort reminding me of Anna and of Lippendorf and home. She steps back a fraction but keeps hold of both my hands as if she is afraid I will disappear. 'I'm your Aunt Magdalene. You need not fear. We will look after you.' She turns to the kitcheness and words fly between them, their hands flashing. Fascinated, I watch the rapid movements, punctuated by quick glances towards me, and wish I knew what they were saying, their smiles the only comfort.

The tall nun turns back to me. 'I will take you to the abbess now. She also has been looking forward to your coming. We trust you will be happy here.' At the doorway she signs to the kitcheness again, then whispers to me, 'Don't worry, you will learn to sign in time. For now, take care not to raise your voice; in the quiet that prevails here, a murmur will be sufficient.'

I want to ask 'Is it hard not to talk?' but am not sure the question will be welcome.

As if she reads my thoughts, she says, 'Those who must have contact with the outside world may speak when necessary.' A glimpse of a smile. 'It is sometimes a relief.' Then, as if she recollected herself, 'But for the most part I am content with quiet.'

We pass another low building, little different from the rest. I wouldn't know it was the church but for the statue of Our Lady that guards the door and the sounds spilling out through the tall windows. A disjointed phrase, sung, stopped, sung, the silences between broken by single notes ringing out from one true voice. Aunt Magdalena waves her hand.

'The choir, practising for Sext. The chantress tries her best, but we are not overly musical here.' The choir strikes up again, this time the music continuing for several minutes, one voice like a bell with a crack in it, another a little behind time. I make a face and she raises her eyebrows in an unspoken question. 'They would welcome a new voice … as would we who must listen.'

I shake my head. Whatever else I must be here, I don't want to be part of that.

She regards me for a moment, and I think she knows my capabilities, but she doesn't press. 'No doubt we will find a niche to suit you.' A pause, a glimmer of a smile, as if the contrast is deliberate. 'And if it is as a chambress, looking to the lavatories, that gift too is needful.'

The abbess also hugs me, but with a little more restraint, before stepping back and also holding me at arm's length, her gaze direct. Again I have the uncomfortable feeling that she sees right into me – perhaps that is the gift of an abbess – but I meet her gaze without flinching.

'Well, child? You have the look of your mother. I trust you will prove to have her character also.'

It is the undoing of me. Tears spill down my cheeks,

impossible to stop, however much I rub at them with my sleeve.

Her voice is gentle. 'How long is it since someone spoke of your mother?'

'Not since home.'

'That is something I can remedy. It is my privilege to speak when required. Something you will share in the meantime. We are not ogres here.' She thrusts a handkerchief at me. 'Private communication by signing is a rule you will find strange at first, but' – there is a twinkle in her eyes – 'the benefits of silence often outweigh the inconveniences.'

She waits for me to dry my cheeks, hand back the handkerchief. 'You understand what it means to come as a postulant, Katharina? The changes that must be made?'

I look down at her sleeve and can't resist touching it. The wool is surprisingly soft, the weave straight. 'Yes,' I whisper.

∞∞∞

At Brehna I loved the music; here I want to shut it out: the melodies that jar, the discordant notes, the painful mis-timings. I bury 'linnet' along with my hope to be a chantress, and make my voice unremarkable, so that no one suggests I join the choir. At Brehna we children rose in time for Prime, now I struggle from bed in the deepest hour of the night and stumble to the church, my feet slipping on the damp flagstones, to shiver my way through Matins and Lauds, coldness seeping up from the stone floor numbing my feet. Magdalena von Staupitz, among the oldest here, stands directly opposite me, her face tilted upwards, and though her eyes are shut I know by her expression that it is prayer she focuses on and not her discomfort. That shames me.

I'm neither old nor arthritic, yet all I can think of is the ache in my legs from standing and the desire to escape back to my cell to curl up like a snail, the thin blankets wrapped tight around my ears, blocking out the constant call of the bells.

Sister Magdalene's voice is kind, her touch on my shoulder light.

'Don't fret, child, the discipline will get easier with time, I promise you.'

But it doesn't, and when I confide in Eva as we stand in line waiting for the brothers to take our confession, she smothers a laugh and whispers back, 'Me too. But at least it saves having to imagine some other sin to confess. And the penance is light.'

Later, as we kneel side by side in the garden, harvesting herbs, I say, 'I can't confess to the same thing every week.'

She shrugs. 'Why not? Probably most of the sisters do. Anyway, you can alternate: difficulty waking one week, difficulty keeping the rule of silence the next. There aren't many sins to commit here. No parents to fail to honour, few possessions to covet.'

In the next row Eva's sister raises her eyebrows. 'There are other commandments.' A pink tinge spreads across her cheeks. 'They say the well has many secrets to keep.'

We have none of us noticed the abbess. 'That's enough. Come with me, Marta, such talk is unseemly.'

She scrambles to her feet, her face now flooded with colour, and follows as the abbess strides away, her back stiff.

Eva rocks back on her heels, whistles. 'Wonder what penance she'll get for that?'

I'm still thinking of my own guilts. 'What if I'm not good enough for this?'

'How often have you been brought before the abbess?'

'I haven't.'

'Well then.' She grabs her basket and mine, glances up at the sky. 'Come on, there's half an hour before Vespers and I know where there's some early blackberries.' As I still hesitate, she tosses her head. 'If you're worried, say a few more *Hail Marys*. If Our Lady will not listen to us here, in the convent of her throne, where else?'

CⓍⓍⓍD

I wish I was Eva. Observant to the rule of the bells, but not held captive by them. We have had two months to prepare for our installation and her elfin smile remains the same, laughter still twinkles behind her eyes, and her prayers lie light on her. Not on me. My prayers are feverish, diligent, more frequent than our strict rules demand, yet I derive no comfort from them.

We are practising signing in pairs, the silence between us filled with gestures and grimaces. When Eva can't make me understand what she's trying to say she tosses her head and whispers, answering Sister Magdalene's reproving look with an apologetic smile that draws a smile in return. There are few who do not smile on Eva.

Later, when we are grading the apples in the storehouse, I ask again, 'What if I'm not good enough?'

She shrugs. 'Maybe none of us are. But the choice has been made for us.' She brings her head close to mine.

'Besides, there are worse things than a cloister. We have a cousin who was forced to marry an old man because my uncle had little to spare for a dowry. He had more hair growing out of his ears than on his head and was bow-legged and as fat as a bishop. She cried for a month before the wedding, and probably didn't stop then.'

'Don't you have *any* fears for what lies ahead?'

'Why should I? Whatever we may look like on the outside, inside I will still be me and you will still be you. Friends forever.' She stands up, strikes a novice-teacher pose. 'Protected from the world. Your duty only to the cloister.'

'And to God,' I say.

'Chastity and poverty and obedience to the *Hours* will scarcely be difficult in our circumstances.' She grins. 'Except for getting up in the middle of the night. Though I'm not sure that God would worry if we slept till morning.'

'Eva!'

'What difference should it make *when* we pray?'

Her God is still the kindly grandfather of our childhood, and I wish I could believe in Him, instead of mine, who seems to grow colder with the weather, his demands more impossible to fulfil, whatever Eva says.

The draught creeping under the door of my cell makes me shiver as Sister Magdalene strips me of my clothes and dresses me in the white postulant's robe. As she parcels up my own things to take away, she favours me with a smile, her fingers flashing reassurance. Automatically I sign back.

'See?' Her smile broadens, her signing emphatic. 'You *are* ready.'

We file into the church for our formal installation, outwardly calm. I am ahead of Eva and as the ceremony proceeds I do all that is expected of me. Kneel when I must kneel, stand when I must stand and make my petition for admission to the order without stumbling over the words, my voice clear. I sense the pride of the novice-teacher and for a moment my heart swells, to be swallowed by shame, for is not pride one of the deadliest sins? I look down at the habit that engulfs me but see only a stranger. I know that both of my aunts have their eyes on me and that it pleases them to have me here, but I wish with all my heart that I was as sure about God. I think of home, of Hans and Anna and little Franz, who won't be little any longer, and Father, and Frau Seidewitz and the unborn child who drove me away, and struggle not to hate them all.

Chapter Eight
Nimbschen, October 1509

'Hatred is an uneasy bedfellow, Katharina. Believe me, I know.' Aunt Magdalene halts in her crushing of lavender heads, the scent rising around us, and meets my eyes, understanding in her gaze. Her fingers convey gentleness, with no hint of reprimand for my breaking of the silence that normally accompanies our work. She looks down at her hands, and begins to work the pestle again. Running her tongue around her lips, she casts an upward glance at the plaque of Our Lady that adorns every chamber here, as if in supplication or apology, before she says, 'You may have good reason for your feelings, but here you do not hurt anyone else by them, save yourself. Hatred leads to bitterness, and bitterness can grow inside you until you can scarcely breathe for sake of it. Pray that you may be able to forgive, if forgiveness is needed. It is by far the best way.'

I have prayed: in the church when I should have been listening to the readings or concentrating on the prescribed singing, and kneeling by the side of my bed until my knees ache from the cold. But either God isn't listening, or my prayers are in some way deficient, so that they fail to reach past the ceiling.

It's as if she sees right into my head. She reverts to signing. 'God is always listening, child. But sometimes he chooses not to answer.' A pause, then, 'Or not in the way we expect.'

I want to say 'Why does he torture us so?' but choke off the words, for I don't wish to shock and I know it is comfort she seeks to offer, the fact that she has broken the rule of our order to speak to me an indication of her depth of feeling. I sign back, 'I'm sorry, it's just there are times…'

She reaches across the table and rests her hand for a moment on mine. 'We all have times of doubt, but with Our Lady's help we can overcome them.' She lifts the mortar and shakes the crushed lavender into the open box, closing the lid as if to signal the end of the conversation. I envy her assurance but cannot find it in myself.

⊗⊗⊗

The bell rings for Sext. We have reached an accommodation, the bells and I. They punctuate my life, marking out the days and hours, but I no longer wince at every stroke, since I discovered that it's possible to hear yet not listen.

'A useful skill in many circumstances,' Aunt Magdalene had signed, when she saw me telling Eva. I didn't understand her then. I do now. It is an art we all practise, as a protection from the petty jealousies that spring up from time to time to threaten the smooth running of our order.

As I hurry along the path towards the church, other sisters appear from every direction, the slip-slap of shoes on the flagstones a familiar counterpoint. But today there are no forbidden whispers to be masked. Instead, the air is full of the fluttering of many hands, one sentence constantly repeated.

Abbot Balthazar is here.

I feel the unease in my stomach his name always arouses, reinforcing, as it does, my sense of unworthiness. He's standing at the chancel steps, his expression stilling the hands of even the most garrulous of us, his eyes far from kind. His castigation likewise, reverberating around the church. It is as if he speaks directly to me, as if he knows of our conversation.

'God does not favour disobedience,' he bellows, 'and it is most displeasing to me to hear of your laxness in keeping the regulations of your order: your Godless chatter, your faulty observance of the *Hours*.' He leans forward, the spittle flying from his mouth, the abbess flinching as it lands on her cheek. 'Repent of your sins, whether of commission or of omission, and root out the guilty, from the youngest to the oldest, lest God bring a judgement upon you.'

I shrink into myself, sure that he must see into my soul and know that I have caused my aunt to sin also, but the corners of Eva's mouth lift a fraction, as if she struggles not to laugh. I tramp on her toe, opening my eyes wide at her. It's no laughing matter. As we file in silence towards the refectory for the noontime meal, the two monks from Pforta who live within our compound appear. Eva's hands flutter briefly. 'It seems our good fathers do not confine themselves to taking confession. No doubt it is they who

69

are the abbot's spies.'

True or not, it's a dangerous thought.

The abbot himself presides over our meal, spreading across the bench between the abbess and the infirmaress, picking the bones of salt herring from between his teeth. Under his glare the nun whose turn it is to give the reading of the day stumbles over her words, the Book of Hours shaking in her hands, and I look down at my food, afraid that he will see the uncertainties I feel.

Eva nods at my untouched plate, raises her eyebrows in a question. I shake my head, push it towards her. I don't like Abbot Balthazar, fear him even, yet his words have pricked me to the heart. Though there is no reprimand registered against me in the records of our convent at Grimma, I know I don't meet the standard he demands. And if not his, who is only a man, how can I attain to God's? When we are dismissed I slip back to the church, to prostrate myself on the stone slabs, repeating the prayer of the penitent, again and again, until my muscles ache with the cold and my teeth chatter. Before I know it, the bell chimes for *None* and I scramble to my feet, remembering the duties I should have performed, add that lapse to the list of sins I must confess.

At Brehna I counted out the weeks, marking them off in a line of cherry stones placed around the base of the potting shed at the far end of the gardens, where no one but me would notice. By the time word came for me to leave, the line had stretched around three sides and was almost back to where I had started. Occasionally, when it is my turn

70

to help in the orchard, I think of them, whether any might have grown into saplings, and if someday the shed would be smothered in blossom. Then, I kept count so that when I returned home I wouldn't be taken by surprise by the change in my brothers. Now, knowing that there will be no such return, I choose not to mark the passing of time, but allow the days to blend into weeks and the weeks into months, seeking salvation in the ordered routine of our lives. And as the seasons turn and the months drift into years, I take solace in the cycle of saints' days and church festivals, wrapping observances around myself like a blanket to counter the ice-blast of Abbot Balthazar's thunderings.

Of all the tasks I am given, two remain my favourites: assisting in the infirmary, where Aunt Magdalene teaches the healing properties of plants and herbs that we grow in the physic garden, and how to prepare the decoctions and unguents that are needed for treating the various ailments that beset us from time to time; and working in the brewery, the smell, which Eva wrinkles her nose at, failing to bother me. Of the tasks forbidden to us, I regret only one: that I cannot tend to the pigs.

'That is for farmhands, Katharina,' the abbess says, when I ask if it may be part of my training.

'But why? Is it not also honest toil?'

'Honest, yes, but not seemly.'

I try Aunt Magdalene, but she refuses to be drawn.

'Rules are made for a reason, our duty but to follow them.'

Eva is no help, shrugging her shoulders. 'I don't know.' She pinches her nose between finger and thumb. 'And why would you want to look after such dirty, smelly creatures? Getting rid of the brewery smell is hard enough, but the pigsty! Anyway, they're ugly and snort and roll in the mud.'

'Don't you think the piglets sweet?'

'All young animals are sweet, but mostly they don't stay that way long. I, for one, am glad we can't work the farm.'

'And I.' Marta von Schonfeld appears behind Eva, amusement in her eyes.

'I still don't see why not.'

'Don't you?' Her signing is exaggerated, as if to someone dull-witted. 'We are female. The farmhands are male. Of course we aren't allowed to work with them.' She rolls her eyes. 'Who knows what consanguinity might do?'

Torgau: 1552

Someone is playing a lute, the melody haunting. I shut my eyes, allowing the sound to lap at the edges of my brain, like a tide. I have not seen the sea, but one of the sisters at Brehna talked of it. I remember the wistful expression in her eyes as she described the soft shush of the waves as they advanced, the rattle as they sucked back the shingle, then carried it forward again, how each time they swallowed a little more of the land; the picture she painted so vivid that I felt as if I was there. And now I am: high up on a cliff edge; and far beneath me the sea glistens, welcoming. I dive downwards, seeking its embrace, the water all around me, on my forehead and my cheeks, sliding between my breasts and my thighs: cool, soothing. I shiver, strain to make out the voices.

The first is soft, hesitant. 'Is it too much? We do not wish to give her a chill.'

The second I recognise. 'She already suffers a chill, the fever a sign of it, and all the more dangerous for that. We must reduce it.'

I nod, proud of my daughter. She has learnt well, and I want her to know I agree, but she doesn't seem aware of my affirmation. I feel her roll me onto my side, and I make a movement to protest, the pain in my hip travelling down towards my foot, but she doesn't seem aware of that either. Perhaps someone is, for I hear the first voice again, doubtful.

'The Herr Doctor...'

Margarethe is dismissive, trailing a damp cloth over my shoulders and down the ripple of my spine, giving relief from the fire that licks at my skin. 'He doesn't know everything.'

I laugh at that, a belly laugh that starts deep in my abdomen, building as it climbs, shaking my chest and shoulders; but as it bursts from me it isn't laughter that comes out, but rather a paroxysm of coughing. She props me up, her arm about me, and pats my back, as she might a child. Opening my eyes to smile my thanks, I see relief in her face and feel her grip tighten. 'I'm here, Mutti. I'm here.'

Of course she is. But where are the others? Lizzie and Magdalena? Outside the light is fading, the square of window disappearing into the shadows.

The first voice again, 'What time is it?'

Margarethe's reply is scarcely more than a whisper. 'About nine, I think.'

Nine o'clock. The hour for Compline.

CHAPTER NINE
NIMBSCHEN, OCTOBER 1515

'All people that labour to come to God, other than
through Christ, walk in horrible darkness and error; and
it helps them nothing that they lead an honest, sober kind
of life, affect great devotion, suffer much ... they remain
always in doubt and unbelief, knowing not how they
stand with God.'

Martin Luther

Compline. I slip into my place, a little behind time, dart
a glance of apology to the abbess, who nods, as if in
understanding. Today is the last day of my novitiate, the
last opportunity to draw back; tomorrow I will become a
Bride of Christ. I look around at the sisters, searching their
faces for contentment as they sing the Office. In some I
surprise serenity, chief among them the oldest of us all,
who, it is said, also came as a child and knew no other
place, which gives me momentary encouragement. In
others I sense resignation; which raises doubts to threaten
my peace.

As I file out of the church, one of the older nuns plucks at my sleeve and leads me into the shadows of the orchard, signing, 'I have something to share with you before the morning.' I think perhaps that she has sensed my hesitation and that she risks punishment to whisper some word of encouragement, and I prepare to be grateful. The apple trees are old, each trunk split, marking the point at which stems from a good fruiting variety had been grafted onto sturdy stock. We stand close under the low branches and she begins to sign.

'There are worse fates than to be shut away in a convent, worse marriages.' She hesitates, her fingers still, then begins again, the expression on her face matching the impassioned flashing of her hands, so that it seems the pain of years spills out of her. An echo of Eva, but with the force of experience, and I'm not sure that I want to hear her confession, afraid that it will only increase my own sense of unworthiness, but there is no polite way to halt her. I hadn't expected tears, nor her agitation, and find it hard, in the dim light that filters through the branches overhead, to follow the ever-increasing speed of her signing.

Dusk is falling, stars appearing as pinpricks in the vast blackness of sky, and she glances upwards, then draws a deep breath and begins to speak. Her voice is husky, but whether from lack of use or the pain of her words I cannot tell. I touch her arm, say, 'There is no need…'

She places her finger against my mouth, continues, 'I do not think God will censure me for this breach. It is by far the least of my sins and I will confess it freely. On the outside I lived so long with guilt that I was sure God had forsaken me: for what I did not feel for my husband and for

76

what I did feel for another. And to my shame I prayed for release. In my lowest moments it was my husband's death I prayed for, but mostly it was for my own. Yet when he did die, it didn't bring me the freedom I had yearned, nor the opportunity to love as I had wished. Despite that my own love was still free, still wished to marry me, and that I now had the means to make it possible for us to live in comfort, I found I could not do it. I felt nothing but relief at my husband's death, and that itself was a guilt hard to bear, but worse was the conviction that burned within me, that far from profiting from my widowhood, I should suffer for the failure of my marriage, for the blame was surely mine. Convinced I didn't deserve the future that was offered, I feared to grasp it, lest it be at the cost of the one who meant the most in the world to me; for did not my husband's death by his own hand indicate that I was flawed, incapable of giving happiness?' She took another deep breath. 'I came here as an act of contrition, a way of seeking forgiveness, from God and from my husband. But what I found was a way of forgiving myself.'

I shift, my buttocks sore where the gnarled graft on the trunk of the apple tree I'm leaning against is digging into me, and try to still my impatience, for though her circumstances are not mine, I know she means well.

It is as if she reads my thoughts. 'You have come as a child, with no past to trouble you. We all tread different paths to this point, but from here our paths converge. In the days to come you may be troubled with dreams of what might have been, with longings that cannot be fulfilled. You may not always find joy in your calling...' She pauses, and I sense an internal struggle as if she weighs honesty against encouragement, before she continues.

77

'Few I think do, but most find contentment, and that a blessing that many outside our walls would envy.'

She falls silent and I don't know if she expects a response, but I have nothing to say. After a moment she reaches out and grasps my hand in both of hers, massaging it gently. 'I do not mean my history to be a burden to you, but the world is not always kind, to women especially, and a convent can be a salvation, in this life as well as the next.' Then she is gone, fading into the shadows, and for a moment I wonder if it has been a dream or a visitation, if God Himself is speaking to me.

As I pass the kitchen on the way back to the dormitory, the door opens, the kitcheness beckoning me, holding one finger to her lips. I am struck by the irony of it, that on this, the night before my consecration, two of the sisters are laying aside the rules on my behalf.

Her encouragement is in keeping with her figure, her signing spiced with humour. 'This isn't the easiest life, but not the hardest either, and for those with little fortune it is at least a guarantee of bed and board. The food, as you know, if not exciting, is wholesome: the bread without weevils, the cheese without mould, the small beer nourishing.'

I stifle a laugh and see an answering glint in her eyes as she turns to the stove and lifts a tumbler of hot milk, the scent of honey rising from it as she passes it to me.

'Drink this, it may help you sleep.'

Despite her kindness, I lie on my bed, the darkness deepening, the hour of my 'marriage' creeping upon me, and perhaps because of what had been said to me in the orchard, I find myself thinking of families who had once been of our acquaintance, one of whose sons, had it not been for Frau Seidewitz' intervention, I might have grown up to marry, might indeed have already married and borne his children. And hard on that thought, a memory of our mother, of the candles guttering in the wall sconces in her chamber as we were summoned to make our goodbyes. Her eyes huge against the pallor of her face, her voice no more than a whisper. The priest anointing her, mumbling the last rites, accepting the coins my father presses upon him before stepping back from the bed to give way to my brothers and to me. Father standing me on a stool, my hand creeping into hers, the surprise I feel that, though her hair is damp and sticks to her cheeks, her skin is hot and dry. The hurt when she turns her face away, allowing my fingers to slip free, her last breath a sigh.

Anna, breaking the silence that follows, 'There is little more dangerous than childbirth and women expected to shoulder that burden more times than is good for them.'

It was the first time I heard her say a critical word of my father, the only time I saw a tear in his eye, and it comes back to me now, as clear as if it were yesterday. This marriage, which I am about to pledge myself to, is at least free from dangers of that kind. And whether it is the effect of the milk and honey or the comfort of knowing that the sisters welcome me into their ranks, I slide into sleep, clinging to the thought that it is a better thing to embrace the life laid out for me than to imagine what might have been.

There's a chill in the air when I wake, and I shiver as I disrobe to wash myself in the water brought to me in a pottery ewer by the kitchen maid, who struggles under the weight of it. It chills me to the bone, bringing home, as nothing else can, the enormity of what I am about to do. The chambress, come to shave my head and help me dress, nods her encouragement as she drops the white woollen habit onto my shoulders.

'Are you ready, child?' Her fingers are, for once, hesitant, as if to give me one last chance to pull back.

'I am ready,' I sign, straightening my shoulders and turning to the door. Then, in a burst of honesty, 'Though I do not feel worthy, but I will pledge myself to try.'

She nods again, signs, 'It is those who think highly of themselves who are most likely to fail. Humility is the better way.'

In the church I lie prostrate on the floor, as I have watched others do before me, coldness seeping upwards from the flags into my bones. A draught, funnelled from the arched doorway, rolls over me in waves, and my shaved head aches. It is a shock how difficult it is to lie prone, how tense my muscles become as I hold my arms outstretched while prayers are said and the formalities followed. I'm glad that my face is hidden, that no one can see the doubts that still trouble me. When the abbess raises me up, the cramp in my legs and arms turns to pins and needles, and I struggle to remain still as the scapular is placed over me as a sign of the acceptance of my vows, the black a stark contrast to the white of the habit. The girdle is tied around my waist, the rosary swinging and settling at my side. And finally the white wimple and black cowl, and I am glad of them, for the relief they give to my head and ears.

The procession winds down the nave and through the

archway towards the door that leads to the cloister, the choir trying their best, and for once I don't focus on the less than perfect harmonies, the cracked notes, but instead try to drown in the words they sing. The church is ablaze with candles: mounted on every pillar and held aloft by the nuns who process behind me. As I pass each sconce the flames dip and rise again as if in acknowledgement of my consecration, and I begin to feel that perhaps I do belong here. That what my father ordained might be God's will also. Outwardly serene, inwardly I pray a final, anguished prayer that one day I may prove worthy.

All the way down each side of the nave are the altars before which our relics are displayed. I have looked on them so many times that to my shame I have come to barely notice them, but today is different, each one gaining in significance: a heritage in which I now share. I come to the reliquary that holds a vial containing St Paul's blood and, momentarily distracted by the miracle of its preservation, stumble on an uneven flagstone, the abbess' hand reaching out for my elbow to steady me. It isn't just for my sake that she wishes no ill omen to mar this day, but for the whole community, for we are a superstitious lot, and apt to see signs and portents in any mishap, however small. For if God is here, of a surety the Devil is too, seeking to destroy God's work, his presence a canker that mustn't be allowed to root.

Behind me, the music swells to a crescendo as I approach the door to step out into a new life. Dawn is breaking, the sky suffused with colour, the blossoming clouds edged with rose. I pause on the doorstep, take a deep breath. One final step and it is done, irrevocable. Above me a shaft of light, breaking through the clouds, pours over my head and shoulders and down to my feet, spreading out in a pool around me. The abbess beams, my stumble forgotten, the other nuns breaking ranks and crowding round me to offer congratulations. They are like a flock of birds, their hands fluttering like wings, messages flying backwards and forwards, so many that I cannot catch them all. I turn first one way then another, my rosary swinging from side to side, refracting the new light into a myriad of miniature rainbows arcing across the path, and I think perhaps it is a confirmation that I am not making a mistake. Yet when the music falters and stutters to a stop, I am possessed by another fear: that I was wrong to turn my back on the role of chantress, that I may have forfeited God's pleasure by hiding my gift.

CHAPTER TEN
NIMBSCHEN, JUNE 1516

The man who comes from the village demanding to speak to the abbess is dressed soberly, a badge of office sewn on his cloak. I am on duty at the inner gate and so bring him to the abbess' chamber. Showing him in, I station myself outside the half-open door. Whether it is to protect the abbess' honour, or to ensure the good behaviour of the abbess herself, is not stated in the book of rules, but the principle is clear enough: it is forbidden for any member of the community to meet with a man in private, save in the confessional, and there the grill between them safeguards both.

It appears he is angry, and, stoked with a sense of his own importance, prepared to give vent to his anger. He speaks, it seems, for the whole village. They are suffering from a lack of fish, caused, so they suppose, by the diverting of the river to run through our fishpond and thereby trap many of the fish.

'You harm not only those whose living depends on the fish stocks, but indeed many among the population who cannot readily supplement their diet to compensate.'

The abbess is polite. 'Will you sit, that we may discuss the matter more amicably?'

Ignoring her offer, he leans over the desk that separates them, and, with a backwards glance at the half-open door, thumps the Book of Hours with his fleshy hand. 'Are our children to starve because of the greed of your nuns? Is this Christian behaviour? Where is your charity? Your dedication to doing good?' He puffs himself up to his full five foot two inches, which leaves him still an inch or two short of the abbess. 'It is a sin of commission that God will not overlook, nor will the abbot, should we be forced to report the state of affairs to him.'

The abbess rises, bends her head towards his as if she would speak in his ear, and I can no longer see her expression, but hold my breath, her closeness to him making me uneasy. I hear what seems like a whisper, but cannot be, for her answer follows, the tone conciliatory.

'Perhaps it is needful to provide an alternative watercourse. Should the town council wish to come up with a plan, we will be happy to consider it.'

I see his shoulders relax and think I sense a softening, the thought quenched by his gruff tone. 'No doubt they will wish it, and when they have consulted I will return with their plan.' His voice rises again. 'And rest assured we will appeal to Pforta, should we not receive speedy recompense and the restitution of our rights.'

He pulls the door wide and thrusts past me with every appearance of annoyance, but something in his stance makes me suspect it may be for my benefit, and as I glance beyond him into the abbess' chamber I see her slide a paper from the Book of Hours and conceal it in her desk, her lips curving into a smile.

She looks up, sees where my gaze rests and signs, 'When you have shown our visitor out, come back, I would speak with you.'

She is standing by the small window, resting her arms on the sill, and turns as I reappear in the doorway, her hands signalling, 'Come in … and shut the door.'

Thinking that she might be cross with me for my earlier inquisitiveness, I sign back, 'I wanted to check that you were unharmed. He sounded so angry.'

'I know.' She comes to me and lays her hand on my shoulder, guiding me towards the chair. 'It's not to reprimand you that I have called you back.' Her fingers are long and slim, lending a certain elegance to her signing that sparks a momentary flash of envy in me. Her expression is thoughtful, as if she debates what to say. 'What I shall tell you now is not to be gossiped over, nor to be shared without my consent. You will understand the trust I place in you when I explain.' She sits down, leaning her elbows on the desk in an uncharacteristically informal pose and closes her hands together, the tips of her fingers touching her mouth. The Book of Hours is lying face up between us. 'You need not have feared. The man who came from the village did indeed bring a message about the fish stocks in the river, as you heard, and that is something we will have to address. But his anger was feigned. The fish story, though true, but a pretext for bringing me this.' She reaches into the desk drawer and brings out the paper that I saw her conceal. She sets it down where I can clearly see the lines of dense writing that cover it. It is a measure of the significance of it that her hands remain still, and instead she speaks aloud.

'Cloistered we may be, but the affairs of the world outside do not entirely pass us by. And, on occasion, it behoves us to know what is happening.' She taps the paper. 'This is one such pamphlet.' She draws a deep breath, continues, 'It comes from the prior at Grimma, who as you know is uncle to two of our young sisters, and was entrusted by him to the man you allowed entry. It seems the whole town is made alight by the controversy. I do not know as yet what I will do with this, but I am grateful for it nonetheless.' Her tongue flicks across her lips. 'If even one quarter is true, it is an iniquitous business.'

She is resting her chin on her linked hands, her eyes focused on the paper. 'God knows the sale of indulgences is not new, but this...' She shakes her head. 'Full remission of not only one's own sins, but those of deceased relatives also. See how this man Tetzel seeks to sway the credulous...' She slides the paper towards me, jabbing at a paragraph in the middle.

Do you not hear the voices of your parents and ancestors clamouring for help: We are suffering unbearable punishments and torments. You can buy our release with just a few alms, but you will not.

'No doubt it is a tug to the heartstrings and a sop to the conscience many will pay dear for. His mission attested by the Pope and Archbishop Albert.'

'But...' I begin, thinking of our own relics: more than three hundred of them, including a straw from Jesus' manger, a thorn from his crown, and, most treasured of all, a shred of cloth from the Virgin's veil. I have never before dared voice my lack of confidence in them, or my

86

discomfort at the income we derive from pilgrims who come to gawp, but I am close to it now.

The abbess nods, as if she follows my thoughts. 'Neither are we blameless, and perhaps we should set our own house in order before we condemn others.' She draws a deep breath. 'The wind of change is blowing in the outside world and will buffet us in due time. And perhaps sooner than we think, for it is our own provincial vicar, the Reverend Dr Martin Luther, who makes the challenge, and I find myself tempted to agree with his sentiment, if not his rhetoric.' She slides the paper back into the drawer. 'Suffice to say, if our confessing fathers were to learn I have received this, or to report it to the abbot, it would not be to our advantage. I can count on your discretion?'

It's my turn to nod, though I can't help thinking of Eva and of how hard it will be to remain silent.

'How we respond to the current turmoil is a question I must ponder, for I have a responsibility for us all.' She summons a smile, and reaching forward she touches my shoulder, indicating for me to rise. 'I have spoken to you as your aunt and not your abbess, but I shall not trouble you any further with my musings.'

At the door I hesitate, questions multiplying in my mind, but her expression silences me.

She reverts to signing, 'Before you return to your duties, please ask that the infirmaress come to me.'

Chapter Eleven
Nimbschen, March – August 1517

Words run like quicksilver among us. Not mine, or not at first, for I keep my promise, but that's of no consequence, for the gossip of our farmhands and the artisans who hail from the villages around is whispered from ear to ear and flies from the tips of every finger. It begins with what I already know from the abbess: of Tetzel and the Basilica in Rome; the extravagant promises made to those who will pay. It sounds more preposterous each time we talk of it.

'Remission of a thousand years!' Eva laughs. 'For a long-dead great-grandmother? No one will fall for that.'

But it seems she is wrong, and the abbess is right, for hard on the heels of the first whispers come rumours of the credulous travelling from near and far to buy remission of their sins.

'More fool them.' Eva is perched on the corner of the table in the sewing room, one foot swinging.

Lanita, the most timid of us, darts a glance towards the door, whispers, 'Don't you find it sad? That this Tetzel can prey on the poorest, and with the Church's blessing?'

It's a measure of her strength of feeling that Fronika, whose signing is normally rapid and fluent, chooses instead to speak. 'It's a disgrace! Our uncle Wolfgang says...' She breaks off at the sound of footsteps in the corridor, and though I desperately want to know what she was about to say, for the opinion of the prior of the monastery at Grimma is surely valid, I bury my head in the basket of embroidery threads, only emerging, clutching a skein of cerulean blue, when I hear the sacrist entering.

Her gaze encompasses us all but focuses on Eva, her signing censorious. 'Why are *you* here? I did not set you a task today. And get down at once. Tables are not for sitting on. Nor' – and this she directs at us all – 'is this an opportunity to gossip. We aren't paid to produce shoddy workmanship. Indeed we may not be paid at all if the altar-cloths you embroider do not meet the standards that are expected of us.' She turns again to Eva. 'But if you are so keen, perhaps you could return after Sext. No doubt I could find some suitable work that will save you from the need to distract others.'

I sense an agitation in her signing that cannot be explained simply by annoyance at Eva's presence, reinforced as she continues, 'You would all do well neither to listen to idle chatter, nor to repeat it. The traditions of our Church will no doubt prove stronger than the current controversy.'

Later, in the hour for our recreation, I draw Fronika aside.

'What *does* your uncle say of this?'

She hesitates, as if she regrets her earlier outburst, then, glancing around to see that we aren't overlooked, signs, 'He is proud. That the first real challenge to Tetzel has come at Grimma, that it is our provincial vicar at the heart of the matter. He says that the Church is ripe for reform, that change is coming, that even we, who are protected by the cloister, will feel it and should be ready to embrace it.' She hesitates again, and then, slipping her hand inside her sleeve, produces a tightly folded piece of paper. 'Here. This was enclosed in the letter he sent us.'

It's a copy of Dr Luther's letter to Albert, Archbishop of Mainz, and though the print is tightly packed, the sense is clear, and I cannot disagree with any of it. Nor, when I think of the abbess, once serene, going about with a permanent pucker between her brows, can I disregard Fronika's uncle's assessment.

⬡⬡⬡

Change is coming, and far from lagging behind, we, who have more time to ponder the matter, are swept early into the controversy, the divisions among us growing as the months wear on. Now it isn't only we young that cluster in corners and whisper together behind our hands, but some of the older sisters can also be found gathered in twos and threes, their hands flashing in animated discussion, cut off abruptly when anyone else appears. I, who have counted half a dozen of those closest to my own age as my particular friends, sense a new distance between us, signalled by awkward silences and a reluctance to sit with me in the gardens during our rest hour after Sext.

Aunt Magdalene is sympathetic, but unsurprised, when I go to her. 'Did not our Lord say he came not to bring peace, but a sword, to turn fathers against sons, brother against brother?' There is a twist to her mouth.

90

'I do not imagine it is any different for sisters.' She is looking down at her hands as she signs, but whether to ensure her accuracy, or to avoid meeting my eye, I'm not sure.

'These past months have been a testing time: for us, as for the outside world. And disagreements within a community such as ours are magnified by our seclusion.'

'I haven't expressed disagreement with anyone. Why should they shut me out?'

'You are the abbess' niece, and mine. That alone must make you suspect.'

'But the abbess…—'

Aunt Magdalene, with a swift look over her shoulder, cuts me off, her hand signal emphatic. 'Whatever you may know, or think you know, of the abbess' opinions, do not share them with anyone. It is for her alone to comment when she feels ready.' Her fingers still for a moment. 'And my responsibility, for the time being at least, is to follow her lead.' She allows her shoulders to relax. 'Talk to Eva and the others. You cannot blame them that they are wary, but whatever you feel inside, on this, or any other matter, share it with them openly. Friendship is a valuable commodity and one you should cling on to.' Another twist of her mouth. 'Though what good it may do any of us to think for ourselves is debatable, if all that is achieved is that we become discontented with our lot.'

'Sister Agnes says the Church will prevail.'

'She may well be right, and the disruptions we now suffer be but a small storm that our order and the Church will weather. If, however, Dr Luther's words are of God, neither we nor anyone else will be able to halt their effect.'

It seems that Abbot Balthazar is determined to try, his visits becoming more regular. Sometimes it's only the abbess and the prioress who suffer his admonishments, but today we are all ordered to attend in the church immediately after the noontime meal, forfeiting our permitted hour of relaxation, to share the brunt of his censure. He's in full flow, proclaiming from a Latin instruction of his own making, which in future is to be read aloud four times a year, the abbess responsible for explaining the minutest of details and ensuring that we keep to its strictures.

Beside me the chantress sighs and closes her eyes, as if by so doing she could block out his words, and I suspect she shares my view that this complaint is petty.

'You have a missal containing the proper and regular songs which must be sung. Accepted in all your houses, it is a sacrilege to add to them. Does our Church add to the psalms as heretics do?'

My attention wanders, to be caught again when he turns to the vow of silence.

'...Silence is the key to religion, disobedience a sin that will be called to account, for in this you do not merely dishonour God, but your order also, and the memory of the blessed St Bernard who set your rules.'

Eva's hands flash, 'Pity Balthazar hasn't taken a vow of silence,' her comment, though intended only for me, earning a glare from the sacrist, who clearly caught the movement.

He raises his voice further, puffs himself up like a turkey-cock, his face reddening, and I sense that this is the crux of his complaints. 'Furthermore, it has come to my attention that some among you harbour sympathies for this upstart priest who challenges the authority of the Church. And it is rumoured that some of his heretical writings have penetrated the cloister.'

There is a stir among us, an awkward shifting of feet and the whisper of robes brushing the floor. Several of the sisters closest to me look down and I see the raised colour on their cheeks, aware of heat in my own. It seems that Abbot Balthazar has also noted it, for as his gaze sweeps over us, he lingers longest on those of us whose heads are bowed, relish in his voice.

'If it be so, they should be surrendered to the abbess to be consigned to the fire and appropriate confession made.' His attention swings to the abbess. 'I shall expect a report to that effect and should it prove necessary a search can be made.'

The abbess' mouth is tight. 'I will deal with it and you will have your report.'

There is a self-satisfied smile on his face. 'From henceforth you will be protected from such influence. The replacement latticework I have ordered to be installed in the parlour will see to that.'

Chapter Twelve
September 1517 – November 1518

Abbot Balthazar's satisfaction is short-lived, despite that he got his report, the abbess making a show of burning several tracts which had apparently been left outside her door. Under the watchful eye of our confessing fathers, she thanked those, whoever they might be, who had taken the abbot's words to heart, and trusted that no further heretical writings would be found.

I see Eva's mouth twitch, her fingers moving on her lap. 'Take that how you will…'

On my other side, Fronika turns a snort into a fit of coughing, causing the sacrist to look across at us, her eyes narrowed. And month by month, just as wind slips through the smallest of cracks, so news of the turmoil outside continues to seep into the cloister. Some is unsurprising: Luther's removal from his position as provincial vicar. Some shocking, or indeed exciting, depending on preference: the burning by students of eight hundred copies of Tetzel's rebuttals of Luther's theses. Some barely believable: that the theses themselves have spread throughout all of Europe and beyond, that even the

English king has read them.

I'm in the brewery, cleaning out a vat, when Eva sticks her head around the door. She places one finger against her mouth and beckons to me, radiating excitement. I shake my head and signal towards the rear passage to indicate that the fratress is there. Eva holds up five fingers and raises her eyebrows as a question. I'm almost done, so I nod and resume my scrubbing.

The door behind me opens, and the fratress, looking out the window and seeing Eva disappearing towards the garden, is betrayed into a smile and to signing, 'On you go. I can finish up here.'

I dip my head in thanks, and pulling off my apron, I hang it on the hook before rushing out. I often find it hard not to envy Eva the ease with which she has won over all but the sternest of our community, the indulgent attitude that most of the older nuns display towards her. But today I'm glad of it and that I can answer her summons without delay, for though the renewal of our friendship seems to be holding, it isn't so long ago that I feared for its loss, and I'm not altogether confident of my place yet. The air is November-sharp, my breath curling in front of me, and the parts of the path that are shaded are silvered with frost, so that I slip and slither as I run to catch up.

When I skid to a halt beside the girls clustered around Eva there is a pain in my lungs and I bend double to recover. Fronika holds out her hand to raise me up and I grasp it, grateful for even the smallest sign that I belong among them again. We pass through the gate into the garden and settle ourselves on a pair of benches in a patch of sunlight, which takes the edge off the cold. The garden is empty, the silence complete. I risk, 'What is it that we cannot look at it indoors?'

'This.' The paper has been rolled so tightly that it curls again as Eva unfurls it, so that she catches the corner and stretches it out like a proclamation. 'The Holy Father has upheld Tetzel's claims for indulgences and Luther must recant or face trial for heresy.'

'Where did you get it?'

Fronika says, 'From my uncle, wrapped in a handkerchief.'

'Will Luther recant?'

'He thinks not. He says that if Dr Luther didn't crumble when faced by Cajetan at Augsburg, he won't give up now.'

'Luther is a brave man then.'

'Or a foolish one.' Eva's sister, Marta, is uncharacteristically serious. 'The disputation will not stop with Wittenberg; every church and monastery in the land raises money through indulgences. Including our own. I trust we won't have to tighten our girdles as a result.'

'But if the points he makes are true?' Else voices what we're all thinking. What has been eroding the peace of the cloister for months now.

'If what are true?'

Magdalena von Staupitz, the novice-teacher, has come on us unnoticed and holds out her hand. Eva, who had attempted to hide the paper in her sleeve, passes it over with an apologetic glance towards Fronika. I steel myself for the reprimand and perhaps a punishment, or that we'll be reported to the abbess, for we all know the respect Sister Magdalena has for the Church and for the rules of our order. She reads to the end, her lip caught between her teeth, then turns to Fronika, her signing tentative. There is a new uncertainty in her demeanour that sends a shiver through me.

'Does your uncle have a copy of these theses? Perhaps I should read them for myself. For if there is truth in them, everything must change.'

Tomorrow is the saint day of St Martin, and I don't sleep between Lauds and Prime, anticipation clawing at my stomach like an ache. The abbess is to make her annual trip to collect monies due to the convent and to make certain purchases of provisions and other goods that we cannot provide for ourselves, and I am to accompany her. It will be the first time I've left the safety of the cloister since I arrived nine years ago, the first time I've slept anywhere other than my own hard pallet, and I don't know how I shall feel to be outside. No one aside from the sisters has seen me in my nun's habit, and sometimes even to myself I still seem a stranger. I don't know how I will feel if I meet someone I know.

As we leave the church I share my fear and Eva laughs. Even without the laugh I'd know I amused her, for she has the gift of communicating emotion though her signing. It's as if I hear her voice in my head.

'Supposing you did, they wouldn't look twice at you, nor likely recognise you if they did. When you were outside, what did *you* see when you passed a nun?'

'The habit. If it was white or black.' I pucker my forehead, trying to think back, and have a vision of a group of nuns in the square at Lippendorf, one much taller than the rest, with an awkward, stooping stance as if she wished to shrink. 'If they were tall or short, fat or thin.'

'Nothing more?'

'We weren't encouraged to stare.'

'Exactly. She gestures downwards. The habit renders us almost invisible. Besides, no one you know has seen you for ... how long?'

'Fourteen years.' As I say it, I feel very small inside, as if I am that child again outside the door at Brehna, looking over my shoulder as Father remounts to ride away. For a moment I feel my hair, loosened by the wind, tumbling down my back, a few stray curls escaping from my cap. She's right. No one I used to know will recognise me now.

'You're fortunate to have been chosen to go. Think on that. And take care to look and listen well: for we'll all want to know what the fair is like.' She glances around to see if we are overlooked. 'And to hear the latest of this Dr Luther. If he has been thrown to the lions yet for his heresies.'

Despite my worries, I laugh also. 'Hardly. And as for the fair, I don't know if it is to that we go.'

'Of course you will go. You'll have to, if the abbess is to buy everything that is needed. Yesterday's shopkeepers in their own place will be stallholders at the fair tomorrow.' Her sigh is heartfelt. 'I do so wish I was you.'

To be envied is a new sensation, for normally it's me wanting to be Eva, and I give her a hug, though I'm not sure if I mean it as commiseration or appreciation. She pushes me towards the gate into the outer courtyard. 'Go on. The abbess will be waiting.' And as if she has read my thoughts, 'Pretend you *are* me. That way you may be able to properly enjoy the outing.'

Torgau: 1552

Paul is here, standing by the window, looking down onto the street. They have been good, Paul and Margarethe, readily giving of their time to sit by my bedside and watch over me. It is time, I think, to tell them that I no longer need such care, for surely, the pain in my hip diminished, I will be up and about soon enough. I miss Magdalena, but when I asked for her, they were evasive: no doubt she has other, more important things to do. As they may. I stare at the back of Paul's head, the wave in his unruly hair so much a mirror of his father's that I cannot but smile. He, of all of them, is most like Martin, in character as well as appearance, and I must tell him so, for it is something to be proud of.

There is a knock on the door, and as Paul turns I narrow my eyes to a slit, so that he won't see I'm watching him. A girl whom I don't recognise is standing on the threshold. They change their servants frequently here, which is not the sign of a well-run household. Forgetting my pretence of sleep, I pull myself up, make a decision. It's time to return to Wittenberg, to our own place, to those that we know and love. The cloister won't run itself, and though Dorothea is beyond suspicion, I cannot trust Martin to manage the other servants, nor to keep a firm hand on the accounts. A child could rob him blind and he wouldn't see it, and if he did would likely think they had good reason, and add alms to what they had already taken.

The girl, after a quick glance at me, directs her words to Paul, her tone apologetic. 'I'm sorry, Herr Luther, the Fraulein is out and the merchant is here, demanding payment. I wasn't sure what you would want me to do.'

Martin will be amused when I tell him that his youngest son is addressed thus, though it may make him feel old.

Paul's shoulders stiffen, with pride I imagine. 'I'll speak with him; you may tell him I'll be down directly.'

I stifle my desire to laugh at his pompous tone, but as he turns his head, I see a furrow of worry on his brow and long to reach out to him, to say, 'I will do it', but I don't wish to spoil his moment.

The girl barely has time to turn before the door bursts open revealing a man short of stature but large in voice, his indignation clear.

'Herr Luther, you cannot live forever on the memory of your father. I won't be fobbed off any longer, whatever promises you may offer…'

In the draught carried towards me, I taste the whiff of fish.

Chapter Thirteen
Nimbschen, November 1518

'It is a great blindness of people's hearts that they cannot
accept of the treasure of grace presented unto them.'

Martin Luther

The horses are already harnessed, the abbess seated inside
the carriage. And with her, my aunt and the novice-teacher.
I don't know why I should feel uneasy, for all three smile
a welcome, my aunt shifting sideways to make more
room on the seat. Our wagon at Lippendorf had a wooden
bench seat, and I can still remember how hard it felt when
we bounced across ruts on the track. This one is buttoned
leather, padded with horsehair, and I expect it to be more
comfortable, but I'm wrong, feeling the imprint of the
buttons on my buttocks with every jolt, despite the close
weave of my habit. Trotting behind are two spare roans, to
alternate in the pulling of the carriage, and we make three
short stops for feeding and watering and changing them
over, which provides a welcome chance to get down and
walk about a little.

Aunt Magdalene is solicitous. 'Stiff, Katharina?'

I rub at the base of my spine and stretch. 'A little.' It seems strange to speak openly. The others have been conversing quietly throughout the journey; mostly about practical things: the likely increased cost of supplies for the schoolroom, the hope that the convent dues would be forthcoming without delay and the need to settle accounts with Herr Köppe. At the mention of the fish merchant, their conversation falters briefly, as if each have their own, private thoughts, and I surprise an almost furtive glance passing between them.

After a moment the abbess says, 'You may wonder why we have brought you, Katharina? The reason is simple. There is much to be accomplished and our time in Torgau so short, I thought it best that Sister Magdalene take on some of the tasks that must be done. And as it isn't seemly for any of us to go about alone. Your aunt will accompany me and you will go with Sister Magdalena.'

Clearly mistaking my growing excitement for nervousness, she echoes Eva. 'Do not fear that anyone will give us a second glance, the good people of Torgau are well used to beguines. And we look very little different.'

The driver is encouraging the horses, his gruff voice accompanied by loud cracks of his whip. And looking out I understand why, for clouds are building on the horizon: purple and black bruises on the dimming sky.

Sister Magdalena voices a new fear. 'What if we don't reach it before dark?'

The abbess waves her hand. 'Of course we will. It isn't far now.'

I stare out of the carriage window, not wanting to miss the first sight of Torgau, my stomach churning. It's so long since I've been in any town that the prospect both daunts and excites me in equal measure. And this isn't just any town, but the centre of Saxony, the place that our electors have chosen to make their home … if I were to see Duke Frederick … that *would* be something to tell Eva and the others. Off to the right of us, tantalising glimpses of water are visible through the clumps of trees, and here and there, huddled among them, thatched cottages, likely the houses of those who make their living from it. Dusk is falling, light leaching out of the sky as the town comes into view: a clutter of red roofs, spiked with steeples, in the distance a tall church, its bell tower standing out on the skyline. The abbess has not said so, but I wonder if it'll be there that we make our devotions, or if, with the pressures of other business, we'll be spared the usual Offices. A pleasant thought, speedily overlaid by guilt.

Almost directly in front of us, taking my breath away, is the Schloss Hartenfels, with its towers and gables and serried rows of windows that catch the last rays of light, the reflection dazzling. There are signs of further construction and I feel dwarfed by the scale of it and stifle my dream: of course I won't get to see the duke. Below the castle a wooden bridge spans the river and disappears into the trees on the far bank. For the convenience of the hunt perhaps? I stare at the rickety structure, fascinated by the conical stacks of tree trunks, like up-ended woodpiles, that support the planking, and the flimsy arches that march along each edge. And I'm glad that we're on the town side of the river, where only small arms of the Elbe, remnants of earlier meanderings, snake among the flat meadows, so that our crossing point is narrow. We turn into the town through the Fishergate, the road ahead stretching

103

straight to the marketplace, watched over by the church of St Nicholas on the south side and the Rathaus on the northern corner. The carriage rattles over the cobbles as we skirt the perimeter of the square, already crowded with stacks of trestle tables and poles and rolls of canvas ready to be erected in the morning. We turn and turn again, coming to a halt in a narrow street below the castle. As we step down, a door opens, the woman on the threshold curtseying to the abbess.

'Reverend Mother. Welcome.' She ushers us into a wide hallway and indicates the table ready-set. 'No doubt the journey has been wearisome. I trust a bite of supper will revive you.'

She trusts wrong, in my case at least, for whether it's the unaccustomed heat from the stove, or the thick potage, or my wakefulness of the previous night, I find sleep creeping upon me, my eyelids drooping. I stifle a yawn and the abbess rises with a smile.

'I think perhaps we should all retire. Today has been long, and tomorrow may be also.'

The market is in full swing and I don't need to pretend to be Eva. Used as I am to the silence of our cloister, at first the noise seems deafening, as all around us stallholders cry their wares: vying with each other, making more and more extravagant claims for the quality of their goods or the efficacy of the remedies they peddle. It's as if I am a child again, at my first Martinmas fair: clutching tight to mother's hand, round-eyed, while at her other side Hans and Klement strain for release, like hounds on a leash.

We pause by a stall piled high with smoked sausages of all shapes and sizes. The novice-teacher glances at the stallholder, her mouth twitching, and bends her head close to mine.

'I cannot imagine they're as tasty as he claims, for going by him they'll not be making anyone fat.'

It's a new side to her, a glimpse of mischief, of what her character might have been had she not been sent into a nunnery, and I smother a giggle. She shakes her head and draws me away, but her smile remains. At a clothier she rummages through a basket of embroidery threads, picking out skeins of reds and blues, greens and purples, yellows and ochres and a rich burgundy-black.

'Hold these.' She delves deeper, and brings out a skein of silver, which glitters as it catches the light. 'The sacrist will be pleased with this.'

The stallholder, his attention caught, halts his sales patter and fingers the money pouch swinging at his waist. 'You'll not find better, I guarantee you that. Brought from Rome, from the workshops of the weavers who see to the robes of the Holy Father himself.' He pauses, and when Sister Magdalena remains silent, hurries on. 'And seeing as it's for you, Sister, the price will also astound.'

Again the mischievous curl of her mouth. 'So high, you mean?'

He contrives to look offended, gestures at her habit. 'How could you think it? That I would cheat a religious?' His gesture is extravagant. 'Here, take them.'

For a moment I'm startled, until I realise this is an elaborate game, that in a moment they will begin to haggle. And so they do, and to judge by the smiles when the novice-teacher finally hands over five pfennig, they finish with a price that's fair to both. We hurry from stall to stall, passing some without a glance, pausing at others to examine the goods, and if they satisfy Sister Magdalena, to argue over the price until a suitable settlement is made. By the time we turn out of the square, my arms are full of packages, my brain packed tight with sights and sounds: the crush and the crowds, the patter and the gossip, the half-heard conversations swallowed in a volley of cursing or a burst of laughter. Threaded through them all, one name, spoken variously in approbation or disdain: Martin Luther. It rings in my head also, filling my thoughts, unsettling and exciting in equal measure, which hurry ahead to my return to the convent and all that I shall have to share with Eva and the others.

We turn out of the square into the relative quiet of Leipziger Strasse and halt at an elegant townhouse, the ground floor one large room stretching the width of the building. As Sister Magdalene rings the bell above the door announcing our arrival, a young man appears from behind a stack of barrels wiping his hands on a rag and stations himself at the marble slab that forms the counter.

The novice-teacher has reverted to her usual seriousness. 'I trust the merchant Köppe received my message?'

He nods and gestures towards a doorway at the rear of the shop. 'My uncle is expecting you. If you will follow me.'

The queasiness in my stomach is not because of the smell of fish, though that is strong, but rather that I sense this visit is what has brought the novice-teacher to Torgau, confirmed when, breaching protocol, she says, 'Perhaps, Katharina, you would wait here. My business with Herr

Köppe shouldn't take long.'

As they disappear, I count the creaking stairs, tread by tread, as I used to when Anna visited the merchant's store in Lippendorf and we children were sent upstairs to take cordial while the business was being done. The ceiling is higher here, the flight of stairs longer, a measure of Herr Köppe's status. As the footsteps resume, coming downwards, I study the floor, afraid that I shall betray an awkwardness in the man's presence. He coughs twice, forcing me to look up, then gestures towards a bench in the corner – 'Perhaps you'd like to sit?' – before he retreats, betraying his own unease at being left alone with a nun by the vigorous way he rubs at the already gleaming counter with a rag that smears rather than cleans. After a few moments he disappears, to return with a tankard of weak ale, which he proffers without speaking.

I notice his hands, the fingers long and slim, and blurt out, 'Are you a musician?'

He flushes. 'At home, yes... I play the lute.' There is a wistfulness in his voice as he returns to the counter. 'I wish...' He shakes his head. 'I am a merchant and will always be so.'

'As I am a nun.' I look away from him towards the street and the open doorway of the church opposite. 'I loved to sing once ... but we cannot always choose what we do.'

'No.'

This time the silence that falls between us is that of two people who share a common regret. Mindful of Eva's last instruction and the look I intercepted when Herr Köppe's name was mentioned in the carriage, I risk, 'What do you know of this Dr Luther?' And then, by way

107

of explanation, 'His name is on everyone's lips, or at least it seemed so in the market.'

He glances towards the inner door. 'I have heard him preach, and when he speaks it is with fire, despite that he is so thin you could almost count his bones.'

'But do you think him right in what he says?'

'How should I know? I can read and write our own tongue, which is more than most, but I am no student of theology.' He crumples the rag and flings it aside, and afraid that I've offended him in some way, I look down again and so don't notice he has moved until he's standing over me, a folded paper in his outstretched hand. His smile is tentative.

'Here. You're a religious. Read his words for yourself.' A pause, as if unsure whether to say more. 'My uncle believes him. That much I do know.'

When I hesitate in my turn, he says, 'Take it. I can easily get another.'

There is the sound of footsteps on the stairs, and somehow the paper is in my hand and I stuff it inside my sleeve as Sister Magdalena reappears, Köppe behind her.

He sees us to the door, bows. 'Thank you for your continued custom, and if I can be of further assistance, don't hesitate to send.'

As she dips her head in return, I sense they aren't talking only of fish, and I consider showing her the paper I've been given, but she hurries me into the street in front of her and the moment is lost.

They cluster around me like sparrows seeking crumbs,

firing questions from all sides, and I shut my eyes to remember every detail. The furthest fringes of the fair noisy with livestock: makeshift pens with sheep and cows, geese and hens gobbling and clucking as they peck at the bars of cages, and best of all, a sow on her side, grunting with pleasure, ten piglets fastened to her, feeding. The square filled with the rows of stalls, their striped canopies flapping in the wind; spilling over into the streets beyond, each section dedicated to a separate trade. A flesher, with smoked hams slung on hooks and the boy with the sausages that had so amused the abbess. Fishmongers and baxters, brewers and costermongers, and besides them, the crafts and guilds. A blacksmith selling scythes and pitchforks, a pewterer with tankards and pails and milk churns. The apothecary, his stall an extension of his usual place, the simples he displays guaranteed to cure everything from warts to toothache. Weaving through them all, constantly on the move lest they fall foul of the guildsmen, the peddlers, trays slung from their shoulders heaped with lace and ribbons, combs and tweezers.

Else asks, 'What was your favourite?'

'Silversmith,' I say, without hesitation, remembering the drinking vessels, the trays as smooth as mirrors, the pomanders hanging from fine chains and, reminding me of Mother, the brooches and hairpins, set with stones that flashed as if with inner fire.

Eva stares into the distance when I describe the clothier spinning out, with practiced hands, the satins and velvets and brocades for the prosperous wives of the merchants who linger to finger the bales and exclaim over the rivers of colour that flow across the trestle top. When I stop, she looks down at her habit, her sigh long and drawn-out,

109

reducing us all to silence.

I produce the paper, like a conjuror, but keep it folded, savouring the moment. It's Fronika who snatches it from me, and, opening it out, begins to read.

'...seek not to avoid the penalty of sin, but rather the sin itself...'

Despite that she's whispering, Luther's words still have the power to cut to the heart, as they did the first time I read them, in the privacy of the closet in the Torgau house.

Else says, 'I wonder what he's like. If his presence is as powerful as his sermon suggests.'

I think of how the young man in Köppe's shop described him. 'They say he looks half-starved, as if a puff of wind could blow him over, but listening to him is like being caught in a storm, all thunder and lightning and relentless rain.'

Eva attempts a laugh. 'A bit like our abbot then, except that it would take a whirlwind to lift him.'

By the catch in her voice I think it an effort to distract from what I suspect is in all our minds: that we'd like to hear this Luther, however uncomfortable the experience might be.

Chapter Fourteen
Nimbschen, April - October 1520

I'm in the storeroom, helping the kitcheness with her regular spring clean, when we hear the rumble of wheels on the cobbles and a voice calling out, 'Whoa.'

There is the snorting of horses and the jingle of harness and the creak of an axle followed by the slap of shoes on the ground.

The kitcheness surveys the empty shelves and the barrels shoved against the far wall, a smile hovering around her lips. 'Herr Köppe is timely, it seems. We can be doing with a delivery.'

One of the younger girls, here for schooling, sticks her head around the storeroom door. 'You're wanted in the yard. The fish merchant is here, with a delivery of herring.' She wrinkles her nose. 'Four barrel-loads. Enough for a year of Fridays.'

The kitcheness laughs, her hands flashing. 'We'll have to eat them faster than that, for salted or not, I'd prefer not to rely on their keeping for that long.' She nods at the child. 'You can tell Herr Köppe we'll be with him directly.' Wiping her hands on her apron, she makes a face at the streak of dust they leave, then grasping an empty barrel turns it on its side and rolls it towards the door. I turn back to the shelf I've been working, but she grasps my arm, signs, 'Leave that and come with me. A barrel apiece will halve the number of journeys.'

Herr Köppe is standing in the rear of the cart, the tail dropped to form a ramp, issuing instructions to a young man who has his back to us. Something about the set of his head is familiar, and as he turns I see a corresponding flash of recognition in his eyes. He drops his gaze immediately, as if he feels it inappropriate to look at me, but not before I see the ghost of a smile on his face. We roll the empty barrels over to the cart and up-end them again and are turning to head back for the others when Herr Köppe leaps down and holds out a folded paper to the kitcheness.

'We'll get the remainder when we put these barrels in for you. If you will just check the list to see that everything is in order. The usual place?'

The kitcheness nods, and with a practiced turn of his wrist Herr Köppe cowps the first barrel as easily as if it were empty and heads for the store. The younger man follows suit, as the kitcheness, unfolding the paper, clicks her tongue. She passes it over to me, shaking her head.

'Perhaps you could check this? The writing's too small for me without my glasses.' She runs her tongue around her lips, then, as if an afterthought, 'Maybe I should fetch them, in case there's anything you don't understand.' She disappears towards the storeroom and I think of reminding her that her glasses are lying on the workbench in the kitchen, but I reckon she'll discover that soon enough for herself. I turn my attention to the list, comparing it to the goods piled beside the cart, and am still ticking things off in my head when she returns. Leaving the Köppes to take the last of the barrels through to the store, she reaches out for the list, signing, 'Is everything in order?'

'I think so. I've just the contents of the box for the schoolroom to check.'

Herr Köppe comes up behind me, his eyebrows raised.

The kitcheness translates my signing and he responds with an emphatic shake of the head.

'No need for that. I checked the contents myself when we collected them. All is in order.'

I begin, 'But shouldn't we—'

'Katharina.' The kitcheness speaks aloud, clearly for the merchant's benefit, a note of reproof in her voice. 'We have no reason to doubt Herr Köppe. Perhaps you can inform the infirmaress and Sister Magdalena that their supplies are here?'

When I return, the cart has gone, and the kitcheness is busying herself making soup for our evening meal. She pauses in the chopping of onions and looks up, her expression serious.

'You met Herr Köppe in Torgau. Is he to be relied upon?'

I don't understand why, or indeed what she's asking, for if she didn't think to query the merchant while he was here, why would she do so now? I shrug my shoulders and say, 'I don't know. It was more than a year ago, and in any case I saw him only briefly, when he came to the shop door to give us goodbye.'

'But you were with Sister Magdalena were you not, while she conducted her business?'

I hesitate, unsure how to reply, for to tell the absolute

113

truth seems disloyal. Honesty wins. 'I waited in the outer shop while she spoke with Herr Köppe.'

She sucks in on her lip, then changes tack. 'You passed on my message to your aunt and Sister Magdalena?'

'They'll be here directly.' I'm about to go through to the storeroom, to finish the task I was working on before the merchant arrived, but she stops me.

'You've worked hard today. There's no need to stay longer. I can finish up.'

'I don't mind, really.'

She shakes her head, 'No more do I,' and, glancing past me to the square of sunlight pooling on the floor at my feet, says, 'Go on, enjoy the sunshine while you can.'

❈

Fronika is already in the garden, pacing up and down as if she cannot settle. I catch up with her, teasing away at the question as to why the kitcheness was so eager to get rid of me when there was still plenty of work to be done. 'You're finished early?'

She glances around, then bends her head close to mine and whispers, 'I offered to help Sister Magdalena check the supplies for the schoolroom but was sent away.'

'Likewise.' From the other side of the hedge we hear rapid footsteps and I freeze until Eva appears around the corner. She's breathless, but not from running.

I suspect the answer before I ask, but ask anyway. 'Have you been let off your work too?'

'Yes, I was about to open one of the boxes that had arrived for the infirmary when your aunt told me to run along, saying that she would do it herself. What about you?'

Fronika and I both nod. 'The same.'

I say, 'There's something else. The kitcheness asked me if I thought Herr Köppe *reliable*. She cannot have been talking of his commercial activities, for he's served the convent well enough for longer than we've been here, and apparently his father before him.'

Fronika tilts her head to one side. 'You had word of Luther from his nephew. My uncle has slipped us snippets from time to time. But that hardly accounts for the rumours and gossip that have multiplied throughout the cloister these two years past. What if…' – she's thinking aloud, her words disjointed – 'What if it isn't just the talk of our lay labourers at the root of them… What if Herr Köppe is also supplying information… If the kitcheness is querying its likely accuracy … or his discretion?'

Eva's brow puckers. 'What did you tell her, Kat?'

'I said I didn't know, that I hadn't been party to the novice-teacher's dealings with him, but had been left to wait outside.'

'Pity.'

'It was the truth. What else could I say? I could hardly share what was no more than a vague suspicion, especially when it concerns a senior.'

'I suppose, but what if the kitcheness was sounding *you* out, not Herr Köppe? Whether *you* could be trusted? He may have brought word of something we'd all like to know.'

⬡⬡⬡⬡

It seems he has, confirmation of it coming from the least

115

expected source: Abbot Balthazar, who pays us another visit. I'm crossing the courtyard towards the infirmary, seeking a remedy for a tooth that pained me, when the porteress ushers him through the inner door. The abbot stops me, orders, 'You there. Fetch the novice-teacher to the abbess' parlour. I wish to speak with her.' His eyes bore into me. 'Immediately.'

Sister Magdalena draws a deep breath, sighs and signs back, 'Immediately?' She looks at the pile of breviaries and the tub of glue on front of her on the desk. 'I daresay these can wait, though it is a task I had hoped to accomplish today.'

On impulse, I offer, 'I could mend them.'

She nods. 'Thank you. They have been in want of attention for some time and the longer they're left the worse their condition will become.'

I watch her from the doorway as she hurries towards the abbess' quarters, tension obvious in the set of her shoulders, then get to work. It's a straightforward task and allows me ample time to think, my mind drifting to Herr Köppe and the secrecy surrounding his recent deliveries. I wonder if Eva is right about the kitcheness' intention in quizzing me, if she too is beginning to question our mode of life, and am unable to suppress a twinge of regret at the way I responded to her. I run out of glue and go to look on the shelves in the alcove at the back of the room for more. The top shelf is too high to see from floor level, so I drag across a stool and am standing on it, staring at the pile of pamphlets I've found, when Sister Magdalena

116

returns. I swing round, startled, the stool cowping, and I fall, dragging the pile with me. She helps me up and leads me back to the desk.

'You'd best sit down while I look at your ankle.'

'I'm sorry,' I blurt out, 'I was looking for glue... I didn't mean to pry.'

She glances at the empty glue tub, at the papers scattered around us. 'I know.' Her head is bent over my foot, so that I can't see her expression, but there is a weariness in her voice as she continues. 'Those pamphlets. As you may have gathered, they are all Luther's writings and thus forbidden. Now that you've seen them, I will not ask you to act against your conscience, nor will I hold it against you if you feel you must report the matter.'

Not knowing what to say, I shake my head, intending it as reassurance, but she's focusing on my ankles, not my face, running her hands over them simultaneously, comparing them, assessing the degree of swelling. I wince as she presses around the bone.

'Wait here. This may be broken. I'll get the infirmaress.'

I'm still clutching the top pamphlet in my hand, *A German Explanation of the Lord's Prayer for Ordinary Layfolk*: the title intriguing and exciting in equal measure. It was the first I'd seen or heard of Luther writing in our own tongue, and for everyone, not just for churchmen or students of theology. I turn the page and am shocked to see not only that it was published almost a year ago, but that it's been reprinted many times.

The door opens, my aunt rushing to kneel and take my foot in her hand. Seeing her glance at the open pamphlet, I colour, closing it and laying it on the desk.

She shakes her head. 'Time enough to deal with that

matter once your ankle is sorted.' Her fingers are cool, a welcome relief from the burning of my skin. As she probes I catch my breath and she looks up. 'Can you wiggle your toes?'

I try, but fail, barely able to suppress a gasp at the pain that shoots upwards towards my knee. 'Is it broken?'

She purses her lips. 'I think so, or badly sprained if not. I can strap it, but you should keep it up for a day or two, until the swelling reduces. I'll know better then.'

⬡⬡⬡

I've been in the infirmary three days when my aunt confirms that the bone does appear to be broken. She reapplies a poultice designed to draw the heat out and to reduce the swelling. 'You'll be here for some weeks, I'm afraid, for if you attempt to put weight on it too soon, even bandaged, you may do more damage.' When I grimace at the prospect, she signs, 'Count your blessings. It could have been your back that is broken.'

'It's just…' I begin.

'Boredom, I know.' One of the novices is folding clean bandages and adding them to a pile in the corner. My aunt nods her thanks, clearly waiting for her to leave before saying anything more. 'Here.' She produces a sheaf of leaflets that look very similar to the ones I'd seen in the schoolroom. 'Some reading material that I don't think you had time to look at earlier.' There is a glimmer of a smile on her face. You'll have plenty of time now. Best make good use of it.'

I stab my finger at the top pamphlet. 'If Luther can explain the Lord's Prayer to common folk, then perhaps I

118

will be able to understand it also.'

My aunt perches on the edge of the bed, careful not to bump my foot, her gaze steady. 'There are many things in these writings that a careful study will make clear. But I trust you will take care with whom you share that knowledge.'

'Are these Sister Magdalena's?'

'No, they're mine, and though you may guess how I obtained them, that too is information I'd prefer you not to share without my permission. There may be a time coming when these matters can be discussed freely, but it isn't here yet, or not in the cloister at any rate.' She draws breath, a twinkle in her eye, then disappears into her storeroom, returning with a pamphlet in Latin. 'There is one other that perhaps you should see. We are all allowed to read this. In fact, we have been forced to listen to it three times over on Abbot Balthazar's orders. But since you've been spared that pleasure through lying here, you may wish to experience it for yourself.'

'What is it?'

She flips to the final page, shows me the impression of the papal seal at the foot. 'A papal bull, to be proclaimed in every town and bishopric where the Church has authority, denouncing Dr Luther and his writings. It depicts him as a wild boar, and his supporters as foxes ravaging God's vineyard, and calls for his books to be publicly burned.'

I can't help but smile at the image of the kitcheness and Sister Magdalene as foxes, but my aunt's expression becomes serious. 'In truth, it's no laughing matter. The word is that there have been bonfires as far away as Mainz and Cologne. This brings the likelihood of Luther's excommunication ever closer. When that happens...'

'When it happens? You are that sure?'

She lifts one shoulder. 'I cannot see any other outcome.' She indicates the pamphlets. 'And when you have read all that he has written you will understand why. He hasn't confined himself to theological discussion or condemnation of the abuses of the Church. If that were the substance of it, many, even those he counts as enemies, might be persuaded to absolve him.' She sifts through the heap of papers and picks out two, entitled *The Papacy at Rome* and On the *Babylonian Captivity of the Church* and lays them on my lap. 'These he cannot escape.'

'But if he is cast out of the Church, surely his influence will wane.' Even as I make the suggestion I feel a pang, as if of sadness.

She shakes her head, her expression even more sombre than before. 'I very much fear there will be no going back. And if it is to come to a split in the Church we will all need to be sure in our own mind which side of the divide we wish to be on, for the consequences will affect not just our thinking, but our whole way of life.'

I wish I *was* sure in my own mind. My ankle is proving
slow to heal, and lying in the infirmary, my foot strapped
and supported on a pillow, I have plenty of time to study
and to think about what Dr Luther says; and it serves only
to unsettle me. I find I miss the devotions of the Hours, my
own private repetitions of them, while I lie prone, failing
to give me any comfort. Else and Fronika are constant
visitors, appearing in odd moments between their other
duties, to sit on the edge of my bed, one of Dr Luther's
pamphlets spread out between us, discussing and debating
what is meant by it all, if what he says can really be true.
Abbot Balthazar's reading of the papal bull has proved a
catalyst, though not in the way he intended, others of the
sisters slipping in and out of the infirmary on the pretext
of aches and pains and, while waiting for my aunt to
examine them, devouring Luther's words as they would
a forbidden sweetmeat. His ideas on Christian freedom
– that the Pope is no more than the vicar of Rome and
every priest of good standing equal to him, their opinions
on theological matters as valid as his – are as shocking as

they are novel. The resulting discussions are impassioned and vigorous, with one unintended consequence: my increased appreciation of the value of our rule of silence, for, as my aunt says, 'What isn't spoken aloud, cannot be overheard.'

It's a salutary warning that not all in our cloister are sympathetic to Luther's teachings, the disagreements of the outside world mirrored within the confines of our walls.

Eva blows in and out, her natural scepticism at the validity of the strictures of convent life finding many echoes in Luther's opinions. I am not so easily persuaded, for a doctrine based on rules is clear-cut. Keep them and salvation is ours. Fail to do so and God's judgement will fall. I wish I knew what the abbess thinks of it all, whether she favours Eva's view or mine, but she keeps her own counsel. When I ask my aunt, she says simply, 'Whatever her private thoughts, the abbess has responsibility for all in the cloister and it is a burden she isn't yet ready to lay down.'

Autumn moves into winter, and fully recovered from the accident, I try to regain my lost peace, to see God in the rhythm of the seasons and our Offices, seeking consolation in the order and regulation of our lives. I want to, but I cannot, for it seems that every month word of some new controversy reaches us, Dr Luther and his writings no longer a flickering flame of dissent, but a raging fire which, it seems, may engulf not only Germany but the entire Christian world. Our lay workers talk more openly now, their tongues loosened by the tide of public opinion swinging in Luther's favour and by the appointment of a new abbot as our overseer, who seems less inclined to criticism. And though it's clear that Duke George and the cardinals and other Church dignitaries don't love Luther, the people do, for he is seen as a champion of the poor, his thunderings against the papacy interpreted as licence for ordinary folk to challenge authority and to refuse to pay their dues.

'I'm not sure that's what he means.' Else and Fronika and I are sitting on the floor of the infirmary, rolling bandages cut from the edges of sheets that have worn through in the centre, a copy of Luther's *Address to the Christian Nobility of the German Nation*, the latest of Herr Köppe's offerings, lying between us. It's already months old, the date on the flyleaf, August, but new to us, smuggled, as usual, into the convent in the schoolroom supplies. Else expertly tucks in the loose end to keep the bandage from unravelling, and sets it aside, continuing, 'It's clear from this that Luther doesn't despise the nobility, far from it.'

Fronika is dismissive. 'What he means matters less than what people *think* he means. He may not challenge the authority of the nobles, but in encouraging them to seek reform of the Church he challenges the authority of the Pope, which in many people's eyes comes to the same thing. If the Pope, who is God's representative on earth, can be challenged, mere human authority is fair game.'

Else, who of all of us likes to think through every issue in detail, is about to retort, when my aunt appears, signing vigorously. 'While I appreciate your willingness to be of help, I do not expect nor indeed want you to give up

123

your recreation hour. Besides that I would be failing in my duty as the infirmaress if I allowed you to waste what sunshine there is.' She scoops up the pamphlet, folds it over and, pushing the door shut, continues, her expression serious. 'If you are to congregate here when you should be outside, there will be questions asked.' There is a momentary hint of a curve to her mouth. 'Especially as you aren't all noted for a love of extra work.' Her mouth straightens again. 'Our new abbot may not be as much of an ogre as the last, but we are still Cistercians, expected to accept and to follow the teachings of our order and our superiors without question. Remember that there are many here who would wish to protect that heritage at all costs, and who would hardly consider the writings of an heretical monk as prescribed reading.'

It isn't Luther's own writings that cause the next stir among us, but news of his burning of the papal bull and various other Church documents. Word of it comes to us in a letter to the abbess, with the instruction to share it with our whole community, so that if there be any among us tempted to see Luther as an Elijah, challenging the prophets of Baal, we might think again. Listening, as the abbess reads aloud how he called on the students of Wittenberg to build a bonfire at the Elster Gate, where it was customary to burn the clothes of plague victims lest the contamination spread, I can almost smell the smoke and see the flames licking at first one book, then another, and another, until with a roar the bonfire caught, lighting up the December sky. And though I think him justified

124

in his protest, I feel a pang for the burning of books, whatever their content.

Fronika is the first to express her opinion. 'I applaud him. To defy the Pope so openly is the act of a courageous man.'

Else is more thoughtful. 'But is it the act of a reasonable one? To burn the papal bull perhaps, and the writings of those who denounced him, but the canon law and the guide for priests hearing confession – is that not taking the protest a little far.'

Eva's opinion is clear. 'He is merely fighting fire with fire. The Pope ordered his books to be burned and he's responding in like manner.' A draught is funnelling along the nave, chilling us all, and she adds, as if in an attempt to lighten the conversation, 'We could do with a good bonfire ourselves.'

The year turns, the darkness of December giving way to the brilliance of a landscape cloaked in snow. The hollows on the hill behind us are smoothed out, the river below sluggish, swollen with slush. Wind blows through the valley, piling the snow in drifts, obliterating the track, neither workers nor visitors able to reach us. Within our walls, ice hangs in long fingers from roofs and windowsills, and crusts the tops of fences. Paths turn to glass and stray stems of plants snap like kindling when trodden on. In the orchard, branches bow under the weight of snow, sweeping the ground, so that we fear for their survival, and the root vegetables we would normally harvest as we needed them are set into ground so hard they are impossible to shift. Outside, the water in the troughs freezes solid, so that fresh supplies from the well must be drawn daily for the animals, and indoors, standing water forms a thick skin overnight. With no prospect of any new supplies arriving, the kitcheness rations what we have, the loaves smaller, the soup thinned.

Trapped inside by the inclemency of the season, the atmosphere in the cloister is as tempestuous as the weather, and with little else to distract, Luther and his writings find their way into every corner, whipping up dissensions, dividing us, it seems irrevocably, into three camps: those who are in sympathy with what he has said and done; those who are equally vociferous in their condemnation of him, and who cite the hardness of the frost as a sign of God's displeasure; and those who refuse to be drawn onto one side or the other, insisting that as we are removed from the world, what happens in it has no relevance to us. These last claim the greatest piety, with sanctimonious talk of praying: for us, whom the Devil is winnowing, for the Mother Church which is under attack, and yes, even for that renegade monk, whom God in his mercy may yet lead to recognise the errors of his ways. And saint or apostate, it seems that Luther's name is mentioned as often between us as Our Lady's is invoked for our protection.

Torgau: 1552

The maid is lighting the lamps and closing the shutters, blocking out the last remnants of the day. I shiver at the sound of the bar dropping into its socket, my breath catching at the thought of the long night ahead. For they will come, I know they will. I shut my eyes against the flickering of the candles but cannot block out the shufflings and scufflings, the creaking of the door as it opens and shuts. I sense they're here, shadow-people, crowding around me, their presence oppressive, their mutterings like the buzzing of bees worrying at my ears. I would talk to them, if they would only come in the morning, when I am less wearied, more able for visitors.

Margarethe appears at my shoulder, straightening the covers, tucking the sheet around me. I wave my hand towards the figures at the end of the bed. 'Send them away,' I say. 'Ask them to come tomorrow.' I'm pleased that my voice is becoming stronger, even if I still sound as if my mouth is full of gravel, pleased that Margarethe no longer needs to place her ear on my chest to hear me.

'Is it the maid, Mutti? I will send her away.'

I shake my head. 'Not the maid. The others.'

Her face smooths out, becomes bland, expressionless, her voice gentle. 'There's no one here, Mutti, only us.'

I speak slowly and distinctly, as if to a child. 'Look. Over there. Amsdorf and Melanchthon and Karlstadt...' There is another man who has his back to me. I think I recognise the set of the head, but his name eludes me. I do know he is no friend, of theirs, or of my dear Martin.

She perches on the side of the bed, takes my hand in hers, strokes it, as one would pet a kitten. 'Mutti ...'

I snatch back my hand, turn my head towards the men. They are shouting now, and though I don't want to listen for it makes my head ache, I can't stop myself. Karlstadt is facing up to the third man, his cheeks red, Amsdorf placing a restraining hand on his shoulder. 'Please,' I interrupt them, 'what is it that the Herr Doctor has done now?'

They don't acknowledge me, but my question is answered nonetheless, the third man stabbing his forefinger at Karlstadt's chest.

'To seek a disputation: fine. How else can our students learn if not by debate? But the theses should have remained here, in Wittenberg, not be spread abroad, for all to argue over.'

Amsdorf steps between them, his tone placatory. 'To challenge indulgences, to suggest reform, what is wrong in that?'

'To challenge the monastic way of life, the priestly vows, is to put at risk the whole fabric of our Church. Or is it that you wish to revoke your vows?' The third man has joined in, and I put my hands over my ears but I can still hear him. 'Duke Frederick wishes fame for our university, not notoriety.' He slaps a folded paper against his leg, 'And as for this latest blast. Luther goes too far. Bad enough that he criticises the Church, but the Pope? Mark my words, he will be called to account for this and trouble will follow.'

Margarethe is ushering the maid towards the door and, distracted, I turn my head. When I look back they've gone, but I know now what they were arguing about. I beckon Margarethe with a smile. 'It's all right,' I say, 'they've gone, but the third man was right. There was trouble.'

128

CHAPTER SIXTEEN
NIMBSCHEN, MARCH – MAY 1521

'Pray, not for me, but for the Word of God.'

Martin Luther

The thaw is late in coming, but when it does arrive it brings with it a flood of rumour and counter rumour: Luther has been summoned to the Imperial Diet at Worms; Luther is banned from the diet at Worms; the Pope has sent out the Bull of Excommunication; the Bull has been suppressed; Duke Frederick supports Luther; Duke Frederick has abandoned him. Our new abbot, Abbot Peter, makes several visits to the cloister, and though it's clear he does not favour Luther, neither will he condemn him until the proper procedures have been followed, his more measured approach a welcome contrast to the fire and brimstone rhetoric of Balthazar. He expresses himself glad that Luther has been summoned to attend the diet in Worms, to answer to the Estates with regard to his books and his teaching, and hopes, though it isn't at all certain, both that Luther will go, and that what is decided will provide guidance for us all. My aunt has concluded that the infirmary is no longer a safe place for those of us who wish to discuss the merits of Luther's writings to congregate, the novice-teacher offering the schoolroom instead.

It's Easter before we hear anything more, but the information is reliable, enabling us to sift truth from falsehood. The prior at Grimma writes to his nieces, describing Luther's attendance at the diet. I find them with Eva and Else in a secluded corner of the garden after Sext, Fronika clearly bursting to share her news.

'The command from the emperor for Dr Luther to attend the diet was addressed to "Our noble, dear and esteemed Martin Luther".'

'Not how I'd expect someone accused of heresy to be addressed.'

'That's not all, Kat. He entered the city led by an imperial herald and they say some two thousand of the townsfolk turned out to conduct him to his lodging.'

'The people do love him then.' There is an undertone of concern in Else's voice. 'No wonder the emperor treated him with courtesy.'

Fronika queries, 'Isn't that good?'

'Not if it's a sign that the emperor fears him.'

'Why should he fear a priest who seeks only the reform of the Church?'

'I don't doubt that may have been Dr Luther's original intention, but if he has gained such a following, who knows where it will end.'

'Who knows, indeed.' The novice-teacher has come on us unnoticed. 'You do well to be concerned, Else.'

It is as if there is a weight pressing on my chest,

constricting my breathing. I sign, 'Is there other news?'

Sister Magdalena nods, signs back, 'From my brother.' For a moment her hands are still, then, 'The Augustinians have a new overseer.'

'But your brother was much respected. Why would he be displaced?'

'He resigned. Months ago, apparently. Lest he be forced to send Dr Luther to Rome.' She pauses again. 'He has written a lengthy letter concerning the diet at Worms. If you wish to read it in its entirety I have it in the schoolroom, and though he doesn't say so, I can tell he is most uneasy.'

'About the people or the authorities?'

'Both. In the preliminary discussions the electors of Saxony and Brandenberg came to blows and had to be separated, and the mood in the city was so incendiary, the streets awash with cartoons, images of Luther for sale on every street corner, that the emperor feared insurrection if he was not allowed a proper hearing.'

Eva expresses the curiosity I suspect we all feel. 'Does he include a drawing?'

Sister Magdalena shakes her head. 'He may no longer have a position of authority to lose, but he is still a monk, and if his letter had fallen into the wrong hands it would have been dangerous to have an image of Luther enclosed within it.'

Eva's face clouds briefly, then clears, her natural optimism surfacing. 'Herr Köppe is due to make a delivery soon. Perhaps he will be less constrained.'

And so he is, the papers smuggled in with his resumed deliveries breathing life into the facts the others had presented.

I am in the schoolroom helping with the younger girls when the boxes arrive. Sister Magdalena sends me into the storeroom to see to the unpacking, while she finishes the lesson, and I find my hands shaking as I search through the supplies. The package is in the bottom of the first box, with a note attached: 'These papers and others that I thought too dangerous to send were circulating in Worms both before and during the diet. You may find them disturbing, but I know I do not need to ask that you take good care they don't fall into the wrong hands.'

The first is a parody of the Apostles' Creed, and it catches my breath. Schooled to believe the Creed as important as Scripture, it seems like blasphemy. *I believe in the Pope... under his power truth suffered, was crucified, died and was buried... I believe in the Romish Church, in the destruction of faith... in the resurrection of the flesh in an Epicurean life...* I stuff it to the bottom of the pile, but the words run round and round in my head, a devilish litany that I wish to dispel. There are a sheaf of cartoons: Luther pictured with a halo and a dove above his head; Luther and Hutton carrying a chest inscribed 'The Ark of the True Faith', Erasmus leading them, dressed as David playing a harp; the Pope and cardinals being bound by soldiers of the guard. Underneath them I find a head and shoulders line drawing of Luther himself, his face carrying more flesh than I expected, indicating he might run to fat in due course. On the back of that paper, Köppe had added a comment: 'His pictures are everywhere, women hiding them in their bosom or kissing them openly.' It made me look more closely, even as I chide myself that such an interest is not seemly.

Buried at the very bottom of the box was Köppe's

summary of the events at Worms, based, he said, on accounts of those who were there, and who, though he could name no names, could be relied on. Spiced with Luther's own words, Köppe related his refusal to repudiate his writings; his clever appeal to "my Germans" and his claim of tyranny, evidenced in the number of Spanish troops patrolling the streets. The admission that when referring to certain individuals he had perhaps been "more caustic than comports with my profession" countered by his argument that it wasn't his life that was being judged, but rather the teaching of Christ.

'Perhaps more caustic? Little doubt of that, I think,' Else says when I read the letter to them, but Eva laughs. 'Better honestly held strong opinions, than none at all.'

We are none of us laughing as I read the final paragraphs. 'The emperor has vowed to proceed against Luther as an heretic, citing tradition: "A single friar who goes contrary to all Christianity for a thousand years must be wrong." His followers are also to be condemned and his books eradicated from the memory of man.'

Else, ever practical, asks, 'Where does that leave us?'

'Exactly where we were before,' Fronika says, 'though I don't know how easy it will be to be content.'

The last news to filter into the cloister, brought by a new postulant seeking entry to our order, is even more shocking. Luther was set upon in the woods at Eisenach on the way home from Worms and is thought to be dead, though no one has claimed responsibility and no body has yet been discovered.

CHAPTER SEVENTEEN
NIMBSCHEN, JUNE 1521 – AUGUST 1522

For a time speculation rages among us, but gradually a lethargy sets in, a sense that the past years of turmoil were as nothing and we must settle again to the life laid out for us. Those who had been against Luther feel vindicated, some of them ready to say so, but others are more charitable, seeking to mend the relationships that had faltered in recent times. Among my particular friends I say little, but in the privacy of my cell I renew my vows, praying more frequently and fervently than ever in an attempt to regain my peace.

We are scrubbing the chancel steps when Eva drags my opinion from me.

'In these last months you've been very quiet, what do you think, Kat?'

Without looking up I say, 'I think if Luther was of God surely God would have protected him? If he is dead then the Church fathers must be right and our interest in Luther's writings a sin. That troubles me, for I cannot even seek the release of confession, for that would threaten us all.'

She pauses in her scrubbing, rocks back onto her heels. 'Say rather, an honest error, which, if penitent, God will surely forgive, whether confessed to the priests or not.' She gestures at the painting of St Sebastian, his body peppered with arrows, his many wounds dripping blood. 'Besides, the Church is full of martyrs whom we are to revere. Luther may be one such.'

'Or he may be the Devil incarnate, come to devour us all.' The thought is in my head, but I don't say it aloud, for what use is it to share my torment.

She touches my arm, smiles her elfin smile. 'Because we have heard nothing means little. He may be alive and well and hiding somewhere until the dust has settled.'

I wish I could think that, for it would give credence to the attention we have paid him in these last years, but I cannot, the daylight hours troubled by an image of a tonsured monk with horns and a forked tail, my sleep disturbed by a recurring dream in which I'm stretched out like Isaac on an altar built of books, flames leaping around the base, and standing over me the Holy Father, knife raised.

The summer is long and hot, the cloister airless, and aside from the Offices of the Hours I spend as much time as I can outdoors working in the herb garden, finding in the monotony of tending to the plants a semblance of content. But as the leaves begin to fall and the air sharpens, frost silvering the grass and glittering on the paths, our day labourers bring fresh word. His friends have received letters headed: "From the Wilderness" and "From my

Isle of Patmos", and they spawn new rumours: Luther is alive and well and in hiding. Luther is alive but not well, suffering many illnesses of the mind as well as the flesh. But wherever he is and whatever his physical state, one thing seems clear: it doesn't stop him working, for a torrent of writings attributed to him are slipped to us concealed in Herr Köppe's deliveries. The man at the centre of it all is invisible, yet the outpourings of his mind appear, like the writing on the wall at Belshazzar's feast, weighing the Church in the balances and finding it wanting. Our forms of worship, confession, the Mass, the veneration of saints, the images and icons in church buildings, the distinction between priest and people, even the outward symbols of clerical garb are all challenged.

And though I find myself drawn to his latest ideas, it troubles me that the peace which had begun to return to the cloister is disturbed afresh. The world outside, it seems, is in greater foment than before, the secrecy surrounding him producing an additional frisson. I share my concerns with the novice-teacher, who has taken on the role of mentor. 'If Luther wishes everyone to know he's alive and his work to be spread abroad, why does he remain in hiding?'

She gestures me to a window seat, and we sit together in silence. Her signing is hesitant, as if she considers each word before framing it. 'You must understand Katharina, Dr Luther faces great dangers. If he were to reappear in public his safety couldn't be guaranteed. Which is why Duke Frederick…' She breaks off, as if she has said something she shouldn't, and I think perhaps she has information that she has chosen, thus far, to keep to herself.

After a pause she continues. 'There have been death threats, and though I understand from my brother that Luther's desire has always been to return to Wittenberg, his friends will not allow it. Those who remain at the university consider the reform of the Church is better served by his quill than by his presence.' A smile flickers on her face. 'And perhaps they are right.' She pauses for a second time and studies her hands. 'They carry on the work of disseminating his ideas and building on the foundations he lays, and aside from the many pamphlets and tracts that find their way to us, there is word that he has undertaken a more substantial task: that we will shortly have the New Testament in our own tongue.'

Something moves inside me, but whether it stems from excitement or fear I'm not sure. 'A Bible that everyone may read for themselves?'

'Yes. And who knows' – this time her smile is broad – 'perhaps Dr Luther has been set aside for such a task as this.'

The harvest is long since in, the season of Advent approaching, when we hear the latest scandal. It begins with a tract *On Monastery Vows*, in which Luther advocates that anyone who wishes should be permitted to leave the cloister, insisting the vows are unbiblical, and cannot be considered binding. It seems his words have struck a chord, for Augustinians are leaving the order in droves to resume a secular life.

They strike a chord with me too, a flicker of envy that I seek to suppress, and when I recognise a similar yearning

137

in Eva, I sign, 'It may be fine for a monk to step out into the world, for he at least has a prospect of employment, but not for us.'

She crumples the paper, signs back, 'Why is everything easier for men?'

I shrug. 'It has always been so and nothing we may do will change it.'

With the coming of the new year the cloister is caught in the grip of winter, the roads into the valley once more impassable, so that for a second time the kitcheness counts and recounts the jars and sacks in the storeroom, gradually reducing the portions she serves. We live in semi-darkness under lowering skies, the temperatures too low for outside jobs, the daylight hours insufficiently bright for inside work, unless supplemented by candles, also in short supply. A commission for bishop's vestments has to be set aside, the sacrist despairing of finishing them in the time promised, and with little to do other than the usual Offices, tempers fray and minor irritations become major grounds for complaint. Luther's tract, smoothed out, is hoarded with the rest on the top shelf in the schoolroom, and though we haven't discussed it again, the thoughts expressed in it remain with me, an itch that begs to be scratched.

It is March before the thaw comes, and for a time the roads remain treacherous, the melting snows turning the hard-packed earth to rivers of mud. The workers who straggle back to resume their duties talk of carts bogged down to the axles, and horsemen brown from head to toe, as if they'd swum through treacle, and gloomily predict that the supplies we so desperately need may be a long time in coming. But when the first snowdrops push through the grass in the orchard and the blackbirds return to pull worms from the softening soil in the kitchen garden, the atmosphere changes. Perpetual scowls are replaced by smiles, and even the most staid among us seem to have a spring in their step.

A messenger from the prior at Grimma is the first to arrive, with a letter for the abbess, asking how the cloister has fared through the winter, and enclosed with it personal notes for Fronika and Margarete. It seems that events in Wittenberg have set the whole of Saxony abuzz. The word is that in December Luther slipped home incognito, bearded and disguised as a knight, and though he stayed only a few days before returning to his hideout, lent courage to his followers, among them Melanchthon and Karlstadt. And on Christmas Day almost the entire population of the town, some two thousand people, drawn by rumours of what was to come, turned out to witness Karlstadt's officiation at the Lord's Supper. He wore a plain black robe, the first time a priest had administered the sacrament without vestments, and though that in itself was startling, it was his sermon that had proved most controversial.

Fronika seeks me out in my cell during our recreation hour, her uncle's letter hidden inside her sleeve. 'You must see this, Kat.' She thrusts it at me, and as I read, it is as if I am in the Castle Church hearing Karlstadt preach, his words washing over me like a cleansing flood: "… there is no need for fasting and confession, only faith and a deep sense of contrition." I have read Luther's words on faith a dozen times or more and each time struggled to comprehend them, but now, through Karlstadt, the sense of them comes to me with the freshness of morning dew, the imagined taste of both the bread and wine of the sacrament sweet on my tongue. When I first entered the cloister I had determined never to allow anyone to see me cry, but with this new revelation I fall on my knees, my tears flowing freely, and I begin to understand that they are worth more to God than all my years of observances and set prayers have been.

Fronika crouches down beside me and hands me a handkerchief, whispering, 'That's not all, Kat. Our uncle included this.' There is a tension in her that the title of the tract she's holding out cannot explain.

I lean my back against the wall. '*The Estate of Marriage*. Why send us this?'

'Read it and you'll see.'

It's been newly printed at Grimma, but in a much smaller format than usual, almost as if it had been designed for illicit distribution. I can sense Fronika's impatience as she waits for my reaction, but the words are dancing in front of my eyes and I find it hard to focus. Luther has already challenged our vow of obedience, now it seems he challenges celibacy also, urging priests to marry, maintaining that as a symbol of the Church, it is not only good, but the highest calling possible.

Fronika bursts out, 'Our uncle says that monks and priests alike are finding new joy in marriage.'

I hand the tract back and summon a smile for her, to hide my overwhelming sadness.

We scramble to our feet as the bell rings for Terce..'Think of it,' she says, 'Faith … freedom … and marriage. Can it all be possible?'

Sister Magdalena also has news, which she shares with us after Prime. Her brother writes, *'the English king has entered the fray, referring to Luther as "that lecherous monk" and suggesting that all his ideas of reform stem from his own licentious desires. I cannot but laugh,'* he continues, *'for who among kings is upright in this respect? Henry should look to his own behaviour before presuming to traduce more worthy men.'*

Fronika tosses her head. 'Who cares what the English king thinks?'

Else looks up from the cross she's embroidering for an altar-cloth. 'I imagine it isn't because of what Henry thinks that von Staupitz writes, but rather to illustrate how far afield Luther's writings have travelled. If he is right in what he says, how privileged Germany is to be at the heart of it all. How fortunate we are to learn of his ideas.'

'More fortunate still if we could act upon them.' Fronika is devouring the tract on marriage for a second time, Eva looking over her shoulder, her hands still, as if she can't quite take it in. I don't want to think about it, for it seems so far beyond what is possible, serving only to threaten what little contentment remains to me. I look at Eva: pretty and vivacious, full of fun; for her maybe there could be a chance of marriage, but even supposing I could leave, who would want me, awkward and some would say prickly, and well past my prime? For a moment I remember the shop in Torgau and Herr Köppe's nephew, Leonhard: his kindness, the momentary spark of fellow feeling between us, but dismiss it. It was likely nothing and a long time ago besides.

Eva and Fronika become the centre of a new group, including some who had previously taken little part in discussions of Luther's views but who are attracted to them now, rekindling, as they do, previously suppressed dreams. And however hard I try to distance myself from them, to lose myself in the work of the cloister, to find fulfilment in the lot laid out for me, I find that the observances on which I previously depended have become dust and ashes in the face of the freedom of my new-found faith.

Chapter Eighteen
Nimbschen, September 1522 – March 1523

It is a turning point from which there is no going back. There are twelve of us who yearn to be released from our vows, and daily we come together in the hour after Sext, under the pretext of helping in the schoolroom, to discuss what we should do. Eva and some of the others are for breaking out of the cloister immediately, with little thought of what might come after, but Sister Magdalena, who aside from her position as novice-teacher is the oldest among us, counsels caution. All of us came to the cloister as children, and her suggestion, that we write to our respective families asking that they buy our release, has the mark of sound sense. Those whose families are in Electoral Saxony write their letters with a feeling of optimism, for there is a mood of reform throughout Duke Frederick's territory. Those who hail from Ducal Saxony understand that the possibility of success is less, Duke George favouring tradition, but are determined to try.

My position is difficult, for, Father dead, I cannot expect any joy from my stepmother, and I know my brothers will have little or no money to spare. I dare not ask the abbess to write to my mother's family, but I do speak to Aunt Magdalene, who is sympathetic but not encouraging.

'These past years have troubled us all, Katharina, and if you wish to seek release I cannot blame you, but neither can I hold out much hope of success. The von Boras are a noble family, but you wouldn't be here if your father hadn't fallen on hard times. I don't imagine your brothers will have managed to swell the family coffers sufficiently to afford to buy you out. But write to them, by all means. There is nothing lost by trying.' She runs her forefinger across her palm, as if tracing the lifeline, then signs, 'Do not fear that I will share your desire with anyone, so that, if in the end your lot is to remain here, there will be no scope for recriminations.'

⬤⬤

A flurry of letters are presented to the abbess, who betrays no reaction, though I suspect she's well aware of their contents. Once or twice as we leave the church after Prime, I sense her eyes upon me, as if she would speak, but each time the moment passes.

Aunt Magdalene welcomes me into the infirmary and sets me to preparing an unguent of oil of roses and chamomile mixed into a base of beeswax and oil. The repetitive motion soothes me, as I suspect she intended, but it doesn't dispel my need to ask. I ladle the cream into a jar, bite my lip.

'The abbess,' I begin, but Aunt Magdalene presses my hands together, stilling them, and signs,

'She cares for you, Katharina, and sympathises with

144

your struggles, but were she to share your full confidence it might prove difficult for her. As things stand she cannot be held accountable for what she hasn't been told. Nor can it be dragged out of her. I think it for the best, however often she may have been tempted to speak, that she refrains.'

'She knows what's in my mind?'

'Guesses, I imagine, but that's a very different thing. Without the dangers that knowledge carries: for you, as well as for her.'

'I've...'

She stills my hands again, shakes her head, and I see a tear trembling at the corner of her eye. 'Don't, please. You have long known where my sympathies lie, but like the abbess, I have responsibilities here that I cannot ignore. If I were younger, if I were not the infirmaress, perhaps...' She summons a smile. 'Whatever lies ahead for you, Katharina, whatever you may hear of us, know that you have our love, always.'

The von Zeschau sisters are the first to get a reply, passed on to them in another letter from their uncle. Fronika, recognising his handwriting, snags her nail in her haste to break the seal. We cluster around, suppressed excitement giving way to despondency, as we see the colour drain from her face.

Margarete whispers, 'He can't have refused. He can't have?'

Fronika holds out the letter. 'See for yourself.'

'But surely our uncle...'

145

'He says he tried, but Father hasn't the money to seek a papal dispensation and will not risk the consequences of proceeding without one.' She turns her head away, as if she can't bear to look at any of us, and though I've never seen her weep, not even when the inner door to the cloister blew shut trapping her finger and snapping the bone, I suspect she is close to it now.

Herr Köppe brings word to Sister Magdalena, her hopes similarly dashed.

In the safety of the schoolroom, Eva's signing is vigorous, expressing the disquiet I imagine we all feel. 'If they cannot convince their families of the validity of the case, what hope is there for the rest of us?'

I have misjudged Else. She surprises us all, exhibiting a patience and a resolve that rallies us and gives us renewed hope. 'We have none of us come to this decision lightly. If some have success we must all rejoice with them, but for the remainder, we will find another way.'

Three of our group receive guarded replies, indicating that if they were to leave the cloister of their own volition, a place would be made for them at home, but no prior assistance is offered. For several others the answer is an emphatic 'No', while two of us hear nothing at all.

Else, accepting that no reply is as good as a refusal, suggests a new plan, the confidence in her signing an indication that it's something she has carefully considered. 'We must appeal to Dr Luther. His teachings have brought us to this point. Surely he cannot ignore the pleas of those who wish to follow them.'

It's a confidence I'm not sure I share, but her logic is clear. We all look at Sister Magdalena, as Else continues, 'Who better than you to write to Luther to present our

146

case? Age and experience alone should commend you, and convince him that we act from conviction.'

Conviction of what, I wonder, but dismiss the thought. Uncertain of the root of my own desire, who am I to judge the others?

Eva echoes my thought, her eyes also fixed on the novice-teacher, 'If any of us were to write, he might be justified in questioning our motives, but yours he cannot.'

Sister Magdalena's eyes are glistening, but whether it's because she's moved by Eva's compliment or apprehensive of the task I don't know. She looks down at her hands as if noting the fine lines in her skin, like crazing in the faulty glaze of a water pitcher, and taking a deep breath, she signs back, 'I will write to him, on behalf of us all.' Her gaze rests on each of us in turn. 'And you must pledge to make this a matter of private prayer and the utmost secrecy. If it is God's will, He will accomplish it.' She looks around again, her signing slow and deliberate. 'To preach that vows are not binding is one thing, and I daresay there are many who share Luther's thinking, but to aid our escape is quite another, and it carries grave dangers. It won't only be Luther that will be put at risk, but everyone who plays a part in it, however small.' She pauses, as if unsure how much to say.

I fill the void, my signing also tentative. 'What *is* the penalty for aiding an escape?'

She runs her tongue around her lips. 'It will be considered an abduction, not an escape, and the penalty for that,' she pauses again, 'is death.'

The word hangs in the air between us, and I dare not meet anyone's eyes lest I see my own doubts mirrored there. Else brings us back to the practicalities.

147

'How can we get a message to Dr Luther? How do we know who we can trust?'

Sister Magdalena shuts her eyes for a moment, as if in prayer, then signs, 'It is a lot to ask, but I think Herr Köppe is our best chance. Indeed' – she looks towards the window and the narrow shaft of light it casts across the floor – 'likely our only one.'

The bell rings for None and we slip from the schoolroom in ones and twos, joining with the rest of our company as they make their way to the church. Eva is clearly still worrying away at the problem, for despite that her gaze is focused on the path, she fails to see the uneven slab and trips, landing heavily. I help her up, expecting to see annoyance, but instead she flashes me a smile, whispers, her usual self-deprecating humour resurfacing, 'I'd best not break my leg, or I'll have no chance at all.'

Torgau: 1552

The room is in darkness. I call out, for the servant, for Martin, for Muhme Lena, but there's no response. As my eyes accustom to the gloom, I make out the features of the room. Not my chamber at home. No wonder they don't answer. I stretch my hand out from under the covers, the air nipping at my fingers, struggling to find recognition in something, anything here. There is a half-inch stub of a snuffed candle on the windowsill, the only light a thin sliver slipping around the edge of the shutters. Moonlight? Daylight? Perhaps if I knew that... I try to swing my legs over the edge of the bed and manage with the first one, but the second stubbornly refuses to follow, pain shooting from my hip to my ankle. I think I must have screamed, for the door opens and a girl appears, her nightgown stained a pale yellow in the flickering light from the candle she carries. She sets the candle in the niche by my head and tucks my arm back under the covers.

Her eyes are dark in the pale oval of her face and there is concern in her voice. 'Don't try to move, Mutti.'

With her words comes realisation. I'm in Torgau, after the accident. With Margarethe and Paul and half the university. And my pelvis is broken. I settle back against the pillows. 'I'm fine now. I woke and forgot for a minute where I was.'

'Is there anything you need?'

'No, no, you go back to bed. Except ... would you open the shutters for me?'

I hear the doubt in her voice. 'Shouldn't you rather they remain closed against the night airs.'

'Please. I want to see the moonlight.'

'If you're sure?'

'I'm sure.'

The hinges creak as she folds the shutters back against the wall and I hold my breath, for fear of the noise.

She rests her fingers on my shoulder for a moment, her touch feather-light, then turns to go. In the doorway she pauses, smiles, blows out the candle. As my eyes adjust to the moonlight I see the others streaming from the church towards me. In the brazier the fire has burned down to a few glowing embers, but it is enough to stop me shivering as I wait to acknowledge their nods of affirmation, each sister touching my shoulder in passing. If they sense my excitement it will be thought no more than a justifiable pride in the role I have played in our Easter celebrations. Eva hangs back until the last, and as we move along the path together I'm surprised I can't hear her heartbeat, for mine thuds in my chest as loudly as if it were the new convent clock that stands in the abbess' chamber marking time.

Ahead of us, Sister Magdalene slows, allowing us to catch up. Her fingers flash encouragement in the moonlight. 'Tonight we have celebrated Christ's new life. Tomorrow we will honour it by a celebration of our own.'

CHAPTER NINETEEN
NIMBSCHEN, APRIL 1523

'You have done a new work that will be remembered…
You have liberated these poor souls from the prison of
human tyranny at just the right time: Easter, when Christ
liberated the prison that held his own.'

Martin Luther

There is an air of expectancy throughout the cloister as
preparations proceed. The Paschal candle is already in
place, and outside the church a farmhand, released from
his normal duties, is setting a fire in the brazier. I pause to
watch, my heart thudding in my chest, the abbess' words
ringing in my ears, unintentionally prophetic.

'Tonight you will light the Easter fire, Katharina, to
herald in the new beginning.'

We stand in the darkness, the moon obscured by cloud as
I set the spark, and I hold my breath until the first flicker

151

becomes a steady flame, leaping into the night sky. Eva presses my hand, as if in need of reassurance, and I press back. It will be all right. It must be. One by one we enter the church, each of us lighting our own wick from the Paschal candle, the repeated cries of 'Lumen Christi' echoing throughout the nave. On the stroke of midnight the abbess leads us in a prayer of exultation, and in the moment of silence that follows, candles, lit simultaneously by the more senior of our sisters, flare all around the church. As the light increases I lose myself in the swell of sound, my voice soaring in the Easter Proclamation, the triumph of Christ's resurrection more meaningful than ever before. It's hard to think it will be the last time I will sing it in this company, but when the notes fade away, and we process down the nave, I'm buoyed by the hope that is in me, despite the uncertainties ahead.

There is perhaps one hour to wait, and we gather in the garden unwilling to risk missing the call, clustering in the shadow of the cloister wall, hiding from the moonlight that reflects from every window, illuminating the path leading to the gate. Behind us a single light burns in the abbess' chamber, and I wonder if she looks out, if she senses what is happening, if she regrets the position she holds. We stand in silence, hands clasped, afraid even to whisper while the novice-teacher checks the gate. The bolts slide back without a sound and I sense her relief as she leaves it on the latch. In the darkness breathing is magnified, a single cough as loud as a pistol shot, every movement, every rustle of clothing seeming a danger. Beside me, Eva shivers and wraps her shawl more closely around herself, and I touch her shoulder to offer her mine, for I feel as if my body is on fire, but she shakes her head. It

152

is an eternity, thoughts of every possible disaster running through my head: a wheel coming off Herr Köppe's wagon, a stranger seeking hospitality hammering at the front gate and waking the cloister; the sacrist, walking the corridors unable to sleep, finding our empty cells. I feel as if a band is being tightened around my chest, constricting my breathing, and my legs are in cramp and I can't stop myself whispering, 'Please God, let them come soon.'

On my other side, the novice-teacher leans into me, her mouth close to my ear. 'Have faith, Katharina, they will come.'

And, as if on cue, we hear the creaking of an axle and the slap of canvas and the clip-clop of two pairs of horses on the track outside. The horses halt and an owl hoots three times. The novice-teacher lifts the latch and as we slip, one by one, through the open gate, I feel the band loosening around my chest and take in great gulps of air.

Herr Köppe's nephew holds the horses steady as the merchant lifts the canvas flap and hustles us into the cart, whispering instructions, his teeth showing white in the darkness. 'It won't be the most comfortable of journeys, for we'll be travelling on back roads to avoid being seen.' He nods to Sister Magdalena. 'As you'll remember, part of our route passes along the edge of Duke George's territory, and until we're well past that we are in particular danger. I will give it as wide a berth as I can, but there is no safety in any of this, especially in that garb.' He gestures at our clothes. 'So, please, if you can remain silent, it would be better.'

'If you can sleep,' Sister Magdalena suggests, 'that would be best of all.'

I must have dozed, for the next thing I know we seem to

be deep in woods, for all around us I can hear the cracking of twigs and the rustle of undergrowth. Remembering the previous journey, the carriage taking the widest tracks through open farmland, this sign of secrecy convinces me as nothing else could of the seriousness of what we do. The cart is slowing, the spare horses at the rear shifting, and as I straighten I hear Herr Köppe's whispered, 'Whoa, whoa.'

Sister Magdalena is shaking my shoulder and indicating to me to lie down.

I start to ask 'What's…' but she clamps her hand over my mouth, silencing me, jerking her head towards the noises coming through the canvas. There is little space and we squeeze down together, our knees tight to our chins, Eva shifting sideways in an attempt to make more room for me. Sister Magdalena pulls a rough blanket, jaggy with horsehair, over us, and I struggle not to sneeze, thinking of Duke George and the forces he has at his disposal. The voices are closer now, the sounds clarifying into snatches of conversation punctuated by a low whistling. The Köppe's are arguing, young Leonhard for keeping going and meeting head-on whoever is coming our way, his uncle wanting to stay put and perhaps be passed unnoticed.

'If we are found, having left the path,' Leonhard insists, 'it will only add to the likelihood of the discovery of our business. If we continue, we can maybe talk ourselves out of trouble.'

'You'd best polish up our story then.' Herr Köppe clicks his teeth and guides the horses back onto the track, urging them forward. The metal band running along the side of the wagon is pressing against my shoulder and my buttocks are sore with bouncing against the base-boards. We hear a single shot, Eva jerking sideways, her elbow jabbing into my ribs. The cart judders as if the horses at the front and the rear are pulling against each other. There is the sound of someone dropping to the ground, Herr Köppe's voice soothing the horses and Leonhard calling out a greeting.

The response is surly, the smell of burning match-cord drifting through the canvas lacings. 'What's your business?'

Leonhard's tone is reasonable, as if being held up on a track in remote woods is the most usual of occurrences. 'Similar to yours, I imagine,' he says.

'What do you know of our business?'

'Nothing … specific' – a slight pause – 'but I could hazard a guess, and no doubt there are those who would pay for such information.' There was a chorus of low growls, the cart shifting again as the horses stirred. 'Not that I wish to guess.' Leonhard stops as if to allow the assailants, whoever they are, time to absorb the thought, his voice, as he continued, if anything more pleasant than before. 'We will forget entirely we have seen you, if you do likewise.' Another pause, in which I imagine his lopsided smile. 'And if some bottles of wine should happen to fall from the back of our cart, we won't notice their lack until it's too late to seek to recover them.'

There is a guffaw of laughter and a 'What say you boys? Did we meet anyone in the woods tonight?'

Another voice calls out, 'Not that I saw.'

And a third, 'Nor I.'

'That's it then.' Leonhard's voice is slightly raised, as if for our benefit. 'My uncle, here, will just check the fastenings on the wagon and the spare horses and we'll be on our way.'

A fourth voice cuts in, and a shiver runs through me.

'Perhaps I should help him check, in case the load has shifted.'

We lie extra still as footsteps approach the back of the wagon.

Leonhard's voice again, deliberately easy. 'No need for that, we are all friends here, are we not.'

There is a moment of silence and then the first man says, 'I say we let them away, we've wasted enough time already.'

Through a slit in the blanket I see the edge of the canvas lifting, and I cannot breathe until I recognise the edging on Herr Köppe's sleeves as he lifts out a clinking box. The canvas falls again, the cord jerked tight, followed by the sound of him clambering back onto the wagon seat.

'We give you goodnight,' he says, and with a click of teeth we move forward again, Leonhard urging the horses into a trot. My back and legs are aching, my head likewise and I dearly want to sit up, but dare not move until we hear a whispered, 'I think we are safe now. You can remove the blankets. It won't be long until we're past the boundary of Duke George's territory, then we'll stop to change the horses and you can all get out to stretch your legs.'

◇◇◇◇

Dawn is breaking, light filtering through the canvas, when we hear the sound of bells carried on the breeze.

The horses slow and Herr Köppe unlaces the canvas and gestures at the outline of the city in the distance. There is pride in his voice, and a hint of relief as he announces, 'There it is: Torgau. Your freedom.' He waves towards the track ahead of us, dotted with people and carts all heading for the city. 'I wanted you to get a glimpse of it before I must ask you to remain quiet again, for your own safety. Even here it would not be politic to draw attention.'

The cluster of roofs and towers and steeples are painted on the skyline, their outline softened by the early morning haze. Above it, the castle towers, larger than I remember, my thought echoed by Eva, who says, a catch in her voice, 'I had not expected Schloss Hartenfels to be so huge!' She starts to laugh, her shoulders shaking uncontrollably, and I put my arm around her in an attempt to still her, but it makes no difference, her laughter coming in great gasps, as if she's choking. Sister Magdalena leans over and slaps her cheek, leaving a bright red palm-print. We all recoil, but the laughter stops, and after two, long, shuddering breaths, Eva says, her voice hoarse, 'Thank you.'

Herr Köppe nods to Sister Magdalena. 'I'm sorry to have to shut you in once more, but my inn is on Leipziger Strasse, one of the main routes into the town. It will be half an hour, no more, and the worst will be over.'

Cocooned inside the covered wagon, I glance at Magdalena and wonder if she too is thinking of our previous visit, if the seeds of what we are doing now were sown then. The temperature is rising, heat bleeding through the canvas, and I feel sweat trickling between my breasts, but whether from the heat or nervousness I'm not sure. The noise outside is increasing, Leonhard's voice, as he shouts out an occasional greeting, adding to the general hubbub. The horses slow again, come to a standstill, and there is a saliva rush in my mouth, my stomach cramping

157

as if it were my monthly course. I press my fist against it, fighting the irrational fear that it may all have been for nothing. A fear that others clearly share, Lanita grasping my hand, her fingers biting into my palm.

Sister Magdalena smiles a reassurance, signs, 'Don't worry, it'll just be the crush at the gate.'

As if on cue, we lurch forward again, the momentary dark indicating that we're in the shadow of the gateway, but it's only when we emerge on the other side, the light filtering through the canvas once again, that my tension drains away. The wagon is making a sharp turn, and we slide together, then apart again, before we come to a final halt.

Herr Köppe folds back the cover and hands us down into a cobbled yard while behind us a boy pulls shut the tall arched doors leading to the street, the sound of the bolt shooting home an unwelcome reminder of what we have left. A man in clerical garb is framed in the doorway from the shop, Herr Köppe clapping him on the shoulder, pleasure in his voice. 'Gabriel, I had not expected you so soon.' And to us, 'This is Gabriel Zwilling, our preacher, who also has your best interests at heart.'

Zwilling bows, his smile as he straightens encompassing us all. 'I came to greet you, to commend your bravery and to assure you of God's blessing on your new life.'

Magdalena takes a step towards him as if she is going to curtesy, but instead her legs crumple under her and I rush to grip her arm, holding her up.

A dumpling of a woman, with a face wreathed in smiles, appears at the top of a short stair and bustles down to us. 'Welcome, welcome.' And to Herr Köppe, her tone that of a mother scolding a thoughtless child, 'Do not keep them standing, they have had a long journey and are in need of rest.' She nods encouragement. 'You should be safe now. Nevertheless, the sooner you change out of those habits, the better.' There is a twinkle in her eye. 'The clothes we have for you may not be the best of fit, nor fashion either, but at least they will not betray your origins.' She gestures towards a row of windows overlooking the courtyard, a note of apology in her voice. 'I'm afraid we cannot give you our best rooms, for those overlooking the street were already taken, but perhaps…'

Sister Magdalena waves away her apology. 'We will do very well here, thank you, and indeed are more in need of quiet than of comfort.'

The women's relief is obvious. 'Well then, I trust, despite the celebrations of the day, it will be sufficiently quiet here to suit your needs.'

She moves towards the stair, indicating for us to follow, but Sister Magdalena puts a hand on her arm to halt her, before turning to Gabriel Zwilling. 'A prayer for us if you will, before we step into our freedom.'

Chapter Twenty
Wittenberg, April 1523

We arrive at Wittenberg, the valley of the Elbe stretching out wide and flat on every side to a faraway horizon furred with trees. The air is crisp and clear, the sky a cloudless blue, as if the whole world is rinsed clean, and looking up, I cling to the thought that it is an omen, a sign of God's approval of what we have done. This time Herr Köppe is in the back of an open wagon with us, his nephew, Leonhard, driving as before. He pauses at the first sight of the town, the castle rearing ahead of us, beyond it the tower of a church.

I wave towards the steeple. 'Is that the church where it all started?'

Herr Köppe nods. 'I don't think anyone imagined then what would come of Dr Luther's theses. But we may pray it will be a better world as a result of them.'

Magdalena's hands are clasped tight, her 'Amen' heartfelt.

As we approach the crossing we join a throng of people and carts and animals, all making for the city. The closer we get, the more the noise increases: voices raised in argument or greeting, harness jingling, axles creaking, the protests of sheep and pigs as they are herded onto the bridge. I grip the edge of the bench to stop my hands from shaking and concentrate on breathing slowly to suppress the unease in my stomach, for if I thought the Torgau bridge rickety with no one on it, this one, identical in construction and crowded, must surely be unsafe. Leonhard is pressing forward, urging the wagon through the stream of other travellers, using liberal cracks of his whip both to encourage the horses and clear our path. I begin to relax as we reach the town side of the river, the ground sloping down towards the arched gateway, the horse's hooves ringing on the hard-packed earth. A bullock cart is heading straight for us, heaped with steaming dung, and I expect Leonhard to give way, but for the second time he demonstrates that behind the reins he is not the diffident young man I remember from the shop. Fronika wrinkles her nose as the stench from the dung reaches us, my stomach, which had begun to settle, reacting afresh, so that I clap my hand over my mouth and nose to avoid retching. The wagon driver's shout is lost in the surrounding hubbub, but the accompanying rude gesture makes his meaning clear. Leonhard's return gesture is less rude, but equally clear. The bullocks lumber towards us, the horses growing increasingly restive as the gap closes, the forthcoming contest a source of amusement and good-tempered wagering among the passers-by, some calling encouragement to the cart driver, others to Leonhard, but all regarding us with frank interest.

Else shakes her head. 'Can we not give way? I do not like to be stared at so.'

Herr Köppe, with a glance at her white face, taps

Leonhard's shoulder and he pulls the wagon off to the side, the driver of the bullock-cart losing no time in taking his advantage.

As we wait, it seems that every eye is on us, and Magdalena asks, 'How will the townsfolk receive us?'

'I hope well, Fraulein.'

She flushes, like a young girl receiving her first compliment. 'I never thought to be addressed as such.'

'It is your due.' Herr Köppe is gentle. 'And you should enjoy it.' His smile broadens. 'It may not be for long…'

She waves away his words, but her flush deepens and I feel shamed that I have no idea what it is she hopes for in this new life. We young ones have discussed it among ourselves – where we might go, what might happen to us – but we none of us thought to consider Magdalena.

The show over, we are on the move again, the dirt track giving way to cobbles as we pass into a street lined with buildings on both sides. A tree, smothered in blossom, overhangs a wall on our left, and Lanita, looking up, says, 'I wonder whose garden that is? I do so like cherries.'

I cannot help smiling, that even in this circumstance she thinks of her stomach, while I, though with the same emptiness in my belly, cannot contemplate food.

Herr Köppe is smiling also. 'The garden belongs to the Cranachs, one of Wittenberg's wealthiest families. And as they are well disposed towards Dr Luther, you will likely have the opportunity to sample their produce.' As we pass through the market square, he points out the town hall, squatting in the centre, half-timbered, the framing filled in with brick. At ground level, the façade is punctured with arches, leading, I imagine, into small shops. Behind it there is the beginning of a new building, surrounded by

162

piles of timber and uncut stone and mounds of sand and lime, with great bites gouged out of their sides. Off to one side a mason sits, mallet and chisel in hand, dressing blocks, slivers of stone covering the ground at his feet. He looks up as we pass and, raising one hand, wipes at his forehead, cutting a damp smear through the dust coating his face. The neat stack of tooled blocks that is growing beside him is so familiar, so ordinary, that I think perhaps it will not be so hard to rejoin the outside world after all.

Curious at the scale of the foundations of the new structure, I ask, 'What are they building?'

Leonhard laughs. 'They pull down their barns to build bigger.'

Herr Köppe interrupts him, a note of mild censure in his voice. 'Since the opening of the university Wittenberg has outgrown its Rathaus. The new one will be both bigger and stone-built, as befits the town's increasing status. Indeed, there is much improvement taking place throughout the city, for the council, concerned about the risks of fire, have decreed that all new building work must be of stone or brick. It is a wise move and one that is being replicated in many towns.'

I look around, comparing the square, not to the coarse buildings of the Marienthron, but to the houses I remember in Lippendorf, and wish that I could return to see what has been made of my birthplace. Leonhard pauses the cart again, as the sound of a bell rings out from a church on the east side of the square, with twin towers stretching heavenward, and between them, on a sloping roof section, a painting of the Virgin and Child. It's the first time I've seen a roof used in this way and I cannot help but stare.

Herr Köppe gestures towards the painting. 'It is

unusual, is it not, but, I think, effective, though I'm not sure that I would have liked to be the one who had to work at that height.'

'That's the Town Church?' Eva asked. 'Where Karlstadt…'

I finish the sentence for her, '…officiated without robes and gave the people both elements of the sacrament.'

I have a suspicion Herr Köppe is amused by our enthusiasm, but if he is, he doesn't say so, his tone matter of fact. 'The town council made an order that both elements are always to be given now. I think Wittenberg is the first to do so.'

I see the longing in Fronika's face and, sharing it, say, 'If only *we* could have been here yesterday.'

'You will have many more Easters.' Magdalena is looking up at the painting, her expression pensive, and I wonder if it hides an element of regret.

Eva exudes confidence. 'We all will.'

Leonhard shakes the reins and we move on again, thrusting our way through a constant tramp of people and carts and horses. Fronika's sister Margarete startles each time someone calls out a greeting or pauses to speak. Used as we are to almost total silence, the hustle and bustle of the Wittenberg street is deafening. I press her hand, remembering my first moments in the market at Torgau.

'You'll get used to this in no time. Soon it will be silence that will seem strange.'

All along our route people turn to stare as we pass, and I feel colour creeping into my cheeks. Some seem curious, others amused, and one or two, hostile. I try to see us as they see us: an odd assortment of women of varying ages, our clothes, hurriedly found for us in Torgau, mismatched and ill-fitting, no trace of any hair escaping around the edges of our caps. I look down at my hands, the nails cut square and short, the skin dry, palms calloused, the backs of them covered in scratches from cutting back blackberry canes. More likely to be a drain on the parish purse than an asset to the town, it's no wonder they stare. I have to ask. 'Do they know who we are?'

Herr Köppe shakes his head. 'Not the ordinary townsfolk. It was thought best that it should not be noised abroad, save among the better of our families, whose help Luther desired, lest word leak out and cause the enterprise to fail.' His glance sweeps over us. 'But you will be the talk of the town tonight, for it isn't everyday a cartload of women arrive as you have done.'

Eva as usual takes a lead. 'Where will we stay?'

'At the Black Cloister, for tonight at least.'

There is an empty feeling in the pit of my stomach, a fear of returning behind walls. 'Who else is there?'

'Only Dr Luther and one other of the original brothers, I believe, but—'

Magdalena straightens her shoulders. 'Then I think it is not fitting.'

Else says, 'No doubt Dr Luther has thought of that.'

Marta grins, whispers in my ear, 'If he hasn't, there's more than us will be the talk of the town.'

On my other side Fronika snorts, quickly turning the sound into a cough, and I think: all the months and weeks of hoping and planning have not prepared any of us for this.

Herr Köppe finishes his interrupted sentence. 'You need not worry, there are servants also.'

165

He is there to meet us at the entrance to the cloister. The tension, which has been building in me as we passed along the Collegienstrasse, dissipates as I see there is no surrounding wall enclosing it, only a fence separating the cloister grounds from the street. Leonhard brings the wagon to a halt, Herr Köppe leaping down to drop the tailgate and hand us onto the cobbles one by one. Eva is first, unable to conceal her excitement, Fronika following, and after her, Magdalena, stiff from the journey.

I come last, jumping down without help, my curtsey an unfamiliar movement dredged from my childhood. 'Herr Dr Luther. We are grateful for all you have done.' I gesture to Magdalena, who is leaning on Eva's arm. 'But as you see, some of us require the opportunity to rest, for the journey has been arduous. Our fear that we might be apprehended remained with us until we passed from Duke George's territory. Will the Elector Frederick give us his protection?'

Luther bows. 'The elector is mindful of your needs and will, I trust, do all in his power to meet them. But once you're rested, Herr Cranach and his wife, who are among our foremost families, have graciously offered refreshment. It is but a short walk…'

Behind me I hear Lanita's sigh of satisfaction, and clearly Dr Luther does too, for he pauses, as if to give her a chance to speak.

Herr Köppe fills the momentary silence. 'I pointed out the Cranach house on our way from the crossing' – there is a twinkle in his eyes as he glances at Lanita – 'no doubt the ladies will be pleased to make their acquaintance.'

166

Luther nods and continues. 'There are a number of households that have expressed themselves willing to accommodate you, so soon as arrangements can be made, but for tonight at least you'll sleep here.' His gaze sweeps over us all, and I note, without surprise, that it rests a moment longer on Eva than on anyone else, the beginnings of a smile playing around his mouth. Clearly, even without hair he finds her pretty. Once it is grown she will outshine us all.

It's a thought that I return to in the Cranachs' house, when, the meal cleared, we remain seated around the table as Luther and Cranach talk of what may be done for us.

Herr Cranach is quite clear. 'There are only two possibilities. No doubt you each have some skills, and it may be that they will enable you to find positions in which you can support yourselves, but it is by no means guaranteed. There are those, even here, who would be reluctant to employ an escaped nun for fear of the consequences.' He smiles as if to remove any sting from his comment. 'The easier solution may be to find a husband.'

I flush, but Eva's eyes sparkle.

Frau Cranach shakes her head at him, as if in reprimand. 'It's not something that must be decided in a day or two.'

'Indeed, I but thought to prepare the sisters for the difficulties that may arise.'

'Better we look to celebrating what has already been accomplished.' Her voice matches her smile. 'Whatever may lie ahead, today should be a joyous thing, without alloy.' She rises and gestures to us to follow.

As we cross the hallway, I hold back a fraction and hear Luther say, 'Some folk in town will help these sisters, but not many. I have done nothing but ask on their behalf since I first knew of their coming, and it has been a disappointment that some, even among those I counted friends, have not supported the venture. I had to appeal to the elector to ask for money to feed them for ten days or a fortnight to allow time for them to be suitably placed.'

'And his response?'

'He sent it. But others must help too, or it will be too much for us to handle.'

Cranach's reply is indistinct, and I can't hold back any longer, but as I follow the others upstairs I struggle with the thought – we are not wanted here. Perhaps it was a mistake to seek release. Our escape may have been straightforward enough; our path into the outside world seems likely to be less so.

Frau Cranach is talking over her shoulder as we follow her across the hallway and climb the staircase. 'No doubt you were grateful for the clothing Herr Köppe found for you at Torgau, but I trust I can do better.' She opens a door into a tall upper chamber, sunlight spilling through the leaded windows, painting circles of light onto the gowns laid out on the bed. 'You must take your pick and find what fits you best. We knew only how many of you to expect, but not anything of size or shape.' She dimples 'Indeed, that would, I think, have been rather too much information for the good doctor to handle.' A wider smile. 'It took every ounce of diplomacy I could muster to make a collection that might meet all requirements.' She looks at each of us, her eyes narrowed as if she calculates, and I guess at her thoughts. We are much as any group of women might be: a mix of short and tall, slender and stout.

'To begin with it was only those of slender build who offered gowns. Perhaps because others did not wish for me to know how tightly they were laced into their clothes. I had to promise anonymity before I could persuade those of more ample proportions to part with anything. I trust you will not be so coy in choosing.' She stands back, as if to give us space and the dignity of choice.

Eva is the first to break free of our huddle, and crosses to the bed, lifting first one gown then another, holding them against herself, each time turning with a questioning look in our direction. It's impossible to advise, for everything suits her, the colours glowing against her pale, flawless skin.

'That's a good choice,' I venture, when she holds up, for the third time, a full-skirted gown in periwinkle blue, the white bodice criss-crossed with perfectly matched narrow ribbons.

'Do you think so?' Her tone is unusually tentative, unsure, as we all are, of fashions and colours and style.

Frau Cranach, with a motion of apology, takes over. 'Perhaps you will let me help? It can be hard to choose for yourself.' She nods to Eva. 'That *is* a good choice for you; it complements your eyes, emphasises their colour.' She turns next to Magdalena, perhaps in recognition of her senior status, and, picking out a gown in soft burgundy wool, holds it up. The neckline is high and plain, the simple sleeve caught into the wrist with a row of silver buttons. She cocks her head to one side like a sparrow, nods. 'This has a certain elegance that I think appropriate.' One by one she draws us forward, passing over some gowns, and lifting others, choosing with unerring ease, clearly deriving satisfaction from matching the dress to

169

the person. As I wait my turn I'm surprised by a fear that perhaps there won't be anything pretty left. It's the first time in my life I've been concerned by appearance, and I find the stirrings, of what I barely recognise as a desire to be attractive, somewhat disconcerting. She offers me a gown in a tawny brown and I stifle my disappointment, for it seems rather plain, the only ornamentation the black velvet piping edging the square of muslin inset at the neck and the up-turned collar. I summon what I hope is a suitably grateful smile, but raising my eyes to her face, I catch a hint of amusement in her eyes which makes me hesitate, think of refusal. Poor I may be and without means of support, but I'd rather have one gown, ill-fitting or not, given out of genuine compassion, as those in Torgau had been, than be paraded in better for anyone's amusement. Magdalene, as if she reads my thoughts, shakes her head. I hold the gown against myself and as I half turn to face the others, the cloth shimmers under my fingers, the colour changing in tone as it catches the light. Surprised, I turn back and back again, delighted by the subtlety.

Frau Cranach smiles. 'It is a feature of the cloth, a subtle undercurrent, which has its own attraction. At least, I always found it so.'

Ashamed to have so misjudged her, and to cover my embarrassment, I speak for us all. 'We are grateful for your efforts and for everyone who has given so generously to clothe us.' The others nod and murmur with me, but she waves away our thanks. There is an ironic twist to her mouth.

'The benefit is mutual. For most of us it is an excuse to have something new of our own. These aren't the latest fashions, but will, I trust, serve in the meantime.'

Stockings and undergarments are draped over a chest by the window, an assortment of shoes and boots on the floor beside them. 'No doubt you will wish to sort through these yourselves; come down when you're ready. I'll be waiting in the Stube with the others.'

I am not mistaken. When we reappear in our new finery, Dr Luther's eyes go straight to Eva. Afterwards, when we return to the Black Cloister and retire to a large chamber overlooking the town wall, where a makeshift dormitory has been set up for us, she laughs at my suggestion, dismissing him with a shrug. Her sister, Marta, is more pragmatic. 'If we must all find positions or husbands, why should you despise the doctor?'

She flares out her skirts. 'I did not escape from one unfulfilling marriage to enter another one perhaps equally restricting.'

Else is thoughtful. 'We owe him a debt that perhaps marriage might repay.'

'You marry him, then. I've no intention of doing so.'

'Eva!' Magdalena shakes her head.

'Oh I know he's a good man, and without him we would none of us be here and free of our vows. But he's an *old* good man, and I wish to find a *young* one.'

Fronika is standing by the open window listening to the rise and fall of voices and the accompanying bursts of laughter carrying from the university precinct, the sounds magnified in the still night air. 'There may be many prospective husbands among the students here. If only we can get to meet them.'

171

Magdalena sounds a note of caution. 'We are not all young, indeed none of you are as young as most girls who seek a husband. And an escaped nun may be considered too dangerous a choice for many. Best that we think of how else we can support ourselves.'

'What would *you* like to do?' I ask, for if any of us are too old for marriage, Magdalena certainly is.

She is staring into the middle distance, yearning in her voice. 'I would wish to run a school, for girls, where they could be taught without the restrictions of a convent, where their future lay without, not within, the walls.'

'Is such a thing possible?'

'I believe so. The abbess talked of one such at Grimma. I intend to ask Herr Dr Luther if he can speak for me there.'

There is the sound of a door banging downstairs and Luther's voice. '…You may be sure there will be repercussions, but I've no intention of hiding my part in this and have already written my defence.'

Frau Cranach asks, 'What of the merchant, Köppe?'

'His too. It was a brave and good thing he has done this day. I will do everything in my power to see that he doesn't suffer for it.'

172

The censure isn't long in coming, Luther presenting Magdalena with a letter from Spalatin, Duke Frederick's secretary, enclosing a copy of the protest that the abbess and Abbot Peter sent to Duke George. She reads it out to us and I think of my aunt, on the day of our escape, reaffirming the love that she and the abbess have for me, exhorting me, whatever happened, to remember it always. I hadn't known it then, but I see now it was a message to comfort me in this circumstance, confirming my suspicion that they had both been fully aware of our intent and had chosen to ignore it. Lanita is shifting on her seat, her hands trembling.

Magdalena folds the paper, her composure unruffled. She reaches out to Lanita and stills her hands, but her gaze is fixed on mine as she says, 'They have little choice but to protest, or they too would be implicated in the escape. Do not fear that they will press any further.'

Else asks, 'What of Duke George's reaction? Should we fear that?'

Luther is holding out another paper. 'We already

173

have it. This is a copy of his letter to Elector Frederick, demanding that those responsible for abducting nuns from a convent in his territory be surrendered to justice.'

Lanita begins to shake again and Magdalena puts her arm around her. 'What will happen now?'

'The elector has refused his request. He won't give me up, despite that I have taken full responsibility.'

I'm thinking of the snippet of conversation I heard in the Cranachs' house. 'What of the merchant Köppe?'

'He too is safe, and though he has lost the trade from the Marienthron, he has gained new custom from those who wish to display their support.' Luther's gaze flicks towards Eva. 'And my defence has been framed in such a way as to allow your reputations and honour to remain intact.'

He has done his best, but the reality is somewhat different. And though we remain in the Black Cloister only a matter of days, it's clear that in some eyes we are already tarnished. Divided among the best houses in town, some of those who open their homes to us take pains to emphasise that they do so at the risk of their own good standing. It's an attitude that clearly annoys Dr Luther, but one which he can do little to alter.

I am more fortunate, taken in by Philipp and Elsa Reichenbach. Elsa welcomes me with an open generosity, so that I come close to tears. With a quick upward glance at my face, she sweeps me away, taking me to a chamber high under the eaves, her voice brisk as she apologises for its small proportions. If her intention is to divert me from emotion by focusing on the practicalities, she is successful, and I'm thankful for it. I look at the iron bedstead, its thick bedding topped by a brocade coverlet, at the rag rug on the floor and the carved chest under the window, and manage, 'There's no need for apology. This is a palace in comparison to my cell at the convent. I will be more than comfortable here. Thank you.'

As the days pass, I begin to realise just how fortunate I am, for Philipp Reichenbach is the town clerk and their house on the Burgermeisterstrasse is always busy, so there's plenty to distract me, both from doubts about what we have done and fears for the future. Yet it remains clear that though Wittenberg is the centre of the changes that are sweeping our land, there are many here who are troubled by our presence, who think that Luther has gone too far in aiding our escape. Some express their disapproval in subtle ways: stepping sideways on the street as I pass, lest I brush against them, or whispering behind their hands while I wait my turn in one of the shops under the Rathaus. Others are more vocal, their critical comments clearly meant to be heard. But none dare to stand in open opposition to the Reichenbachs, so that I'm shielded from much of the antagonism that others face while Dr Luther redoubles his efforts to find a solution to our plight. He and Herr Cranach are frequent visitors in the Reichenbach house, spending many hours closeted with Philipp, Dr Luther's voice reverberating along the corridor, reaching the Stube. I have to strain to hear the others but cannot stop myself trying to listen.

At first he is optimistic, clearly hoping that he has only to ask in the name of Christ and many of us will be able to return home; his frustration when his requests are refused, equally clear. 'They talk of a desire to follow Christ and yet refuse sanctuary to their own offspring? Shame on them.'

Herr Cranach is more understanding. 'Not everyone has your courage, Martin, nor your convictions. And we are here, with the protection of Frederick. For those in Duke George's territory it's a different matter.'

'And what of those families also under Frederick's control? What excuse can you make for them?'

Herr Reichenbach sounds impatient, but whether with Luther or the personal inconvenience of accommodating me I'm not sure. 'Think why these women were placed in the convent in the first place. Most likely to avoid the necessity of providing a dowry for them. And that may have been more a case of economic necessity than any intentional cruelty. If their own families cannot or will not support them, we need to find another solution, for we cannot keep them here indefinitely.'

Frau Reichenbach rises and shuts the door. She comes to sit beside me. 'There are those who will take a good wife on her own merits, without a dowry. And where better to find such a husband than in this town, with a university full to bursting point with young men.'

I think of Eva, her chances likely good, but am much less sure of my own.

⟨⊗⊗⟩

The Reichenbachs' hospitality is renowned, their circle of friends large, and it's easy to make myself useful, for my time in the kitchens at Nimbschen made me a mistress of the basics, if nothing more elaborate. But their cook is happy to share her skills with me and I find it rewarding to be able to produce new varieties of soups and sauces, and make bread and fancies of all shapes and sizes. At Nimbschen we ate to survive, nothing more. At the Reichenbachs', meals are joyous occasions, the appearance and flavour of what is served as important as the goodness it provides. The silverware and napery on the table are a glittering accompaniment to the lively conversations, reminding me of the market at Torgau, of the silversmith whose work I'd so much admired.

Some of the household furnishings are more unsettling, stirring painful memories. The rugs on the floor, the pictures hanging in the Stube, the painted ceilings, all reminiscent of the manor at Lippendorf and the family I have lost.

Frau Reichenbach is perceptive. 'When you're settled, and know where and how you are to live, you will be able to invite your brothers to visit you.'

I bury that hope deep within me and concentrate on making the necessary adjustments to this new life, trying not to dwell on the thought that, had my father not sent me to Brehna, it might have been mine all along.

To begin with, I still wake at two in the morning and have to force myself to remain in bed, tossing and turning until six. I miss the others, especially Eva and Fronika and Else, for though we see each other from time to time, when out shopping or at church, the snatched moments are nothing compared to the constant companionship of our Nimbschen days. I miss our recreation hour when we sat in the convent garden sharing our grumbles and frustrations, and latterly, our hopes and dreams. Eva is a short walk away at the Cranachs', but we are neither of us sufficiently confident in our position to suggest calling on each other socially as gentlewomen do. I miss the Offices of the Hours, the dividing up of the day with devotions, so that looking back they begin to take on a rosy glow they'd didn't have when they were an obligation.

Frau Reichenbach is sympathetic when I share such thoughts. 'You were under that discipline for so long, naturally it will take time to adjust. But do not think that we, who do not observe such rigours, have any less gratitude to God, only that we show it in different ways.'

To begin with I have other difficulties also. I find it hard to think of myself as a single person, rather than as part of a community, and I struggle to choose in even the simplest of situations: whether to take beef or pork at dinner, fruit or a pastry for dessert, which of my two shawls to wear going to the market. It's a freedom I've never had, and at times it overwhelms me. Often, when asked a question, my hands start to fly before I recollect that I am allowed to speak. And, ironically, considering how often I was tempted to break the rule of silence in the convent, initially speech itself disappoints, for it seems slower than my hands, as if it can't keep up with my brain.

That too, Elsa, as she instructs me to call her, says will come with time. 'I don't mean to insult you, Katharina, but in some respects you must regard yourself as a child, learning all over again what to do, how to behave.' Her gaze is direct. 'How to be happy.'

The question pops out before I can stop myself. 'Are you happy?'

'Yes, yes, I am. But that's a question you must realise isn't always appropriate. There are many who will resent such directness.' She touches my shoulder, as if to show

I've caused *her* no offence, her words but a warning for my relations with others.

As the days and weeks pass I settle into a new rhythm. Philipp I scarcely see, apart from at mealtimes, for his duties as clerk keep him busy, but my reliance on Elsa grows into a friendship that is as welcome as it is unexpected.

I've been there a month when she comes to me in the herb garden as I'm picking rosemary to add to a stew.

'Why not stay with us. When a husband is found for you we'll be happy to provide your wedding feast, and until then you're welcome here. Indeed, I will take it as a kindness if you will think of yourself as part of the family, for I would miss your company if you were to leave in any other than the best of circumstances.'

A cloud moves across the sun, and although I want to throw my arms around her, I'm aware that others in the household might not share her view, so ask, 'What of Herr Reichenbach ... the other servants?'

She places her arm around my shoulder, pulls me against her side. 'I can deal with them. In other circumstances we would have been friends, why not in these?' She falls silent and I'm not sure if she expects a response, but after a moment she continues as if she feels the need to convince me. 'We have the means, Katharina, and have been blessed with children. Nevertheless, there is room in this house for a daughter such as you.'

CXXXD

I'm right about Eva, though it isn't a scholar she sets her heart on. She darts over as we leave the Town Church

179

after Sunday worship and whispers, 'I've something to tell you. Can you walk with me?'

I cast a questioning glance towards Elsa and she nods, saying only, 'Don't be overlong delayed. Philipp, as you know, is always impatient for his meals.'

Eva pulls me aside as folk spill out of the church and mill in groups on the street. The crowd is slow to disperse, for the weather is kind, and with little wind there is a warmth in the pale sunshine that encourages loitering. She looks about and, grasping my arm, pulls me to the opposite side of the street, which is less busy, and bends her head close to mine. I don't need to ask what she wants to share, for her eyes are dancing, but I'm desperate to know who it is. With so little contact between us, I've no idea who she might have met in the Cranachs' house, but I imagine that they, like the Reichenbachs, are happy to entertain students and teachers alike from the university.

'Do I know him?'

'Kat! Don't be a spoilsport. You weren't supposed to guess.'

'How could I not? You're like a cat who's got the cream.' I grin at her, ask again, 'So, do I know him?'

'I don't think so.'

'Not Dr Luther then?'

She makes a face at me. 'Of course not. Basilius is a pharmacist and assistant to Lucas Cranach.'

'And young?'

'Young … and kind.'

'Handsome?'

The dimple is coming and going in her right cheek. 'No. Not especially, but Herr Cranach says his work is excellent and with diligence and a little help along the

180

way he may go far. Barbara … Frau Cranach, assures me the help will be forthcoming and that his reputation is untarnished, which, it seems, is of the utmost importance, especially in our situation, but best of all he makes me laugh.'

'Just as well. I can't imagine you with some sober-sides insisting on seriousness at all times.' I hesitate, but curiosity gets the better of me, and I blurt out, 'How does he make you … feel?'

She looks down, pink tingeing her cheeks, and I sense an embarrassment, normally so foreign to her. 'I can't describe it, Kat, except that every bit of me tingles when he comes near, and when he offers me his hand to lead me in to supper, the touch of his fingers is like a burn.' She squeezes my arm. 'You know what I hoped for, and though it may not have been an assistant to an apothecary, Basilius is so much more than I expected. Sometimes just hearing his voice makes me breathless.'

It's my turn to look down. I'm glad to see her happy, of course I am, but I can't help feeling a twinge of envy that shames me. Eva has always been good at guessing my thoughts, and I don't want her to know this one, so as a distraction I think of Dr Luther and the way he watched her when we first came, and I concentrate on feeling sorry for him instead.

A group of Wittenberg matrons pass us and we nod a greeting, pretending to be unaware of the critical undertone in their scrutiny.

Eva waits until they're out of earshot, and with unerring instinct she says, 'You needn't feel sorry for the good doctor.'

I lift my hands in protest, but she wags her finger at me,

and for a moment I see her as she might be in ten, twenty years' time, the prosperous wife of a burgess, confident in her position in society and comfortable in her own life.

She has regained her normal colour, and mischief has replaced the uncertainty in her voice. 'Had I waited for Dr Luther to declare an interest ... supposing I wanted it, which as you know I didn't ... I'd likely have died without a husband.' She glances around, lowers her voice. 'I overheard the Cranachs discussing the matter ages ago. It seems you may have been right: apparently Luther said, if he was to marry any of us, I would be his choice, but he is resolved to remain single.'

'I wonder why? When he is so adamant that marriage is good.'

'That's what Frau Cranach asked too, and according to Lucas, he thinks he is too old and feels his life so precarious that it would scarcely be fair to take a wife who might be left a widow at any time.' A pause and a grin. 'A lucky escape, it seems.'

I can't resist it. 'For both of you.'

'Undoubtedly!' We both dissolve in laughter, and I bend over, pressing against the stitch in my side and wiping at my eyes. A worthy standing at the corner of the square glares at us and we turn away, attempting to smother our mirth. This may be a Reformation town, but laughter on a Sunday is clearly as suspect here as it had been at Nimbschen.

Torgau: 1552

I wake to a clip-clop, clip-clop on the cobbles and turn my head towards the window. A girl is sitting beside it, a shaft of light from the half-open shutters falling across her lap, illuminating her sewing. Her head is bent, her hand crooked, the needle between her forefinger and thumb stabbing the cloth, in and out, in and out, the dimples on her pewter thimble casting tiny circles of light onto the ceiling. I try to drag myself up in the bed and push away the covers, but the movement causes my chest to convulse and I begin to cough, a harsh rasp that brings her to her feet immediately. She bends over me, tugging at the coverlet, a strand of hair straggling loose from her cap, touching my cheek.

It smells of vinegar and I wrinkle my nose and brush at it. 'What are you doing?' I take hold of the edge of the cover to thrust it aside again, but she doesn't let go.

'Help me up,' I say, but she shakes her head.

'Frau Luther.' Her speech is slow and patient, as if she speaks to a child. 'The Fraulein is out and asked me to sit with you. You have lost your covers and I thought to remedy that, lest you catch cold.'

'I didn't lose them. I put them off. I'm too hot.'

She bites on her lip and I see a tooth beginning to blacken at the tip and fix on it, determined to distract her, to get her to release her grip of the cover. 'You should have that tooth removed, or the infection might spread to others.'

She puts one hand up to her mouth, her answer muffled, and I see how young she is. 'I'm afraid it will hurt.'

I speak sternly. 'You don't wish to lose more?'

'No, but…'

'Paul will do it,' I say. 'Where is he?'

'At his studies, Frau Luther.'

'Ah yes. Later then. I'll tell him.' The ring of horseshoe on the cobbles is louder now and I remember what I wanted. 'Open the shutters.'

'The Fraulein said…'

'What Fraulein?'

She takes a deep breath, a knot of worry on her forehead, her tone uncertain. 'Fraulein Margarethe. She'll be here presently, and if she finds you uncovered…'

I curl my fingers around the edge of the coverlet, push at it again. 'I am not a child, to be told what to do.'

She takes hold of the cover again, attempting to draw it up to my chin. 'You are not well, the Fraulein…'

It's a tug of war, each of us determined not to give way, and in other circumstances I would admire her, for she has spirit. 'All right,' I say, 'I'll keep the sheet, but not the cover. And don't worry, I'll see to the Fraulein.'

She sighs, retreats to the chair and picks up her sewing, the thimble winking on her finger.

'Please,' I say, and she is on her feet again in an instant. 'Is it him?'

I can tell she doesn't know what to say and feel a flicker of sympathy for her. I look back at the window. 'If you will just open the shutters and tell me if it's him.'

She hesitates, 'Who…'

'Jerome Baumgartner. If he is back I must go to him.' I want to explain, but there's no time, the hoof-beats receding. 'Quick,' I *say, sliding towards the edge of the bed, ignoring the pain in my back and legs, my chest constricting.*

There is a flicker of panic in her eyes and she nods, thrusting aside the shutters. 'What does he look like?' she says, leaning out.

'Tall, young…' I smile at her bent back, remembering, '… handsome.'

CHAPTER TWENTY-TWO
WITTENBERG, MAY 1523

'The heart of a human creature is like quicksilver, now here, now there; this day so, tomorrow otherwise.'

Martin Luther

Even from above he's handsome, disturbingly so. I'm sitting at the open window enjoying the warm air which drifts in, carrying the smell of fermenting hops, reminding me of the brewhouse at Nimbschen and my labours there. Many would think me strange to hanker for the hard work of the brewing, as against mending a tear in one of Philipp Reichenbach's shirts, and I know I should be grateful for so light a task. When Elsa relinquished the mending to me her relief was visible, and it's an easy enough way to repay her kindness. For though it wasn't my favourite occupation at Nimbschen, my stitches were precise and even, the envy of many in the cloister.

The sound of horse's hooves catch my attention and I set aside the shirt and lean out through the open casement, resting my elbows on the broad sill. Below me a horse high-steps on the cobbles, the gold threads in the emblem on the saddlecloth catching the sunlight, the feather in the rider's soft bonnet waving in the breeze. Dark hair curls on the collar of his cloak, which looks to be of finest wool, the weave tight. A sudden gust lifts the corner, blowing it aside, and I see a velvet jacket and the glint of embossed buttons. Clearly a young man of my own class, one that, in other circumstances, I might have met. I narrow my eyes, half squinting at the monogram, but still can't make out the design, and chiding myself for my interest, I turn away from the window, for I am a lifetime away from my childhood at Lippendorf, a world away from such as he. Out of the corner of my eye I see a flash of fur as a dog darts across the street startling the horse. It throws its head up, front hooves lifting, then clatters down again and dances sideways, skidding on the cobbles. There is a musical lilt to the rider's 'Whoa, whoa, easy now, easy,' as he soothes the horse, and it opens a pit in my stomach that I refuse to acknowledge. Hurriedly I reach out to shut the casement, and as I do so the thimble slips from my finger, bouncing off his saddle and dropping onto the cobbles below. As he looks up, his mouth curves into a smile and there is a flicker of amusement in his gaze. Heat flooding my face and neck, I step back, cross at my carelessness, even more cross that he sees my blush. I wait until I'm sure he's gone, the sound of the hoof-beats receding, before I fly down the stairs to retrieve the thimble – but it's no longer there. I'm sitting staring at the window frame, wishing I were as pretty as Eva, when Elsa appears and jolts me out of my reverie. I know I should confess to the loss of the thimble, but I don't want to mention my folly in watching the young man, so say nothing.

187

'I came to give you warning that we will have a visitor at supper.' There is a liveliness in her voice, a suppressed excitement, reinforced when she says, 'You will perhaps wish to wear your best.'

Despite the Reichenbachs' status, we aren't normally so formal, and there have been plenty of other visitors coming and going without ever a thought of changing in their honour. I run my mind over the events of the past few days in an attempt to guess who it might be. There was word of the duke coming to Wittenberg, so I ask, my stomach lurching, 'Someone from the court?'

Elsa shakes her head but offers no clue. In an attempt to play her at her own game I try, 'The King of Sweden perhaps?' It's a jest, but has a grain of possibility in it, for there's talk that he's interested in Luther's teachings and may one day come in person to hear him. And that he isn't above lodging in a rich merchant's house. If that rumour be true, who better than the Reichenbachs to entertain him?

Elsa's eyes are dancing as she twirls the keys that dangle from the cord about her waist. 'Not quite. A former student, returned on a visit. His family and ours have been acquainted for many years.'

'And you would have me dress up for him?'

'He's handsome, well bred, with a good fortune, unmarried, and not contracted to anyone so far as we know... I think he might do you very well.'

I feel the colour creeping into my cheeks again, but determine to snuff the flicker of hope that threatens to flame within me. 'But would I do for him? Would he not expect more than this?' I hold out my hands, the skin chapped from the ammonia used in the bleaching of sheets a few days before, the nails clipped short, lest they snag the fine lawns and cambrics that I spend a good deal of time sewing.

Elsa takes them in both of hers. 'Why not? You are also well bred, well educated, can sing and sew and bake and as capable of managing a household as anyone of our acquaintance.'

As so often when I am unsure, I resort to sarcasm. 'I am also twenty-four and less pretty than most. No doubt the bride every well-favoured young man seeks?'

Elsa ignores my tone. 'If he has sense, yes.' She looks towards the window. 'I'm surprised you didn't see or hear him, for he passed not long since…' She pauses, a teasing note creeping into her voice. 'Or perhaps you did, and that was why you didn't hear me when I called for you.'

I affect a shrug. 'There was a man passed by, when the window was open. I noted him only because his horse needed some handling.'

'With a burgundy cloak and a feather in his bonnet?'

'The same.'

'Well then, is he not well made?'

'To be truthful' – I turn away to hide my expression, for the words might be true, but the thought behind them certainly isn't – 'he was almost passed before I noticed, and the top of one man's bonnet looks much like another. All I could say, if pressed, was that he had a good seat and held his back suitably straight. Beyond that he could have been the Holy Roman Emperor himself and I wouldn't have been able to tell.'

She laughs. 'Thank God he isn't, but he is here for supper, and it is your opportunity to shine.'

My stomach somersaults again and, as much to

convince myself as her, and as a defence against the disappointment I feel sure is to follow, I say, 'I can hardly expect him to be interested in me.'

We have been in Wittenberg barely six weeks, but already several of the men of the town have come sniffing around, their interest evident in the youngest and prettiest of us, and as a result some have already found a prospective husband and others cherish hopes in that regard. None have come for me, and I've no reason to think that this young man will be any different.

They say an eavesdropper never hears anything good of themselves, and I well believe it. I am crossing the courtyard towards the privy, when I hear Philipp Reichenbach's voice carrying clearly from the chamber above. There is no mistaking of whom he speaks.

'Baumgartner could have the pick of Saxony. Why should he be taken by an escaped nun, besides that she is well past her prime and not the prettiest of the pack.'

Elsa, though she speaks more quietly, is insistent, and while I think her opinion likely of no account, I bless her for it.

'There are those who prize maturity and capability over a winsome face and an empty head.'

Philipp is dismissive. 'And you think he is one such?'

'He hasn't fallen for any chit thrown at him up to now, and I daresay there have been plenty. That indicates some sense at least.'

'Perhaps. But he is young and handsome and of good family. All of which will influence his choice, and not to

Fraulein von Bora's advantage.'

'Can we not try to show her in the best light possible? Her family is well enough and she would make a good wife.'

'For a widower with five children perhaps. But for a young man of Baumgartner's status? I think not.' There is a pause, through which I remain standing beneath the window, despite that I've already heard enough to make me want to run back to my chamber and shut the door and not emerge until this Baumgartner fellow has left. Philipp begins again. 'I wish her to find a place as much as you, but a good family is of little account when a dowry is lacking, except to those tradesmen and such who may wish to raise their status by the match. Find me an honest costermonger in want of a wife and I'll gladly lend my support, for she is competent, I'll give you that.' I hear his footsteps crossing the floor towards the window and, too late to escape, I shrink back into the shadow of the wall, willing him not to look out.

There is a whisper of skirts as Elsa comes to join him. 'Philipp…'

He cuts her off. 'She is rather too fond of her own opinions and willing to share them. Most men, and I don't imagine Jerome to be any different, would prefer someone more pliable.'

If it is a barb directed at Elsa, it has no effect, for her voice is as firm as ever. 'She has had many years in which to form opinions. You cannot expect her to throw them off in an instant, along with her habit.'

'What she thinks is her own concern, what she voices another. There have been times at our table when I have thought her an embarrassment, the saving grace that the

191

whole town knows she is none of ours.' He is pacing up and down and I don't move, wanting away but afraid I will be spied.

'Baumgartner's parents are among our oldest friends. Do you think they would welcome our intervention on her behalf? Were he my son I would have higher ambitions than Katharina von Bora, however worthy and clever she may be.'

It's his final word and I hear the sound of a chair scraping across the floor and flee to the privy, my face flaming, sitting longer than necessary to allow time for my colour to subside and my irritation to fade. Philipp has been unfailingly polite to me in the time I have spent in their home, and I thought the distance between us only what is natural between an older, married man and a single girl who is a guest in his house. His reserve more than made up for by the friendship that Elsa so generously bestows. Clearly I am mistaken, his true opinion of me one I would rather not have heard.

When the time comes for supper I don't change my clothes, sending a message with the maid who comes to call me that I have a headache and wish to be excused; the thought of making polite conversation with this Jerome Baumgartner under Philipp's critical eye more than I can bear.

I bargain without Elsa. She sweeps into my room without knocking, a breach of courtesy that indicates the strength of her feelings, and drops a burgundy gown on the bed. It has a pretty latticed bodice and full sleeves, and I recognise it as her best and bend my head to avoid her accusing gaze.

'What's this nonsense about a headache? You were

192

perfectly well when I spoke to you an hour ago.'

'It came on of a sudden. I will be better remaining quietly here. Besides…'

Her eyes narrow. 'You overheard my argument with Philipp?'

I colour, for to admit to that is to admit not only to eavesdropping, but to the invention of a headache, but I have already been untruthful enough and cannot compound it. 'Yes, and no doubt he says only what most people feel, even if they don't voice it.'

'Just because most people think something doesn't make it right. You of all people should recognise that. Leaving Nimbschen wasn't exactly in conformity to what most people think.'

'And perhaps that was a foolishness I will live to regret. It is one thing for Dr Luther to talk in the abstract, another for us to act on what he says.'

'Do not think that. There are many in this town who support what you did and who applaud your courage and resolve. And look what your example has done. Without it, Luther could not have written the pamphlet justifying both your decision and your escape. And think of the many others you have inspired. The sixteen nuns who fled Wiederstedt no doubt bless you for the lead you gave. My husband, for all he has embraced the teachings of the good doctor, thinks too much of his position, and of the opinions of others, to have your courage. But you must not let that hold you back. Others are not so blinkered.'

'In religion perhaps, but in marriage? If he speaks for the majority then it's as well I do not meet handsome young men who are out of my reach. Besides if I come down now, all I will be able to think of are his comments on the matter. How can I face this Baumgartner thinking of that?'

'The same way you've faced all your difficulties up to now. With your head held high. Where Philipp sees only problems, I see opportunity. We have known Jerome for a long time. You'll like him, I'm sure, and there's no reason why it shouldn't be mutual.' She grips my hands. 'You are no girl in your father's house to be led to the altar like a sacrificial lamb. You have a choice and owe it to yourself to make use of it. If you do not, you are less a person than I think you. Lanita von Golis has had the offer of a good marriage, why should you be less fortunate?'

'Lanita is pliable, unlike me, as your husband so kindly pointed out.'

'She is a renegade nun, whose family has renounced her, and, pliable or not, carries that burden. It didn't prejudice her chances, why should it yours?' She lifts the gown. 'There is little time to waste. Put this on. It's easier to take pride in yourself when you are well clad.'

'I cannot masquerade in your best clothes as if they are my own. What will Philipp think?'

She brushes aside my protest. 'You can and you will. I am determined on it. Philipp may not even notice.'

'And if he does?'

'What can he say without making a scene? And that would be beneath his dignity. He will not wish anyone to know that his wife disobeys him.'

I think of afterwards, of what he might say or do then, but Elsa is already unlacing my bodice.

'Thank you, for your concern and' – I run my hand down the skirt, enjoying the feel of the brocade under my fingers – 'and for this.'

194

Despite that it is May, the stove is lit, Philipp standing close to the hearth, talking to the young man I'd seen on the street. As we enter I see the fractional tightening of his lips, the speculative look in his eyes as he glances first at me and then at Elsa. She gives me an encouraging prod, then links my arm and leads me towards them. The young man's smile for Elsa is wide. He embraces her then turns to me as she makes the introductions. 'This is our guest, Katharina von Bora.' The emphasis on the 'von' is slight, but unmistakeable and I am grateful for it. Poor I might be, and dressed in borrowed clothes, but Elsa is right, I have nothing to be ashamed of in my ancestry. I shoot a glance at Philipp and straighten my shoulders. If Elsa can stand up to him, I won't let her down. Jerome is bowing over my hand, his breath warm on my wrist, and as I rise from my answering curtsey, our eyes meet. His are brown, flecked with gold, with a hint of mischief in them that is unsettling.

'Fraulein von Bora.'

He keeps hold of my hand for a fraction longer than is necessary for courtesy's sake, his smile disarming. Behind us I heard the creak of the door as a servant enters to call us to supper. Elsa touches Jerome's arm and indicates we should move through. He steps to the side, and as I precede him across the hallway I sense him so close behind me that I'm afraid his feet might catch my skirts.

Elsa waves me to a seat and, with a glance at Philipp, as if daring him to object, sets Jerome by my side. She opens the conversation. 'It's so long since we saw you,

Jerome, we thought you lost to us.' She opens her eyes wide at him. 'Or is there some special reason that keeps you at home?'

He grins. 'Not of the sort you think of.'

I'm studying my plate, but I feel his glance on me, as he continues, 'Indeed I begin to think it may be a happy chance that has brought me here today.'

I dissect my slice of beef into ever-decreasing slivers, so that they slip down my throat without the need for chewing, for I've always been embarrassed by the sound of it, fearing that anyone close to me might find it jarring. I take a sip of wine as Elsa asks, 'Do you stay long?'

Jerome leans back in his chair. 'As long as I'm not needed at home.'

Philipp interjects, 'Your parents are no doubt glad of your presence. They are well?'

'Very well. They thought to accompany me, but some small circumstance kept them at home. They said to tell you they hope to visit themselves within a month or two.'

Elsa cuts in. 'It will be good to see them. When you're writing, please assure them of our welcome.'

'Of course.'

A servant appears to clear the table, Elsa rising first, and, as if to pre-empt Philipp, she suggests, the evening being fine, that Jerome might wish to take a walk in the orchard. 'The trees are particularly pretty just now, a mass of blossom.'

He glances at me, a smile hovering at the corner of his mouth. 'Perhaps Fraulein von Bora…'

Elsa avoids Philipp's eye. 'Katharina will I'm sure fulfil our obligations of courtesy and accompany you. I'm a mite tired, and Philipp, I know, still has business to take

196

care of.'

Annoyance flickers on Herr Reichenbach's face, and I suspect it's his pride that stops him from outright contradiction. Instead, he says, 'My business won't take long, and perhaps thereafter I can join you.'

Whether he means it as a warning or not, it serves to add to my awkwardness as we walk in the orchard behind the house. He has not offered me his arm and I don't know whether it should have been customary, nor even if I wish it. We wander through the trees, the only sound a chaffinch singing its heart out. Above our heads sprigs of apple blossom stir in the light breeze, petals drifting down onto our shoulders. When we reach the end furthest from the house, Jerome halts and, turning, indicates the rows of trees.

'There will be a fine harvest come the autumn...' He pauses. 'I remember helping with the gathering-in once.' The mischief is back in his eyes. 'And dropping one on purpose, that I might have the excuse to eat it.' His smile becomes a grimace. That is until I tasted it and realised it was a cider apple I bit into, strong but by no means sweet.'

He reaches up to a branch of the nearest tree and pulls off a sprig of blossom. 'It was, I daresay, divine retribution for my deceit.'

I lean against the trunk of the tree and find myself smiling back. 'I don't think God is interested in punishing small boys for the theft of an apple, and what you did could scarcely even be called theft.'

His laugh is hearty and genuine. 'I daresay not ... had I been a small boy. But I'm afraid I was a student of somewhat more mature years who should have known better.'

197

Answering laughter bubbles inside me, but I choke it off, afraid to drop my reserve any further. He is toying with the apple blossom, removing the petals one by one.

'There is a more recent theft on my conscience that perhaps I should confess.'

I strive for an even tone. 'Indeed.'

He slips his hand inside his jerkin and brings out the thimble. 'This, I believe, is yours.'

I drop my gaze, aware that my breathing has quickened, that colour is staining my neck and cheeks. I want to retaliate, to turn the tables, to embarrass *him*, so I say, 'Not mine. Frau Reichenbach's.'

'Ah. Then it's fortunate I'm returning it, so you don't have to confess to its loss.'

I flush again and he laughs. 'So I am right. You haven't told her yet?' He flips the thimble up into the air, catches it again, then taking my hand turns it over and, placing the thimble in the centre of my palm, closes my fingers over it. 'Well, now you don't have to.'

I snatch my hand away. 'If you'd left it where it fell I could have retrieved it myself.'

'Unless someone else got it first … some light-fingered urchin perhaps.'

I ignore the amusement in his voice and attempt to deflect attention away from me, indicating the petals on the ground. 'Are you intent on diminishing this year's harvest?'

His eyes are on mine, the mischief gone, to be replaced by a seriousness that makes a heat rise in me, as if I flushed from the tips of my toes to the top of my head.

'Not,' he said, 'if you will take it upon yourself to remind me of my duty.'

198

I cannot look at him, afraid this time of what he might see in my eyes.

The musical lilt is back in his voice, but with a new uncertainty, and he stretches out his hand as if to tilt my face upwards. 'Fraulein von Bora?'

In the distance the orchard gate creaks, Jerome pulling back his hand as if from a scald. He takes a step away and leans back against the opposite tree, his head turned towards Philipp, who approaches us, his tone over-hearty.

'There you are. The orchard is flourishing, as you see. We have had a good spring, and if the bees are plentiful and do their part, we should have a good autumn also.' He is looking back and forward between us, and I suspect he has noted my flushed cheeks, but his words are reasonable enough. 'Perhaps you could excuse us, Katharina, I have some business to discuss with Jerome. Elsa is in the Stube and would value your company.'

I incline my head to Philipp and turn to go, glancing at the bland expression on Jerome's face, telling myself there is no reason for my heart to race, that what passed between us was meaningless. The kind of dalliance any aristocratic young man might indulge in.

He takes my hand, bends over it. 'Fraulein. Thank you for your company. No doubt we will meet again tomorrow.'

Chapter Twenty-Three
Wittenberg, June – July 1523

He is a frequent visitor, much to Elsa's satisfaction. Philipp's disapproval is equally clear to us, though he hides it well in Jerome's presence. I understand now what Eva couldn't explain, and I don't know what to think or hope for, only that I hold my breath every time there is a knock at the door, my heart starting to race. When he does come, his presence unsettles and exhilarates me in equal measure: I'm afraid to speak in case I say the wrong thing, afraid to keep silent lest he interpret that as disdain. At night I dream of his hand on my cheek, his lips brushing mine, my whole body alive with the thought of it. I want his touch and fear it, and I have never felt so out of control in my whole life. When he is gone I feel his lack as an emptiness in my belly that nothing can fill.

At odd moments when I'm baking bread or stirring a stew or stretching a newly laundered sheet over my bed, tucking it under the mattress, I imagine it is for us, in our own house, and my stomach curls at the thought of it. Schooled in the convent to think of physical desire as a sin, my thoughts are troubling, and I keep the copy of

Luther's pamphlet on marriage under my pillow, referring to it frequently, clinging onto his statement that it is the highest calling possible, that the marriage bed is pure. 'Only two possibilities,' Herr Cranach had said, and I know now with a certainty that it is marriage, and Jerome, that I want.

I'm in the kitchen, helping Elsa and the cook set down a new stock of pickles, the smell of vinegar sharp in my nostrils and catching at my throat.

'In season and out of season,' Elsa says, laughing, when a servant appears to announce him. 'Go on then.'

I sniff my fingers and the sleeve of my gown. 'I cannot receive him reeking of vinegar.'

'If you are to make him a good wife he will need to be prepared for worse, you both will. Besides' – she laughs again – 'maybe he likes pickles.' Then, relenting, 'Give your hands a good scrub with soda and rub in some lemon juice – that should sort the smell. You'll find an unguent in my bedchamber to take the roughness off them, for no doubt he will not wish to kiss a blacksmith's file. Put on the green silk, and allow a strand or two of hair to escape your cap. And take your time. It won't do him any harm to have to wait a little before you appear. I'll entertain him in the meantime' – there is determination in her voice – 'and sing your praises.'

I wish she wouldn't, for I'm still uncomfortable as the centre of attention, and I worry that if too much is made of me, it will scare him away, or worse, that as he gets to know me better, the reality won't match his expectations.

CRXXD

As usual we go to the orchard, where we can have time alone without fear of gossip, for it is bounded by a wall at the rear and the herb garden in front, and thus not overlooked from either house or street.

'Walk and talk,' Elsa had counselled. 'Search out his character, allow him to learn of yours; for you are not chattel to be disposed of without any consideration of your feelings, nor is he so young that he can't make up his own mind. It is a freedom of choice bought by your courage and you must not waste the opportunity, for it is a luxury denied to most.'

Instead of keeping to the paths, we wander arm in arm through the trees, passing in and out of the dappled shade, shards of sunlight catching the gold threads in the monogram on his jacket and breathing life into the auburn tint in his hair. I imagine sliding my fingers through the unruly curls, the thought bringing a warmth in my belly. Would it feel as smooth as it looks? Or would it be coarse to the touch, as Hans' hair had been. I have thought of my brothers often since our escape from Nimbschen, and long for the time when we might see each other again. Even Klement would be welcome, though it is Hans whom I remember with real affection. What would he and Jerome make of each other? Would they be friends? I hope so.

It's as if he can read my mind. 'You haven't spoken of your family, Fraulein. Do you have brothers and sisters? Parents that I might meet?'

I stop in the shade of an ancient cherry tree, picking at the gnarled trunk. I assume he knows my history, the most recent part at least, but this question goes to the kernel of it. 'My mother died when I was very young.' I bite on my lip. 'And when my father remarried I was sent into a convent … for my education, they said.'

He places his hand over mine, stilling it. 'That must have been difficult, to feel pushed out of your own home.'

'I didn't understand at first, though I hated *her* as perhaps only a child can. But I told myself it would only be for a while, that once I'd learnt my letters and singing and sewing and whatever else was expected of me, I'd be brought home again. Even though Klement warned me.'

'Klement?'

'My second brother. He said I was destined to become a nun, but I imagined it was just his way of taunting me. He enjoyed to tease.' I shut my eyes, remembering Klement brushing aside Hans' protest. 'It wasn't until I was moved to Nimbschen that I knew he'd been right all along. And for a time, however unfairly, I think I hated him for that.'

He's looking down at me, his expression pensive, and I fear that, though he is undoubtedly sympathetic, he is thinking of my family in terms of what such a connection might entail, and I feel a flush spreading across my neck and up to my cheeks.

But when he speaks, it is with a gentleness that flows over me like balm. 'Sometimes we try to hate, in order to mask our hurt. You were only a child. You must not blame yourself.' He is stroking the back of my hand, the touch of his fingers warm and dry. 'You say second brother. How many do you have?'

'Three. Hans is the eldest, then Klement. Franz was just a baby when I was sent away… I hope someday to see them again.'

'They haven't visited since your…' He breaks off, as if he doesn't wish to refer to my circumstance.

203

'No. Elsa says…' It's my turn to hesitate, not wishing to talk of a home of my own lest it appear presumptuous, but he picks up my sentence and finishes it for me.

'When you have a home of your own you'll be able to invite whomsoever you like.' His smile seems to give extra meaning to his words, and warmth spreads through me, reaching from the top of my head to my toes. He turns my hand over and draws a circle on my palm with his finger, saying, 'We are friends, are we not? And need no longer be formal.'

I look down at the trampled grass, at the blossom blown off in the last high winds, the petals beginning to turn brown at the edges, and am afraid, despite that he still has hold of my hand, that I may be imagining more in his words than he intended.

'Katharina?'

A tentative note creeps into his voice, as if he is as uncertain of me as I am of him, and it gives me the confidence to lift my gaze to his and smile in return.

The grass hasn't been cut, and as the evening dew falls it clings damp against my skirts. We pause at the farthest end of the orchard as usual, to lean against the warm stone of the wall and watch a pair of magpies strutting under the trees as if an omen, their white breast feathers contrasting with their coal-black heads and the gleaming iridescence of the wing and tail feathers.

'They *are* beautiful,' I say.

He is winding a loose strand of my hair around his finger, tugging gently and then releasing it, so that it springs back against my face. 'Fishing for a compliment?'

I flush. 'No! I…'

He laughs, the same hearty laugh of our first walk,

when he confessed to the stealing of an apple. 'I'm sorry,' he says, but his mouth twitches, belying his words. 'It is unfair of me, but I cannot resist to tease.' He trails the back of his hand along my jawline, bringing it to a rest against my cheek. 'For you are so quick to rise.'

I want to think of a witty reply, but all that's in my head is the feel of his skin against mine, and how I want to tangle my fingers in the curl of his hair on his collar and bury my face in his jerkin, breathing in the faint scent of musk. He lifts the strand of hair again and sniffs at it. 'My mother always swore by vinegar for rinsing her hair, but…' He allows my hair to drop and captures my hand instead, bringing it to is lips, his eyes alight with mischief. 'My preference is for the scent of lemons.'

I blush again, thinking of the time Elsa had alone with him in the Stube, and what she must have said, and he clearly notes my heightened colour, for this time his laugh rings through the trees.

'I do like pickles, as it happens, but I do not look for my mother in you, but something else entirely…'

I study my feet, afraid once again of what he might see in my eyes, and without conscious thought I pull the strand of hair towards my nose.

'It doesn't smell of vinegar, I promise you.' His tongue slides across his top lip, his expression suddenly serious. 'And even if it did, a preference for lemon or not, I wouldn't care.' He turns me to face him, one hand gripping my arm, the other tilting my chin so that I cannot avoid looking into his eyes. 'You know what I want, Katharina, what I have wanted from the first day I saw you.'

I don't answer, for I am in uncharted territory, unsure of what is meant; if it is just what they say any man wants, or if he offers me more than that. Something of my uncertainty must have been revealed in my eyes, for his darken. 'You cannot think I would ask anything that is not proper? I'm asking you to be my wife, Katharina. I want you in my life, in my home, and yes' – he leans forward, his forehead touching mine, his breath warm on my cheek – 'in my bed.'

I want to say, 'Yes, oh yes,' but I can't seem to get the words out, and in the momentary silence he lifts his head, asks again, the note of uncertainty back in his voice. 'Katharina?'

Tears are shining in my eyes, threatening to spill over onto my cheeks, and lest he misinterpret them, I stretch upwards, my voice no more than a whisper. 'I want it too.'

Chapter Twenty-Four
Wittenberg, July 1523

The bees have done their part and the clusters of young fruits are showing on the trees. Philipp is right. It looks to be a good harvest come the autumn, but I have begun to hope that I will not be here to see it. There is a pattern to Jerome's visits now, a regularity that clearly pleases Elsa almost as much as it does me. He is my first thought when I wake, my last as I go to sleep, and as much a part of my dreams as he is of my days.

July has come in warm and dry, and day after day the sun rides high in a cloudless sky. And evening by evening I thank God for my freedom, for the weather, and most of all for Jerome, and the happiness that it seems is within my grasp.

Sometimes we talk as we walk and sometimes we stroll in silence, increasingly at ease in both. And though my body is unruly, reacting to his slightest touch, whether intentional or accidental, I grow skilled at keeping my desire within bounds, my yearning for him largely hidden, from anyone else at least. I learn of Nuremberg, of his family's position, of his parents and their ambitions for their son; and though there is a hesitancy when he talks of them, I push it to the back of my mind. Whatever my recent past, my lineage is as good as his, my family of equal standing in the community. I talk of Father, of how I hadn't seen him since I was five years old yet still felt a sense of loss when he died. My stepmother I don't wish to speak of, for I cannot claim to have truly forgiven her, and I prefer not to dwell on my sins.

I am sitting in the Stube, on a rare damp day, watching the raindrops slide down the windowpane, my sewing lying untouched on my lap. Elsa comes to sit beside me and pats my shoulder, and I can't stop myself saying, 'He won't come today, will he?'

'Perhaps not, but the rain won't last forever. Tomorrow will likely be bright again, and his desire to see you the greater.'

'Is it wrong of me to think so much of him? In the cloister…'

'Forget the cloister, Katharina. You are here, in the real world, and God as much with you now as He was then, indeed likely more, for you have gained a truer understanding of Him.'

'It's just… at Nimbschen devotion was easy to measure … in the keeping of the Offices, the observance of the Hours…' I'm not sure how to explain my uncertainties, or even if they can be explained to someone who hasn't experienced enclosure. 'When we left, I thought it was because of Dr Luther's teachings, because we had come to accept that faith alone was necessary, that we did not truly serve God in rote and ritual. But sometimes I fear that it was a more selfish thing, that I wanted … this.'

She pats my shoulder again. 'Remember it was God's

leading released you from the bondage of the convent, and He who brought you to Wittenberg. It isn't wrong to enjoy the freedom you have been given, nor to think on the blessings that may yet be to come.'

There is a knock at the outer door and a stamping of feet in the hallway, as if someone is knocking the rain off their boots, and I feel my stomach lurch.

Elsa stands up. 'I'd best see who has braved the weather to call on us, and you' – she gestures at the sewing – 'had best tidy your work away and prepare to make them welcome.'

He towers over me as I rise to greet him, droplets of water shining in his hair and glistening on his nose and cheeks. He bends over my hand. 'Fraulein Katharina. You didn't brave the weather this morning?'

I search my memory for some particular reason for venturing out, but come up with nothing. 'Should I have?'

'There was a disputation in the Town Church to mark the visit of two visitors from Orlamünde bringing word of Karlstadt's latest teachings, and your absence was commented on by some of the students. They say you have an interest in such things.'

Beside me Elsa stiffens, and I feel a momentary pang of guilt that I have hidden this from her, fearing that she wouldn't understand my need; for it wasn't the student's faith I questioned as I listened to the debates, but the depth of my own. She is searching his face as if to determine what he's thinking, and I sense she's afraid he will think me unwomanly and all her efforts on my behalf come to

209

nothing.

I'm not sure how he'll react either, but answer truthfully, for I cannot be anything but honest. 'Sometimes, yes. If the topic is of relevance to me.' I touch Elsa's shoulder as if in apology. 'You have been good to me and have treated me like a daughter and I am grateful for it' – I hesitate, then, despising my momentary cowardice, finish – 'but I did not leave my mind in the cloister, and there are times I need something more to occupy it than the household tasks that are my responsibility. And whether it is meet or not, listening to a disputation fulfils that need.' I look down at the rug on the floor, concentrating on the strength of the colours, afraid that I may be a disappointment to Elsa … to Jerome.

'Well then'– far from censure, there is a hint of a deepened interest, and I think admiration, in his voice, and relief floods me – 'you should have been there. Luther and the visitors were going at it hammer and tongs, to the shock, I believe, of all those present.'

Elsa waves him to a seat, and he settles himself before continuing. 'It seems that Karlstadt has taken Luther's ideas in a direction and manner that are not pleasing to the good doctor.'

'Andreas Karlstadt? But he is one of Dr Luther's closest followers.'

'So he may have been, but if his opinions have been truly represented, then he has moved far beyond what Luther teaches.' He is leaning back in the chair, his legs crossed, his tone relaxed, as if it is but an academic discussion he relates.

I have an emptiness in my stomach and my voice is no more than a hoarse whisper. 'What were they saying?'

'That he refuses to be called Herr Doctor, and refers to himself simply as Brother Andreas. That he has discarded all clerical garb and wears only a plain grey coat, such as the meanest of burgesses might have.'

'Is that all?' My stomach is beginning to settle, my voice to return to normal. 'Oversensitive perhaps, but surely not an issue to raise Dr Luther's ire, for it is but an extension of his "priesthood of all believers".'

'Had they stopped there, I daresay you'd be right. However, that was but their introduction.'

Elsa, as if the conversation is too much for her, rises. 'I'll leave you to your disputation, for I must see that the supper is in hand.' She smiles at Jerome. 'You'll stay, I take it.'

He rises with her, hands her to the door. 'If I may.'

Returning to the chair, he waits until we hear the door to the kitchen quarters groaning on its hinges and the sound of her footsteps fading before continuing. 'He has refused his salary and insists on supporting himself by the plough.'

'He's become a farmer?'

'Yes, and while he fulfils his preaching obligations, he considers himself but one of the flock, contending that a peasant who studies the Word may know as much as a preacher.'

'And Dr Luther?'

'Was predictably derisive.' There is amusement in Jerome's voice that relaxes me still further. 'His counterargument – that the preacher who does not devote all his time to the Word will end up knowing no more than the peasant.'

I don't need to have been there to imagine the manner

of Dr Luther's rebuttal, for I have heard him often enough in the Reichenbachs' Stube to know how forceful he can be. But it doesn't seem enough to explain a rift between them. I pucker my brow, question again, 'There must be more to it than that?'

'Luther thinks it an evasion of responsibility that is inexcusable. '

'But Luther himself has advocated the value of honest toil, saying it is a reflection of God's character.' I tap the arm of Jerome's chair. 'He sat here, not a month since, speaking of it. "God is a tailor," he said, "clothing the deer; a butler, setting forth a feast for the sparrows". "Our Lord was a carpenter. Even so must we labour in our callings."' The memory of Philipp's face as Luther spoke makes me smile. 'I think Philipp thought it somewhat flippant, but the point was clear enough. Why then would he criticise Karlstadt for working?'

'Because he considers Karlstadt's calling is to be a preacher and working the land a failure to fulfil it.'

He falls silent, his expression sober, and I need to know what it is he keeps back. 'What aren't you telling me?'

He edges his chair closer to mine, places a hand on my arm, a new seriousness in his voice. 'It is his new theology that caused the real friction.' He pauses and I feel a constriction in my chest.

'Go on.'

'Apparently he denies the real presence in the sacrament and rejects infant baptism.'

'He has become an Anabaptist?' I look down at my hands, surprised to see them balled into fists.

'This news troubles you?'

'It's…' I take a deep breath, release it again, allow my shoulders to settle. '…I know it is Luther we have to thank for all that has happened, but without Karlstadt's preaching I wouldn't be here … for I had read Luther's writings over and over at Nimbschen, and though in my head I accepted what he said, it wasn't until we received a copy of Karlstadt's Christmas sermon that it penetrated my heart. I find it hard to believe he would desert the teachings he once helped to promote.'

'He would say it is Dr Luther who steps back, lacking the courage to follow them through to their obvious conclusion. Or at least that is what his disciples claim.'

'Perhaps if Karlstadt himself was here … perhaps I would be better able to judge…'

Jerome uncurls my fingers, takes both my hands in his. 'You mustn't let this trouble you, Katharina, or I shall blame myself for passing it on. Besides, he may have been misquoted, or their understanding of what he means faulty.' He hesitates, as if he's unsure if he should say more. 'Thanks to Luther we have the Scriptures in our own tongue and can read them for ourselves. It's hardly surprising that it leads to differences of interpretation. And if they are not of essentials, we shouldn't be disturbed by them. Who knows who will be proved right in the end, but whatever the case, faith depends on the Word, not on who preaches it. You know that. If we depend on a person, however great, we may find ourselves disappointed; for any of us may one day prove to have feet of clay.'

CHAPTER TWENTY-FIVE
WITTENBERG, AUGUST 1523

I'm in the Stube with Elsa when the note arrives. She breaks the seal. 'Frau Cranach has invited you to supper.'

I start to smile and then remember that Jerome is expected, that we thought to share our desire with the Reichenbachs this very evening. My reluctance to accept the invitation fills me with guilt, for if the invitation had come two days ago, I would have jumped at the opportunity to spend the time with Eva, who I so sorely miss. It should be no different now.

Elsa hands me the note. 'The von Zeschau sisters are to return to their uncle's house at Grimma and Barbara thought you would wish to see them before they go.'

'Yes, yes, I would. It's a kind thought. If I can be spared?'

'Of course.'

I don't know why I blurt it out, perhaps to avoid other conversation, but I find myself saying, 'Each time one of us leaves, it's like a bereavement, but it will be especially hard to say goodbye to Fronika and Margarete – they were among my closest friends.'

'That's why you must go.' She lays her hand on my arm. 'I know it has been hard these past weeks to see so little of your friends, but we thought it best that you all became more detached from each other and thus more able to bear the partings when they came.'

I look at her, startled. 'I thought—'

'That you didn't have the standing to go visiting as gentlewomen do?' She purses her lips. 'I'm sorry, Katharina, perhaps I should have said something earlier, but this is new territory for all of us, and I hope that what we have done will turn out to have been the kindest in the end.'

I slip onto the floor by her feet, and rest my head against her knee, my voice muffled by her skirts. 'You've been more than kind. I couldn't have asked for better.'

I can't see her face but I know she's smiling when she says, 'I hope to be kinder still.'

I sigh, thinking of Jerome, of what I cannot say without him beside me. It's as if she can read my mind. 'Don't worry about Jerome. If you're not here when he comes, it will but increase his desire to see you again. And meanwhile I can sing your praises, let him know how good a wife you will be for someone.'

The mischief in her voice makes me laugh, and I think perhaps I should tell her of our understanding, in confidence, but I know it wouldn't be fair to Jerome, for though I have no father, and it should be a formality only, he wishes to do the honourable thing and seek Philipp's permission.

Elsa acknowledges my laugh. 'That's better.'

The air coming in the window is cooler now, the sun dipping towards the west. I scramble to my feet and move to close the casement. In the square the town clock chimes the hour.

She nods 'Off you go. And don't feel the need to hurry back.'

We say our goodbyes, Fronika hugging me fiercely, Margarete holding herself stiffly, as if any sign of weakness will be the undoing of her. At the last moment, as we stand by the door, she says, as much I think to convince herself as us, 'This is what we wanted, to be able to go home, to start life all over again. Be glad for us.'

I am glad, for them and for the others, as, one by one, their futures are secured. Magdalena gets her wish and finds a position in the school at Grimma, her letters frequent and cheerful, full of anecdotes about her pupils and the townsfolk, and it's clear that she's happy there. Marta settles at Brunswick and Else in Thallwitz. It's only Eva and I who remain in Wittenberg, visiting each other regularly now. It seems we too will soon be settled. Eva's attachment to Basilius Axt is common knowledge. She colours prettily when I tease her that they are the talk of the town and must surely be married before long.

'You do like him, Katharina?'

'Of course I do, not that that's important. It's what you think that matters.' I grin at her, happy that our old companionship is renewed. 'And he *is* what you were looking for – a *young*, good man. I'm sure you'll be happy.'

She grins back. 'We aren't the only ones to be gossiped over. I hear whispers about you everywhere I

216

go. Only last night Dr Luther dined with the Cranachs and I heard him express his satisfaction at your attachment to Baumgartner.' Then, her tone suddenly serious, 'Who would have thought that I would end up as an apothecary's wife and you married to an aristocrat. I shall miss you though. I wish Nuremberg was nearer.'

I bite on my lip. 'Luther spoke of it?'

'Yes. And the Cranachs are delighted also.'

'I didn't think... How do people know these things? We haven't been seen together outside of the house and gardens."

'How could they not? Jerome spends so much time at the Reichenbachs' he might as well be living there. And no one thinks it's Philipp he comes to see.' She laughs. 'Oh, Kat, you surely didn't think that you could keep Baumgartner's interest in you a secret? This is a small town and thrives on gossip, and he is a particularly tasty morsel.'

'We have an understanding...'

'I knew it.' Her pleasure is obvious. 'Go on.'

I think of the previous evening, as we strolled arm in arm in the orchard, stopping by the wall facing the last of the apple trees, the young fruits beginning to swell. Of Jerome, leaning back against the warm stone, slipping his arm around me to pull me against him, his eyes dark as sloes. How he cupped my face in his hands, his lips feather-light, our breath mingling. And how, when we began to talk of the when and the how and the where, his voice was husky, as if he started a cold.

I'm not sure if I want to share that moment even with Eva, but I think of how much we have meant to each other and haven't the heart to disappoint her. 'Last night we talked. But we haven't had a chance to say anything formally to the Reichenbachs yet and Jerome insists on it. Though if the entire town already knows, it scarcely matters.' I'm smoothing down my dress, tracing the faint figuring in the silk, deciding *what* to share. 'He asked me if I could be happy in Nuremberg. Away from everyone I know.'

'You told him yes?'

'I told him "Where you go, I will go. Where you live, I will live, and there will I be buried".'

She laughs. 'Oh, Kat! Wouldn't a simple "Yes" have done?'

'For you, Eva, perhaps – not for me. When we came to Wittenberg I felt like Ruth, still do. Penniless, a widow of a sort, not the youthful bride folk might expect for someone of his standing. His offer of marriage is far beyond anything I could have hoped for.'

She struggles to keep her face straight. 'How did he respond?'

'He smiled and touched my cheek and said, "I trust you'll have a long life, if I'm to be your Boaz…"'

She laughs again. 'So he *can* concentrate on a sermon even while he's watching you … I wouldn't have sworn to it.'

I think of his last words to me, the promise he made, and sigh.

She is contrite, as if she thinks I'm hurt by her amusement. 'What's wrong, Kat? The Reichenbachs aren't in the position of guardians and so cannot object, even should they wish to.'

'I know, but … he spoke because he has been called home, and though he assures me he'll seek his parents' approval and be back soon to make all the proper arrangements, I can't help fearing that once he is away…'

'He'll not forget you.' She jigs my arm. 'You are neither of you sixteen and foolish. Why should anything go wrong?'

The window is open, voices floating up from the street below. I can make out snatches of the conversation, enough to know that it is a wedding party, a cluster of young men accompanying the groom to his betrothal. The voices are young, their words punctuated by laughter, so that I decide it is a wedding that both parties desire, the thought pleasing. In the distance a church bell is ringing, and I wonder if it is in their honour, if his bride is waiting in a house nearby, if her heart is fluttering in case he does not come, or if she is confident, happy that the day is here at last.

In the chair beside the bed Margarethe has not stirred, and I stretch over to shake her arm. 'Wake up! We must get ready.'

She's rubbing the sleep from her eyes, and I think it must be the confusion of being only half-awake, so I'm patient with her, even though time may be short. 'If you dress first, then you can help me.'

She pats my hand, gestures downwards. 'I am dressed, Mutti, but I can help you if you'd like to get dressed, to sit in the chair for a time? The doctor says your pelvis is healing, that you may soon be on your feet again.'

I can see the thought pleases her, as indeed it does me, for if I wasn't getting better I wouldn't be able to go. She's rummaging in the chest under the window and emerges with my brown day dress, shaking it out and laying it over the back of the chair before delving into the chest again. I don't understand how she can have forgotten, and I struggle to keep the irritation out of my voice. 'We mustn't be late.'

She turns from the chest, a linen underskirt in her hand, and comes across to the bed, her forehead puckered. 'Late for what, Mutti?'

'The betrothal of course.' I finger her skirt, the coarse wool scratching my hand. 'You cannot attend in this. Nor I in that.' I wave my hand at the dress laid out for me. We both need our best. To honour the occasion.'

She bends over to stroke my hair, her voice soft, as if I were a child to be soothed. 'It isn't today, Mutti.'

'Of course it is. Listen, there is the bell.'

She shakes her head. 'The bells are for someone else.'

'Are you sure?' I say.

There is one last peel and something akin to relief flickers in her eyes. 'I'm sure.' She pats my hand. 'We don't know this couple.'

Maybe she doesn't, but I do. I concentrate on the voices, separating them out by accent and tone. One emerges, clear and distinct above the rest, and I can't help smiling. 'Listen,' I say. 'It is him. He isn't handsome, nor wealthy, but Lucas says he has prospects. Though I don't think she cares, for she is so happy.'

The uncertainty is back in Margarethe's voice. 'Who, Mutti?'

'Eva, of course.'

CHAPTER TWENTY-SIX
WITTENBERG, AUTUMN 1523

'It is the highest mercy of God, when a married couple
love each other with their whole hearts.'

Martin Luther

We are all invited to the Cranachs' house, the first time I've
been there since the departure of Margarete and Fronika,
only this time it is for a happy occasion: to witness the
betrothal of Eva and Basilius Axt. Eva flies to meet me,
taking both my hands in hers.

'Oh, Kat, I'm so glad that you're here.'

Her eyes are moist and I know what she isn't saying:
that she misses Marta and Fronika and Else. I return her
pressure on my hands, say, 'They will be here for the
churching, won't they?'

She nods. 'Marta will, at least, and I hope the von
Zeschaus – the invitations have gone out; though we
haven't yet had a reply. Barbara says I mustn't fret, that
there's plenty of time. And you'll never guess!' She
jiggles my hands.

'What?'

'Barbara invited Magdalena von Staupitz, and she also will be here.'

'It will be like a reunion, but it's a pity…'

'That Else cannot be here. I know. But she sent me the loveliest note. She's happy for me, as we were for her.'

Basilius appears at her shoulder. He takes Eva's arm and, bowing to me, says, 'Fraulein von Bora, my apologies, but Bugenhagen is ready.' His gaze flicks to Eva. 'And so am I.'

The ceremony is simple and short, Eva beaming throughout, Basilius keeping a firm grip on her hand as if he fears she might disappear. I am honoured to be called as a witness, and as they pronounce their vows I think of Jerome and pray it might be soon that we too will stand in the presence of our friends to be joined together before God.

Lucas and Barbara Cranach are generous hosts and the meal that follows is a merry one, Eva and Basilius the centre of attention, their happiness evident to all. When Lucas Cranach stands up it is the signal that everyone has been waiting for, and we all stand as Basilius leads Eva from the Stube, followed by Lucas, who is the chosen witness for the bedding. Eva cheeks are flushed, and I see the faint tremor in the hand that rests on Basilius' arm, and so I smile an encouragement as they pass. Nervous or not, I see a flash of the old Eva as she winks at me in return, and then the door shuts behind them and I feel part happy and part bereft.

Barbara Cranach sits down beside me. 'It will be your turn next.' She glances across to where Luther is deep in conversation with Bugenhagen and Philipp. 'No doubt when the time comes you will have everyone's blessing.'

'There is nothing settled,' I say, blushing.

Barbara's smile is almost mischievous. 'The whole town expects daily to hear of your engagement, and I for one think it a fitting end to all that you have suffered in the past.' She nods towards Elsa sitting by the window. 'As Elsa does.'

'The Reichenbachs have been kind to me, Elsa in particular. I hope someday I can repay them.'

'Their friendship with the Baumgartners was a happy coincidence, and your marriage will be almost like a joining of the two families. I'm sure that will be thanks enough.'

I think of Philipp's reservations, which, though not openly expressed, were clear enough to me, but for Elsa's sake I say nothing.

A small group has formed around Luther and I hear the name Leisnig, my interest quickened. 'Isn't that the town…'

'That sent to ask for Luther's support for their ordinance for the organisation of their parish? Yes. Luther wrote the foreword and Lucas is proud to have had the printing of them. I suspect they will be widely circulated, for Luther thinks it the pattern that all parishes should follow.'

'Isn't anything he writes widely circulated?'

'Indeed yes.' A faint shadow clouds her face. 'It's not unusual to have to reprint a pamphlet seven or eight times. And while we benefit from the proceeds, I do wish Luther himself would accept some payment.'

Bugenhagen is on Luther's right, nodding in agreement to whatever Luther is saying, Philipp clearly less convinced. We turn and catch the tail end of a sentence.

'…a common chest to hold all income and from which all expenses will be drawn.' Philipp leans forward, his sense of what is practical and proper clearly offended. 'An account surely?'

'No. I imagine they don't have much trust in bankers. At any rate' – I sense that Luther is enjoying Philipp's discomfort, which isn't surprising, for all the town knows that money means nothing to Luther, but rather a lot to Philipp – 'they say it is a sturdy chest, kept, for safety's sake, in the church.'

Philipp jumps on what he obviously thinks is a flaw in the argument. 'But if they keep the church locked, as surely they must, does that not defeat the evangelical principle of free access to God.'

Luther shakes his head. 'Oh, the church isn't locked, but the chest is – fourfold – and all of the keys are needed before it can be opened.'

The whole room is listening now, and Luther, acknowledging the interest, raises his voice a fraction. 'No section of the populace has been forgotten, for one key is held by a representative of the nobility, one the council, one the townsfolk and one' – he pauses and I recognise his desire for the theatrical – 'the peasantry.'

Philipp's shoulders tense, but he asks, reasonably enough, 'Who decides who should hold the keys?'

'Men are chosen from among the trustees, themselves elected by the parishioners. All very democratic, it seems, and organised in such a way that fraud is well-nigh impossible. Meticulous records, open to all, are kept and updated weekly.'

Bugenhagen's approval is also clear. 'A far cry from the abuses which used to prevail. It is a paradigm for parish governance that every town would do well to follow.'

I'm curious to know more and am about to ask Barbara if I could have a copy of the ordinance, when Lucas Cranach reappears, nodding to show that all is well with the newly-weds, which is the signal for the party to disperse. Dusk is falling as we stroll through the market square and past the Rathaus. I lag a little behind Elsa and Philipp, my thoughts full of Leisnig and the earlier snippets I'd caught, of regulations on parish relief and on schools, and wish I could know more. If it were not for Jerome, if I was not to be married, then I think I'd settle for being a teacher, for having my own school, as Magdalena does. The church bell tolls the hour, the sound rich and sonorous, and I wonder if music is in the prescribed curriculum. Perhaps when Magdalena comes for the formal celebration of Eva's marriage she will be able to enlighten me.

⬤⬤⬤

I don't have to wait that long, for Luther appears at the Reichenbachs' on the following evening, and as we sit at supper Philipp raises the topic I am desperate to hear.

Luther thrusts his hand inside his gown. 'I thought you might be curious, so I brought a copy along with me. You can peruse it at your leisure, lest we bore the ladies.'

'You won't,' I blurt out, earning a frown from Philipp and an amused glance from Elsa, quickly concealed.

Luther looks at me, his gaze assessing, as if it is the first time he has truly noticed me, and I colour, but hold my head high, for I am not ashamed of my interest, nor prepared to pretend that there is nothing in my head but fripperies.

Philipp begins, 'My apologies, Martin, I'm sure Fraulein von Bora didn't mean…'

Luther, still looking at me, cuts him off. 'On the contrary, Philipp, I suspect she betrays a genuine interest, which perhaps we should indulge.'

My face is flaming, for I'm not sure if he is mocking me, but I'm determined not to be cowed into silence. 'It is particularly the organisation of the distribution of food and the plans for the schooling of girls that I'd like to hear more of.'

'As for the food, that is a radical notion, which in general I approve, though I'm surprised they manage to make it work. Everyone that is able to work must do so, and if they cannot, the parish must supply their needs. The church is both a distribution point and a storehouse and they have a custodian to oversee all. It is an admirable system, for no man should have to suffer the humiliation of begging.'

In the time we have been at Wittenberg it has not been hard to admire Luther for his cleverness, his knowledge of the Scriptures; but hearing his enthusiasm as he talks about Leisnig, I warm to him in a way I haven't before, for he seems somehow less austere, more human.

Philipp is looking somewhat bored, but Elsa, I think, is as interested as I am, Luther pleased to have a receptive audience. He nods at me, as if to acknowledge that I share his opinion. 'It is their proposals for education that I find most appealing. I have long advocated schooling for girls as well as boys, as you well know.'

This last comment he directs at Philipp, who is quick to take the opportunity to break into the conversation. 'As

227

I do too, of course, though, as we have found, even here it isn't easy to get the council to release the funds required.'

I'm thinking back: to Lippendorf, to how different things might have been if there had been a school for me, and say, 'If only everyone of means would contribute. Perhaps then it might be possible.'

Luther turns back to me, an odd expression on his face, as if he isn't sure whether to think my contribution unwomanly, or to treat it as he would a comment from one of his students. 'Indeed.' An ironic note creeps into his voice, but I suspect he is not altogether jesting. 'Perhaps if we elected women to our councils something of the sort might be achieved.'

Chapter Twenty-Seven
Wittenberg, October 1523 – April 1524

It has been three months now, and no word from Jerome. Our last conversation plays and replays in my head, his 'feet of clay' a refrain. He didn't mean himself, but nevertheless, it seems he may have been unintentionally prophetic. Elsa tries to be encouraging, but I see my own worry mirrored in her eyes. 'There could be many reasons why Jerome's return is delayed. I do know he was here for much longer than originally intended and probably had many things to see to on his return home.'

Philipp says nothing, even when Elsa calls for his support, and I know I will receive no sympathy from him.

Eva, when she calls to see me, confident in her new status, is insistent. 'Write to him, Kat. You had his promise. Give him a chance to keep it.'

'I have written, three times, and heard nothing in response.'

'Write again. Your letters may have gone astray, or his to you. Perhaps he thinks *you* have forgotten *him*.' She hesitates, then, 'Did Herr Reichenbach write to his parents, supporting your engagement?'

'Elsa wanted him to, but Philipp said it was something that Jerome must sort out for himself.'

'But surely…'

'Philipp has never been in favour of the attachment, I knew that from the start, but thought it wouldn't matter, for as Elsa said, we are both old enough to know our own mind. And without the money problems that might have been a difficulty to some, she was confident he would keep his promise, especially when the match had the approval of Luther and all his old teachers.'

'The approval of all who know you,' Eva says. 'The word in the town is all of when he might return to claim you and how fortunate a day it was for you both when he returned to Wittenberg for a visit.' She frowns. 'What is it that Philipp has against the match? Aside from the household saving that your departure would produce, I would have thought he'd be pleased to relinquish his responsibilities towards you and see you well settled.'

'It is precisely the money issue that concerns Philipp – he thinks it too good a match for me, that in my circumstances I should not have set my sights so high. That and his friendship with the Baumgartners, which he feels has been compromised.'

She's indignant on my behalf. 'What right has he to judge?'

I try to be fair, though inwardly I find it hard not to resent his attitude. 'They gave me sanctuary and have supported me all these months, that surely gives him some right?'

'As for the help they gave, you know you have Elsa to thank more than him. Though I imagine his position in the town made it well-nigh impossible to refuse Luther's request. Think of the gossip if he had.' She bends her head close to mine and opens her eyes wide, her voice a perfect mimicry of the most notorious gossip in the town. 'It is a disgrace. A slur on us all that we have a town clerk who is too penny-pinching to take in a destitute nun. He should look to his position, or he may not hold it for very much longer.' She reverts to her own voice, her scorn evident, and I signal her to speak more quietly, for I don't wish Elsa to hear.

Eva tosses her head, but she does lower her voice. 'I daresay it suits his self-esteem to consider himself charitable.' She's swivelling her wedding ring, faster and faster, and I appreciate her feelings on my behalf. 'As for the Baumgartners, surely they will wish their son to be happy? And they are of the reform party. If they favour Luther's views on the Church, why would they not agree with him in this respect also?'

'Religion is one thing, and for many folk for one day a week only. Marriage is another, and touches every aspect of a life.' I hear the note of bitterness that creeps into my voice. 'As you say, I am a destitute nun. What have I to offer but a taint on their family name?'

'Your family is as good as the Baumgartner's, better perhaps than the Reichenbachs. Perhaps it's Philipp's lack of a "von" before his name that makes him so down on you.'

I should feel guilty at the turn of conversation, for I do owe much to the Reichenbachs, and however much Elsa might have wished to provide assistance when we arrived, without Philipp's agreement she could have done little.

Eva touches my arm and I know she means it as encouragement. 'I'm sure Elsa is right. If he were to speak

231

for you, to lend you his support, then perhaps it might yet come right. If he will not, then I hope…'

The door from the servant's quarters opens and I hear Elsa shooing the cat out from between her legs. I put my finger against Eva's lips. 'I don't wish to hope anything that will hurt Elsa, but' – I give Eva a hug – 'thank you. For the reminder that there is no shame in my parentage, and for caring.'

⟨⊗⊗⊗⟩

I cannot stay. I'm coming down the stairs when I hear the raised voices in Philipp's study. Hesitating in the hallway, unsure if I should return to my chamber, curiosity, or perhaps fear, keeps me pinned to the bottom step. There have been many occasions of late when I've come into the Stube and found conversations cut off mid-word, Philipp looking angry, Elsa refusing to meet my eye. But this is the first that I've heard an outright argument, and I cannot bear to listen; I cannot bear *not* to listen though, for I'm sure it's me they argue over. And so I tiptoe to the kitchen, leaving the door open a fraction. Philipp is adamant, his feelings clear and unmistakeable.

'Not another word, Elsa. I will not do it.'

She continues to plead. 'We encouraged the attachment, Philipp. We cannot desert her now.'

'*You* encouraged her. I was against it from the start, as well you know, and I see no reason to change now. In fact, every reason not to.'

'She has been ill-used in our house and by our friend's son. Does that mean nothing to you?'

'It was a foolishness that should have been stopped

232

before it started. And the sooner she realises that, the better.'

'I cannot see her so miserable and do nothing to help. She hardly eats and does not look well.'

'She won't look any better while she continues to hope for something that's clearly not going to happen. You do her no service by refusing to make her see sense.'

'It isn't just me. Everyone can see how much this hurts her. Lucas and Martin called in yesterday, and when Lucas heard she was out and that therefore he could speak freely, he questioned me about her wan appearance.'

'And did you importune them to intervene on her behalf as you do me?'

'It isn't my place to ask them.'

'But it is to instruct me?'

'Not instruct, Philipp, suggest. As, indeed, does Martin himself.'

'So you did discuss the matter with them.'

'I said nothing of Jerome, but Martin suggested a letter from you to Jerome's parents would be … helpful.'

'I have no intention of being "helpful", as you put it. I think it an ill-judged attachment and clearly the Baumgartners agree with me, or Jerome would have returned long since. I will not stand against the wishes of those who are our friends, not for you, not for Luther and most certainly not for her.'

There is a clatter of dishes in the kitchen which blocks out the sound for a moment, and when it stops I hear Elsa say, '…Katharina is also of good family and good reputation. Why must she continue to suffer for what was done to her as a child?' I hear the swish of her skirts as she criss-crosses the room, then a pause before her voice hardens. 'If you won't write to Jerome's father, *I* shall write to his mother. Perhaps she will be more sympathetic, if not to Katharina, at least to her son.'

Philipp's response is quiet, but his tone is chilling. 'You forget yourself, Elsa, and I warn you, if you write to Frau Baumgartner encouraging her to act in defiance of her husband, as you seem determined to do to me, it will be the last letter you write from my house.'

I hear the latch lifting on the study door, and the bang as it swings back against the wall, then Elsa's rapid footsteps in the corridor. She stops outside the Stube but doesn't come in, and after a few minutes I hear her climbing the stairs. It's a relief not to have to face her, not to have to pretend I don't know the difficulties I've caused between them. The study door slams again and this time it's Philipp's heavy tread that causes the floorboards in the hallway to vibrate. Hurriedly, I push the kitchen door against the jamb, not daring to shut it properly in case the noise betrays me, and scurry to the window seat, picking up my sewing and beginning to hum, as if I've been occupied all afternoon and am oblivious of the conflict. It's only when I hear the front door shutting that I set the sewing aside and stare at the ashes of the fire, my hopes likewise crumbling to dust.

Each day, the atmosphere at mealtimes becomes more strained, conversation withering almost before it has begun, so that I take to excusing myself when I know that Philipp will be present, and forage in the kitchen thereafter. The cook places a plate in front of me without comment and I'm grateful for her reticence. Even with Elsa I'm uncomfortable, wanting to talk to her but not knowing what to say. I appreciate her desire to help, but

I want to tell her not to say anything more, for I cannot contemplate gaining a marriage for myself at the cost of hers, supposing her intervention would be successful, which, in my calmer moments, I think unlikely. I cannot even thank her for what she has already tried to do, for that would reveal I'd been listening as she argued with Philipp, and I fear it would only serve to increase the embarrassment between us.

I go to Eva, thankful that it's she, of all the Nimbschen sisterhood, who remains in Wittenberg, and confident that, although she appears to have changed since her marriage, her matronly demeanour is but a veneer that she polishes daily lest the gossips of the town find anything to reproach her with, while underneath she is still the same Eva and my best friend.

I burst into her parlour and am disappointed to see Barbara Cranach sitting with her.

'Oh, I'm sorry, Eva, I'll come back later. I hoped...'

'To find her alone?' Frau Cranach's voice is gentle. 'You don't need to leave on my account, Katharina, but if you have something private to say to Eva, I can call again another time.'

'No.' Eva puts out her hand to stop Barbara rising. Her tone is unusually serious. 'I think we both know why you're here, Kat, and' – she casts an apologetic look at me – 'and indeed must confess to talking of you before you arrived.'

I tense, prepare for flight, angry at Eva for gossiping about me, angry at myself for allowing the situation to develop that makes me a matter for gossip, angry that I find myself wishing Frau Cranach, who has never been other than kind to me, anywhere but here.

She detaches Eva's hand from her sleeve, comes across to me and places her hand on my shoulder. 'Don't be angry with Eva, Katharina, she didn't tell me anything I didn't already know. Men are often the biggest blabbermouths, and both Lucas and Martin shared their concerns with me.'

I shift, try to pull away but she doesn't let go.

'Do not blame them either, they feel a responsibility for your well-being, as they did for all of you, and would wish nothing more than to see Baumgartner fulfil his promise to you.' Her mouth tightens. 'I thought Jerome an honourable man – we all did – and your attachment entirely suitable.'

I can't bear to hear anyone talk ill of him, however hurt I am. 'He is honourable, I'm sure of it. There must be some reason that keeps him away, something he cannot avoid.'

Eva begins, 'Perhaps, Kat, you should…'

Frau Cranach shakes her head at her and draws me to the bench. 'Sit down, Kat.' Her voice is once more gentle, as if she doesn't wish to startle me into running away. 'There is another reason for your visit, I think. Whatever it is, perhaps we can help.'

It is her use of the diminutive that breaks me, and before I can stop myself I've told them of the Reichenbachs, of Philipp's ultimatum, of my fear that Elsa might disobey him, that I might be the cause of a marriage rift. Eva has moved to my other side and has her arm around me, pressing hard. When I finish, my words petering out, Frau

Cranach also puts her arm around me. This time her tone is firm, as if she won't accept any contradiction.

'You must come to stay with us. We have more than enough room. In fact, you would be doing me a service because, now that Eva is married, I find myself lacking in companionship.' And with a sensitivity that soothes my agitation she finishes, 'And have no fear, Lucas, were he here, would agree.' Her brow knots as she works something out. 'In fact, you must come now. We can send to the Reichenbachs' for your things.'

'I cannot leave Elsa without a goodbye. She has been so kind to me and…'

'Then I shall accompany you while you give her your thanks and take your leave.'

'What of Philipp?'

'What of him?' Eva is scornful. 'He's not worthy of your courtesy. And if his reputation suffers as a result of your leaving, it is no less than he deserves.'

⟢⟤

Autumn slips to winter, winter to spring, and when I walk in the town I cannot fail to notice that folk turn to stare as I pass, almost as much as they did when we first arrived. But now it is pity I see, and I find it as hard to bear as censure once was. Elsa I glimpse once or twice in the market, and each time she turns away as if she cannot speak, and I will not force myself on her. She suffered for me once and it may be that she suffers still. Jerome has not come back despite that I have written to him many times, and though I cannot forget him, I have determined I will not write to him again.

The Cranachs, husband and wife, welcome me as if family, their kindness a balm. Their children, too, are friendly, their liveliness an antidote to my despondency. Lucas, whose portraiture is thought to be particularly fine, asks if he may paint my likeness, and as I sit for him, the quiet of the studio penetrates my soul. Barbara goes out of her way to involve me in all of her activities and I throw myself into them with as much enthusiasm as I can muster, for I know she hopes to moderate my pain. Eva is outraged on my behalf, and her white-hot anger against Jerome and against the Reichenbachs for failing to write to the Baumgartners alternately soothes and upsets me.

Holy Week is almost upon us, and as I see the blacksmith setting up a brazier in front of the Town Church, I wonder who will have the honour of lighting it, if the ceremonies here will be very much different from those we were used to in the convent. The abbess' voice rings in my ear, 'A new beginning...' and I realise that she did know what we were about to do and that, though she couldn't acknowledge it openly, her words had been meant as a benediction.

I seek out Eva, and we walk together down to the river. She is the only person here who, despite her own happiness, might understand why, as the anniversary of our freedom approaches, I find myself thinking of the closing of the outer gate of the convent, which had in the past always signified a shutting *in*, as a shutting *out* also. There is no wind, the reflections of the trees on the other bank shimmering in the water, the only sound the occasional plop as a trout rises and drops again as they did in our fish pond at Nimbschen. I break the silence. 'I miss my aunts and wish there was some way to have news of them.'

She hugs me. 'How can you not? They are your family, Kat, however cut off from you.'

'Last year, though I knew it was impossible, I wished we could have lingered in Torgau for the Easter celebrations, but because we could not, I expected this year to feel only joy.' I don't know how to say that there are moments when I miss even the sternest of the sisters, those who made it their business to spy on us and relished every fault they found, but I don't have to, for it's clear she knows what I'm thinking.

'They were part of our life for so long, Kat, it is inevitable we will think of even the harshest of them, and perhaps it is a healthy thing to remember their best qualities, not their worst.'

She hugs me again. 'When Sunday dawns I'm sure it *will* be joyous, and at least we too will be together.'

It's my turn to guess at her thoughts: of the others who escaped with us, how they are, what they're doing. She tilts her head to one side, a stray curl lying against her cheek. 'I shouldn't tell you this, for it was to be a surprise, but Barbara has ordered a new gown and bonnet for you as an anniversary gift, and I shall have one too. We shall be very smart.' The dimple appears in her cheek. 'It will be hard to be miserable in new clothes. You won't tell her I told you about the gown?'

'Don't worry, I won't spoil her surprise. She is very generous and I should be … am grateful for it.'

I focus on gratitude, to the Cranachs and to our Lord, as we move from the triumph of Palm Sunday into the sombre commemorations of Holy Week itself, but despite myself, I find that thoughts of those who are *not* here break though at odd moments to disturb my peace.

It is Thursday, the lull before the storm of the Passion, when the letters arrive. Lucas brings them into the Stube and cascades them into my lap, his, 'See, they do not forget you,' an indication that he too has noted my abstraction.

Fronika is full of talk about the farm, about the piglets that broke from their pen and escaped into the woods and how it took two days to find them all; Margarete of the responsibilities of running a household, the difficulty of dealing with a mother-in-law who has her own ways of doing things. And although the tone of the letters is light, in both I sense an underlying unease, reinforced by mention of the loss of a plough-hand, a replacement proving hand to find. Magdalena von Staupitz speaks fondly of the girls in her school and it's clear that she is happy in her new life, though she too talks of her brother's concerns regarding the disputes among the Reformation party and his fears that they might lead to greater troubles.

At the bottom of the pile, a letter from Nimbschen, written by the abbess, her words clearly carefully chosen, so that I wonder if it has to pass an inspection by the abbot, and if that is our doing. *You are in our thoughts, as we are sure we are in yours. Our prayer for you, that despite our differences, that your faith in our Lord is unshake*n. Mention is made of Aunt Magdalene and I wonder if there is an underlying message there, if she too has thoughts of leaving … *she has added to the role of infirmaress that of novice-teacher, though there are no new postulants at present … she hopes to write to you soon.* The final paragraph is disturbing. *There has been some unrest in the countryside around – farmers that are refusing to pay their tithes, workers who fail to fulfil their obligations, or* *demand a wage for their labours – but I think we are, for the moment, safe.*

As I stand beside Barbara in the Town Church, the Paschal candle burning brightly in front of the altar, the anthem celebrating Christ's resurrection swelling around us, I thank God anew for my freedom, and pray with all my heart that God will protect those we left behind in the Marienthron.

Eastertide is no sooner past than Barbara is possessed of a desire to spring clean the entire house, no corner left undisturbed, so that I overhear Lucas asking Basilius, who has called on some business matter, if there are spiders marching down his stairs in protest also? And in all the busyness May creeps up on me almost unnoticed, so that I have no time to brood as the anniversary of my meeting with Jerome approaches. But on the morning itself I wake early and, unable to settle in the house, walk past the old Franciscan monastery to the corner of the wall which bounds the Reichenbachs' property. Over the top of the wall I can see the apple trees, smothered in blossom, and imagine him leaning against a trunk, sunlight dappling his hair, his eyes full of laughter. A gust of wind drifts blossom onto my shoulders, and as I brush it off I think of Eva's advice, 'Forget him, Kat. He isn't worth it.'

I cannot forget anything of what passed between us: the feel of his hand on my arm, the touch of his finger on my cheek, the taste of his breath mingling with mine; arrow-sharp memories that I fear will never be blunted. To the world and to the Cranach household I hide behind

241

indifference, forcing myself not to jump up every time we hear a messenger at the door, and painting a smile on my face, which I cannot quite get to reach to my eyes. Only with Eva do I allow myself to reveal the loss I feel, the sense that I will never be complete again.

Chapter Twenty-Eight
Wittenberg, Spring 1524

There is a new face at the Cranachs' table: Caspar Glatz, a pastor newly converted to Luther's teachings who has come to Wittenberg to seek help in finding a place. I know what Eva would say of him, for from his appearance he is of that age when his character, his mannerisms, his likes and dislikes, must be already set. I, who have no interest in him beyond the intellectual stimulus his conversation might provide, am prepared to wait in judgement until I know more.

Word comes of Karlstadt. He has not drawn back from any of his more controversial teachings and it seems that the parishioners of Orlamünde are determined to follow him, for they have requested his appointment be made permanent. We learn of it at supper, for Dr Luther, disturbed and, I think, disappointed that their ideas have diverged so widely, is open in his opposition to the appointment.

'It pains me to see the errors into which Andreas has fallen. I have spoken to Spalatin, asking that he advise the duke to refuse the request and to summon him to

Wittenberg, that he may be set straight. If that may be accomplished then I will be pleased to see him lead the good folks of Orlamünde back into the fold.'

'And if he cannot be persuaded? What then?' Glatz' face shows only a mild interest, such as could be explained by a desire to understand the religious implications, but as I turn towards him I think I catch a glitter of excitement in his eyes. I cannot be sure, though, for when he sees me looking at him he shifts his gaze, and when I catch his eye again, his expression is bland.

Luther is unequivocal. 'If he will not teach sound doctrine, there is no place for him, either in the university or a parish.'

I don't know the Karlstadts personally, for they left Wittenberg shortly after our arrival, but nevertheless I can't help myself. 'But his wife, his child, surely you wouldn't have them left without support?'

Lucas intervenes. 'We none of us wish to see anyone suffer. Let us hope that sense will prevail, that he will answer the duke's summons and come to be convinced of the right course.'

It has been raining for days, the Elbe lapping at the top of its banks, the council watching anxiously lest it overflow, when more news comes. Dr Luther blows into the Stube, dripping on the polished floor, Glatz, who has become almost his shadow, trailing in his wake.

Barbara rises to greet them, and though she fulfils the formalities, there is an element of exasperation in her voice. 'Was there no servant in the hallway to take your

244

cloaks? I'd prefer you not to soak my floor.' She opens the Stube door and summons a maid, then gestures the men towards the stove. 'An extravagance, I know, in May, but the weather has been so inclement and we so miserable with it, that I thought heat would be cheering.'

Glatz bows, obsequious. 'And so it is.'

I feel my stomach curl and am filled with guilt that I suspect his tone and doubt his motives, but my quick sideways glance at Barbara confirms that she shares my distrust.

Lucas appears from his studio. 'Martin. I heard your voice – what news from Orlamünde?'

'Karlstadt is determined to remain within the parish and has resigned from his position as archdeacon and from his role in the university.'

'He refuses the duke's summons?'

'Not exactly. He will not come to give testimony at the duke's behest, but he has sent word that he will come to hand in his letters of resignation in person.'

I cannot conceal my interest. 'And you will meet him?'

Luther looks across at my interruption, nods. 'Of course. We were good friends once and I would wish that we could be so again.'

At his side Glatz nods in unison. 'No doubt, Martin, if you cannot, it won't be to your blame.' He stretches out his hand towards the stove, bestows a smile on Barbara, asks, 'What will happen to Orlamünde now?'

'Nothing,' Luther dismisses the question. 'Until, that is, we have heard what Andreas has to say. After that... He is still pastor at Orlamünde, but it is in the duke's gift. If he will not come to his senses there will have to be someone else found to take on the responsibility.'

'I do not wish to push myself forward' – Glatz assumes a suitable diffidence – 'but I would be happy to offer my services. To restore the Church and the people to a true understanding.'

'I'm sure you would.' Barbara's whisper is intended only for me, but Lucas clearly catches it, for he turns his head sharply, signalling silence with his eyes, and interjects,

'Time enough to worry about Orlamünde once we have had a chance to hear what Andreas has to say for himself. And theology aside, I shall be glad to see him again.'

'And I.' Barbara is staring at the stove as if she sees memories reflected in the tiles. 'He was always a welcome guest, his conversation entertaining, his company good.'

I am thinking of what he has meant to me. 'Other than in the pulpit of the Castle Church, I only saw him the once, at the Reichenbachs', but I owe my presence here to him.'

Again Luther glances at me, this time with a mixture of surprise and interest.

'We had studied your teachings within the cloister for some time, Herr Doctor, and of course they were an influence, but it was the report of Karlstadt's Christmas Day sermon that brought me to my final decision.'

'Indeed.' Luther's face clears. 'You owe him a debt of gratitude, then.'

'A good man, no doubt.' Glatz gives all the appearance of sorrow. 'But if he is now a deluded one, then the souls of others are at stake.'

Lucas betrays irritation. 'His contribution to reform must not be forgotten, and however far astray he may have wandered now, it will be by conviction and from the best of motives.'

'Of course. Of course.' Glatz acknowledges Lucas' comment with the smallest of nods, then turns his gaze on Luther, as if addressing him alone. 'But those of us privileged to understand the Scriptures bear a great responsibility to share our knowledge and lead others to the truth. And if that means standing against those who are less well versed, then our courage must not fail.'

We watch from the window as Luther and Glatz pass out of our line of sight, heading for the Black Cloister.

I sigh, uneasy that I may be distrusting him without cause. 'Is it just me? Or is there something false about Herr Glatz?'

'You sense it too?' Barbara is pulling at the tails of the ties that criss-cross her bodice, the knot coming loose. She knots them again more firmly. 'He professes an interest in the spiritual condition of the parishioners of Orlamünde, but I cannot but think it is the wealth of the charge that is his primary concern.'

'Eva says…' I stop.

'What?'

'Nothing. It's only gossip. She had it from her maid, and the maid from a friend, so I shouldn't repeat it. It's hardly fair to judge a man on third-hand information.'

'Judge him as you find him.' Lucas has returned from seeing our visitors out and moves to place his hand on Barbara's shoulder.

She reaches up to cover it with her own and asks,

'How do *you* find him?'

'Penny-pinching and ungenerous, and though *what* he says may be in order, I do not like the *way* he says it.'

It's important to me that I have some justification for my instinctive dislike of him, so I ask, 'Do you have evidence of his parsimony?'

Lucas moves to stand with his back to the stove, and takes a moment before answering. 'Some, yes, but' – he casts a glance of apology towards Barbara – 'it isn't my story to share, or I would share it with you.' And this to me, 'But I have it on good authority, you can be assured of that.' He pauses again. 'Martin does not see it, for it isn't his gift to understand a man's heart, only to hear his words, but I'm sorry to say I do not think Glatz a man of integrity.' He draws in a deep breath. 'And though I should be ashamed to admit it, for the sake of those on whom he might be afflicted, I hope that Martin finds him a place soon, and one not overly close to Wittenberg.'

It's the longest speech I've ever heard Lucas make, the first time I've heard him criticise anyone so openly, and I suppress a desire to hug him, for the relief he brings me.

Barbara speaks for both of us. 'We have not judged Glatz too harshly, then.'

'I think not.' Lucas' affirmation is primarily directed at Barbara, but he includes me in it. 'Never underestimate your own instincts, and in this case, believe me, they are right.'

In the moment of silence that follows I realise the rain has stopped, the only sound a steady drip, drip from the eaves, and I have an overwhelming desire to get outside, to feel the freshness of air on my face. 'Now that it's drying up, may I go to call on Eva?'

'Of course. You know you don't need my permission.' Barbara looks towards the window. 'There is still some light left, but if you wish to linger, no doubt Basilius will see you safely home.'

A watery sun peeps through the clouds, turning the damp cobbles to jet, and I pick my way with care, avoiding the worst of the puddles that lie in the dips. Overhead, swallows dart and swoop in a joyous sky-dance, as if they too celebrate the return of the sun, and looking up, I think I might like fine to be a bird.

There are footsteps on the stairs, the rattle of a bowl on a tray. I turn my head as I hear the latch lifting and summon a smile for the woman who enters. Steam is rising from the food she brings, in it the scent of rosemary and thyme. I cannot bear the thought of mutton again, but try not to wrinkle my nose, however little I feel like eating, for without the generosity of Frau Karsdörfer, we would be in grave difficulty for want of funds. The money that is daily expected from the duke has not yet arrived and I suspect that Herr Brück holds it back to emphasise his power as chancellor. I hope it will come soon, for Frau Karsdörfer's culinary tastes are not mine, but I cannot say so to her servant who has come to feed me.

'Where's Margarethe?' I say, for if I do not like what food has been provided, she will not press me against my will, whereas I do not have the strength to withstand this woman.

'She took a message to the Chancellery, and I thought to spare her the time by seeing to your supper.' She props me up against the pillows before settling down on the edge of the bed, the tray balanced on her lap, a cloth spread over the coverlet in protection. I do my best to swallow the spoonfuls of broth she puts to my lips, for the sooner I manage it, the sooner the ordeal will be over and I will have peace again. She prattles on, a constant stream of names of people I don't know and snippets of gossip, which interest me not at all. I try to look as if I'm listening, for I know she means well, nodding and shaking my head at regular intervals, hoping that I have chosen aright, my mind elsewhere. Her voice is rising, the note of indignation

penetrating my thoughts, stirring memories that I thought long buried.

'…I told her, it is a disgrace that children should be trailed from place to place …Frau Karlstadt should not allow it…'

'Karlstadt?' I say, 'Anna Karlstadt?'

She stops mid-flow, as if confused, and colours, 'She bides on the Spitalstrassse. If I had thought you'd know her, I would not have presumed to criticise.'

'It was a long time ago … I was sponsor to one of her children … and a right clip he was.' She is looking puzzled, so I try to explain. 'Not at the first of course, but later, when the countryside was ablaze. They were our first house-guests, but we had to plead with Herr Dr Luther, for he thought Andreas had betrayed him.'

She sets aside the bowl, wipes the corner of my mouth with a cloth. 'Perhaps it is not the same Karlstadt.'

'We are none of us the same but' – I shake my head – 'I cannot think ill of Andreas. I owe him too much.'

Chapter Twenty-Nine
Wittenberg, May 1524

'This Satan of Allstedt ... he raves about the Spirit –
where are its fruits?'

Martin Luther

Karlstadt doesn't come, his journey thwarted by roads still blocked by high water, his failure a disappointment to the many who remembered him with affection from his time at Wittenberg. It seems there will be no disputation with Luther, no opportunity for them to reconcile their differences. I am saddened by the thought, for my faith is still a fragile thing and I need the foundations of it to be solid, this open disunity among the reformers disquieting.

Barbara is more pragmatic. 'You cannot expect that centuries of misrepresentation ... or misunderstanding, if you chose to be charitable, of the Scriptures can be swept away without debate as to what must be put in their place. And good and sincere as all these men are, they are but human and prone to error as any of us may be.' She places her hand on the copy of the German New Testament which has pride of place on the table by her side. 'Remember the words of Gamaliel, *What is of God cannot be overthrown, what is of human origin will fail.* In time it will become clear whose views are right, but just now my concern is for Anna Karlstadt. Andreas may be acting out of conviction, but I trust he has also thought of the consequences for his family, and should he be forced to give up the living of Orlamünde, that he has made some provision for them.'

I share her concern, maybe even surpass it, for I know only too well what it is to be dependent on others for everything. 'It is only the permanent position that has been refused him … there is no thought of him having to leave altogether?'

'Not as yet, but it is hard to see a good outcome in all this. I fear for Anna, for them both.'

It seems her fears may be well grounded when Lucas appears at supper-time, throwing himself into his seat, his annoyance clear.

Barbara pours him some beer and he takes a long swallow, then, 'I do not want that man in my house again!'

'Who don't you want?'

'That fellow Glatz. As you know, I didn't take to him from the first and I like him even less now.'

'What has he done?'

'According to Justus Jonas, he is constantly putting himself forward as a suitable replacement for Karlstadt at Orlamünde.'

'He has access to the duke?'

'No, but he spreads the word about the university, and the more a thing is talked about, the more likely it is to come about.'

Lucas accepts the plate Barbara offers him and begins

253

to dissect a slice of beef.

I'm struggling to understand why he is so incensed by something we have known for months, when Barbara, as if she reads my mind, says, 'This is old news, Lucas. There must be something more to so annoy you now.'

He takes another swallow of beer. 'He has the ear of Martin, and daily drips poison into it, suggesting that Karlstadt differs from us in more than theology. I fear that he may turn Martin against him altogether.'

'There are other influences in Wittenberg, and of much longer standing: Bugenhagen, Melanchthon, Jonas. What is Glatz against them?'

He studies his plate and Barbara probes again. 'What aren't you saying, Lucas?'

'It's this fellow Müntzer. Since he was chosen as pastor at Allstedt…'

We all start as we hear the stamping of feet in the hallway and Martin's voice booming a greeting. 'Am I too late for supper? I trust Frau Cranach will not mind that I have brought Melanchthon and some of the students with me.'

Barbara is laughing as she throws open the door, and I suspect it is at least in part that she hopes they will distract Lucas and improve his mood.

'Martin! Philipp! We have started, but I daresay we can find a morsel or two for you.' She stands back and inclines her head to the three young men that troop in behind them. 'You are all welcome,' she says, before disappearing towards the kitchen.

I set five extra places and Lucas draws more chairs to the table, as Barbara reappears, a servant in tow. The conversation begins well enough, though I'm surprised that Lucas does not immediately return to what he'd been about to tell us when we'd been interrupted by Luther's arrival. Instead, all his talk is of commerce, of the businesses that wish to come into the town and the new regulations for taxation the burgesses are proposing. Although they aren't unusual topics for our table, they are of little relevance to our guests and it is unlike Lucas to talk of his own concerns at the expense of the interests of others. His tone is forced, and I wonder if he is afraid of the consequences should the conversation take a wrong turn.

Despite the cheeriness of his greeting, Dr Luther seems preoccupied, his first tankard of beer still half-full, and it is the only time in all the meals I have seen him share at the Cranachs' table that he has not dominated the conversation.

Barbara, when Lucas dries up, begins to talk of mutual acquaintances, of the damage that the Coelius family sustained when their cellar had flooded in the recent rains; of how Justus and Katherine Jonas were looking forward to the enlargement of their family; of the aptitude Basilius Axt was showing for both the apothecary and the printing business. Luther stirs at that, and I think of Eva and wonder if she was wrong about him, if all his talk of being too old was but a smokescreen to hide his own disappointment at her marriage. A servant hovers at his shoulder with a jug of beer but he shakes his head and waves her away. I have never seen Luther drunk, nor even merry, as Philipp Reichenbach sometimes was, but neither have I seen him refuse a drink as he does now, and it troubles me. There have been rumours that he is not always well, that he suffers with his stomach and with insomnia, and perhaps worse, but up till now I have seen no evidence of it.

Barbara is also watching him, her tongue poking between her lips, as it does when she is uneasy about something, while Lucas drums on the table with his fingers, a sign that he is searching for some other safe topic. He is beaten to it by one of the students who leans across the table towards Luther and says, 'Word is that Müntzer has taken control of the council of Mühlhausen. Does he have *any* right on his side?'

Luther throws down his napkin. 'None whatsoever.'

Lucas' head comes up and he wags a finger at the student, but he, either ignoring, or unaware of the warning signal, persists. 'They say he displays a silk banner in the church with a rainbow and the motto "The Word of the Lord Abideth Forever" on it and calls for the faithful to rally to the call of God and the cleansing of the nation.'

The second student cuts in. 'It seems his following grows daily. If he were in error, surely his cause would falter.'

'You are forgetting the words of Christ.' Melanchthon speaks quietly as if in an attempt to defuse an explosive situation; that many will prophecy in His name who are none of His.

There is a moment of silence, Barbara picking at her food, Lucas passing a platter of cheeses to me and indicating for me to hand it on.

Luther ignores it, characteristically abrupt. 'Müntzer is a mad dog and should be treated as one. We are not of the Old Covenant but of the New.'

The first student chimes in again. 'But did not our Lord say He did not come to destroy the law but to fulfil it?'

I do not want the discussion to stop, for this is the sparring I have come to expect when Dr Luther and other of the university join us, and I'm grateful I've the opportunity to eavesdrop on it.

Once again Melanchthon is swift to reply, and I have the sense that his intention is to moderate the discussion, to keep it within civilised bounds. 'Indeed. The rich young ruler is told to keep the commandments: Do not murder, do not steal. It is a pity that Müntzer advocates both, and more.'

'A pity? An outrage rather.' Luther's colour is rising, as the third student, a little slow in following the direction of the debate, cuts in.

'But did not Christ also cleanse the temple, throwing over the booths of the money-changers? Is not Müntzer following his example in seeking similarly to cleanse the Church?'

Luther's knife follows his napkin, the point scoring the surface of the table as he tosses it down. Whatever the reason for his previous distraction he is fully involved in the debate now. I see Barbara tense; had it been a member of our household her censure would have been immediate and sharp. As the culprit is Dr Luther, she has no option but to bite her tongue, though I imagine she's already thinking of a preparation of powdered rottenstone and linseed and wondering if it will be enough to remove the scratch.

He thumps the table with his fist, the platters rattling. 'The money-changers made the house of God a den of thieves and were rightly chastised. You are correct that what our Lord has done, his ministers may do also.' He pauses, but only to draw breath. 'As indeed we did when

257

we challenged the exploitation of relics and the rapacious greed of those who peddle indulgences. And rightly so, for ours was a just anger; but a rampaging mob such as Müntzer inflames, that I cannot support.' He looks around the table as if he dares any of us to disagree with him. 'Nor have I ever advocated the tearing down of images, the sacking of churches. It is reform I want, not revolution.'

Melanchthon opens his mouth to speak and I see a sliver of beef trapped between his teeth. 'We lit a fire, Martin. We must bear some responsibility for how it burns.' He reaches out a hand as if to lay it on Dr Luther's arm, but, seeming to think better of it, lifts his tankard instead and takes a drink. 'It is hardly surprising that your views on the ills of the monasteries have been taken as licence to despoil them, nor that your insistence that prayers to the saints go no further than the ceiling, should lead to the destruction of icons. The logical conclusion is that they are at best a distraction, at worst idolatry.'

Beside him, Dr Luther is like a coiled spring, and Barbara's hands on her lap are clasped tight, the skin stretched over her knuckles, the tendons taut.

Lucas, with a glance at her white face, makes one last attempt to direct the conversation into calmer waters. This time, however, his choice of topic is ill-judged, his 'What news of Andreas?' drowned out by Luther's explosive response.

'He is an instrument of Satan and beyond all help.'

'He is misguided.' Melanchthon attempts to placate Luther. 'When he has had time to consider, no doubt good sense will prevail.'

I'm thinking of the conversation cut off as our visitors arrived, if this was the poison that Lucas had referred to.

'Karlstadt surely cannot support Müntzer?'

Melanchthon glares at me and I know what is in his mind, that though he suffers me as a guest of the Cranachs, and someone for whom Dr Luther feels a responsibility, I should know my place, and it assuredly isn't to debate with clerics such as these.

Chapter Thirty
Wittenberg July – August 1524

Müntzer is the name on everyone's lips, the topic of gossip on every street corner and at every shop in the arches under the Rathaus. His challenge to Luther, to the value of Scripture itself, has become more virulent and personal, and that is sufficient to set the whole town abuzz. His pronouncements are to some shocking, to others amusing, to many, bordering on the blasphemous. 'Luther is "Dr Easychair", "Dr Pussyfoot"; more interested in currying the favour of princes than in encouraging and strengthening the elect.' Müntzer refers to Scripture as 'Babble, Babel, Bubble' and 'But paper and ink', insisting that those who rely on the letter of it, a clear reference to Wittenberg's theologians in general, and Dr Luther in particular, 'Are the scribes against whom Christ inveighed.' His primary claim, an equally plain reference to himself, is that 'The elect are Spirit-filled, those to whom God gives direct revelation, and only they can interpret the Bible aright.'

He is the subject of conversation at our table too, replacing the problem of Jerome's continued silence in everyone's mind but mine. And indeed I am glad of it, for although I appreciated the sympathy I saw in Barbara's eyes every time Jerome's name had been mentioned, I prefer to keep my pain private, rather than be the subject of pity.

Lucas, although not directly involved, betrays his increasing concern regarding Müntzer. 'Everyone at the university felt he had such promise, and Martin had no reservations in recommending him to the pulpit. And this is the way he repays the teaching and encouragement he received. He sees himself as the new Elijah. It will not be long before he is calling down fire from heaven to consume us all.'

I rouse myself from my reverie, in which I have been wondering what Jerome makes of Müntzer, if he worries of the consequences for Nuremberg, as we do for our own city, and ask, 'How can he advocate violence? On what biblical text does he base such a call?'

'He takes the words of Christ *I have not come to bring peace, but a sword* and twists them to his own ends. He claims the elect cannot enter into their inheritance without a struggle, and that struggle is to slaughter the ungodly.'

I'm thinking of the talk in the market, of his mocking of Dr Luther. 'He cannot think Dr Luther ungodly?'

'He thinks anyone ungodly who does not share his vision of the Church and of the world.'

'Perhaps,' Barbara says, 'this is the fulfilment of the predictions that Melanchthon talked of.'

'Predictions?'

'Didn't you know Melanchthon dabbles in astrology, Katharina? Apparently the planets are conjoined in the constellation of Pisces, and to those who study such things it presages disaster. There have been more than

261

fifty pamphlets published predicting that 1524 will be the year when the world will be deluged in misery and woe.'

Lucas is dismissive. 'He should know better. Astrology is for the credulous, not for those of a sound faith. Whatever misery and woe comes, it will not be the movements of the planets we should blame, but rather a cause much closer to home.'

I know that Lucas speaks of Müntzer, of the religious controversies he awakes, and that my concerns are far from his thoughts, but nevertheless his words are like a knife opening a wound in my chest, and I need to get away before I disgrace myself by crying. I stand up, make my apologies. 'If you will excuse me' – I press my hand against my stomach – 'I have a pain. I think I must lie down for a bit.' I suppress my guilt at the deception, for it's true, in its way, but not in the sense I intend them to take it.

Barbara also rises. 'Would you like me to accompany you to your chamber?'

I shake my head. 'No … thank you … I'll be fine, I just need…' I don't have to say anything more, for she touches my arm and nods, her coded message of both sympathy and understanding clear.

'I shall come to you later then, in case there is anything you need.'

I must have dozed, for I surface from a confused dream in which Müntzer is haranguing Jerome for the misery he has brought on the world. Luther is standing behind him, likewise shouting. His German New Testament is open in his hand, his forefinger stabbing at the page, and his face is as red and as round as a beetroot. I don't know which man his anger is directed at, but I hope it isn't Jerome, for though I may have cause for complaint, I don't wish for him to suffer anyone else's censure.

I disentangle myself from the cover I'd pulled over me when I lay down, and swing my legs over the edge of the bed. Dusk is falling, and outside the window I see bats swooping and darting, as if chasing shadows. I'm thankful I'm inside and safe, for a memory from my childhood, when one flew so close to my face that I fell backwards, cracking my head against the barn door, still has the power to fright me.

'I will not listen to him, though he has swallowed the Holy Ghost, feathers and all!' The voice is Luther's, and I stand up, shaking the creases from my gown, and, padding across the floor, slip my feet into my shoes. Though I haven't admitted it to anyone, for fear of censure or mockery or both, I continue to be disturbed by the fierceness of the disputes springing up among the reformers, as if they are packs of savage dogs prepared to rip each other apart. I need to be convinced in my own mind whose opinion I accept, for my new-found faith is still fragile, its roots not yet fully established. Schooled as I have been to think of peace as paramount, I am almost sure that Müntzer must be wrong, but I want to hear Dr Luther's arguments for myself.

Barbara rises as I enter and indicates that I join her on the settle. Dr Luther and Lucas don't have to stand up, for they are already standing, one on either side of the table, as if they too are antagonists in a sparring match. Lucas turns to greet me, his smile painted on his face.

'Katharina, you're feeling better?'

'I am, thank you.'

Barbara cuts in. 'You're still flushed. Are you sure you're all right?'

I put my hand up to my cheek and feel the heat in it. 'I fell asleep. That's all.' I can see she isn't entirely convinced.

'It was not the raised voices that woke you?'

'If it was, I'm glad, for I wouldn't wish to find myself awake at midnight having slept too long now.' I settle down beside her and tuck my feet under the bench. 'And I cannot but be curious as to what was being discussed so heatedly.'

'Müntzer, of course.' Luther spits out the name. 'And his outrageous claims. I say again he is an agent of Satan, and if Andreas Karlstadt has been seduced by him, then he too must be condemned.'

'We don't know if Andreas has any connection to Müntzer.' Lucas' voice is controlled, his words chosen with care. 'We cannot condemn a man without a hearing.'

'There is little doubt about the league Müntzer has formed at Allstedt. Nor that his claim of others supporting him also has truth in it.'

'It doesn't mean Andreas is implicated.'

I haven't noticed the letter lying open on the table until Dr Luther lifts it and waves it in Lucas' face. The arms of the electors of Saxony are emblazoned across the top and bring a saliva rush to my mouth.

'Would you question what Duke John has said?' Luther straightens it out, begins to read, *'I am having a terrible time with the Satan of Allstedt... Kindliness and letters do not suffice... Karlstadt is also stirring up something and*

264

the Devil wants to be Lord.'

Lucas takes a deep breath. 'I do not dispute the trouble Müntzer is causing for us all, but the part that refers to Andreas is unspecific.'

'He has been deprived of his position at Orlamünde yet refuses to leave. Is that specific enough for you?'

Beside me Barbara tenses, tries to interject with, 'Will he still have the farm?' but neither Luther nor Lucas seem aware of her interruption, continuing their argument as if she hadn't spoken at all.

'The rumour is that Müntzer invited Andreas to join him, but he refused.'

Luther slaps the letter down on the table. 'And you would listen to rumour rather than to Duke John?'

'I cannot believe that Andreas would foment rebellion. Indeed, I have it on good authority that he wrote back saying that such a league as Müntzer proposes is against God's will, and that the Orlamünders have no wish to become criminals and rebels.'

'You have seen this letter?'

'No, but I believe it to have been written.' Lucas fills a tankard and holds it out to Luther. 'Why not go to see Andreas, hear what he has to say for himself? He may differ from us in doctrine and feel that your reforms go neither far nor fast enough, but we have known him a long time, Martin, and though impetuous, and always wishing to run before he could walk, I do not think he would become embroiled in this.'

Luther sets down the letter, accepts the beer, and Lucas, clearly keen not to lose the advantage, continues. 'You have promised the duke that you will undertake a preaching tour through the villages to reinforce sound doctrine; Jena is already on your route and Orlamünde is not so far away. It would be the ideal opportunity to meet with Andreas and learn for yourself the truth of the matter.'

We are sitting in the garden, hulling beans, the August sun burning the back of my neck. Barbara pushes aside a strand of hair that has escaped from her cap and I see the beads of sweat sparkling on her forehead. I lean back against the bench. 'Shall I fetch a drink?'

'I should not wish the sun away, for it will be autumn soon enough, but I *am* rather hot.'

As soon as I step through the rear door into the corridor behind the kitchen I hear the murmur of voices. I cannot make out what is being said, but I can distinguish the speakers. Justus Jonas is there, along with Lucas and Bugenhagen. I pause at the entrance to the pantry, consider going to greet them, to offer them a drink also, but they sound subdued and I suspect this isn't a social call, and that perhaps they'd prefer not to be interrupted, so I lift a jug of peach juice and two pottery tumblers and slip out again into the garden. Something of my unease must have registered in my face, for as I hand Barbara the drink, she asks, 'What is it, Katharina?'

'I'm not sure. Justus Jonas and Bugenhagen are here to see Lucas, and their greetings were not...' – I pause, trying to think how to describe what they sounded like – '...cheerful. I think they have news.'

She is ahead of me. 'Of Martin's meeting with Andreas?'

'Perhaps. But if it is, I suspect it didn't go well.'

'I hope it did not go so very badly, for I would hate to think of Andreas losing his place now, with one child already to his credit and Anna expecting again.'

'I wonder what *she* thinks of his opinions?'

Barbara shrugs. 'Who knows, but she is loyal, and if her thoughts *are* critical she won't allow them to become known.'

'Do you agree with her in that?'

'Of course.' Her hands are clasped around the tumbler and I see her grip tighten. 'I do not subscribe to the belief that a wife should have no views of her own, but whatever she may say to her husband in private, it is right that in public she supports him.'

'However wrong his views may be, or however difficult that may make her life?'

'Difficult or easy, Katharina, marriage is based on vows taken before God and they shouldn't be lightly set aside.'

I think back to the vows I took at the Marienthron and shiver.

She sets the tumbler down and reaches out to grasp both my hands in hers. 'Do not equate your convent vows with a marriage that God may yet give you. You were a child without choice when you were sent to Nimbschen. You are a woman now and with the freedom to make your own decision in this regard. Pray God that you get the chance.'

I want to ask her what she means, when Lucas appears.

'This sounds serious.'

Barbara looks up with a smile. 'Lucas.' Her smile fades. 'We were talking of Anna and Andreas and wondering

267

how Luther's meeting with him went.'

Lucas throws himself down on the grass at Barbara's feet. 'Jonas says at first it was awkward, both of them prickly, as if they had not been close once, or perhaps because of it. It hadn't helped that the tour itself was less than successful, supporters of Karlstadt disturbing the church services, heckling Martin's sermons, so that it was hardly surprising that they met as strangers, facing each other across a table in an inn. Andreas protested his innocence in regard to Müntzer and Martin appeared to take his word. In the end they agreed on a written debate on the pace of reform. It seemed that it was a worthwhile meeting after all.'

I sense the reservation in his voice. 'Seemed?'

He doesn't answer and I'm not sure that I want to know what it is he's reluctant to say, but ask anyway. 'What else has happened?'

'Martin was no sooner home than he wrote to Spalatin, and as a result Andreas is to be banished from Saxony.'

There is a choking sound and I turn my head to see Barbara sliding off the bench and crumpling on the ground. Lucas is on his knees beside her, loosening the neck of her gown, shaking her gently by the shoulders, murmuring her name.

I'm part way up the path, calling back, 'I'll get salts,' when he halts me.

'No need, she's stirring.' He's supporting her head in the crook of one arm, holding the tumbler to her lips.

Her face is white, her eyes huge. 'Anna,' she says, 'and the child…'

268

I'm in the pantry, clearing a shelf to make space for the preserves that the cook is setting down, when Barbara appears in the doorway.

'Leave that for now, Katharina, I need to talk to you.'

There is an odd note in her voice that makes me uneasy. 'What…'

She looks over her shoulder towards the cook and shakes her head. 'Let's go outside.' There is a basket lying by the door and she picks it up. 'Last night's storm will likely have brought down apples. We can check for any that have fallen while we talk.'

A thousand thoughts race through my mind as we head for the orchard. I want it to be good news of Jerome, but I suspect by her serious expression that I am not to have that joy.

'Remember, Katharina, when we were talking of the Karlstadts?'

I nod. 'Is there ill news of Anna? Or Andreas? Of the child?'

'No. It is our discussion on marriage I was thinking on

269

… and its responsibilities.' She catches her lip between her teeth, continues, 'You know the hopes we all had for you, Katharina …' She breaks off, and then in a rush, as if she's afraid if she doesn't tell me quickly she won't be able to tell me at all, 'Martin has brought news of another offer of marriage, indeed the person concerned is here and wishes to speak to you.'

Again a pause, again another rush of words. 'You know you have a home here, Kat, and have no need to accept any offer that isn't to your pleasing. And though Martin thinks he is suitable – a pastor, evangelical, of sound doctrine…' It's as if the name is stuck in her throat.

I bend down to pick up an apple, smoothing it in my hand, checking for bruises, afraid to look at her. 'It cannot be Glatz?'

She rests her hand on my arm. 'There is no suggestion that it should be soon, for as you know he does not yet have a place, but he has already asked Martin for his approval and is here now to seek yours.'

I start to shiver, the apple shaking in my hand, and in an attempt to focus on something … anything else, bring it up to my nose and inhale deeply. 'This will have a good flavour.'

She is sliding her hand up and down my arm as if to calm me. 'Katharina. This must be faced.'

'No. No! Had it been anyone else, perhaps I could have considered, but you know what I think of Glatz.'

'I know' – her words are a sigh – 'and *you* know we share your view. Lucas was sitting with a face like thunder as they put the proposal, and if Glatz had been alone, or with anyone but Martin, he would have shown him the door immediately. Martin, however, insists that you at

270

least hear him out. And it's difficult to gainsay him.' She is biting so hard on her lip I see a bead of blood. 'I think it best if you get it over with. Once you have refused him, hopefully that will be the end of it.' A pause, then, 'We did try, Katharina, Lucas and I both, to tell Martin our opinion of the man, but he doesn't see it.' She sighs again. 'For such a clever person he can be so stupid in some things, so full of vision where theology is concerned, so lacking in it in other respects. I warned him you wouldn't look on Glatz with favour, indeed, that you would likely refuse to see him, but he chooses to take that as an indication of unwarranted pride on your part. If you are to retain his good opinion, I think you must see Glatz. Nothing we could say would convince Martin to make Glatz retract the offer, for in his opinion it would be most suitable.'

'It is impossible. He is impossible. You saw the way his eyes glittered at the prospect of the living at Orlamünde. I may not be able to marry for love' – I shut my eyes for a moment – 'but I must be able to respect my husband. From what we have seen of him, Glatz is avaricious and proud and…' I falter, thinking of his eyes on me when he was last at the Cranachs', of how I felt as if his gaze burned through my gown, '…when he looks at me I think it lust I see in his eyes, and the touch of his fingers on mine turns my stomach… I am not suited, neither by character, nor inclination, to be a helpmeet for him. Or he me.'

'I know,' she says again. 'Wait here and I will send him to you. Refuse him with as much grace as you can muster and we will try once again to convince Martin how unsuitable it is. But whether we succeed or not, he cannot force you to marry against your will, nor do I think he would wish to. It's just…'

271

'That I alone remain as a burden Dr Luther wishes to shed.'

'That is unkind, Kat. He has a concern for you, that is all.'

In my heart I know I am being unjust to Luther, but the idea of Glatz as a husband is so repugnant that I nurse my resentment that he should even think of it. I set the apple, now burnished to a shine, in the basket. 'Do you think it all lost with Jerome?'

This time Barbara is brisk. 'Whatever may or may not happen in the future with Jerome, it is Glatz you must deal with now. And remember, Kat, you are of as good a family as his, or better, so you can refuse him with your head held high. But choose your words carefully, for these things have a way of getting out, and gossip is rarely kind. While we none of us care for Glatz' reputation, we wouldn't want yours to be tarnished.'

'Fraulein von Bora.' Glatz bends over my hand, the touch of his fingers damp, and it takes all my resolve not to pull away too quickly for courtesy.

I bow my head in acknowledgement. 'Herr Glatz.' Withdrawing my hand I take a step backwards.

He indicates the path that winds round the circumference of the garden. 'Shall we walk?'

I'd rather stay where we were, in full view of the workshop, but I have no reason to refuse and so move into step with him, keeping distance between us, my gaze lowered, pretending I haven't noticed his proffered arm. I'm busy trying to find a form of words that will leave him in no doubt of my refusal, when the time comes, without stretching the bounds of politeness too far, and so fail to see that he has steered us into the path that leads to the arbour, until it's too late to suggest otherwise. This path is narrower and he edges closer, his arm sliding around my waist.

'Herr Glatz!' I step sideways and quicken my pace in order to free myself from his grasp, but my foot catches on the edge of the grass and I stumble, unable to conceal an involuntary intake of breath as pain shoots through my ankle. He is quick to take advantage, grasping my elbow on the pretext of steadying me.

'You are hurt, Fraulein?'

I force myself to place my foot flat on the ground, ignoring the pain. 'No.' I try to pull away, but he snakes his arm around me again, his face flushed.

'Fraulein … Katharina. Frau Cranach has told you why I am here. I think in the circumstances your name is permissible is it not?' He presses his fingers into my side to draw me closer.

My stomach is protesting, acid rising into my throat, and this time I do succeed in extricating myself. I make myself as tall as possible and look straight at him. 'I am aware of the honour you wish to do me, but I'm afraid I cannot accept.'

'Come, come. You need have no maidenly reluctance with me.' His tongue flicks across his top lip, leaving it glistening, and my stomach heaves again.

'I wish to make you my wife, Katharina. To the pleasure I'm sure of all of our acquaintance, and…' his tongue flicks out again, his eyes travelling from my neck to my waist to my toes, as if in his mind he undresses me

273

'…to our mutual joy also.'

I take another step back. A mistake, for it takes me into the arbour, the seat pressing against the back of my knees and unbalancing me, so that I can do no other than sit down.

He is by my side in a flash, filling the seat, pinning me against the wooden frame, one hand cupping my chin. His tone is pious, as if he is in the pulpit. 'Marriage is an honourable estate and the marriage bed pure.'

I hear Barbara's voice in my head, suppress my desire to tell him what I really think and strive for the grace she advocated. 'I do not think I am suited…'

He ignores my interruption and slides one finger downwards, allowing it to rest for a moment on my neck before trailing it around the edge of the muslin infill of my gown, halting at the hollow between my breasts. 'I'm sure we can do very well together.'

His face is close to mine, his breath hot on my cheek, my whole body in revolt at his touch. I try to stand up. 'Herr Glatz, please…' But he fastens his hand on my breast and squeezes, and in an instant all my resolve, all the politeness Barbara advocated deserts me. I put both hands against his chest and push hard, catching him off-guard, and leap to my feet as he rocks back. His head cracks against the side of the arbour, a stem of a trailing rose swinging against his face, the thorns raking his cheek, drawing blood.

He staggers to his feet, his hand against his face. 'You…'

I push him again, knocking him backwards, anger lending me strength. 'No. You listen to me. I was prepared to be civil, despite that I find you repulsive in person

and in character, but you have forfeited any right to consideration. You have shown no respect, for me, or my person. Why should I treat you differently? I was mistaken in talking of honour, for your offer does me no honour at all, and I'd rather return to the convent than marry you.'
A thin trickle of blood has reached his chin and he wipes at it and then stares at his palm as if surprised. He looks at me, his colour flaring again, his fist clenched at his side, and I determine to have the last word. 'From the first moment we met I thought you avaricious, hypocritical and ungenerous – now I see that you are lustful also. You do no credit to your profession, and I despise you for it. And if you do not want me to share your behaviour with Dr Luther, I suggest you do not come back into the house. Not today. Nor ever.'

I tell Barbara I've refused him, but I don't share the details of our interview with her, for when I think of his hand on my breast, I burn with shame, despite that I know it was not my blame. The new gown, which Barbara had intended to raise my spirits, seems likewise soiled, so I revert to wearing one that I had been given on my arrival in Wittenberg, ignoring the worn cuffs and the faded colour in the folds of the skirt. It had been destined for rags, and when I appear in it at supper-time, Dr Luther having long since also departed, I see the speculation in Barbara's eyes, but she doesn't quiz me, saying only, 'I see we must wait awhile for a new rug for Lucas' study.'

I bless her for her reticence. I do not think Glatz will return, but I fear what he will say of the terms in which

I refused him, and so daily expect to hear Dr Luther's booming voice in the hallway and receive his censure for my temerity in turning the proposal down. Every time I hear a knock at the front door I flee to the kitchen or to my chamber, emerging only when I am sure it isn't him who has called. A week passes with no word of any sort, in which I barely sleep or eat, so that when I see the notice of a disputation I resolve to go to the university, a plan forming in my mind. I think of the kindness with which Herr Amsdorf has always treated us, the sympathetic expression in his eyes and I know Luther respects his opinions.

I remain when all the students depart, standing quietly in the shadow cast by the half-open door as Herr Amsdorf tidies away his notes. When he turns to leave I step forward, blocking his way, and he halts, clearly unsure of how to respond.

'Fraulein von Bora, this is … unexpected.'

I plunge straight in for fear I will lose my nerve. 'I hope you will forgive the intrusion, Herr Amsdorf, but I have need of your help. You are a good friend to Dr Luther and have proved yourself a good friend also to all of us who sought refuge in Wittenberg.'

He waves his hands in deprecation. 'I have done no more than many others, and a good deal less than some, but if I can be of assistance, I will be happy to do so.' He turns back into the lecture hall, indicates for me to sit, his voice soft. 'Something is troubling you.' It's a statement, not a question, so I wait for him to finish. 'I've watched you grow in the time that you've been here, Fraulein' – he pauses – 'and have seen you cope with both good fortune … and bad. Whatever it is that is disturbing you now, you

276

may speak freely, for I am no man's judge.'

I colour, heat rising in me. 'I have not come seeking the confessional.'

I see his shoulders relax, and he nods in encouragement. 'Go on.'

'Pastor Glatz has made me an offer. I refused, but I'm afraid that Dr Luther may try to persuade me to accept, and I cannot.' I shut my eyes, repeat, 'I cannot.'

There is a light touch on my arm. 'Fraulein?'

I open my eyes and find myself staring into his, inches from my face.

He straightens up and relinquishes my arm. 'For a moment I thought you'd fainted…' His brow is puckered, as if he is considering how best to continue. 'You cannot think a doctor and pastor of sound doctrine an unsuitable match?'

The question is simple enough, but I think I sense distaste in his voice, and I'm not sure if it's directed at me, or the proposal. I strive for an even tone. 'It is not his profession, nor his intellect that offends me, for both are admirable. Were you or…' I cast about in my mind for some other doctor or pastor equally unlikely to wish to marry me '…Dr Luther to seek my hand, I would not refuse.'

He laughs at that, and it gives me the courage to continue. 'I swear it is not pride that makes me refuse him and I beg you to plead my case.'

He becomes serious again. 'If I am to speak for you, I need to know the basis of your objection.'

There is no point in being less than truthful, and though I cannot bring myself to tell him all, the memory of Glatz' touch still shaming me, I fix my eyes on his and

277

confess my lack of love for him and my reservations as to his character. I finish in a rush. 'As regards his personal qualities, both the Cranachs share my opinion of him, but as to what I feel in my heart, that I am solely responsible for.'

There is a moment of silence in which I drop my gaze and focus on the cracks between the floor tiles, afraid that my appeal is in vain, before he touches my shoulder and I look up to see his outstretched hand. As he draws me to my feet, his grip is firm, his skin dry and warm, a welcome contrast to Glatz' palm, slick with damp. He radiates understanding and I don't need to hear his promise to know that he won't fail me, though I'm pleased to have it nonetheless.

'Have no fear, Fraulein. I will speak to Dr Luther.'

A surge of relief sweeps through me, and though it isn't in the least amusing, I have to stifle an almost uncontrollable desire to laugh.

Torgau: 1552

'Shall I read it to you, Mutti?' Margarethe is perched on the side of the bed, a letter in her hand. 'Mutti?'

I look up at her fresh eighteen-year-old face, ripe for disappointment, and tap the folded paper in her hand. 'Do you have a suitor, Margarethe? Is this from him?'

She flushes. 'You know I don't, Mutti.'

'Who then?'

'Aunt Eva. She writes to ask of your health. Would you like to hear what she says? She gestures towards a small table in the corner, to the inkpot and quill. 'I could write a reply for you.'

'I wrote so many letters. So many. And no response.' A tear squeezes out of the corner of my eye. 'If there had been even one, to explain, it would have been easier to bear.'

'What letters, Mutti?'

'Eva counselled me to write, and I did, every month for almost a year, and every month waited and waited for a reply. Or for him to come back.'

'But when Father was away he wrote to you often. You always read us his letters.' There is a mischievous twinkle in her eye. 'Or the parts of them you thought proper for us to hear, at least.'

I shake my head. 'Not your father.'

Sunlight is playing across the embroidered coverlet, and I trace the outline of an apple with one finger. I can feel the warmth of the sunshine on my neck and Jerome's hand under my elbow as we stroll among the trees. He's talking, but I'm not really listening, for I'm thinking of Eva and of how she hugged me when I confided in her, how she'd said, 'He is everything anyone could want, and you, of all people, deserve that.'

He looks down at me, his voice the music of water trickling over a streambed. 'What have I said?'

I smile up at him. 'Nothing.'

'You were laughing.'

'I'm just ... happy.'

There is a hand on my shoulder, a new voice, intrusive, uncertain. 'Mutti? Who are you talking to?'

'Jerome, of course. Jerome Baumgartner. Have you met him?'

'No...'

'I should introduce you.'

Her grip tightens. 'He's not here, Mutti, no one else is here.'

'No? Perhaps it's for the best. Philipp thinks so. He says I should not have hoped for so much.'

'Philipp Melanchthon?' She sounds bewildered.

'Reichenbach.' I toss his name at her and hurry on with what I want to say, for she is of an age now that she should know such things. 'It's so easy to believe what you want to be true. Everyone thought ... I think he even believed it himself...' I run out of voice, take a deep breath, begin again, for this is important. 'Remember, Margarethe, promises are as nothing if they are not made binding.'

When I say her name her expression changes to a mixture of relief and curiosity. She sits down on the edge of the bed, curiosity winning. 'What happened, Mutti?'

'With Jerome?' I feel a need to reassure her. 'It doesn't matter. Not anymore. It wasn't an end, though I thought it so at the time. It was a beginning' – I reach up to touch her cheek – 'of Martin, and of you.'

280

Chapter Thirty-Two
Wittenberg, Autumn 1524

'What devil would want to have her then? If she (Katie)
does not like him, she may have to wait a good while for
another one.'

Martin Luther

The harvest is past, the leaves beginning to curl and drop.
Nothing more has been said of Glatz, which gives me hope
that Herr Amsdorf's intervention on my behalf may have
been successful, but I don't know for sure and can't ask,
for he has been called to Magdeburg. It is a year now since
Jerome left, and in my head I know he isn't coming back,
that I must find some other future for myself, but in my
heart I'm not yet ready to accept it. Every time I bite into
an apple I think of him, as, laughing, he shook a branch
above my head, the blossom falling onto my shoulders,
and of how he picked off the petals one by one. Though
his touch was light, and his fingers didn't stray, even in
memory I can scarcely breathe. In church I hear his voice
in the singing of the hymns and see him haloed in light as

he steps forward to accept the sacraments. And when the rain comes to trap us indoors, I think of the window seat in the Reichenbachs' Stube and remember his teasing. I don't share my thoughts with anyone, for they are always tinged with guilt, my petty problem as nothing compared to those in the world at large.

Müntzer has been summoned to Wittenberg by the elector, to defend his inflammatory views, but has refused to come, insisting that his place is at Allstedt.

Dr Luther is incensed at his effrontery and thunders his opposition from the pulpit of our Town Church.

'It's as well it's solidly built,' Eva says, laughing, when we step out into the sunshine at the end of the service, 'else it might have collapsed under the weight of his oratory.'

'It's no laughing matter.' We turn to see Lucas immediately behind us, his expression sombre. 'There is word of trouble springing up in many areas and Müntzer at the heart of it. I fear where it will end.'

Barbara, who has lingered to ask of the health of one of the Cranachs' old retainers, catches up with us as we reach the corner of the Markt.

'Eva, Basilius. Why not dine with us today? We will all benefit from some cheery company, to drive away thought of the ills that surround us.'

It's easy to be cheerful in Eva's company, for however circumspectly she may behave in public, as befits a matron with a husband of some standing in the community, at home with the Cranachs her irrepressible nature reasserts itself, and she entertains us with the latest gossip, gleaned in the market, her mimicry of some of the stallholders and the women who try to get the better of them, perfect. Even Lucas, who can be somewhat straight-laced where

282

mockery, however gentle, is concerned, lets loose the occasional guffaw, grateful, as we all are, for Barbara's suggestion.

When it seems that Eva's anecdotes may be coming to an end, Basilius, with a glance towards Lucas, asks, 'May I mention the latest pamphlet?'

'Why not? It will be common knowledge soon enough.'

Barbara opens her mouth as if to protest at the introduction of business to our conversation, but Lucas holds up a hand, a mixture of pride and sorrow in his expression.

'This will interest you all, I promise you.'

'Another of Dr Luther's?' I ask.

'No...' Basilius has that same odd look, as if he isn't sure whether to be proud of the publication, or ashamed that it should be necessary. 'Florentina von Oberweimar has written her story, and Martin has asked that we print it along with an open letter to the Counts of Mansfeld.' He tightens his lips and I see that shame wins. 'It makes for sober reading.'

I think of Florentina, the latest escaped nun to seek sanctuary in Wittenberg – of how ill she looked when she first arrived from Eisleben and how she flinched when I went to help her remove her habit to replace it with one of Barbara's gowns. How she refused to meet my eyes and asked that I leave her to manage for herself. The glimpse I had of her emaciated arm as she took the dress from me, shocking. She has been the subject of much gossip and speculation, and it grieves me, for however much I wished that those in the town who are at the forefront of such things would divert their attentions from my concerns, I didn't wish it to be at the cost of further suffering for such as her. In her first days, Eva, who knows the family she is lodged with, reported that she perched on the edge of the chair, as if she were always on the verge of flight, and every time a door creaked behind her she startled at the noise like a frightened animal. It had taken weeks before her cheeks filled out and the dark circles around her eyes faded, and each time I saw her I ached for her and wished I could do something to speed her recovery.

Barbara, with characteristic sensitivity, decreed we must respect her desire for privacy until she felt ready for social contact. 'Exactly how much she has suffered we may never know, but we must pray that given time, and quiet, and God's help, she will be able to embrace this new life as you have done.'

Now it seems we *are* to know, as Eva, with the same mixture of pleasure and pain as Basilius and Lucas had displayed, takes up the story. 'I accompanied Florentina to the press last week, for she wanted to see how it was done, and though she betrayed some nervousness, no fear remained in her eyes.' For once Eva is entirely serious. 'Her freedom may be Luther's finest achievement.'

'She is doubly brave, first to suffer and then be willing to share her experience with the world.'

'She feels she owes it, Kat, to those who remain in convents, held against their will, and to God who saved her from that fate, and she says that if the publication will protect even one person from the abuse she experienced, it will be worthwhile.'

Afterwards, when we three take a stroll in the garden, while Lucas and Basilius are engaged in some further discussion of business, we return to the topic of Florentina's story.

Eva is once more serious and I see how deeply it has affected her, see also that she has a new capacity for compassion, a willingness to empathise that she once lacked, and I wonder if it is age, or maturity or marriage that has changed her, or simply Florentina.

Whatever the cause, there is no doubting her sincerity now. 'It shames me when I read her story, to think of how *we* agonised, how we feared what might happen to us, and thought ourselves ill-used.' Her tone becomes passionate. 'It was nothing, nothing compared to the cruelties she suffered: the privations, the beatings, the imprisonment...' She stops, and I see tears shining in her eyes. 'Do you pray for the abbess, Katharina, for your aunts and the kitcheness, that knew our intent and did not try to hinder us?' She pauses again. 'Since I have read Florentina's experience, I do. With thankfulness.'

We have reached the end of the garden and turn back. Ahead of us the house glows in the last of the sunshine, as Eva passes on another piece of news.

'You know that Karlstadt is heading for Basel?'

Barbara answers for both of us. 'So we heard, though it seems his route is somewhat roundabout.'

'Yes. And the word is that Anna and the child are not to join him until he is settled.'

'It will be children before long. Is there any word of how she fares?'

'Only that there are plenty in Orlamünde who are willing to support her for the sake of her husband.'

'Andreas was always popular, if nothing else.'

'What is Anna like?' I ask. 'We didn't have a chance to get to know her before they left.'

'You'd like her. Most folk did. And she was a good

foil for Andreas, in the home at least, providing a dose of common sense to moderate his eccentricities.'

We have reached the bench where we were sitting when Lucas brought the news of Karlstadt's banishment, and I see by the shadow that flits across Barbara's face that it is in her mind also.

As if to dismiss the thought, she says, 'At least she's safe and well-looked-after and will have support when the babe is born.'

There is a new light in Eva's eyes and a hint of a smile.

'Eva!' Barbara beams. 'You didn't say anything. When do you expect the birth to be?'

'In the spring. I wasn't sure until a week ago, and I'm still nervous about spreading the word lest something goes awry.'

'Does Basilius know?'

'I told him last night' – laughter bubbles up – 'he looked astonished, as if he had no idea how babies come about. But once he got over the shock he seemed pleased, though I'm beginning to think he may drive me mad with cosseting between now and May. This morning he asked if I was fit to come to church, if the walk wasn't too much for me.'

Barbara is laughing with her. 'It is a temporary aberration in most men at the first. You needn't worry. He'll be looking for his meal on the table as usual before you know.'

I feel excluded, envious, the loss of Jerome a pain that, though suppressed, is still there, and I look away, for I don't want to spoil Eva's moment and I fear that something of what I feel might be visible in my eyes.

'Katharina?' Eva is shaking my arm and I'm not sure

how much I have missed. 'Your turn will come. I know it will.'

I look at my feet, at the scuffed toe on my boot, and think of the cinder paths in the Reichenbachs' garden, but try to be matter of fact, to keep the despair from my voice. 'A year has past now and I've heard nothing.'

Her pressure on my arm increases, and though her words pain me, I love her for the intention behind them.

'There are other men, equally good, equally kind, Kat. Kinder, in fact, for he has not used you well.'

CHAPTER THIRTY-THREE
WITTENBERG, OCTOBER 1524

I am in my chamber when I hear voices in the hallway. Dr Luther's carries, as usual, but the others are indistinguishable murmurs. It is some time since Luther has come to the Cranachs' house, and the talk in the kitchens is that he is suffering from a depression brought on by the opposition he faced from Karlstadt's supporters on his preaching tour. I can well believe it, for when we see him in the pulpit, though his sermon is as lively as ever, he does not look well. His clothing too has an unkempt look about it, not merely threadbare, though it is that, but uncared for, and it reminds me of the sister at Brehna who fell into an illness of the mind and had to be forced to surrender her surplice for washing when the smell became obvious to even the least worldly-wise. I think him thinner also, his skin with a greyish tinge, and when I mention it to Barbara, she is convinced that with only the prior for company in the Black Cloister, they don't feed themselves properly.

Lucas agrees, but his reasoning is different. 'I don't think it is altogether by choice. There are financial problems: unpaid debts that can only be solved with the duke's intervention. Martin will not talk of it, but it's rumoured there are days when the pantry is bare.'

'Then we are also to blame that we do not insist he dine with us more frequently.'

'Believe me, Barbara, I've tried. But you know him. He will not be told what to do, and though pride is a sin he has preached against many times, he is not altogether free of it himself.'

Now, as Lucas welcomes him, I hope that his presence here is a sign that he is recovered, and if so, I will be glad of it for, abrupt as he can be, and on occasion outrageous in his pronouncements, he is a good man.

I'm about to go to join them, my hand already on the door, when Barbara appears in the doorway and motions me to a chair. I feel a tightness grip my chest and blurt out, 'He has not brought Glatz again?'

'Far from it. He has written to Jerome.'

My breathing shallows, colour flooding my neck and cheeks, and I'm not sure if that isn't almost as bad.

'It appears that Nicholas Amsdorf spoke of you before he left and didn't mince his words.'

'Dr Luther told you this?'

'Justus Jonas, actually, and with some relish, Martin's sheep-faced expression confirming every word. Apparently, Amsdorf called Glatz a "cheapskate" and "penny-pinching" and asked what the devil Martin was doing in trying to force you to marry him. It was a kind deed, and I suspect the reason that Martin determined to write to Jerome on your behalf, though how Nicholas came to know of the proposal is anybody's guess.'

I flush again, and her eyes widen. 'What made you

think of it, Kat? And how and when did you appeal to him?'

'When I refused Glatz I feared that Dr Luther was only biding his time and would press me to reconsider, despite that I knew both you and Lucas had spoken up for me. He isn't noted for changing his mind.'

'You're right about that. But why Amsdorf?'

'I thought if Dr Luther would listen to anyone it would be him. There was a disputation at the university and afterwards I remained behind to speak to him alone. He was very...' I was picking through my mind searching for the most appropriate word, when she finished the sentence for me.

'Understanding?'

'Yes. And kind.'

'We have always found him so. He is a good man and Magdeburg is fortunate to get him.'

'When he left, although I'd had his promise, I'd no idea whether he'd had an opportunity to speak for me or not. I hoped he had, but when nothing was said I couldn't be sure.'

'Well, you can be sure now. And as for Jerome, perhaps something will come of Martin's intervention.'

'I'm not sure I want to have Dr Luther begging on my behalf.'

'You would have been happy to have Philipp Reichenbach write to the Baumgartners a year ago, why not Martin now?'

'To Jerome's parents at the time, yes. But after so long and to Jerome himself ... I don't know.'

'Think well of Martin, Kat. In the midst of his own ills, he has thought on yours and taken steps to try to help.

It is a compliment.'

'Or perhaps since my refusal of Glatz he despairs of his responsibility for me ever coming to an end.'

She doesn't contradict me, and I wonder if privately she shares his pessimism at my prospects, but if so, she doesn't admit to it.

'At least this should settle the matter. If Jerome will not respond to Martin, then you will know you must look elsewhere.'

When I still say nothing, she presses my hand. 'One way or another, Kat, this will be for the best, believe me.'

'I am grateful to him' – I take a deep breath – 'but I don't know if I can come down just now. I wouldn't know whether to speak of it, or...'

'He does not expect your thanks. Indeed, when I said I would tell you, he expressly asked that nothing more be said, which was probably as much a command to Justus as to anyone else. So you can join us without embarrassment. No doubt you may feel it a little awkward, but if do not you meet him now, the next time will be harder. Besides, with Katherine and Justus also here, you need not fear to be the focus of attention.'

She's right. To begin with the talk is all of the university, of Melanchthon's increased salary, of how he has been persuaded, somewhat against his will, to concentrate on the teaching of Greek.

Even though I hadn't intended to draw any attention to myself, I cannot stop myself asking Luther, 'Is that so necessary, now that we have your translation of the New Testament?'

He looks at me, a quizzical expression in his eyes, as if he isn't sure what to make of my obvious interest in intellectual matters, and I can't tell whether he approves or disapproves. 'Even more so.' The corner of his mouth lifts. 'I can hardly deny the infallibility of the Pope and claim it for myself.'

At the far end of the table Jonas coughs into his napkin, and I suspect he's smothering a laugh. Dr Luther's self-deprecating humour is an endearing facet of his character that few outside the circle of his closest friends are aware of, and I feel privileged to see it.

He glances at Jonas, then back to me, his face serious once more. 'I think it a healthy thing for any pastor to be able to read the Scriptures in the original tongue.'

Katherine Jonas, in a transparent attempt to turn the conversation to lighter matters, as if she has enough of theology at home, asks of Lucas' latest portrait, and comments on how she has heard young Lucas shows talent and is set fair to follow in his father's footsteps.

'We need have no fear that portraiture will die with this Lucas,' Barbara begins, her voice drowned out by the general laughter at her husband's expression and his,

'I had not thought you so ready to be rid of me.'

'I wasn't...'

Lucas rests his hand for a moment on her shoulder, his smile wide. 'I know,' he says, and watching them, I wonder if I will ever be blessed with an easy companionship such as theirs. Jonas enquires of Lucas' expanding business interests, and how he means to juggle his time between painting and printing and the pharmacy, and I subside into my own thoughts until the mention of Basilius catches my attention.

'He is a good man and I am fortunate to have him.' Lucas stretches back and places his hands behind his head. 'I can safely leave the pharmacy in his hands. He has a natural talent for it, an instinct for delving to the root of an ill and prescribing accordingly. It was a good day when I took him on as an apprentice.'

'And Eva?' Katherine Jonas looks at Barbara. 'How is her pregnancy progressing?'

'Well, so far as we know. At any rate she seems to be blooming and Basilius to have realised that her condition is a natural thing – that she can be allowed to go to the shops as usual, without requiring a cart to carry her.'

We all laugh again, and as the conversation drifts, with no reference to me, or my concerns, I relax and begin to be grateful to Luther that he has put himself out on my behalf. And to hope, foolish or not, that it might make a difference.

Afterwards, when the others have gone and Lucas, Barbara and I are sitting in the Stube, the candles flickering, Lucas says, 'I forgot to tell you, we've been granted our wish, or answer to prayer if you prefer. Glatz shouldn't trouble us any longer, for Orlamünde is his.'

I cannot hide my relief. 'Dr Luther's change of heart or not, I'm glad to see him go, for I would not be able to meet him, even in passing, without feeling a revulsion that would be difficult to hide.'

Barbara smiles at me. 'Well, he's gone now, and you needn't think on him anymore.'

Chapter Thirty-Four
Wittenberg, November 1524

I have had my answer. Or rather a lack of one, which comes to the same thing. Barbara passes on Dr Luther's message and I'm glad I don't have the embarrassment of hearing him tell me himself. It is hard enough to see the sympathy in her eyes and in Lucas' also when he appears for the evening meal. 'It has been a grave disappointment to Martin, for I know he hoped for better of Jerome. To be dissuaded from his original intent, by filial duty as we must assume, is one thing, and that perhaps could be forgiven, but not even to write to explain is something else.'

'Perhaps Herr Reichenbach was right and I should not have looked so high.'

There is an edge of anger in Barbara's voice. 'Think rather that Jerome should not have trifled with your affections. If there is blame to be apportioned it is his. You were unschooled in such matters, without brother or father to protect you, and therefore vulnerable to his advances. He should have been mature enough both to know his family's feelings and to have considered them from the start.'

I think of Philipp Reichenbach's assessment of my marriage prospects and try to make a joke of them. 'Are there any widowers of your acquaintance with five children to their credit, or must I look further afield?'

Barbara remains serious. 'I hope we may do better for you than that, for you have time yet to have five children of your own.'

Autumn has faded to a winter grey when Eva hurries into the Stube without removing her cloak and comes straight to me.

'I didn't want you to hear on the street, Kat. Jerome is to be made a councillor in Nuremberg, which perhaps...'

I finish her sentence. 'Makes me all the less suitable for him.'

She squeezes my arm. 'You know I don't believe that, Kat. He should have been proud to have you at his side, but his parents never had the opportunity to meet you and so may have been swayed by what others might think. But that doesn't excuse him. If he values public opinion more than you, he's a fool.'

'How did you...?'

'I had it from Basilius, and he from Justus Jonas, who came looking for some medicines for his wife. Apparently a new student has come from Nuremberg, and knowing that Jerome studied here, mentioned him in passing, as someone Jonas might be expected to have an interest in. The Nurembergers consider Jerome a popular and worthy choice.' She tosses her head. 'If I had heard it face to face

I would have been sorely tempted to set him straight.'

I hug her, grateful for her loyalty, but say, 'Please, Eva, I need to think well of him. It is hard enough to have my hopes dashed, but to have my memory of him tainted also, that would make it harder to bear, not easier.'

She hugs me back. 'Oh, Kat.' I hear the break in her voice and know there is something more. I don't want to hear it, but I know I must.

'He's married?'

'Not yet, but there is a rumour that his parents have chosen a bride for him, that the engagement may be announced soon.'

I cannot avoid the bitterness that creeps into my voice. 'No doubt she is young and beautiful and wealthy, everything I am not.'

'As to beautiful' – Eva makes a face – 'I've no idea, but she is only fourteen and an heiress. I imagine that is what counts most.' The vehemence is back in her voice. 'I hope he comes to recognise what he has lost and regret his choice.'

Barbara, when she hears the news, expresses her sympathy not in words, but in the gift of another gown, in deep olive, the wide skirt falling in soft pleats. The bodice and sleeves are trimmed in black velvet, the central inset of fine muslin, criss-crossed with ribbons below a coloured band. I feel a prickling sensation behind my eyes as she holds it up against me, my gratitude tinged with guilt because of the dress I haven't worn since Glatz' proposal. 'I can't take this, it is…'

She shakes out the skirt, lays it on the bed, and her voice is firm. 'I want you to have it. Sometimes if we are well presented on the outside, it makes it easier to conceal what we feel inside. Besides, the colour will suit you better than it ever did me.' She darts a glance at my face. 'I want you to be able to hold your head up high, Katharina, whatever gossip may make of your situation.'

Her kindness is almost my undoing, and I brush at my cheeks with the backs of my hands.

She passes me a handkerchief. 'We have guests tonight: the Jonases, Melanchthon and Martin, fresh from Hans Löser's wedding. Wear the dress.'

My instinct is to refuse, for it raises a difficult memory, of similar pressure from Elsa Reichenbach on the night that Jerome arrived, and I'm not sure if I can cope with sympathy.

Barbara holds up her hand to stop me saying anything. 'You cannot hide away, Katharina, and it will do no harm to look your best. Perhaps if you look it, no one will stop to think of how you might feel.'

I run my hand down the velvet trim, the nap springing under my fingers and focus on pleasing her, for I know she has the best of intentions, and perhaps she is right. Perhaps pretending an indifference to Jerome and acting as if the latest news affects me not at all will make it so. As I change out of the plain workaday gown, I try to convince myself that to forget him will bring relief, that I will no longer need to feel my heart thudding in my chest at every knock on the door, or turn my head in hope every time I hear horse's hooves on the cobbles behind me. I brush my hair, smoothing it back beneath the matching net, pull the sleeves down to cover my wrists, and prepare to meet the company.

I am not prepared for Glatz. Barbara turns as I enter the Stube, signalling an apology with her eyes. She hurries across, whispers in my ear, 'I don't know what Martin is thinking of. If I had known Glatz was in Wittenberg, I would have ensured that our invitation stretched no further than those of our own choosing.'

There is a leaden feeling in the pit of my stomach, but for Barbara's sake I try to make light of it. 'It's all right. It's months since he was last here. No doubt someone else will have taken his attention by now.' Whether they have or not, he is clearly intent on embarrassing me, malice sparking in his eyes as they meet mine. In the Stube Barbara directs him to a seat as far away from me as possible, but he ignores her gesture, making a point of coming to stand over my chair.

I detect the relish in his voice.

'Fraulein von Bora, I hear you have had a disappointment and are suffering somewhat.'

I look at Jonas and Melanchthon and Luther, wondering which one of them has made me the subject of gossip. Common sense compels me to accept it may be none of them, but that thought is even less comfortable and I wonder if Barbara has heard anything, if her mention of gossip when she brought me the dress was more than a general comment. Melanchthon, however, avoids my gaze and, convinced that I have him to thank for Glatz' glee, I feel a surge of anger. What right has he to talk of me?

Barbara is also watching him, and I bless her as she wrong-foots both of them. 'We all suffer when the weather is inclement, do we not? Fraulein von Bora no more than the rest of us. Is that not right, Philipp?'

Katherine Jonas backs her up. 'I for one will be glad when the spring comes, for' – she looks towards the

window, to the storm clouds scudding across the sky –
'wind and rain both can be depressing.'

'Indeed.' Justus Jonas nods an encouragement at his
wife, as if he too is aware of the undercurrent of the
conversation, and I'm grateful that he changes the subject,
directing attention away from me and onto their recent
journey.

'And inconvenient also, as we found to our cost. It
was not the pleasantest of journeys to Pretzsch. Had it
not been that Martin was to officiate for the nuptials, we
might not have gone at all.'

Barbara is quick to follow his lead. 'I trust everything
went well, even though the weather wasn't kind.'

'Löser is thoroughly married, Martin saw to that, and
despite the weather, the festivities were enjoyed by all.'

There is a mischievous glint in Barbara's eye as she
turns to Luther.

'I hear Argula Grumbach has been challenging *you*
to practise what you preach. Will it be your marriage we
hear of next?'

He is abrupt. 'I told her no. As I have told many others
before.'

Katherine Jonas looks at her husband, her hand straying
into his, a smile curving her mouth. 'Why not, there are
plenty of your acquaintance who can recommend it.'

He smiles at her, as he might at a child, but brushes
her comment aside with, 'I told her no, not because I am
a sexless log or stone, but because it doesn't seem fitting
to expect a wife to live daily with the threat of death, as
I must.'

I begin to feel a fellow sympathy for him, as Katharine
refuses to be diverted.

'If we were all to follow your lead, the world would soon be empty. And have you not taught us to live as if each day is our last, remembering our Lord may return at any moment?'

Looking at the dust that lies in the creases of his new coat, I can think of another argument she could put to him, but any topic to do with marriage is too close to home for me to risk commenting. I look at Barbara to see if she will continue the conversation, but Glatz, his eyes fixed on me, says, 'You have time yet, Herr Doctor. A man may marry at any age, while a woman, if she does not grasp an opportunity that presents itself, may come to regret it when she finds no one else wants her.'

Colour flares in my face, but though I would have run away when first I saw that Glatz was of the company, now that he has targeted his spite directly at me, I am determined not to be cowed by him. I sit up straighter, tilt my chin. 'Better to remain single than be forced into a marriage without inclination.'

His scorn is evident. 'And poverty with it?'

Barbara's anger on my behalf is unmistakeable. 'We value our friends, married or single, moneyed or not. Our house is always open to *them*.' She faces Glatz down. 'And while we have guilder to spare, none of them will go hungry.' She waves her hand towards Luther. 'As the good doctor can testify.'

Luther is regarding Glatz with distaste. 'Indeed. Without the Cranachs' hospitality, I would often have suffered.'

There is an uncomfortable silence, broken by Justus Jonas, who glances towards the window and brings the conversation back to the weather, the pucker of his

300

brow showing that, aside from sympathy for me, there is something else on his mind.

'Look at the sky, how dark it grows. While we do not wish for ill weather, it might serve us all if the storms were to continue for a month or two more.'

Lucas clearly knows what concerns him and picks up the thread. 'The unrest in the countryside is increasing?'

'Fifty-fold.'

Katherine Jonas shakes her head at her husband, as if to try to halt him, but he continues.

'Müntzer claims he has ten thousand of the true elect ready to answer his call to arms. He is the new darling of the masses, and if his teachings take hold…'

Luther is emphatic. 'The peasantry have been ill-used, of that there is no doubt, but there must be a better way to solve the problem. Someone who could speak *for* them, not rouse them to insurrection.'

Silence falls around the table again and I suspect most of us are thinking the same thing – if anyone could speak for the peasants it would be Luther, though no one has the courage to suggest it.

They all leave together, Glatz' pressure on my fingers too firm for comfort and I am certain he means to hurt. I snatch back my hand and see the mockery in his eyes as he bids me goodbye.

Dr Luther's eyes narrow, his gaze flicking from Glatz to me, to the Cranachs, and back again to me, and for the first time I sense an undercurrent of understanding as he says, 'Pastor Glatz returns to Orlamünde tomorrow. No doubt you will all wish to give him Godspeed.'

I keep my voice to a suitable murmur, though I'd like to shout my satisfaction from the rafters.

Afterwards, Barbara says, 'You did well tonight. The next time will be easier, and the next again, easier still.'

'When I saw Glatz... If I had to suffer his attentions again...'

She puts her arm around my shoulder. 'We all saw the way he baited you, Martin included. I don't think you need fear that there'll be any more encouragement in that quarter. And his absence, at least, will be something to be thankful for.'

Torgau: 1552

I cannot sleep. I am too hot, sweat beading on my forehead and trickling between my breasts, my nightgown sticking to me, yet when I push back the covers I begin to shiver, the moisture on my skin suddenly cold. I pull the blanket up to my chin and tuck it around my neck, thrust it away again, tug it back. I wish Margarethe was here. She might be able to help me escape this round of hot and cold, hot and cold.

Someone has left a pitcher and a tumbler by the side of the bed and I inch towards it. If it is ale, it will likely be weak and flat, but perhaps it may assuage my constant thirst. I can move a little now without feeling as if someone is thrusting a dagger into my thigh, so perhaps it won't be long until I'm up and about again. I hope so, for I am ready to go home. I will be better in my own place and with my friends around me. I miss Martin and fear for what he might say or do when I am not there to moderate his outpourings.

The door opens and Margarethe appears, candle in hand. She sets it on the windowsill and leans over the bed, her unbound hair brushing my cheek. I smell chamomile and smile at her, reaching up to tug on a curl, pleased that she remembers what I have said. That it will bring out the auburn in it and give it a shine, for she will shortly need a husband. Her hair is Martin's, wiry and hard to control, a matter of regret to her. But as it tumbles on her shoulders I think it a pity that convention rules she must imprison it in a cap, for if a young man could only see it now…

She tucks it behind her ear. 'What is it, Mutti? You called.'

I don't think I did, but we have had that argument before and it seemed to upset her, so I don't protest. I think I must go home tomorrow, your father will need me.'

Her tongue flicks across her lips. 'You are not yet fit, Mutti, the doctor…'

'When I am back in Wittenberg I can see my own doctor.'

'He's here, Mutti. Don't you remember?'

'Here? In this house? Why? I do not require constant supervision.'

'He came with the university, as we did, and likewise lodges with Frau Karsdörfer.'

'The university is here? Where's your father then … Paul, young Martin?'

She allows her hair to fall over her face, and I think it is to hide her expression for she only partly answers my question. 'Paul will be here later.'

'Then he can take me home.' I wave at the covers. 'I know my leg is not yet strong enough for me to drive, but Paul is quite competent.'

'Wouldn't you rather rest awhile longer? Until your' – again the slight hesitation – *'leg is fully recovered?'*

Outside, rain begins to fall, hammering against the shutters and drumming on the roof tiles above our heads. She draws a deep breath. 'It is not the weather for travelling. They said there was a storm coming…'

I nod. 'There was.' And it touched us all, Martin more than most, for the man who caused it had once been his protégé.

CHAPTER THIRTY-FIVE
WITTENBERG, APRIL - MAY 1525

'If anyone thinks this is too harsh, remember that
rebellion is intolerable and that the destruction of the
world is to be expected every hour.'

Martin Luther

The arrival of spring is not the joyous thing we might
have hoped. The sporadic rumblings of discontent that
have troubled the countryside all winter become a forest
fire fanned into flame by Müntzer. He abuses his position
in the pulpit to call the elect to arms, his words reported
everywhere, the fear that follows them palpable, for
his interpretation of the elect is restricted to those who
accept his narrow view of religion and of the world,
everyone else deserving of death. I hear them first as I
cross the Markt, heading to the Bugenhagens' house with
a message from Barbara. The man who stands on the front
step of the Rathaus, his fist raised to the sky, is unkempt,
his legs bowed, his hair hanging in thin grey trails like
damp string. Spittle flies from his mouth as he harangues

the crowd that has gathered to listen to him.

'Pity not the Godless when they cry. Remember the command to Moses to destroy utterly and show no mercy!' He pauses as if to regather his breath, his vehemence intensified. 'Your rulers have perverted justice – cast them down! May their carcasses be devoured by the birds of the air.'

I do not want to listen, his vehemence sending shivers through me, and yet, I'm powerless to move on, until he is bundled away by Philipp Reichenbach and another official who grab one arm each and drag him down from the step and around the building to the rear. He does not go quietly, continuing to scream his invective, adding the Wittenberg town council to his list of those who must be cut down, and calling on us to rise up in his defence. It is a relief to see that no one responds to his plea, and as the crowd begin to disperse, it's clear from their muttered comments that they are less interested in the fate of the man than the implications of his message for our own town, and for Torgau, and Duke Frederick.

It is the question in everyone's mind, the opening of every conversation. 'If a mob comes, will we be able to stand against it? Will he?' The duke's health is failing, his resolve to challenge Müntzer rumoured as doubtful, which makes it a concern for us all as word comes of lootings and burnings, violence and destruction on every side. And though it hasn't yet touched Wittenberg, we hear of castles and cloisters in other places reduced to rubble, and visitors who come to the town talk of columns of acrid smoke blackening the sky and blotting out the sun as if there were an eclipse.

Luther loses no time, writing both to the leaders of the

insurrection and to the princes. To the rebels he makes this plea:

Be ye in the right as ye may, yet it becomes no Christians to quarrel and fight, but to suffer wrong and to bear evil.

To the nobles he is equally blunt:

You have none but yourselves to thank for these disorders, for you live in grandeur, while robbing your subjects.

Duke Frederick accepts Luther's criticisms and speaks of 'just occasion' and 'wrongs done', but adopts a fatalistic approach, leaving the outcome to God. Spalatin sends word from Torgau that Frederick has written to his brother, Duke John, *If it be God's will, the common man will come to rule, but if not, we need not fear.*

I cannot help thinking that his attitude is more a reflection of his own state of mind than of serious consideration and say so to Lucas. 'Everyone knows he is dying, and no doubt he has a desire to go to God with a clear conscience, confessing his sins, but to do nothing to suppress the unrest is surely folly.'

'Duke John agrees with you. As I do, along with every thinking man in this town. We may trust his approach is more effective.'

'What has he done?'

'He has yielded the right to collect tithes to the peasants, but I wouldn't wager on it being enough to satisfy.'

His doubt proves accurate, for Müntzer is contemptuous of Duke John's efforts, considering them as no more than crumbs tossed from the master's table. And for Müntzer's followers also it is too little, too late, the carnage continuing.

307

A flurry of pamphlets and cartoons appear: peasants swearing allegiance to the Bund; peasants attacking and successfully plundering a cloister. Some feature Luther: those put out by Catholic sympathisers showing him instructing the peasants, or putting on armour to rise up with them; those that come from Müntzer's party deriding him as double-tongued.

'He cannot win,' Lucas says. 'The Church considers him the root cause of it all, and in favour of the uprising, and with some justice, for there are many Lutheran priests to be found among the peasant forces. Yet the peasants see him as their enemy, and that also with justice, for he is vocal in his condemnation of violence.'

'Where will it end?' I ask, when word of a particularly cruel sacking of a convent emerges.

'There will not be an end until one side is victorious, and only God knows how many will die first.' There are new lines on Lucas' face, and I think of how much the unrest affects us all, despite that thus far we have been spared the terror.

A tract appears, entitled the *Twelve Articles*, setting out the peasants' demands, and with it a rumour that they hope Luther will negotiate with the princes on their behalf.

'And will he?' I ask Lucas.

'He agrees with most of what is in the tract. In fact' – there is a ghost of a smile on his face – 'he could almost have written it himself. But they have moved far beyond what he will support, for he has always believed violence to be unbiblical and he will not change now.'

'He will do something, though?'

'He has been invited to dedicate a school at Eisleben and will follow it with a preaching tour thereafter. It's his way of attempting to calm the situation.'

'Will the people listen?'

'We may pray they do, for all our sakes. If the wind were to blow in our direction…' His gaze rests on Barbara, and in my head I fill in what he does not say – that a mob cannot be contained. And women especially to fear.

At first the news that filters back is hopeful, for Luther is well received, not only in in Eisleben, which is to be expected, but in Stolberg also, where, despite it being Müntzer's birthplace, the town council honours him with gifts of wine and Einbeck beer. But our relief is short-lived, for in many places, where before he was lauded, now he is jeered and jostled on the streets. From some towns he is forced to flee under the cover of darkness, while in others, when he climbs into the pulpit, opponents ring the church bells throughout his sermon to drown him out.

Lucas' mouth is set in a grim line when he brings the news. 'It seems his life is in danger, not just from the Church, which has long hated him, but from the very people he yearned to set free.'

It is the first time he has been openly vilified by ordinary folk, and it seems that it has hit him hard, for though he continues to travel from village to village, preaching conciliation, those with him who send word back to Wittenberg talk of how he scarcely eats or sleeps, and that they worry for his health.

There is worse news to come. Word filters back of an Easter service disrupted by a mob that dragged out a nobleman and his followers and struck them down, the street running with blood.

I fling aside the collar I have been working on. 'How

309

can they make any claim to faith and do such things?'

Lucas shakes his head. 'Religion is a powerful weapon, and it can be used to whip up anyone who thinks themselves ill-used.'

'But can they not see the wrong in such an action?'

'A mob sees nothing but their own desires, and if they can be convinced they have right on their side, then the evil acts they do are justified by the good that will come as a result.'

'What good can come of defiling an Easter service?'

'They have rid the world of an oppressor, or so they see it. And thus a fitting way to celebrate the new beginning that Easter promises.'

Barbara has also set her sewing aside. 'And the implications for us?'

'We have a castle and a duke.'

He doesn't need to say any more, the inference clear. I pick up the collar from the floor and rub it against my skirt, trying to remove the dust mark, but succeed only in smearing. I cast a glance of apology at Barbara, who shrugs.

'It doesn't matter. A soiled collar may be the least of our problems soon.'

It seems she may be right, when two days later she returns from the market with the tale of the murder of the Count Ludwig von Helfenstein at Weinsberg.

'It seems he and some of his soldiers were cut down outside the garrison and stabbed to death, and another twenty-four nobles and their servants who had gathered for the celebration there were stripped naked and made to run a gauntlet of lances, their bloodied corpses dumped in a field as carrion for the crows.' She is picking at the

310

edge of her nail, refusing to meet my eyes. 'Although it is a distance away, the ripples of fear that the report has brought have spread through the university and the town, casting a pall of gloom over the entire marketplace.'

But just as the council prepares for an attack here, there is the prospect of respite, Luther writing jubilantly to the Jonases of a peace treaty signed at Easter between the Swabian League and the leaders of the peasants. And whether it is as a result of the events at Weinsberg, or in spite of them, he sees it as a sign that the worst may be over. Justus and Katherine bring the letter to us, the closing sentence a sentiment we all share.

We should fall on our knees and thank God for it, and pray that their good sense will prevail in our area too.

Barbara asks, 'Will Martin return to Wittenberg now?'

'I'm not sure.' Justus taps the letter. 'However pleased he is at this development, there is no indication that he thinks his work done, and he will not stop until he does.'

Barbara is unexpectedly vehement. 'He will be of no use to the Reformation dead. I hope what he does now won't be at the expense of his own health.'

'You know he thinks little of himself, and there is no one dare tell him otherwise.'

'Argula Grumbach was right. He should marry. A wife might be able to make him see sense.'

Justus laughs. 'I doubt it, or at least it would take a very strong woman to try.'

Unbidden, a thought flits through my mind and is as quickly dismissed.

⬡⬡⬡

It isn't the advice of friends, nor any concern for himself that brings Luther back to Wittenberg, but Duke Frederick. Though his hunting days are long gone, he is at the lodge at Lochau, and the word that comes back is that the physicians have come to the end of all they can do, that it is in God's hands now. But it isn't until Spalatin informs Melanchthon that Luther has been sent for that we know Frederick's death cannot be long delayed. Barbara shakes out her mourning gown, and regarding it critically she decides that it requires only minor repair. Brushing aside my protests, she orders a new one for me from the seamstress, saying, 'No doubt there will be a flurry of orders when the time comes. We will do well to get in ahead of them.'

The end comes more quickly than anticipated, Luther arriving too late to see him alive, and it's clear that though they had never spoken during Frederick's lifetime, his death touches Luther like that of an old friend. Lochau is some fifty miles south of Wittenberg, and the duke's journey home takes four days. Those who ride in advance speak of the clamour of bells in every town and village and of how many throng the streets as the bier carrying the body passes through.

'He was much loved,' Barbara says, smoothing down the nap of her black velvet gown, and well named. Though Duke John is reputed to be a fine man also, Frederick the Wise will be much missed.'

I think of Duke George, another kind of character altogether, and of how when his time comes I won't be there to see it, despite that by birth I am a Meissner and his subject, for he is no friend to the Reformation. And for the first time in perhaps a year, I think again of Lippendorf and of home.

Barbara, as if she can read my mind, says, 'There is no use fretting over what cannot be mended. This is your place now, Katharina, and our house yours. You know that.'

I smile at her. 'I know. But death has a way of raising memories, and I wish…'

'You will see your brothers again one day. I'm sure of it.'

I'm not, but I thrust that thought away, for I owe so much to the Cranachs that they deserve my gratitude without reservation.

Our duke is brought into Wittenberg with due ceremony, every church bell ringing out to alert the townsfolk as the cortège approaches. Lucas has a part in the proceedings, and despite that we know all that is to happen, when we see the procession I find I am both unprepared for and unexpectedly moved by it. I wait with Barbara by the entrance of the Castle Church, as the bier, supported on the shoulders of eight nobles and flanked by twenty men carrying flaming torches and the coat of arms of the Electorate of Saxony, comes into sight, and find myself praying as they process towards the steps that there will be no mishap. The cortège, followed by a succession of dignitaries and prominent residents, passes through the door and comes to a halt in the centre of the nave. Outside, as the bells continue to ring, the timing slightly off, Lucas and another of the councillors distribute coins to the poor of the parish in the duke's honour. I cannot help but smile when I notice an urchin, with a face scrubbed clean like an angel, who, receiving one coin, dives and ducks through the crowd to emerge on the other side and line up

313

again to receive another, his air of innocence protecting him from suspicion. Once the distribution is done, they enter the church, at the head of those of us privileged to have a place within, silence settling over the congregation as the ceremony begins. I have been at only two funerals since the death of my mother and this is a very different experience. Sad yes, but brimful of hope as well and a celebration of the duke's life as well as a commemoration of his death.

At the duke's request, Luther and Philipp Melanchthon have organised the entire proceeding, both today's event and the burial to follow on the morrow. I listen to the hymns and psalms echoing around the rafters and have to concentrate hard to understand Melanchthon's address, for my Latin has become somewhat rusty since leaving the convent, so that it's a relief to find when Luther ascends into the pulpit to deliver his sermon, proclaiming confidence in the resurrection, that it's in German.

The congregation files out, the sound of their footsteps on the flags magnified in the silence. As each person pauses by the bier to make their last personal obeisance to the duke, I see that Barbara is right, for many faces bear the trace of tears. We are the last to leave, and I look back at the sentinels who will guard the corpse until the morning, the silence absolute as Lucas pulls the door shut behind us.

We are up before six the following day, the air crisp and cold, our breath spiralling upwards as we walk to the church to the sound of the bells summoning us to the Office of Matins that is to precede the burial. There is no Mass, and no funeral vestments, Dr Luther preaching again, concluding his sermon with a personal eulogy.

'He was a good man and has been a good friend to the Reformation.' He pauses, and I see his throat move, as if he has difficulty swallowing. 'He was a good man,' he repeats, 'and I have no doubt that he has been received into his rest.'

We watch as the body is lowered into the grave dug beside the altar, while the choir sings *Shall we receive good at the hand of God and not ill*, the words carrying a personal resonance for me and a final acceptance of Jerome's defection.

As we walk back towards the house, I say to Lucas, 'For someone who didn't publicly embrace the new religion, this was an unusual send-off.'

'I imagine privately it was a different story.'

'Why then didn't he come out in favour of Reformation?'

'I think he may have been like the rich young ruler.'

'Who went away sad for he had many possessions?'

'Yes. Only in the duke's case it was likely his many relics he couldn't bring himself to discard. We may trust that God won't hold it against him, for, like Martin, I'm confident the truth was in him. If it was not, he wouldn't have protected Martin all these years, nor instructed that he and Melanchthon preach at his funeral.'

The duke's death has hit the whole town hard, the atmosphere in the market subdued, the talk of the unusual ceremony displacing any wider concerns. There are some who, despite their professing of the new religion, seem to find it difficult, and yearn for the familiarity of the old ways to lend them comfort. It's several days before normality reasserts itself, signalled by the gradual return of the buzz and chatter of the stallholders. It seems that Luther has been affected more than might have been expected, considering the sermons he preached, for following the funeral he retreats into the Black Cloister for three days and refuses all invitations.

As he climbs into the pulpit on the following Sunday, I'm once more shocked at his appearance and turn to look at Barbara for her reaction. It's obvious that she shares my concern, and as he passes us at the end of the service we both take a closer look and find him even more worrying at close quarters.

Once he is out of earshot, Barbara says, her thoughts echoing mine, 'Did you see the colour of his skin and how hollow his cheeks are. He was suffering already as a result of the preaching tour, but I suspect he hasn't been eating since he came home either.' She straightens her shoulders, as she always does when she is determined on something. 'If he persists in closing himself away and will not come to us, we must send food to him, else he'll shortly be no more than a shadow.'

'I'll take it,' I say. 'I owe him a debt that I've never had a chance to repay.'

We fill a basket with soups and bread and meat and cheeses and I walk through the town to the Black Cloister. I haven't been there since our first days in Wittenberg, and though it had been almost empty of inhabitants then, there had been a recent exodus, the atmosphere of community still apparent. Now, almost two years on, the building has a desolate, uncared-for air, and I feel a pang that a building so fine should be allowed to fall into disrepair.

Prior Brisger, the last of the brothers to remain in the Black Cloister with Dr Luther, meets me at the door and, taking the basket from me, expresses his thanks. 'Tell Mistress Cranach her concern is appreciated, and I will do my best to see that Dr Luther will eat, but' – his shrug is eloquent – 'I cannot force him.' As I turn for home I pause to look back at the peeling paintwork and the weeds sprouting though the cobbles and, chiding myself for thinking more of the building than the man, send up a prayer for Luther himself. It is the first time in my life I have prayed on impulse, and without thought either for the words I use, or where I am, and it is a moment of revelation, a long-delayed answer to Eva's childish question all those years ago, 'What difference should it make *when* we pray?' And with it comes a new-found realisation that God is indeed always listening.

CHAPTER THIRTY-SIX
WITTENBERG, MAY 1525

The duke is barely laid to rest before the violence escalates, the peasant hordes on the move once more, not only in the Rhineland this time, but in all of Thuringia and Saxony also. Increasingly out of control, they sweep through towns and villages in a frenzy of burning and butchering, thieving and slaughter, leaving devastation in their wake. At the root of it Müntzer, thundering from the pulpit at Mühlhausen, his words spreading like a canker. 'It is time! At them and at them while the fire is hot. Do not be moved to pity, nor sheath your sword. Throw their tower to the ground...'

Lucas brings a pamphlet home and flings it on the table, the lines on his face deeper than before. Barbara, with a glance at his expression, pours him a drink and he tosses it back as if he were a drunkard in an alehouse instead of a respectable burgess in his own home. I expect a reaction, but she takes the tankard from him and refills it without comment. He drains it a second time and a third, then sets it down, shaking his head to indicate he doesn't want any more. I share both her relief and her apprehension, for there must be ill news indeed to disturb him so. He throws himself into a chair, Barbara moving beside him to rest one hand on his shoulder.

He looks up and covers her hand with his, but he doesn't smile. 'Mansfeld is in an uproar, and it's rumoured almost the entire town has been set alight.'

I don't understand the special significance, until Barbara, tightening her grip on Lucas' shoulder, asks, 'Does Martin know? Is there word of his family?'

'He knows. And according to Brisger, as soon as the word reached him he shut himself in his study, locking the door, the only sound to be heard the scratch of his quill.' He gestures towards the paper on the table. 'I suspect he pens an answer to this foul tract and he'll appear when he's finished and not before.'

'And how long might that be?' Barbara's concern blends into irritation. 'If he does not have a death wish, he certainly acts like it.'

Thinking of my own family, at a distance and with no way of knowing how they fare, my sympathies are with Luther. 'His family are in Mansfeld? Then you cannot blame him for being driven to respond. No doubt he hopes to calm things.'

Lucas turns towards me. 'I wouldn't blame him, Katharina, whether his family were there or not, for we all share his worry at the evil Müntzer is fomenting. But it isn't his intention that concerns me, but what he may write, for words flow from him like a river in spate, and the more furious he is, the faster they flow, and the less reasoned they are.'

'And you will have the printing of them?'

'In all likelihood, yes. But that isn't the issue. It's

the effect they might have. To fan the flames rather than douse them.'

'Will he not allow someone to look them over?'

For the first time since his arrival there is a glimmer of a smile. 'What do you think?'

I think of how passionate Dr Luther is when he preaches, how vigorously he argues a point, how his eyes flash fire … and how unwilling he is to back down or change tack. 'What I have written, I have written?'

'Exactly. Though' – again there is a hint of a smile – 'I don't imagine he would appreciate the comparison with Pilate.'

I flush. 'I didn't…'

Barbara shakes her head at Lucas. 'It's all right, Kat, he'll never know you said it.' Then, serious again, 'Is there a special reason to fear his rhetoric this time?'

He shrugs. 'Aside from the risk to his family, which will touch him deeply, many of the towns and villages caught up in the current unrest are those in which he preached conciliation only last month. He will not admit to it, but this will feel like a betrayal, and I fear he'll react accordingly.'

And so it proves. He emerges from his seclusion with a new tract, which Brisger says was written in the space of two hours. It includes an admonition to the princes, *A Christian ruler should indeed search his heart and exceed his duty in offering terms, for the demands of the peasants for redress for their grievances are fair and just*… but for the most part it is a virulent diatribe against the rebels, and it is this that both sides fasten on. Duke George, who has never supported the Reformation, is more than ready to act on Luther's words now that they are in accord with his own inclination, Philip of Hesse also, while Müntzer denounces Luther as a pawn of the nobles.

We hear it from Dr Luther himself. He stands in the Cranachs' Stube, projecting his voice as if he is in the Town Church, the windows rattling as he reads. The title alone, *Against the Murderous Thieving, Hordes of Peasants*, is enough to send a shiver through me before he even begins, and I see that Lucas and Barbara share my dismay. Luther blasts us with the text, 'Rebellion brings with it a land full of murders and bloodshed ... makes widows and orphans ... Therefore, let everyone who can, smite, slay and stab ... for nothing is more poisonous or devilish than a rebel...' and seems to expect that we will applaud when he is done. Ignoring the silence that follows, he hands the paper to Lucas. 'This must be printed by the thousand and dispersed immediately, for if we descend into anarchy there will be no room left for God in the land.'

There is certainly no room for compromise. All our fears are realised when word comes of a peasant's army some six thousand strong marching on Frankenhausen, Müntzer at its head. The messenger who brings the news to Wittenberg, bolstered by pride in his knowledge, shares it throughout the town to everyone who will listen. And like most gossip, it grows in the telling. By the time it reaches us, the force is ten thousand or more, Müntzer riding on a white charger, the army lead by a pillar of fire.

Lucas, grimly determined to seek the truth concealed within the rumours, finds the messenger and brings him home. He is glad enough of a good meal and swears that any exaggeration in the tale is not of his doing. Lucas dismisses his protests.

'What is said in the town is of no account. Tell the truth here and you will be rewarded for it. Try to fill us full of lies and as a burgess of this town I won't answer for what will happen to you.'

It is an empty threat, but effective, for the lad swallows, his Adam's apple moving in his throat. His voice is steady though, so we believe him when he says, 'It's hard to be exact in numbers, but there is no doubt it began as some six thousand, but more join the rebels every day. Müntzer promises them that they march to Armageddon and that they will overcome; that the worldly authority will be destroyed and the rule of saints begun.' A pause. 'I heard him myself.' There is a hint of pride, allied to a hesitation, that makes me wonder if he had thoughts of joining the rebels, if Müntzer's oratory had tempted him also.

He continues, 'There was a rainbow that stretched across the sky, each arc of colour sharp and clear. Müntzer claimed it as an omen, proof that God is on his side. He promises those who follow him they will not have to fight in their own strength, for the forces of heaven will fight for them. As they did for Gideon when he faced the army of Midian.'

Again I sense his confusion, a fear that he may have chosen the wrong side, and I'm sorry for him, for he is young. 'What of their arms? Have they anything more than pitchforks and staves?'

He looks at me as if surprised by my intervention, not answering until Lucas gives him a nod.

'For the most part, no. But Müntzer encourages them

322

by saying that the missiles of the enemy will not be able to harm them, for God will protect them. He buoys their spirits by his prayers, in which he thanks God for the miracle they are about to see.'

'May God forgive him,' I say, 'for deluding his followers so.'

Again I see the surprise that flashes across the messenger's face, as if he isn't used to a discussion in which women take an equal part. I smother a smile, for it would be amusing if it weren't so serious, and turn to Lucas. 'I have no sympathy for rebellion, but nor can I bear to think of folk mown down because of a madman's rhetoric. What size of a force will they face?'

Lucas' voice is even, controlled, as if to take the horror out of his words. 'It is not the size of the force that will matter, though Duke George and the Landgrave of Hesse will be able to muster at least twice that number, I would imagine. It is the armaments they will face. What are pitchforks against cannon?'

When the lad is dismissed, I ask, 'Will our duke join the Landgrave and Duke George?'

Lucas makes a face. 'I suspect so. At least … I know Martin met with him at Weimar on his way home for the funeral, and if what he said then was anything like what he has now written and if our new elector is inclined to take his advice, then I cannot see any other course for him.'

Lucas is wrong, for Duke John does not march on Frankenhausen, though whether this is by his own inclination or because he has intelligences that inform him he would be too late, is hard to gauge. I cannot help feeling glad that the army opposing the peasants will not be further swelled, but my relief is short-lived, for what he chooses to do instead, when news is brought of the rout of the rebels, is, if anything, more horrific. This time it's one of Duke George's men who rides into the city and clatters to a halt in front of the Rathaus. Drawn to the window by the sound of the horse's hooves, I see him as he passes, his hair wild, his horse lathered, and know by his livery that it must be news of the battle he brings. I cannot rest easy until Lucas returns to the house, but as he enters and I see that he has the man in tow, I have a momentary sense of apprehension, unconnected to the events at Frankenhausen. Barbara, sitting by my side, puts her hand on my arm, and whether she divines my thoughts or not, her touch settles me.

'It is silly, I know, but just for a moment, when I saw his livery, I couldn't help feeling an apprehension … I know he's not here for me, that my rebellion in leaving Nimbschen is as nothing to what is happening all around us, but…' My confession of weakness is interrupted by Lucas, who brings the man into the Stube and introduces us. He's older than at first I thought, so that I place more credence on his assessment of the battle than I might otherwise have done. The news he brings is good, for us, for our town, for all law-abiding citizens, but as he begins to recount the battle and the carnage that followed, I turn away, swallowing with difficulty the acid that rises into my throat.

'The battle was swift,' he says, 'the peasant force no match for our artillery.' He seems amused by the memory and I have to bite on my lip hard to avoid responding.

'Our first volley fell short, and they cheered as if the victory was theirs, but with the second they learnt their lesson, the cannon shredding their ranks. It was enough to throw them into disarray and they turned tail and fled. It was an easy task for the cavalry to chase them down: they left some five thousand of the rebels dead, with the loss of only six of our men.' His pride is obvious. 'That showed Müntzer whose side God is on!'

I shut my eyes against the picture he has drawn in my head: of a field strewn with bodies, tangled in a mockery of makeshift weaponry, the grass underneath them blood-soaked. 'Five thousand as against six! Why did there have to be so much killing? Would it not have been enough to drive them away?'

He waves his hand at me and speaks slowly as if to a child who may not understand. 'Ill-assorted rabble as they were, they had set themselves up as an army in opposition to the rightful authorities. They could not be allowed to melt away as if they had done nothing amiss. That way is anarchy.' Then, turning back to Lucas, 'We need not fear an uprising of this nature again.'

'What of Müntzer?'

The man's contempt is clear. 'He fled likewise, faster and further than the troops he led, but we found him, cowering in a cellar, along with other ringleaders. A quick death was too good for them, Duke George decreeing that they be made an example. They were tortured and executed and their heads displayed at the gates of Frankenhausen for all to see.'

I feel my stomach revolting again and would dearly love to run to the privy, but that would seem cowardice, so

I determine to wait it out, until he has told all.

'Our duke led the battle, but your duke has taken it upon himself to clean up the land.'

I can't stop myself interrupting again. 'What are you saying?'

It's as if he's determined to shock. 'That his men scour the countryside, seeking those who took up arms against their masters, imprisoning them for their rebellion, and as the prisons fill to overflowing, beheading those who cannot be accommodated.'

I sit down abruptly, afraid that if I do not, my legs will collapse underneath me. 'But how can the troops know who is guilty and who is innocent?'

He grins, displaying a mouthful of yellowed teeth. 'There are plenty who will share what they know for a pfennig or two. And the elector isn't short of funds to pay for informers, for he has imposed swingeing fines on any town that harboured a radical preacher.'

Barbara brings the conversation to a close. Her tone is polite, but icy. 'We appreciate you giving of your time to bring us the news, but now no doubt you will wish to wash away the journey and take some refreshment. I'm sure the castle will be happy to accommodate you.'

Chapter Thirty-Seven
Wittenberg, Mid-May 1525

Despite that it is May, the weather, like the mood of the people, has returned to winter, a heavy frost ruining the infant grapes, nuts freezing on the trees. I cannot but feel it is a judgement on us for the savageness of the reprisals that Duke John presided over. There is scarcely a village or a farm untouched by the uprising, the best estimate that Lucas has found for the number of those who have died, some eighty thousand men.

'All those families,' I say, 'the wives, the children – who will support them?'

Barbara's expression is grim. 'There will be many go hungry this year, for want of a father. I cannot bear to think of them.'

Lucas is increasingly abstracted, shutting himself away in his study: emerging for meals but disappearing again immediately thereafter. When I try to quiz him about what he thinks of Dr Luther's reaction to Frankenhausen and in particular the horrific aftermath, he refuses to be drawn into a discussion, saying only, 'Martin has upbraided the nobles for their merciless pursuit of the innocent as well as the guilty, as he should, but he will not retract his earlier writings, which seems to me a mistake.' He walks away without giving me time to reply, Barbara apologising for him.

'You must excuse his rudeness, Katharina – he isn't himself. Recent events have shaken him' – she picks at a fingernail – 'and perhaps his faith also.'

'It would be hard not to be shaken, in person or in faith. I would think less of him if he was not.'

'You feel it too?'

'Yes. When I left the Marienthron, I was so sure that Dr Luther was right. That the God he preached was truly the God of the Bible.'

'And now?'

'I cannot deny that I find it hard to reconcile what he has said of God's love and grace with the carnage that has been done in his name. By both sides.' I pause, unsure if I should say more, but Barbara remains silent, as if waiting for whatever else is troubling me. It comes out in a rush and with more passion than I intended. 'I wish he hadn't written as he did, or at least that he would disassociate himself from those writings now.'

'Have you ever watched an animal when its young are threatened? The fierceness of its defence, often far beyond what is necessary?'

I nod, wondering where she is going with the analogy.

'The Reformation that Martin sought to bring to the Church is his child. As he sees it, the rebels' actions risked the destruction, not only of everything dear to him in human terms, but in spiritual terms also.' She is smoothing out an imagined wrinkle in her skirt. 'I too wish he had been more moderate in his language, but as a mother, I think I understand the depth of his feeling.'

I think of Barbara and her family, of Eva, about to have a child of her own … of Jerome and the end of my hopes, and feel a pang of jealousy for their good fortune, that, in the light of all the deaths that surround us, shames me. To cover it, I say, 'But now that Dr Luther has seen what has come of his rantings, should he not be able to admit he may have been mistaken in writing as he did, however true what he said might have been?'

'Perhaps. But who of us has never said anything in anger that we afterwards regretted but were unable to retract?'

I cannot fault her reasoning and am about to concede, when she continues, 'And if you know yourself to be, at least in part, responsible for actions that you cannot condone, that makes it all the harder.'

It is a perspective on Luther that I haven't considered before, and unsure of what I think of it, I ask, 'What could he do then?'

'I wish I could say "learn from his mistakes", but I'm not sure that he is capable of that either. Clever he may be, but sometimes he's singularly lacking in control. And as Lucas says, his pen runs ahead of his brain. His mouth also, times.' She pauses, as if it's her turn to be unsure whether to speak or not, then, 'He needs someone who could moderate his excesses.'

Something in the way she looks at me makes me wonder just how much Herr Amsdorf shared of our interview, and if she imagined more than I had meant when I'd said I'd marry Dr Luther if asked. She confirms my suspicion.

'He needs a wife, Katharina, and not some pretty little

thing who would be all Yes, Martin, and No, Martin, and Anything you say, Martin, neither. He needs someone who wouldn't be afraid to challenge him if she thought him wrong, nor to shrivel if he reacted badly to the censure.' She stops, as if to give me a chance to respond.

I'm aware that colour is creeping up my neck, and though my first instinct is to laugh off her words, to deny that I want any such task, even if I thought I was capable of it, I find myself saying nothing and am left with the uncomfortable feeling that the conversation is unfinished.

Basilius arrives with word of Eva's safe delivery of their child, and when I visit her, to admire the latest arrival for myself, I look down at the babe as it grasps the finger I stroke across its palm and think of Dr Luther's sermon on the last days, of how the cycle of life, springtime and harvest, labouring and taking ease, will all continue until the end. And it's hard to stifle the unsettling thought that this babe may not have the opportunity to grow up into adulthood, or indeed to grow at all.

The cold snap continues, serving as a brake on the reprisals, and shivering as I go the few steps to the stall under the Rathaus for milk, I think it little comfort to those left destitute and without support, afraid that many will, like the nuts on the trees, be frozen where they lie. There is a desire in the town and the university to find some normality after the horrors of the previous month, and once again the Cranachs' Stube becomes a centre for discussion in the evenings. The heat from the stove is welcome, but it doesn't reach our backs, the draught from the door chilling my legs so that I wish I could turn as a spit does, to even out the warmth.

One evening, when there is a momentary pause in a vigorous discussion between Melanchthon, Lucas and Justus Jonas, I ask, '*Are* we in the last days?' which earns me a glare from Melanchthon, countered by Lucas' more sympathetic glance.

Justus Jonas rests his elbows on his knees and presses his fingertips together, tapping them against his mouth. I cannot read his expression, and wonder if he shares Melanchthon's opinion – that women would do best to be silent – or takes Lucas' more liberal view. Katherine isn't with him tonight, but I know she would favour the latter and perhaps would sway him in that regard. There is a momentary pause before he says, 'We do not know the hour or the day, Katharina, but certainly the signs are all around us. Wars and rumours of wars…'

'Please,' Barbara interrupts, 'can we not think on something more pleasant?'

'But if we are,' I persist, ignoring Barbara's comment, for I have been wrestling with this thought since the defeat of the peasants, 'how should we live?'

Jonas' answer has a ring of finality about it. 'Eating and drinking, marrying and giving in marriage … we can do no other.'

I subside into my own thoughts, and though they are mostly of the situation all around us, occasional images of Dr Luther, and of Barbara's comments that he is in need of a wife to look after him, also intrude.

And as if on cue, Luther himself arrives, blowing in from the Elbestrasse. He rubs his hands together to restore the circulation and blows on his fingers. 'There is no sign of a thaw yet, the river still crusted with ice, and breathing in is like swallowing a fistful of knives.'

Lucas rises and gestures him to his own seat close to the stove. 'Come and warm yourself, Martin, and prepare to be quizzed, for Katharina here is in need of your opinion.'

I look down at my skirt, brushing away a crumb that is caught in a crease, uncomfortable with the thought that Barbara and Lucas may be conspiring to ensure that he notices me. When I hear the creak of the chair as he leans against the back, I risk glancing up. Sitting as I am, off to the side, I have the opportunity to look at him at close quarters without it being obvious, and I can't help noticing the faint lines on his forehead and at the sides of his eyes. Notice also, for the first time, the unruly coarseness of his hair as it curls outwards behind his ears and lies in twists on his forehead. His eyebrows are surprisingly fine, and from this angle his nose has a slight kink in it, as if at some time it was broken, and there is a tiny cleft in his chin. I do want to ask him what he thinks of Duke John's behaviour, but Jonas, as if he doesn't wish a return to the earlier discussion, engages him in conversation about his new lecture programme, and whether there are any among the students who show particular promise. Barbara, with a sideways glance at me that implies some significance in her question, asks if there is any truth in the rumour that he has requested that Duke John find him some accommodation more suited to his needs, now that he and Brisger are alone in the Black Cloister. Studying his face as they talk and watching the tension that was apparent when he first arrived gradually dissipate, I find myself wondering if he knows how good a friend Lucas is to him, and discovering that cap-less and without a tonsure he does not look so old after all.

It is a thought that, having once entered my mind, gradually takes root, so that when he next appears at supper I find myself less at ease than before, but perversely, more determined not to be embarrassed into silence, nor to concealing my own views on the news of the moment. It begins once more, despite Barbara's best efforts to the contrary, with Frankenhausen and its aftermath, and Lucas' suggestion to Luther that alongside his tract condemning the peasants, a new publication counselling moderation from the nobles might be helpful.

The response is sharp. 'Helpful to whom, Lucas? To your workshop, perhaps? To the profit of your enterprise? I do not write other than as I feel, nor as the servant of someone else's need.'

Lucas straightens his shoulders, for once betraying a real frustration, but is given no chance to respond, Luther continuing, 'Besides, I have already written thus. As any careful reading would show. And now there are more pressing issues of theology to be addressed.'

I lift my head. 'What can be more pressing than the

334

fate of ordinary folk? I do not favour rebellion, far from it, but to hurt the innocent along with the guilty, that surely cannot be right.'

Barbara stretches out her hand as if to stop me saying any more, while Melanchthon, clearly annoyed at my temerity, cuts in, 'We do not know for certain that the innocent *are* suffering.'

'Wives and children?' I cannot keep the disdain out of my voice. 'They may not be killed along with their menfolk, but they suffer nonetheless. In this weather especially. We sit in comfort, while others, without any means of support, struggle to survive.'

I am looking straight at Melanchthon but sense Luther's gaze fixed on me as he replies, 'Your compassion does you credit, Fraulein, and you are right – in any war there are always the innocent who suffer. But it is an evil that cannot be avoided.' His voice, which had softened, becomes firm again. 'Those who take up arms against the authorities ordained by God must bear responsibility for the consequences of their actions, for themselves and their families. As the Bible testifies: *Those who live by the sword will die by the sword.*'

'The sins of the fathers visited on the children … do you think that fair?'

'Not fair, no. But it is life. However much we may wish to the contrary.'

Barbara seeks to move the conversation into less controversial territory. 'We can at least pray, both for all those affected, and that the worst is over.'

Luther nods an acknowledgement. 'Indeed, Frau Cranach, we not only *can* pray, but we *must*.'

It seems the worst *is* over, in Saxony at least, Duke John returning to Torgau, his cleansing of the countryside completed. Lucas brings the news when he returns from the workshop, but it is clear from his abstracted expression that there is something else on his mind.

He clears his throat, and I wonder if there is something private he wishes to share with Barbara, if I should leave, but when I stand up he motions me to sit down again. 'There is other news ... of the Axts ... which I suspect will please you both less, as indeed it does me.'

Barbara is impatient. 'Spit it out, Lucas. It won't please us any more for being delayed.'

'Basilius has accepted a post in Torgau and is to start almost immediately.' He pauses again, as if to give us time to react, but when we remain silent, he says, 'I wish it could be otherwise, but they offer prospects that I cannot equal, and he is right to take the chance.'

In my head I agree, for Eva has talked of Basilius' ambition to someday be his own man, but I had not expected it to be so soon, and it is hard not to think of myself in this. For once Eva is gone, I will be the only one left. 'Immediately?' I say. 'How long have they known?'

'It was talked of a month ago, but nothing could be said until Basilius had word that the post was his. And that arrived today.' He looks across at Barbara, but I have the feeling it is for my benefit when he says, 'I invited them both for supper this evening. I thought you would want a chance to speak to Eva for yourself.'

It is a kind gesture, but not perhaps the easiest of circumstances, and I find it impossible either to converse as if nothing has changed, or to ask questions about their move. The meal table is full, all five Cranach children supping with us, even four-year-old Anna, who would normally have been in bed by the time we sit down, and I suspect Barbara has arranged it so in order to spare us the awkwardness that might have hung between us had it only been we adults. Ursula, who at seven has a current obsession with babies, is disappointed that Eva and Basilius have come alone, and compensates by fussing over Anna, who asserts her own independence by refusing everything Ursula offers and demanding the opposite instead. The boys, old enough to recognise the special circumstances and more than happy to take advantage of them, pile their plates high and set to eating with a dedication that is impressive. And as the ale is passed around, I see them sneak a second and third tumblerful, unnoticed by either parent until Hans belches loudly and young Lucas starts to giggle. It is the signal for them all to be dismissed, and as we settle down again in the Stube, the heat from the stove still necessary to counter the unseasonable weather, we hear them above us in the attics, pattering from room to room, their childish voices rising and falling. On any other night Barbara would have checked them; tonight she lets it pass, and I have the feeling that she sees ahead to a time when her own family will not be all around her and is disposed to be indulgent on that account.

Left to ourselves, the conversation, normally lively and free-flowing, is stilted, confined to practicalities. Lucas enquires of Basilius the size of the premises of the pharmacy that is to be his, if he will be taking on an

337

apprentice immediately, if there will be the opportunity perhaps to serve Duke John.

Barbara asks about their accommodation, if it will be comfortable, if it contains the essentials, or if they must provide everything for themselves, and offers, 'If there is anything you need, if we can be of help, you must ask.'

Basilius smiles his thanks, but says, 'We have been promised that everything is in order.'

'Whatever that may mean.' Eva speaks without looking at us, instead concentrating on picking at a scab on her knuckle, betraying a lack of confidence that is out of character. I want to ask if it is the babe she worries for or if it is leaving Wittenberg, now that the idea has become a reality, that troubles her, and noting a slight tremor in her hands, I suspect she is afraid to meet our eyes, lest she reveal her uncertainty.

The undertone of amusement in Barbara's voice dissipates some of the tension, 'Is it a man who has so informed you?'

Eva nods. 'Unfortunately, yes.'

'Ah. Then you do well to be concerned. A woman would have more idea of such things. Does a servant come with the house?'

A flicker of Eva's natural sharp wit surfaces as she repeats, 'Unfortunately, yes.'

'Eva!' Basilius makes a face at her. 'We don't know anything to the detriment of the servant and should perhaps consider ourselves fortunate that we have her at all.'

'We know that she is nearer sixty-five than fifty, and that she suffers somewhat from the rheumatick in damp weather. What better could we wish for?'

338

'It is surely better to have somebody than nobody, at the first at least.' He touches her shoulder, and offers, 'Once we are settled, if she does not suit, you can make your own choice.'

Eva straightens. 'Oh, you needn't worry. I will.' And then, as if she realises how churlish that sounds, she reaches up and places her own hand over his and smiles, though there is a telltale glint of tears in her eyes. 'We will be fine. For all we know, rheumatick or not, she may be the best pastry cook in Torgau.'

We all laugh at that, for it is a quality lacking in Eva, and often lamented by both of them.

CXXXD

As quickly as it came, the cold weather disappears, the sudden thaw turning the paths in the garden to mush, the streams through the town swollen with meltwater, the damp-slicked cobbles even more treacherous than before. I have been at Eva's house twice since they broke the news, helping in the packing up of the few belongings they will take.

Barbara, with an instinctive understanding of what Eva's leaving will mean to me, seeks to be encouraging. 'Torgau is not so far away that you cannot visit and they likewise. There will always be space for them here.'

'I know. But it will not be the same.'

'Nothing stays the same forever, Katharina, and though it may be hard for you to contemplate, whether here or there, your relationship would have changed in any case.'

'Because she is married and I am not? Thus far we have not found it so.'

'It is not so much the marriage that makes a difference, though it can do, but motherhood. You have neither of you had time yet to experience the changes that brings. Both good and bad.' Her glance strays to the family portrait that Lucas had his best apprentice work on as an exercise in perspective, a young child, all in white, in the foreground.

I have never felt able to ask of the child they lost, and cannot even now, though I know it is to that she refers, so answer as if I haven't noticed her focus. 'In the past, whether we talked or were silent, we were at ease together. We knew each other so well it was as if we could read each other's thoughts, and whether in agreement or not it didn't matter. But these last few days our conversation has been like that of strangers. Each time I go I am prepared to share what I feel, and each time I come away having said nothing. Why can I not tell her I will be lost without her? Indeed, that I already am.'

'It isn't always words that speak the loudest, Katharina. She will know how you feel, and no doubt share your feelings, but to admit to them may seem disloyal to Basilius. She is your friend, but she is also his wife. And though the words of Ruth, *Where you go, I will go*, are not in the marriage vows, perhaps they should be, for that is often what is required.'

I think of the others, of how they have all gone, whether following a husband or to find their own place, and acknowledge the right in what she says. But it doesn't make me feel better. Barbara, however, hasn't finished.

'You are helping her prepare. If you can do it without tears, it will be easier on both of you, and when she looks back, that is what she will remember, and with gratitude.' She injects a briskness into her voice. 'It may be your turn

340

soon, and if you also must move away, I would find that difficult, for you are so much like family now that to lose you would be like losing one of my own. But if that day should come, I will be happy for you, as you must be now for Eva, for both your sakes.'

'Mutti?'Paul is standing at the foot of the bed, at his side a girl, sweet colour flooding her face. He takes one step forward, pulls her with him, and I hear the mixture of pride and defiance in his voice. 'Mutti, this is Anna von Warbeck. We are engaged.' Her colour deepens and she curtseys, but as she rises I see a matching determination in her face, and I like her for it.

'Frau Luther, I'm glad to make your acquaintance. Though I'm sorry we meet in these circumstances.'

Her voice is a warm contralto, and I think how Martin would have enjoyed adding her to our ensemble. I want to tell them that, and so begin, *'Your father,'* but Paul, misunderstanding, interrupts.

'I asked Margarethe not to say anything. Anna's father will come round in time, I'm sure of it.'

I am thinking of another father, who did not come round, or so we always assumed, and so don't answer immediately.

His face darkens, defiance overtaking pride. *'Whether anyone approves or not, we love each other and mean to marry.'*

I stretch out a hand to him. *'Margarethe said nothing, and I am the last person on earth to disapprove of you making your own choice.'* I turn towards Anna. *'If you will make each other happy, I will not stand in your way. Indeed, I will rejoice in it. But…'* I tread carefully, for I understand only too well their sensitivities *'…there are practicalities to be considered, and it will be much the easier if you have the approval of your family.'*

He is standing behind Paul, his figure shadowy and insubstantial, but taller than I remember, the feather in his velvet cap sweeping Paul's shoulder as he bows to me. He steps forward, opens his mouth, but I shake my head at him. I look past Paul, addressing Jerome. 'I would have gone to the ends of the world with you, had your resolve been strong.'

'Mutti?' Paul looks over his shoulder, his forehead knotted, then grips my hand more firmly. 'Who are you talking to, Mutti?'

'It doesn't matter,' I say, turning my head, dismissing him. 'He had not your courage, and mine it seems was not enough for both of us.'

Anna, as if she hasn't heard our exchange, says, 'We will try to convince my father. But we won't wait for ever, for it is the marriage that is important to us, not the spectacle, and if we cannot have the wedding we might wish for, we shall settle for less.'

'Well said.' I look back to where Jerome stood, but he is gone, replaced by Martin, not as I last saw him, his hair grey-flecked, his face drawn, but as he was when we stood together in the Black Cloister for our betrothal ceremony, our voices, as we made our vows, echoing in the almost empty chamber. I smile a welcome, ask, 'Do you remember how folk talked? How cross Philipp was.'

Paul is shaking his head, and I touch his arm, try to explain. 'Melanchthon disapproved of our wedding, or so it appeared, but I have thought since that it was a fit of pique, because he hadn't been informed beforehand, nor invited to the first ceremony.' I look back at Martin, who is smiling and nodding his agreement, and I want to share this moment with him. 'We weathered the storm.' I wave my hand at Paul and Anna. 'As they will.'

'Undoubtedly the rumour of my marriage has reached you. I can hardly believe it myself, but the witnesses are too strong.'

Martin Luther

The Cranachs are both out, Lucas at the print workshop, Barbara at Eva's, while I sit at the window, my fingers still, the sewing that Barbara asked me to do lying unfinished on my lap. It is unlike Barbara to ask me to remain indoors and work, while she visits our neighbours or friends, particularly odd that she should choose to go to Eva without me when there remains but two days before their move. She appeared in my chamber after breakfast, muffled up against the biting wind that funnels down the Schlossstrasse, driving wisps of straw and grass and clods of dried dung ahead of it, a parcel in one hand, Lucas' best shirt in the other.

'I need to take this parcel to Eva. It's the shawl I promised for the babe.'

344

I scramble to my feet. 'I'll come with you.'

She shakes her head. 'Would you mind staying this time, Katharina? This shirt needs mending and your stitching is neater than mine. I wouldn't ask you now, but that Lucas wishes to wear it tonight, at the blessing of the painting of Christ and his disciples. I know I should have asked you sooner, but in all the turmoil of the last few weeks I forgot all about it. It probably won't take you long, but I'll be easier in my mind if I know it is done. I won't be staying long at Eva's in any case, for the carter is to be there this morning, and they will have more to do than entertain a visitor, but I promise you may go to see her later, when she'll have more time to talk.'

When the church bell rings the half-hour I'm still teasing away at the issue, going over in my mind everything Barbara said and did this morning, for I don't believe for one minute the excuse she gave, however urgent the task she left me. I pick up the shirt. Whatever the problem, I won't solve it by worrying, and despite her confidence, the tear is a tricky one and will not be so quick to sort. If I am to go to Eva's at all today I'd best get on. I've just threaded the needle and slipped one hand inside the sleeve when I hear a knock at the door and the murmur of voices at the foot of the stairwell. It's an unusual time for a visitor, but it cannot be a tradesman or a business call, for whoever it is, is coming up. The door of the Stube opens, Luther filling the frame.

I stand up and curtsey, wondering why the servant who answered his knock didn't send him away. 'Dr Luther. I'm afraid neither Barbara nor Lucas are here… Do you wish to leave a message for them?'

He bows. 'Fraulein von Bora.' There is none of his

usual confidence in his tone. 'It isn't the Cranachs I have come to see. May I come in?'

I feel myself flushing, a hundred and one thoughts racing through my mind – he surely cannot mean to speak to me. Did Barbara know of his intention? Is this why I have been left alone? Striving to keep my voice even, I say, 'Of course.' I step back, indicating for him to enter.

There is an uncomfortable pause before he says, 'Please Fraulein, sit down. There is something I wish to discuss with you.'

Even I know that this is hardly the usual precursor to a proposal, but nevertheless I have a suspicion that is what's coming. I perch on a seat by the stove and he places himself opposite me. Again a moment of silence, then, 'I believe Frau Cranach is gone to the Axts' house.'

'There was something she needed to take to them before everything is packed up.'

'You will miss Frau Axt.'

From the gentleness of his voice I wonder if he is also thinking of himself, and I find myself annoyed at that thought, my response correspondingly curt. 'Yes.'

He is linking and unlinking his hands on his lap and clears his throat. 'It is hard not to have relatives about you. I understand that. I imagine with the loss of your parents she has been like family to you. As the Cranachs are now, of course.'

I incline my head but don't trust myself to say anything, for thinking of Eva and her impending departure is like teetering on the edge of a cliff, and I have no wish to break down in front of him.

There is another awkward silence as if he also is floundering, with something to say but not knowing how to come to it. He clears his throat again, but when he starts to speak it isn't what I expect.

'You know perhaps that when I was on my preaching round at Eastertide I visited my parents?'

There is a new vulnerability in his face, a lack of assurance that I find somehow endearing. 'Did … did you find them well?'

'They are ageing, and my father particularly cannot hide that in some respects I am a disappointment to him.'

'He is not proud of your achievements, that your teachings are spreading throughout all of Germany and beyond?'

'He is at a stage when posterity matters more to him than achievement. He wishes to see his name live on, not just in me but in my children also. He wishes, in short, to see me married, and I am minded to give him his wish.'

I think of Jerome's proposal, of Glatz', of the saying, *'third time lucky'* and have an insane desire to laugh. Instead I say, 'Why me?'

'I am in need of a wife. You, of a husband. The Cranachs have been kind, more than kind, but I imagine you do not wish always to be in their debt.' He stops, an uncertain note creeping into his voice. 'And I have been led to believe…'

'Is this Amsdorf's doing?'

He looks uncomfortable. 'His … and others…' Then in a rush, reddening, 'Are they mistaken? Or could you consider me as a husband?' Then, as if aware that his mode of proposal perhaps leaves something to be desired, he continues, 'Do not think because I do not speak as a younger man might that I do not esteem you, or that I will not cherish you as a man ought his wife. But we

347

are neither of us so young as to think only of feelings. I have noted qualities in you that I value, honesty and compassion and a lively interest in both temporal and spiritual affairs. I think we could do very well together.' He stops, as if to give me a chance to respond, but when I don't answer immediately, there is a flash of the self-deprecating humour I have lately come to appreciate. 'It is not only our joint predicament that has drawn me to you' – he indicates his creased and dusty robe – 'but my own deficiencies. For as you see, I am not the best at managing and Barbara assures me you have the competence to sort me out.'

It is not the longest speech I have heard him make, and certainly not the most impassioned, and it leaves me in no doubt that what I'm being offered is not the love of Jerome, nor the lust of Glatz, but something more trustworthy, more solid than either, and although I had no thought of it an hour ago, I am ready to accept. For a moment Eva's face flashes before me, her voice ringing in my head, 'Let someone else marry him then … he is an *old* good man…' and I almost laugh again, imagining what her reaction will be.

'Fraulein von Bora?' His renewed diffidence is evident in the way he is rubbing at his palm with his thumb, so that I want to reach out to still his hand. 'I know I have not much to offer and perhaps it is not fair to ask it of you, for every day my life is in danger, but I would count it a blessing if you will consider. If you need time…'

I shake my head, place my hand on top of his, a spark of mischief leading me to echo his own words. 'You have been minded to offer. I am minded to accept.'

Chapter Forty
Wittenberg, 28th May 1525

'You cannot mean it.' Eva spins round from the packing of a crate, the wooden trencher in her hand dropping to the floor with a clatter. 'He is *old*!' The emphasis is clear. 'And serious and … thinks of nothing but his writings and…' She has removed her eyeglasses and is swinging them round and round, so that I fear they will snap. I take them out of her hands and set them aside.

'He is forty-one. Many husbands are that and more. Besides, I am old, as brides go. And now that he has no tonsure and is eating well, he is not unattractive.'

She raises her eyebrows. 'Really? I hadn't noticed.'

'Of course you wouldn't. You have your own life, your husband, your child. While I … I have nothing. Which is more than enough incentive to consider any offer made to me.'

'That isn't what you said about Caspar Glatz.'

'Yes, well, you know what I thought of Glatz. Death by crushing would have been preferable than marriage to him.'

Her voice is very quiet. 'All this time, I kept hoping

you would meet someone you could love.'

I wish she hadn't raised that particular ghost, and I resort to sarcasm to counter it. 'Like Jerome, you mean? Remember how well that worked out.'

She bites her lip. 'If we hadn't been leaving, would you still have said yes?'

I should, of course, deny that her departure had any bearing on my decision, for it's unfair to lay that burden of guilt on her, but I cannot be sure of that and won't lie. 'I don't know.'

She shifts, as if about to ask something else, but I hurry on. 'What I do know is that I respect and honour him. He is a good man, who, if some of his wilder impulses can be contained, may yet become great. If I can help in that, then all that has gone before will have been worthwhile.'

Her natural curiosity surfaces. 'What did he say?'

'To me? That he needed a wife and I a husband and that he thought we would do very well together. To the Cranachs, that he was minded to please his father and spite the Pope.'

Her expression is a mixture of sympathy and doubt. 'That can't have been all?'

'A rough paraphrase.' Then, taking pity on her, 'He also claimed to be aware of my finer qualities and promised to esteem and cherish me as a good husband should.'

'How did you answer a proposal like that?'

'I told him I was minded to accept.'

Her response is halfway between a laugh and a sob. 'Oh, Kat, I will pray you are neither of you disappointed.' Outside the bell rings for noon and she looks around at the possessions still strewn about the floor. 'I should get on, else Basilius will be home and the bags still not packed.'

350

'And I should let you.'

'When is the wedding to be?'

'It was only agreed an hour ago. We haven't progressed any further.'

'You will let me know?'

'You are my oldest friend. Of course I will.'

Chapter Forty-One
Wittenberg, 30th May – 14th June 1525

It is a promise I am unable to keep, however much it pains me, for it seems that, the decision made, Luther wishes it to be done as soon as possible and without telling any more people than are required for the legalities.

He is businesslike when he comes to discuss the matter with the Cranachs. 'I thought the thirteenth would be a suitable day for the betrothal.'

'Two weeks?' Barbara raises one eyebrow. 'What do *you* think, Katharina?'

For a fraction of a moment I think of Jerome and of the grand plans that Elsa Reichenbach once had for me, but I thrust the thought away. In a level tone that draws a smile of approval from Luther, I say, 'If it can be arranged, then let it be so.'

'There is little to arrange.' He is confident. 'I've already spoken to Bugenhagen, and he will conduct the ceremony. Aside from yourselves' – he nods to Lucas and Barbara – 'Justus Jonas and Johann Apel have also promised to attend.'

'No others?' Barbara cannot hide her surprise.

'I have not asked any others. We are in a time of turmoil. Best that it be accomplished without trumpets.'

'But…'

Lucas frowns her into silence, adds a question of his own, 'And the Wirtschaft? That will surely be public?'

Luther nods. 'Of course. I have no wish to dispense with custom, but neither do I think it appropriate to make a show. Two further weeks should be ample time for the organisation required. I have chosen Tuesday the twenty-seventh.' And to me, 'Tuesday, as you may know, is an auspicious day for a wedding.' He turns back to Lucas. 'My parents will wish to come from Mansfeld, and we will, of course, invite any from Wittenberg, town and university both, and others of my and Fraulein von Bora's acquaintance who wish to attend.'

When he is gone Barbara bursts out, 'Why must it be such a rushed affair? Anyone would think…' She breaks off. 'I'm sorry, Katharina, of course we know there is nothing amiss, but to rush it like this is but to invite gossip of the worst kind.'

Lucas is more pragmatic. 'Perhaps it is to give little time for gossip, or for censure, that he wishes it to be so soon. Once it is done, it cannot be undone, and those who might wish to dissuade him … or you, will be too late.'

'Why should anyone wish to dissuade us?'

He was clearly choosing his words with care. 'There are those who will think that now is not the time for anyone to marry, far less Martin. That he should be devoting his attention to the ills of the day, not looking to his own inclinations.'

'But there have been many, friend and foe alike, who have twitted him with his single state and questioned his

353

commitment to what he has written. Surely they would approve of his marrying?'

'He is damned if he does and damned if he does not. And likely you will be too. Are you prepared for that?'

I take a deep breath, and the die is cast. 'I am prepared to stand at his side and pray God I may make a good job of it.'

⬡⬡⬡

The ceremony is simple and short, so that I have no time to wonder if I am doing the right thing, nor to worry about what is to come after. I have a general understanding of what will be required of me, but no idea of how it will feel. I had thought of asking Eva, on that last day, but did not, for fear the contrast between her experience and mine might be so great that it would dispirit me.

Johannes Bugenhagen speaks of Adam and Eve, of procreation, of mutual succour, and we clasp hands and make our vows. And then it is done, and although in my head I know that I am no longer the person I was half an hour ago, I do not feel any different. As we pass through the doorway leading to the staircase, with Justus Jonas preceding us, Barbara steps forward to embrace me and whisper an encouragement.

'Remember, Katharina, God made you for this.'

I hope so, I really hope so.

Jonas leads us to the chamber that has been prepared, for he is our chosen witness, and I bless Barbara for the sweet-smelling herbs sprinkled on the floor and the fresh sheets that cover the mattress. We lie down, side by side, fully clothed, and Jonas pronounces a final blessing before

354

leaving us alone. As the door shuts behind him, I feel a rush of fear and thankfulness combined. Fear of my part in what is to come, and thankfulness that the old traditions are gone, and however difficult or easy the consummation proves to be, at least it will only be we two who will know.

The silence is absolute. Used as I am to the early morning bustle of the square, the quiet of the Black Cloister is strange and unsettling. In that moment, halfway between asleep and awake, fear grips me – perhaps Christ has returned and I have been left behind. I turn onto my side to see the mound that is Martin, relief washing over me like a tide – whoever else might be left, Martin Luther would not. Propped up on one elbow, I watch the rhythmic rise and fall of his chest, and thank God for him and for the events of yesterday. Below his mop of dark hair, the fleshy contours of his neck and shoulders protrude from the blankets, the paler skin in sharp contrast to the weathered appearance of his hands and face.

He stirs, his eyes opening, and I hold my breath, afraid that I will see disappointment in them, despite his seeming content of the previous night, but he turns to me and, placing his hands on my shoulders, says, with an unexpected sensitivity, 'It will be easier next time, I promise you.'

I feel the flush spreading from my neck and throat and onto my cheeks, unsure how to respond.

'Katharina?' It is a request, and though I don't trust myself to speak in case the words comes out wrong, I nestle against his side. His touch is slow and gentle, dispelling my fears, and as our breath mingles, we move together once more and it is indeed easier.

When I wake again it is to full day, light spilling through the leaded windows, painting circles on the floorboards. Martin is sitting at the table, his head bent over a paper, his fingers flying across the surface, the scratch of his quill the only sound. I slip from the bed and pad across the floor and place my hand on his shoulder, and he looks up at me, a smile in his eyes, and despite the discomfort in my loins, I think – if this is how it will be, I am content.

Chapter Forty-Two
Wittenberg, 15th June 1525

I am *not* content with what I find the following day, when, Martin having disappeared to the university, I begin to explore the rest of the Black Cloister. It is two years since I last stayed here and though Barbara warned me, in general terms, of what to expect, that she had time only to clean up a chamber for the betrothal ceremony and likewise for the bedding, the reality was much worse than I imagined. Standing in the dirt and dust of what had clearly been Martin's bedchamber I wished I had taken her advice *not* to be in a hurry to examine the remainder of the house and had waited for the two servants whose services she had offered.

Downstairs the main door bangs and I hear Martin calling for me. I take a deep breath and, staying where I am, call back. Whatever our relative positions outside the cloister, this is my territory and I will claim it now. I hear his quick footsteps on the stairs – whatever Eva thinks, he is not so old, and I prepare to do battle.

'Katharina. I had not expected to find you here. This chamber is not...'

'You're right. It is not clean. It is not serviceable. It

357

is not fit for use for anyone or anything.' I stab at the mattress with the broom handle, raising a cloud of dust. When we have stopped coughing, I ask, 'When was that straw last changed?'

He has the grace to look shamefaced. 'Not for a while.'

'When?' I say again, unwilling to be deflected.

'Perhaps a year...'

'A year!' I cannot keep the incredulity out of my voice and take an instinctive step backwards. I do not see anything moving on it, but I'm sure they must be there.

'It didn't seem important when I lived alone. And to be truthful I never thought about it, but in these past two weeks I had meant to throw it out. And I will, I promise you.'

He is like a small boy caught in a fault, and I'm tempted to laugh. I bite on the insides of my cheeks to keep my face stern. 'No need to promise. You can do it now, that is, if it doesn't walk out of its own volition. No doubt you can make a space somewhere in the garden for a bonfire, for I daresay this will not be the only thing that must go.'

'There is no need to rush at it. We will only use a fraction of the rooms here, what point is there in clearing all now?'

'In the fullness of time we will wish to have guests. I intend them to be ones we have invited, not those who have taken up residence without our permission.' I bang the broom on the floor as emphasis, and out of the corner of my eye see something streak across the room and disappear into a hole at the base of the wall. I nod towards the wall. 'Those of the rodent or insect variety are particularly unwelcome.'

We tackle Martin's study, raising enough dust to turn

both of us into wraiths – face, hands, clothes all become a uniform grey. I do not mind so much for Martin's, for they need to be replaced in any case, but even my oldest clothes deserve better treatment than this.

In the midst of it Melanchthon appears, his normally gaunt face swelled like a turkey-cock, his voice explosive. 'It is true then. You are married. And without thinking to inform your friends beforehand of your intentions.'

Martin touches my hand. 'Katharina, I believe there is beer in the kitchen. Perhaps you could fetch some.'

I am happy enough to be dismissed, but when I reach the top of the stairs on my return and hear Melanchthon's voice still raised, I pause and rest the tray on the windowsill to listen.

'Why that one? She is proud and arrogant and altogether too fond of her own opinions.'

I'm not sure if I want to hear Martin's reply, but I wait anyway.

His tone is more measured, as if he wishes to persuade, not argue. 'So I thought once, but lately I have come to see a different side to her. And while I do not burn with passion, I hold her in high esteem.'

'If there is no passion, why such haste, why such a hole-in-the-corner ceremony without due warning?'

'Because I did not wish to raise a storm, or to give you and others a chance to protest. Besides, when one faces death daily, as I do, time takes on an extra importance. She, and the others from Nimbschen, took me at my word. Do I not have a responsibility for her? If I were to be killed tomorrow, I will have given her a status that cannot be taken away.'

'Alive or dead, tomorrow the world will say she has

bewitched you … or worse.'

'I care little for what the world says, but I do care for your opinion. You are my closest friend and I wish you to grace our Wirtschaft, but if you cannot do so with a smile on your face, then I'd prefer that you do not come at all. I had good reason for this "hole-in-the-corner", ceremony, as you put it, but the solemnisation of our marriage will be before the whole world, with fanfare, bells and feasting, music and dancing, and I wish nothing to sour that occasion.'

I have heard enough, and in the pause that follows, before Melanchthon has time to voice a refusal, I knock on the door, hoping my face does not betray that I have eavesdropped on their conversation. Martin looks over as I enter and I search his face for encouragement. He smiles his thanks and, reassured, I set down the tray, but before turning to leave, I meet Melanchthon's gaze, my head held high.

Barbara appears, to accompany me to the shops. She brushes aside my reluctance. 'You have run the gauntlet of Philipp, you can surely handle the tradesfolk.'

'Does the whole town know already?'

'We thought it best to drop a hint, for if you had been seen entering or leaving the Black Cloister and nothing said, the gossips would have enjoyed to speculate at your expense. And it is much easier to lose a reputation than to regain it.' She links her arm through mine. 'The rumour began an hour or so since, so yes, I imagine by now the whole town knows. Indeed the news may be more than halfway to Torgau.'

I look down at the plain gold band on my finger. 'I hope Eva will not be offended. I made her a promise.'

'She will understand and remember that you told her first, even before us. No doubt they will make every effort to come for the Wirtschaft.' There is a note of determination in her voice. 'And that, I already have in hand. It will be an occasion worthy of you both.'

As we enter the market square, folk turn to stare, and Barbara goes out of her way to speak to everyone in sight, dropping my new name into each conversation, forcing an acknowledgement of my married status. To the flesher and the fishmonger, she says, tapping the counter with her finger, 'Frau Luther will be calling on her own behalf from now on. I trust you will extend to her the same terms that we receive.'

We are coming out of the clothiers, a boy behind us carrying the bale of fabric that Barbara has insisted on buying to be made into a wedding gown for me, when we come face to face with the Reichenbachs. Elsa holds out her hand. 'Katharina. I heard the news. I congrat…'

Philipp cuts her short, his bow cursory. 'Indeed, *Frau Luther*, the whole town will congratulate you. You have made a good *catch*.' The inference is unmistakeable. Elsa flushes and looks down at her feet, and I want to reach out to her, in defiance of Philipp, to show her that I remember her kindness to me and understand that the distance between us is not of her choosing, but Barbara takes a firm grip of my arm, her response barbed.

'It is a good *match*, for both parties. And one that all right-thinking people should welcome.' She tilts her chin. 'As no doubt will all those we chose to invite to the

361

Wirtschaft.'

I hear Elsa's sharp indrawn breath and wish with all my heart that I could save her the hurt that exclusion from the ceremony will cause, but Barbara is pulling me away. 'Come, Katharina, we have much to organise, and little time to waste in idle conversation. Good day, Elsa … Herr Reichenbach.'

Chapter Forty-Three
Wittenberg, 27th June 1525

'Are you ready, Katharina?' Martin bounds into our chamber, where Barbara is adjusting the drape of my wedding veil and brushing imaginary specks from the shoulders of my gown. He waves towards the courtyard. 'Everyone is waiting.'

'May I have a moment?'

He looks surprised but recovers quickly, and I see his sideways glance at the screen, which hides the chamber pot. 'Of course, if you need it. I'll wait below.'

Barbara is also looking towards the screen. 'Katharina, you can't…'

'No. Of course not.' My mind is full to overflowing with people and places and memories – some that I wish to remember, others I wish to forget. 'I just…'

A note of doubt creeps into her voice. 'You do not regret…'

'No,' I repeat, this time with a smile. I press my face against the window, looking down on the crowded courtyard, listening to the voices that rise and fall, greetings and laughter blending together in a murmur of anticipation and pleasure. 'I count myself fortunate.

Only…'

She touches my arm. 'Only you wish you had family and your oldest friends here with you to witness this day.'

She has been so good to me that I'm afraid to look at her face in case I see hurt there. 'I should feel blessed, when I have you and Lucas and the Jonases, and so many well-wishers in the university and the town … and I do … I do. But I miss Eva and my brothers… Is that wrong?'

She turns me to face her, takes both my hands in hers. 'It is only natural. No one will think otherwise. And you know they would have been here if they could.'

The church bell tolls the hour, the crowd outside falling silent and then erupting in a cheer as the bells from both churches ring together to signal the marriage procession. The people below are forming themselves into ranks, stretching out on both sides of the doorway, the musicians who will lead us tuning up their instruments, discord become harmony, and I feel the prick of tears, but whether it is for the folk who are here, or for those who are not, I cannot be sure.

We walk along the Collegienstrasse to the Town Church to the sound of the tambour and flute, the procession of guests, already lengthy, drawing in more people along the way: students and townsfolk, old and young, fit and infirm, all, it seemed, with one desire – to see Luther married. We halt at the portal, the wedding guests fanning out on both sides, the spectators filling the space in front of the church and spilling out into the square. Pastor Bugenhagen steps forward and signals the musicians to stop. We wait for the last notes to die away, and as Martin takes my hand on Bugenhagen's instructions, I look at the sea of faces and begin to grasp how public not only the marriage ceremony but our whole life together will be.

I glance to my left and catch Barbara's eye. She nods, and in my mind I hear her voice, instructing me, and so straighten my shoulders and hold my head high.

The ceremony passes in a blur, the hymns and prescribed readings and Bugenhagen's homily presented in shortened form in consideration of Martin's parents, who stand by his other side throughout, supported by two of the Mansfeld councillors, who have likewise come to add their seal of approval to the match.

'There will be those,' Lucas had said, 'who will think ill of this marriage.' But judging by the reaction of the crowd as the blessing is pronounced, the detractors are not here. For a moment I think of the Melanchthons, conspicuous by their absence, and hope that Martin's breach with Philipp can be healed, for they need each other, and the reformed Church needs them both. The musicians strike up again, accompanied by cheers and cries of good wishes from every direction as we step forward to lead the guests back to the Black Cloister for the wedding banquet. I am proud of what I have made of the refectory, the table scraped raw to remove months of engrained spillages, the floor scrubbed a half-dozen times at least, the bristles of the brush worn down almost to nothing. It will not disgrace us now. A barrel of Torgau beer stands in one corner, brought yesterday in response to Martin's laughing threat that if it wasn't cool and settled he'd make Herr Köppe drink it all himself. The merchant and his wife are in the procession behind us, as honoured guests, and rightly so,

365

for he risked his life for me. Besides the Torgau beer there is a barrel of Einbeck that the town council have provided, a gift that is as important for the approval it indicates as for the beer itself.

We sit down, the smell of roast venison drifting up from the kitchen through the opened windows, and I think with gratitude of the electoral court and Duke John. I still feel heartsick at his actions following the rout of the peasants at Frankenhausen, but today is a time for remembering the generosity and support of the Wettin family, to Martin and to me. Von Dolzig, the duke's representative, is a splash of colour among the menfolk, most of whom are soberly dressed, as befits men of the cloth. Watching him as he leans across to speak to Martin's father, my throat constricts, for his red doublet, the ruched shirt beneath, the embroidered sleeves, the ring on his right hand that flashes light across the ceiling as he moves, are all a reminder of Jerome, of what might have been. Lucas is to my left, Barbara beyond him, and as if she knows what I'm thinking, she says, 'It is a fine company that grace this feast, a sign both of the esteem in which you are held, and of good things to come.' She hesitates, then adds, 'One day you will bless the happy mischance that brought you to this day.'

I look along the table, generously provisioned by others, at the platters of lamb and poultry and pork; the plaited loaves and dishes of butter and curd cheese; the bowls of fruit; and dotted along the centre, dishes piled high with songbirds, Martin's particular favourite. Amidst the smiles and the animated conversations, and the constant buzz, punctuated by laughter, I smile my thanks at her. 'I bless it now and am determined from this moment on, to look forward, not back.'

As I stretch out to carve another slice from the haunch of venison that has pride of place in front of Martin, he raises one eyebrow and whispers in my ear, 'Are you sure? Remember it is our duty to outdance all of our guests and show the world we are happy with our lot.'

I hesitate, want to ask, *And are you?* But this marriage is as yet too young, too tentative a thing for me to be confident of his answer, and I fear to disappoint him, so I set the knife down and lift some strawberries instead.

Bugenhagen nods at Martin and signals to one of the servants, who have also been lent for the occasion. She bends to hear his instruction, then disappears, and on cue we hear the musicians tuning up again outside. Martin takes my hand and draws me to my feet, and up and down the table conversations falter, cut off mid-stream. There is a moment of silence, then a scraping back of benches and a whisper of skirts and the click-clack of boots on the flagged floor as we flood out again, to re-form the wedding procession for the third time.

CRXXXD

The door of the Rathaus is standing open, the frame decorated with trails of ivy intertwined with convolvulus, and we pass from the sunshine through the arch of greenery, the sudden coolness inside making me shiver.

Martin smiles. 'When the dancing starts you'll be glad it's cool.'

I'm glad that it's the dances of honour first, the slow marches that are easy to follow, for I have come late to dancing, and though Barbara has gone through the steps with me several times in the past two weeks, I'm not altogether comfortable with them yet. Martin's parents, as the most important guests, join us first, then von Dolzig representing the elector, and Herr Amsdorf, and following him the Cranachs, the Bugenhagens and the Jonases as Martin's closest friends. Then it is the turn of Herr Köppe and his wife and the councillors from Mansfeld. There is one final march to conclude the formalities, and as we circle the floor for the last time, I think of Hans and Klement, Eva and Fronika, Magdalena and the rest of the sisters who escaped with me, and wish with all my heart they could be here to witness this day.

As the music dies away, the other dancers peel off to either side, forming a guard of honour which Martin and I pass through before coming to a halt at the entrance to the hall. And then it is the turn of all the guests to come forward in turn to present their wedding gifts. This time it is von Dolzig who leads the way, the elector's gift of one hundred gulden more generous than I at least would have expected. The town council are also liberal and, aside from the beer, provide twenty gulden. Wenzel Linck breaks with tradition, folk craning to see as he presents us with a clock. Martin is delighted and thanks him but, inclined to mischief, asks will he also send a mathematician to teach us the workings of it, causing a ripple of laughter all around the hall. The pile of coins in the chest grows, and I am especially pleased that some of the townsfolk have given silverware, though our bulbous reflections on the curve of the cups are hardly flattering. The goodwill the gifts represent is encouraging, but even more so is how far they will go towards the setting up of our household. The last in the line is a man I've never seen before. He

368

steps forward, a clinking purse in his hand. Beside me, Martin tenses and his face darkens.

The man is wearing a Shaube trimmed with velvet, a carnelian on a heavy gold chain nestling against his pleated shirt – clearly important, whoever he is.

Instinctively I put my hand on Martin's arm, but he shakes it off and grinds out, 'You may tell your master I do not want his money.'

Justus Jonas steps forward. 'Martin...' But he is likewise ignored.

Twin spots of colour flare on the messenger's cheeks, his hand moving to his sword hilt. 'Is it your wish to insult the cardinal?'

Martin's answer explodes from him. 'Cardinal Albert has opposed me openly in the past. Does he try to buy me now?'

'I'm sure that is not his intention, Martin.' Bugenhagen's tone is level, as if to defuse the situation. 'Think of it rather as an olive branch that you might do well to accept.'

'You are privy to his counsels now, are you?' Martin is scathing. 'Albert may wish to pretend a friendship, but I will not.'

Bugenhagen tries again. 'This is your Wirtschaft, a day for new beginnings. Why dredge up old ills?'

'Why waste your breath. I will *not* take it.' Martin's bow for the messenger is peremptory. 'Good day, sir.' He turns his back and strides away without waiting for the courtesy response. Or for me.

The messenger takes a step as if to follow, his sword half out of the scabbard, but Justus Jonas moves in front of him and puts out his hand. 'You came with good intentions; I'm sure neither you nor the cardinal would wish this to end badly.'

The man hesitates, as if pride wars with expediency, and I hold my breath until he thrusts the sword home again and turns on his heel. The guests separate to let him through, conversations, which had faltered as folk focused on the dispute playing out before them, beginning afresh. Jonas hurries after him.

'To offer an apology, I imagine.' Barbara shakes her head. 'Why must Martin be so stubborn? To refuse a gift, when he has no income to speak of and a house that will drink every pfennig you put into it, is folly.'

I think of what I have seen of the Black Cloister in the two weeks since our marriage, her support all I need. 'Never mind pfennigs, it will take all the gulden we can muster and more.' I straighten my shoulders. 'Martin may not bend,' I say. 'But I can. And I will.'

❧❧❧

When I come back, having given my thanks and made my apology and begged that the messenger excuse Martin, I drop the purse into the chest. 'Twenty gulden,' I tell Barbara. 'A generous gift and not to sniffed at.'

'Will word of what has happened go back to the cardinal?'

'I trust not. Justus and I both spoke for Martin, and I think we have placated the man. But I cannot be sure.' I sigh. 'It has rather taken the shine off the day.'

Martin is at the end of the room, a mug of beer in his hand. Bugenhagen is remonstrating with him, but I suspect it is with little success, for I can tell by the set

370

of his shoulders that he still simmers. Lucas is giving instructions to the musicians, and Barbara nods towards them.

'The country dancing is about to start and people will expect you and Martin to lead the way. In an hour's time folk will be merry and this will be forgotten.'

'Not by me.'

'Let it go, Kat. You know him well enough by now to understand his temperament. Sometimes his mouth runs ahead of his brain. But with all his faults he is a good man.'

'I know, but today … I wanted it to be special … and it was, until this.'

'It still is, or can be, if you let it.'

'How do I tell him I have accepted the money and make him understand how important it is to us?'

She is fingering the chain around her neck. 'Choose your moment. When he is at his most amenable…' She stops, her expression serious. '*Do not let the sun go down on your wrath* is advice meant for all, but I think it especially important in a marriage.'

As the musicians tune up and the guests fall into line for the country dancing to begin, Martin appears at my side and takes my hand to lead me to the top of the set. At first his steps are forced, and his arms stiff, the signs of tension still in his face, but gradually I see his mouth relax, his expression softening. And when the first dance ends he whirls me into another and another, his enthusiasm growing as time progresses, and we lead the guests up and down the floor, the tempo increasing, until we collapse, hot and breathless, onto a window seat. He lifts my hand and swivels the wedding band on my finger, uncertainty in his eyes. His apology is stilted, awkward, but I can see that he wishes to make amends. 'I'm sorry, Katharina, I do not always speak as I should. I did not mean…'

I think of Barbara's advice and place my forefinger against his lips. 'I know.' There is a temporary lull in the music, the dancers drifting apart, for rest or refreshment, and across the crowded room I see Lucas and Bugenhagen deep in conversation, their heads close together. Lucas looks up, then away again, and whatever it is he says, Bugenhagen also turns to look directly at us, at me. His expression is serious and, as our eyes meet, my stomach lurches. Do they also think this a mistake? I tilt my head, as if to say *It is done now and cannot be undone*. In response his mouth widens into a smile and he nods twice, as if in affirmation, causing a warmth to spread from my shoulders to the tips of my toes. I curl my hand around Martin's, and over his head I smile back at Bugenhagen.

I think of Anna: *Perhaps this is for the best, Liebchen*; of Aunt Magdalene: *There is more than one kind of fulfilment*; of Barbara: *He needs someone who won't be afraid to challenge him … not some pretty little thing who will be all 'Yes, Martin' and 'No, Martin', 'Whatever you say, Martin'*; and of Elsa Reichenbach: *God brought you to Wittenberg, Kat*. I think of Jerome, with his feet of clay, and of Hans and Klement and Franz, who may now be restored to me; and, finally, of my own words to Eva: *He is a good man, who, if some of his wilder impulses can be contained, may yet become great*. I smile again, this time for Martin, and as the musicians strike up, and the sets form for the dancing to recommence, I tug him to his feet, and together we move to take our place at the head of the line.

Glossary

German terms

Rathaus – town hall
Schloss – castle
Shaube – overcoat
Strasse – street
Stube – heated parlour
Wirtschaft – formal church ceremony to solemnise a marriage

Religious terms

Breviary – liturgical texts including psalms, Scripture readings, writings of Church fathers and prayers
Cistercian – A religious order noted for austerity, manual labour and a vow of silence.
'Hail Mary' – a traditional Catholic prayer asking for the intercession of the Virgin Mary, mother of Jesus Christ
Indulgence – considered to reduce temporal punishment after death – commonly sold by church officials in medieval times to shorten the length of time an individual need spend in Purgatory
'Offices' or 'Hours' – Set periods of prayer as follows:
Matins – pre-dawn, c 2.00am
Lauds – 3.00am
Prime – 6.00am
Terce – 9.00am

Sext – midday

None – 3.00pm

Vespers – 6.00pm

Compline – 9.00pm

Purgatory – intermediate state after death in which souls undergo purification to fit them for heaven

Relic – the physical remains or personal effects of a saint or revered person

Author's Note:

Katharina von Bora, the renegade nun who became Martin Luther's wife, is a fascinating and in many ways an enigmatic character. There is debate over her parentage, her birthplace and the circumstances surrounding her admission to two different convents. Her subsequent escape, as one of a group of twelve, is the first recorded 'mass' breakout following Luther's revolutionary teachings, but there is no documentary evidence of her personal reason for choosing to relinquish her vows. From the time of her arrival in Wittenberg onwards, there is much more information on the timing and place of key events, though even that is incomplete, and sometimes differs between sources. Where a choice had to be made, my primary consideration was for the flow of the story and to that end I have taken some minor liberties with chronology. There is little documentary evidence of her personality (only a handful of letters written by Katharina remain, and of those only one contains a personal reference), however it is possible to catch tantalising glimpses of her from surviving letters that are written to her, particularly by Luther, and via the reactions of others, both positive and negative.

There are also several popular legends concerning her. The first – that she and the other eleven nuns escaped from the convent hidden in herring barrels – while entertaining – can be discounted, as it was almost certainly based on a misreading of a contemporary account. The second –

that she was the instigator of their marriage – is based on the attested conversation she had with Herr Amsdorf, in which she said she'd be prepared to marry either him or Luther, but not Caspar Glatz. Whether this was a serious suggestion, or should be interpreted in a different way cannot now be proved. I have chosen an alternative reading of the conversation, which seems to me to fit with what can be deduced of her character. The third – that at their Wirschaft she followed the cardinal's messenger in order to accept the monetary gift that Luther has refused, may or may not have a basis in fact, but it is certainly plausible, given her noted sound business sense and her later, well-documented, attitude to their marital finances. There is, however, one that proved irresistible, namely that her father's remarriage was a factor in her being sent away to the Brehna convent as a young child.

This book *is* a work of fiction, and though based on extensive research, the Katharina depicted here is my own interpretation. I hope I have done her justice.

Her story will continue in a second novel to be published late 2018 – *Katharina: Fortitude*

Acknowledgements

The primary challenge in writing this book, as others have found before me, is the lack of documentary evidence. The closest I could come to Katharina, therefore, was to visit the various locations, to walk where she walked, stand where she stood and seek to see the landscape and surroundings through her eyes. Funding from Creative Scotland made that possible and I am immensely grateful for that.

I also want to thank the many folk in Germany who gave so generously of their time and expertise to answer my questions and to show me around, particularly Bettina Brett, Daniel Leis, Anja Ulrich, Hennie Döbert, Adrian Harte, Helgard Rutte, Cornelia Stegner, Ursula Heinz, Kathrin Niese, Anja Bauermeister and Peter Ehrhardt. My research trip would have been so much less productive without your help. (My apologies if I have missed anyone out, or spelled any names wrongly.)

Finally, I want to thank my editor, Richard Sheehan - meticulous as always, Marjorie Blake, who not only read an early version, but also agreed to proof-read the final text, and my husband, David, who gave me the time and space to write.

Also by Margaret Skea:

The Munro Series (Scottish historical fiction) follows the fortunes of a fictional family trapped in an historic and long-running feud between two clans, dubbed the Montagues and Capulets of Ayrshire.

Turn of the Tide

'It is a dirty business and no one the winner,
save the coffin-makers and clothiers who
aye make good money of men's folly.'

Scotland *1586*. The 150-year-old feud between the Cunninghames and the Montgomeries is at its height. In the bloody aftermath of an ambush Munro must choose between age-old obligations and his growing friendship with the opposing clan.

Intervening to diffuse a quarrel between a Cunninghmae cousin and Hugh Montgomerie, he succeeds only in antagonizing William, the arrogant and vicious Cunninghame heir. And antagonizing William is a dangerous game to play…

A tale of love and loss, loyalty and betrayal, amidst the turmoil of 16th century Scotland.

Praise for *Turn of the Tide*

'The quality of the writing and research is outstanding.'
Jeffrey Archer

'Margaret Skea brings the 16th century to vivid life.'
Sharon K Penman

'More down in the dirt than Diana Gabaldon and as meticulously researched as Philippa Gregory. It's touching, fierce and surprising, with a sprinkling of humour.'
The Bookbag

'Historical fiction that flows, not unlike a Scottish burn, with all the undercurrents, subtleties and smoothness of the finest single malt Scotch.'
Clan Cunningham Society

A rollicking good read ... Skea is definitely a name to watch out for.'
Scottish Field Magazine

'The sheer villainy of some characters will take your breath away.'
Historical Novels Review

A House Divided

'When you must face Maxwell, give evidence
before the King. Have you thought on that?'
'If I do not face Maxwell, I will not
be able to face myself.'

Scotland 1597. The truce between the Cunninghame
and Montgomerie clans is fragile. And for the Munro
family, living in hiding, under assumed names, these are
dangerous times.

While Munro risks his life daily in the army of the French
King, the spectre of discovery by William Cunninghame
haunts his wife Kate. Her fears for their children and her
absent husband realised as William's desire for revenge
tears their world apart.

A sweeping tale of compassion and cruelty, treachery
and sacrifice, set against the backdrop of a religious war,
feuding clans and the Great Scottish Witch Hunt of 1597.

Praise for *A House Divided*

'Captivating and fast-paced, you'll find yourself reading far into the night.'
Ann Weisgarber, Walter Scott and Orange Prize shortlisted author of *The Promise*

'Compelling sequel to Turn of the Tide and a classic adventure story of the highest calibre. Meticulous plotting and authentic period feel grips from the very first page.'
Shirley McKay, author of the 16th century Hew Cullen Mystery series.

'I loved this book - the tension rose and dipped and then rose higher, dipped in brief resolution and rose again – finally to a great crescendo. I was all-in for the journey – and you will be too.'
The History Lady

'Well-paced and told in a compelling voice, A House Divided is a riveting story of family, intrigue, loyalty, friendship, and justice. Vivid, descriptive, tense and suspenseful and filled with action, courage and heart, this is a stellar read that grabs the reader's attention from the first page.'
The Written Word